The Bryant Family Chronicles:
Death and Gold in Zara Zote

Eddie R. Hughes

Deep Sea Publishing

Copyright © 2011 by Eddie Hughes

All rights reserved. Published in the United States by

Deep Sea Publishing LLC, Herndon, Virginia.

This is a work of fiction. Names, characters, places, and incidents either are the product of the author's imagination or are used fictionally. Any resemblance to actual persons, living or dead, events or locales is entirely coincidental.

Deep Sea Publishing ISBN: 0983427607
Deep Sea Publishing ISBN-13: 978-0983427605
Deep Sea Publishing E-Book ISBN-13: 978-0983427629

www.deepseapublishing.com

Table of Contents

Preface

Places

All plotlines in this story, both past and present, take place in Florida. The restaurants in this novel have fictional names, but are based on the great restaurants the author has visited over the years along the Gulf Coast of Florida. Parks such as Cayo Costa, Myakka, South Lido Beach, Blind Pass Beach, and Indian Mound are real and are great places to visit for anyone traveling to the Gulf Coast of Florida. St. Armands Circle and City Island and its spectacular Mote Marine Aquarium are must-see locations in Sarasota.

Technology

This book contains technology from the 1700s to sometime in the near future. Most of the modern technology described in these pages exists at the time this was written or will be available in the next few years. The technologies that do exist now have all been modified by the author from what is offered, but the modifications are indeed possible and are likely in the near future. All technologies described in this book were based on information available to the public from open sources.

Government Agencies

The US and local government agencies represented in this book are very real and do perform extremely valuable services for this nation. Agency investigations listed in this book are completely fictional.

None of the people found in this book that are described as having worked for local or US government agencies exist. They are completely fictional characters. Any resemblance to actual people that may work for these agencies is entirely coincidental.

Dedication

I'd like to thank my family for having endured the long hours spent writing this book. I could not have completed this work without their support and patience.

Chapter 1: *One Last Day of Fun*

Ted Johnson was happy to be moving again. He had been sitting for over an hour in what seemed to be the middle of the Gulf of Mexico. The boat was moving as fast as it could go safely, given that the sun had set and it was pitch black. The glow of lights on the horizon to the east was the only clue to the direction of the nearest land. The waning crescent moon and the backlight from the navigational display was the only light available on the boat itself.

Ted was an overworked marketing manager for a new software company. At thirty years old, he had found his niche in the world. He was elated when he got his bonus and thank-you gift for having catapulted the company into its current leadership role in their market segment. The thank-you was an all-expense-paid trip to a destination of his choice in the United States. The only hitch was that the trip had to be taken now. His wife worked as a teacher for the public schools, which were still in session. So she told him to celebrate and book the fishing trip he had wanted for so long.

Ted had flown down from Atlanta for the sole purpose of doing some offshore fishing. He had been fortunate to be able to book this four-day fishing trip, which was made available due to a cancellation just a week ago. He had arrived at Fort Myers Airport at about lunchtime, and had reported directly to the boat dock where his fishing guide was waiting.

His guide seemed young—maybe in his early twenties. The guide went over the day's plan, which included eating lunch on the way out of Charlotte Harbor. They would try for a few different species over the course of the day. Tarpon, mahi-mahi, and wahoo were the target species, but they would adapt if the bites were lacking.

The only annoyance Ted had experienced was the life vest requirement. The guide told him that all clients had to wear one.

Ted's first thought was of a big orange and cumbersome life vest that he remembered as a child, but he was pleasantly surprised when the guide gave him a slim lightweight vest that automatically inflated when it got wet. It was somewhat irritating that the guide didn't wear one, but Ted decided not to mention it. The vest wasn't so bad, and he soon forgot he was even wearing one.

Ted was enjoying the chicken sandwich, peanut butter on saltine crackers, and ice-cold fresh water as they headed toward their first fishing spot. The food was nothing to write home about, but Ted knew that the blandness was intentional so as to keep the stomach settled on a bobbing boat. The skies were clear, and the waters were much calmer than Ted had imagined they would be. He had on his favorite light-blue Blood 'N Guts brand long-sleeved shirt, his fishing shorts, and his blue Sperry Deck Runners.

Ted popped out his cheap pay-as-you-go cell phone from his breast shirt pocket to call his wife. He bought it just for this trip since it would be no big loss if it got wet.   Plus, it had a loud ringer, in case he got a call while they were motoring around.

"Hi, honey," he said in an upbeat tone. "I made it here to Fort Myers just fine and am heading out to the first fishing spot." He quickly told her the day's fishing plan and when he expected to be back at the hotel. He asked her to give him a call tonight just before the kids went to bed. "Love you too," ended the call.

They had fairly good luck with tarpon near the entrance to Charlotte Harbor, named Boca Grande Pass. The bites were good to the north along Gasparilla Island, which many erroneously think was named after the legendary pirate named Gasparilla. By the end of the day, they had also caught a couple of mahi-mahi for dinner and a myriad of other species several miles offshore.

All in all, it was a good day of fishing and a great day to be out on the water. That is, until the boat motor died as they were preparing to head in. Since they were still getting bites, they had pushed it as late as they could go. The motor problem, which turned out to be a clogged fuel line, had permitted darkness to catch them when they were still six miles from shore.

As the guide worked on the motor, Ted had to just sit in the quiet darkness and wait. The only sign of life around was the momentary obstruction of the moon by what looked to be a bird and a brief but distant hum of a motor. Cell phones didn't work out here, and the radio was mostly static. The staff at the guide service would start calling the coast guard if they didn't hear from the fishing guide within the next twenty minutes. Minutes later, the fuel line was cleared and the motor started effortlessly.

In the pitch black of the night, they were now heading toward the first of the lighted buoys at half throttle. The buoys began more than five miles from the Boca Grande Pass. They were less than a mile south of the buoy at this point. The lighted buoys were about three-quarters to a mile apart and were like a lit runway to the pass.

We'll follow the channel markers all the way back to the harbor entrance," said the guide. "We'll be able to radio home in a few minutes."

"Cool," said Ted.

They had finished their snacks about two hours ago, and Ted knew he'd be hungry again by the time they arrived back at the dock. Ted reassured the guide that the motor problem and falling darkness wasn't worrying him.

"Just another story to tell the family when I get home," he had said with a smile. He knew the guide was worried about his tip at the end of the day. It was typical to tip guides well for a good day of fishing.

As they neared the first buoy, they saw two dim lights just south of the buoy. As they drew closer, they could tell it was actually two boats. One was a sleek speedboat and the second was a fishing boat. Both appeared to be idling in the water.

"Do you think they are OK?" Ted asked.

"Their motors seem to be running, so they are probably OK," said the guide. "I'll call it into the coast guard when we get into better radio coverage."

Ted watched as the guide continued to pilot the boat. He could tell from the change in the guide's body language that something made him nervous as soon as he had spotted the boats.

With some hesitation, the guide sharply steered the boat eastward. Ted soon realized that the guide was making a wide sweep around the two boats' position. Once they were well clear of the boats and back on course to the next buoy, the guide increased the speed of the boat. As he did so, Ted heard the roar of the speedboat's motors. He spun around to see the speedboat come about and accelerate toward them.

"Get down out of view and make sure your life vest is secure," shouted the guide as he pushed the throttle to its limit. "The speedboat is heading our way."

"What the hell is going on?" yelled Ted with a look of worry on his face.

"I don't know," replied the guide. "It could just be a jerk wanting to race us."

"Well slow down and let him win!" said Ted in a loud, agitated voice.

The guide shouted, "I will, once we get within radio distance. But please get down low!"

Ted did as he was told and dropped to his knees. The position was uncomfortable and the pounding from the hull impacts on the waves rattled his bones. *There is something the guide isn't telling me.*

Ted knew from the sound of its motors that the speedboat was gaining on them. The guide continued to look back at the speedboat and then down at his electronic chart display.

"What are you looking at?" asked Ted.

"I added a line on my electronic chart display that is the distance from shore where radio coverage is good," shouted the guide. "The chart display shows we're approaching that line fast."

Moments later the guide picked up the radio and started shouting, "Mayday...Mayday! We're being pursued by a potential pirate threat near the Charlotte Harbor buoy number four. Request sheriff or coast guard support."

Ted broke into a cold sweat when he heard the guide's call for help.

As the guide completed the phrases a second time, Ted heard a staccato of popping sounds similar to firecrackers going off. He peaked up and saw flashes of light coming from the approaching speedboat. *They are shooting at us,* thought Ted. *They must know we're coming into radio range.* The guide made the urgent plea on the radio again as Ted prayed for a response.

The radio crackled, and Ted heard someone respond. But the roar of the speedboat as it overtook them and swerved into their path drowned out the message. The maneuver forced the guide to drop speed to keep from running into the rear of the speedboat. The guide ducked low when another round of bullets was fired in their direction. *The pirates were probably firing into the air as a warning to stop,* thought Ted.

The guide grabbed the radio again and shouted, "This is the *Marlin Hunter*, and we are under attack by pirate boats at channel marker four."

A second motor sound from behind alerted both the guide and Ted that the second boat, the fishing boat, was closing on them. The guide tried to cut to the starboard side and then launch the boat faster to the port side. But with each zigzag move, the speedboat countered. With each attempt, the fishing boat behind gained more, and their own speed dropped. It became crystal clear to Ted that they had been caught.

"Our best hope was to give the pirates whatever they want and be cooperative, said the guide without looking at Ted. "Stay out of site, don't say a word, and let me handle this." The guide then brought the Marlin Hunter to a complete stop.

Seconds later a spotlight shined on them from the aft boat, while the speedboat circled around and stopped a few meters from the bow of the *Marlin Hunter*. Ted saw the guide, looking like a criminal that had been surrounded by the police, slowly raise his hands.

Ted was horrified and was crouching as low in the boat as he could. His knees ached, but he dare not move. The ten-million candlepower spotlight illuminated the guide and a good deal of the boat, but Ted remained solely in the shadows.

The deep gurgling of the speedboat motors stopped, and a voice rang out from one of the two boats.

"What the hell are you doing out here? Why were you watching us?"

"I was fishing out here when my fuel line clogged," the guide shouted back. "It was after dark before I got it fixed. I was just on my way back in when I came up on you. I didn't even know you guys were out here."

"Are you a fishing guide?" the voice asked. "Are you alone?" The guide kept his gaze up so as to not call attention to Ted. Ted could tell now from the direction the guide was looking that the voice was coming from the speedboat.

"I am a guide, but I'm alone. I came out marking fish spots for clients coming in tomorrow."

The guide was smart, thought Ted. *The* Marlin Hunter *was an expensive boat and the fishing gear would outclass most weekend fisherman. If he lied about being a guide, they'd know it.*

"Listen, mister…that light is blinding me, and I can't see any of you," the guide continued. "I don't know what you want of me, but take whatever you want and please let me go. Just point and I'll throw it to you. Here, let me get you my wallet."

The guide began reaching for the floatable tackle box; Ted had seen him stash his wallet there before they set out. A short burst of gunfire rang out, and the guide quickly stopped and put his hands back up.

The voice asked, "Did you call for help?" The guide paused. Ted could tell the guide was clearly torn as to how to answer this question. If the crew on the speedboat saw him with the radio handset in his hand during the chase, they would know he was lying.

"I tried to call the fishing lodge, but I am too far out. They didn't respond."

Smart move again, thought Ted. The tension was so thick, he could cut it with a knife. The shadows cast from the light started moving to the starboard side. *The boat must be moving.*

Just then the radio came on, and a voice clearly said, "This is the US Coast Guard. We received your Mayday, and we have help racing to your position now. Over."

A different voice with a thick accent came from the direction of the light.

"Dead men tell no tales," said the voice.

A piercing noise startled Ted, and he heard the train of bullets first hit the water and then punch through the bow. Ted flinched as the bullets continued their march diagonally to the steering console, hitting first the guide's shoulder and then his temple. Ted watched in horror, in what seemed like slow motion, as the back of the guide's head opened up and spewed its contents. He could hear the pieces of the guide's brain and skull scatter over the water's surface. The guide fell and lay dead, draped over the side of the boat.

Ted had been a few feet from the guide in a fetal position when the gunshots started. But his face, arms, and legs still got splattered with blood. It was all he could do to keep from throwing up. Thank goodness he couldn't see the guide's head. It would have been too much; he would have lost his stomach and likely his life.

He remained quiet and after a moment the bright light went out. Then Ted heard the voice on the fishing boat say, "Sink it, and then get out of here as fast as you can. I've got to get some distance on us. The coast guard will immediately start looking for the boat and then survivors, so we should be fine if we moor tonight somewhere around Pine Island. I will contact you by email in the morning."

With that, the fishing boat roared away to the south.

The navigational display had been hit by the last spray of bullets, and the dim moonlight was of no value for eyes that had been nearly blinded by the fishing boat's bright light moments ago.

When Ted realized that the speedboat would likely fire at the waterline to sink the boat, he jumped over and pulled the guide's body down on the boat deck as quietly as he could.   As he positioned the body closer to him, his leg scrapped the steering console and he picked up a fiberglass splinter from one of the bullet holes.   He could feel blood trickle down his leg and it was quite painful.   But he remained silent.   He quickly crouched low behind the guide's body just as the machine gun Swiss-cheesed the boat. The guide's body twitched as the bullets hit it, but it shielded Ted from the spray. The boat began to immediately take on water.

Ted heard the original voice say, "Mark our location on the GPS so we can come back in the future if necessary. Then start the motors and get out of here." Ted knew what he'd do. He'd let the boat sink, staying behind the guide's body until the pirates left and the coast guard arrived. He had on his life vest, so he'd be OK if the sharks weren't attracted by all the blood.

As the boat filled with water, the guide's body began to float. Ted stayed low and kept the body from drifting, while keeping his feet planted on the sinking deck. It took only about ten seconds for the boat to sink low enough for the water to be at Ted's thighs. In a few more seconds, he'd be totally wet. He heard the voice say, "Start up the motor and let's go."

Suddenly the phone in Ted's still-dry shirt pocket rang.

"Shit!" said Ted in a whisper, while he grabbed his pocket to silence the phone. It rang only once, but the voice on the boat said, "Did you hear something? It sounded like a phone."

Shit, shit, shit, thought Ted. *It's my wife calling!* He pushed the phone into the water to silence it forever. *What else could happen to me?*

Ted could feel the water up to his rib cage as he strained to see the fishing boat. He was beginning to regain his night vision and suspected the people on the fishing boat were too. He was terrified to see several of the men staring in his direction.

Another couple seconds passed and the chill of the water on Ted's chest made him shiver. The chill suddenly made Ted remember what he was wearing. He grabbed at his life vest just as its air cylinder made a loud popping sound followed by the hissing of rapidly moving air. The vest was fully inflated in a few seconds and a bright red flashing light on the vest almost blinded Ted's eyes.

The last thing Ted heard as he began to pray was the deafening blast of the machine gun and the sound of bullets advancing through the water toward him.

Chapter 2: *Oh My Gosh!*

It was Friday noon, and sisters Nikki and Shelli were enjoying the early summer breezes and the char-grilled aromas at their favorite restaurant, the Mango Tango. They were sitting under the yellow table umbrellas at the sidewalk cafe, which was surrounded by large containers of brilliant bougainvillea and the tall palms that lined St. Armands Circle. Normally at this time of year, Florida seemed to breathe a sigh of relief after having endured the onslaught of tourists that visited the state during the winter and spring months. However, the recent massive oil spill in the Gulf and the downturn in the economy had reduced the tourist numbers this year. The streets seemed far less busy than either Nikki or Shelli was used to seeing. Only the occasional Mercedes and BMW, likely locals, drove by during lunch.

Nikki was home from college for the summer. Both girls were excited, since this was their first summer as official Florida residents. The girls grew up in Northern Virginia, but spent at least two holidays a year traveling down to see their grandparents, who lived about thirty minutes south of Sarasota. Sarasota had been like their second home, and they always spent at least one day shopping and eating at St. Armands Circle every time they came to visit. Now they could walk to it from their new home, and nothing made them any happier.

Sarasota is a relatively undiscovered jewel of Florida. It is known for its wide, powder-white beaches, great shopping, awesome seafood restaurants, and low crime rate. St. Armands Circle, in turn, is one of the jewels of Sarasota. St. Armands Circle sits on a small egg-shaped island, known as St. Armands Key, which is accessible by a bridge to its east from the downtown waterfront of Sarasota. The small, picturesque township has a perfectly circular road and garden park at its center. Surrounding the road are upscale shops, art galleries, and restaurants. Ringing the shops in concentric circles are large and expensive homes. Sheltering St. Armands Circle from the

Gulf storms to its west is Lido Key and its long strand of beautiful beaches, which can be accessed by a short walk down John Ringling Boulevard, the main street of St. Armands. St. Armands is the gateway to the exclusive Longboat Key to its north and other beach communities, such as Bradenton and Anna Maria Island. Sarasota had become home for the Bryants long before they moved there, and they never once considered anywhere else to live.

Nikki stared blankly at the white statues of the seven virtues in the garden in the center of the circle while thinking of what she was going to say in her first text message of the day to Cody—her newest boyfriend. Nikki's friend Kelsey stopped by and asked about Cody in between waiting on tables. Kelsey's twin sister, Kristin, worked as a waitress in another favorite restaurant they frequented.

Fourteen-year-old Shelli was talking about, what else...boys. While she was talking about the guy she saw at the beach that looked like Jacob in the *Twilight* movie series, her phone started "singing" her new Katy Perry ringtone. It was her friend Stephanie calling. Stephanie was one of the few girls who talked to her on the first day of classes at her new school, Sarasota High. They immediately clicked and had fast become best friends.

"Oh my gosh, Shelli!" came pouring out of the speaker so fast that mere mortal adults would have never understood it. Without breathing, she continued..."I'm in sooo much trouble! I had my brother Ryan take me on the boat over to Marina Pete's to meet Michelle and Amy, and the motor died. Ryan said something about the rotor snagging a net caused the problem. Anyway, we're stuck out on the northernmost island of Edwards Islands. I can't reach Mom, and I've got to be at dance in an hour and a half. Plus, I gotta pee!"

Shelli couldn't help but chuckle when she heard the last sentence. That's what she liked about Stephanie; she always made her laugh. "Calm down, Stephanie...take a deep breath. Why did you call me? Why didn't you call your dad?"

"He doesn't know we took the boat out!" exploded Stephanie. "You're the first person I thought of that has a boat!"

"Hold on, let me ask Nikki if she can take me," said Shelli. Shelli explained Stephanie's predicament, and after rolling her eyes, Nikki agreed. "

It will take us about fifteen to twenty minutes to get there," said Shelli. "I'll stay on the phone with you while you're waiting. Do you have plenty of battery charge on your phone?

After a slight pause, Stephanie came back. "I'm OK—I've got four out of five bars left."

Shelli and Nikki said good-bye to Kelsey. They had to leave their half-eaten fish tacos and cash for the meal, and raced back to their house. Shelli continued to talk to Stephanie when they entered the house. The large Key West-style house had been love at first site to the family. With Lido Beach and the center of St. Armands Circle being just a five-minute walk away, the house was perfect for the girls.

The girls cut through their large open kitchen and quickly moved to the back porch, down the steps, and along the short white stone path to the boat dock. Nikki unlocked the davit controls and quickly lowered the boat into the water. With the phone resting on her shoulder, Shelli left a quick note for her mom to let her know where they were going. Shelli grabbed her life vest and her sister's from the storage chest next to the dock and jumped into the boat. She was still talking to Stephanie when Nikki started the twin motors and began backing the boat into the canal.

Two minutes later they were at quarter throttle in Sarasota Bay heading eastward. Shelli was trying to get Nikki to speed up, but Nikki reminded her that they were in a manatee zone and had to go slowly. Shelli made a huff sound and kept talking on the phone. The boat was a twenty-eight-foot Mako offshore center console and was fitted with every gadget their dad could get on a boat. Nikki enabled the GPS tracking system so that their parents could track them if they ran into trouble. Nikki's phone rang, and caller ID showed it was an unknown number. She needed to keep her attention on piloting the boat, so she hit End to force the call to voice mail.

Nikki's mind started to drift as they moved through Sarasota Bay. She started to think of Cody. She had finally met a normal guy with nothing weird or strange in his closet. Like her, he loved the water. She could imagine what it would be like to be with him for a long time. Regardless of the outcome, it didn't hurt that he was hot.

Shelli's voice pulled her out of the daydream. She was giggling at something apparently funny that Stephanie had said. Nikki watched her sister as she talked. She was tall with brown hair that matched her thin, suntanned figure. She had aqua eyes and straight white teeth, thanks to years of braces. Unlike other teenagers her age, Shelli was anything but awkward. Years of both dance competitions and kung fu lessons had made her both poised and self-aware of her body. Although Shelli was the splitting image of Nikki at that age, Shelli was more sure of herself than anyone Nikki knew at that age—including herself. She could be a brat sometimes, but for the most part they got along well.

They rounded the eastern side of Bird Key and headed south under Ringling Bridge. The water was a little choppy as the tidal flow began, but it was still crystal blue. As they passed the southern edge of Bird Key, Nikki slowed down a little while looking at the radar map display. Their GPS location showed they were nearing the north bridge to Siesta Key and the entrance to Roberts Bay.

As they passed under the bridge, Stephanie squealed, "I see you...over here. See me?" Shelli spotted Stephanie waving on the small sandy shore along the north side of the island, which sits in the middle of a small bay. To the east was the mainland and to the west was Siesta Key, a large beach resort community known for its large, white, powder-sand beaches.

"Yeah, I see you. Is that Ryan in the water?" Stephanie ignored the question.

"Please hurry up," she said. "I'm about to explode!"

"Tell her we'll come up on her left—on the Siesta Key side," Nikki shouted to Shelli, who relayed the message and asked Stephanie to hang up.

Shelli stowed her phone and prepared to jump off the bow when the boat grounded on the sandy beach. Shelli jumped off with the bowline in her hand and pulled to make sure the boat was secure. Stephanie excitedly jumped up and down with her arms extended and hugged Shelli.

"I am so happy to see you!" shouted Stephanie. Nikki jumped of the boat and immediately tensed as Stephanie hopped over to her for a hug. "Thanks, Nikki—you're a lifesaver."

Before Nikki could say anything, Stephanie spun on her heals and yelled at her brother Ryan to get out of the water and come on. Even though Shelli was good friends with Stephanie, neither Shelli nor Nikki had met Ryan, who was in his final year of college and was home for the first time in many months. Nikki had to keep her jaw from dropping as Ryan slowly emerged from the water. He had been swimming to keep cool and had nothing but his swim trunks on. He had dark hair, was suntanned, and was ripped. Nikki found herself wishing she had stopped by the mirror before leaving home.

Ryan waved, said hi, and went straight to the front of his boat to grab the bowline. He pushed the boat back into the water and walked with the line in his hand toward Nikki. Nikki grabbed the line, hopped in the boat and tied the line to the aft gunwale. Stephanie and Shelli both jumped in as Ryan prepared to push off.

As he lunged forward to push the boat off the shore, his feet sank into the soft sand. Nikki was watching Ryan intently and noticed the grimace on his face. He immediately stopped and grabbed his left bare foot. Stephanie and Shelli were busy talking, but Nikki moved forward to see had happened. Ryan flopped back on the beach still clutching his foot. A small trickle of blood seeped between his fingers.

"What happened?" Nikki asked.

Ryan immediately wiped the grimace off his face when he noticed Nikki was looking at him.

"I stepped on something sharp in the sand," he said. "It's just below the surface."

Nikki leapt off—making every attempt to avoid landing at the spot where Ryan had hurt his foot. She asked to see Ryan's foot, which he reluctantly allowed. The cut was long, but not deep. She asked Shelli to throw down the first aid kit, which she did. A quick cleaning with an antiseptic wipe and a large bandage took all of two minutes.

"Let's go, so I can...go!" Stephanie shouted. Nikki smiled at Ryan and shrugged her shoulders. She started to jump back onboard when she noticed an encrusted metal point sticking up from the sand where Ryan had been hurt. She moved close to it and began to gingerly swipe sand away from the object.

Chapter 3: *Merchandise Movement*

Johnny Gates was enjoying his second skinny margarita at the tiki bar that sits near the Casey Key Bridge on Blackburn Point Road. A seafood restaurant and boat dock share the parking lot next to it. The sun was getting lower in the sky and was making him squint as it reflected off the turquoise waters in front of him. The fans in the hut lazily circulated air, which helped fight off the sweat marks forming on his faded 2009 Redneck Yacht Club T-shirt. Being it was late afternoon on a Friday, the bar was starting to fill with more patrons ready to start the weekend.

At twenty-seven years of age, Johnny thought he had it made. Each day started late—wake up between nine and ten o'clock in his condo off Phillippi Creek. After a shower and an e-mail check, he would visit one of his favorite seafood places, which was conveniently just a walk across the street. He'd usually have a grouper sandwich, stone crab legs, or raw oysters with either a salad or garlic shrimp appetizer, and a beer...or two.

To keep himself fit for the ladies, he would stop by the gym in the early afternoon for a workout and conclude with a swim in the pool. In the late afternoon he would show up for a skinny margarita or mojito at one of the several designated outdoor drop-off locations along the Intercoastal Waterway.

He would meet his business liaison, who would pull up to the boat dock with a blue cooler full of "merchandise." Johnny's job was to exchange a cooler full of money from his car trunk for the blue cooler and then deliver the merchandise up to one of several distribution points in Orlando. He'd then receive funds for the next day's transactions. Every day's merchandise movement plan came as an encrypted e-mail in the morning and was updated by phone text messages as necessary.

Johnny was smart—he didn't sample the merchandise. He stayed clean and sober. He had to work six days a week, if you can call it work, but that was fine by him. He had no one to go home to or answer to, except his boss in Orlando.

Blackburn Point Road is the northern access point to Casey Key. Casey Key is a thin island with a single road lined with million-dollar mansions on the Gulf side and Intercoastal Waterway side. The southern tip of the island is ringed with public beach parks and picnic areas.

The Intercoastal Waterway, or ICW, extends from Norfolk, Virginia, to Miami and also runs up and down a good part of the west coast of Florida. Mostly constructed by nature as a series of brackish water bays, man helped connect the waterways through the use of canals and dredging. In this section of the Gulf Coast, boats can transit all the way from Fort Myers to Tampa safely and without ever entering the Gulf of Mexico. It allows residents and especially smaller boat owners to safely travel to townships and fisheries in sunny and rainy weather.

Johnny and his business partners had found the ICW extremely helpful in moving their merchandise into the country. Sarasota Bay, Venice Inlet, and Charlotte Harbor were the main entrances they used into the ICW. Crime was low in these areas, and as long as there were a few fishing poles on the smuggler's boat and they kept their speed low, they slipped in and out without authorities giving them a second glance.

The shipments were as reliable as the postman. Although the 1,500 miles of open ocean between Columbia and Sarasota was a long-distance commute, the drug cartel had set up a short conveyor operation between islands along the way. This limited information about the overall route from being known by any participant. Each leg of the route was traveled by the same reliable partners. They knew their contacts at their pickup and drop-off points. Divergence from the schedule, the routes, or the players was not accepted.

Shipments started in Columbia and moved to Isla de la San Andres, then Cozumel, the Keys, and then to one of several drop-off locations in the Sarasota area. Johnny had the afternoon shift, and others covered the morning and lunch shifts. The cartel alternated between the designated drop-off points in the Sarasota area so as not to draw suspicion. This meant Johnny rarely saw the same bartender more than once a week. He kept to himself, and as instructed by his employers, he made it a point not to become friends with anyone at these locations.

As Johnny was thinking how lucky he was, he saw the boat ease up to the restaurant dock with two people on board. It was coming today from the south, which meant it had entered the waterway south of Nokomis or through the waterways from Gasparilla Island. Johnny paid his tab with a modest tip. As he walked away to meet his business associates, Johnny failed to notice another patron at the bar who was watching him.

The suntanned forty-something agent blended well, with his faded mossy green cap with fighting tarpon, white sleeveless "Go Gators" T-shirt, khaki-colored multi-pocket swim shorts, and flip-flops. Anyone in the bar would have tagged him as a weekend sports fisherman stopping in for some refreshment before heading back home. No one noticed that he really wasn't texting on his black smartphone, but was instead collecting a close-up video of Johnny's transaction in the parking lot. The small two-way Bluetooth earpiece allowed the agent to describe the events to the team listening on the conference call. The laughter of the other fisherman easily drowned out the agent's comments, which were short but descriptive.

Johnny laughed loudly, shook his head as if he couldn't believe how bad the joke was, and then waved goodbye to his partner and to the boat operator still in the boat. He placed the blue cooler in his car trunk, climbed inside his car, and pulled out of the parking lot. The agent at the bar signaled his surveillance team to follow Johnny. The team consisted of two agents sitting in a pickup truck with Virginia plates, which was parked at the small public library across the street from the bar. Johnny headed to the east toward Route 41 in his late model BMW coupe. Route 41 ran north-south, and although it had long sections of straight roadway, the speed limits on it rarely passed 45 mph. The surveillance team waited a few moments and then pulled onto Route 41 in the same direction as Johnny.

This was the first good break the agent had had on the method of shipment since Johnny was first identified as a drug runner by agents monitoring the cartel in Orlando. Unfortunately, the Drug Enforcement Agency had not had enough time to arrange for a boat, so the agent had to watch the boat runner start his motor and move off to the south. The guys running the cartel were smart—they altered the delivery scheme daily. The DEA was going to need more people and equipment if they were going to be able to intercept all the participants in the ring.

Chapter 4: *Watched*

As Nikki was wiping the sand from the buried object, she was startled by the stomping of Stephanie's feet on the boat deck and her scream of frustration. "What is wrong with you people," she yelled. "Get in this boat right now or face the consequences!" Everyone laughed and immediately resumed the departure. Nikki placed a smooth rock she saw at the edge of the shore over the object so no one would get cut in the future. Then she hopped into the boat, started the engines, and headed toward Stephanie's home on Siesta Key.

As Nikki moved the boat to the west side of Edwards Islands, she gave a quick glance to the right to check for boat traffic. Towing a boat required her to pay extra attention. Her eye momentarily caught a fisherman, who was sitting on the seawall at the park on the west side of the Siesta Key bridge. She returned her attention forward and slowly steered the boats southward. She smiled as she listened to her sister talk to Stephanie.

"Stephanie, why didn't you just go potty on the island?" said Shelli.

"Eeewww," snapped back Stephanie. "There is no way I am going outdoors. Someone might see me!"

"Well, why didn't you walk into the brush to do your business?" Shelli asked.

"Are you kidding? The mosquitoes flying around were huge! I'd be scratching my bottom for a week!"

◊◊◊◊◊

Kyle Thompson was sitting with his fishing pole in his hands, wearing his shades and his beloved UVA cap. His thermal imaging and CCTV camera were hidden in his tackle box, with only the lenses visible at one end of the box. He had been sitting for hours at Country Park watching boats pass through the bridge. Although it was a pleasant day, being stuck in one location for hours without any action—criminal or fish—was tough. He was about to move when he noticed a boat with a single motor sputter and quit in the center of channel. It slowly drifted to the closest of Edwards Islands. The boat's occupants were a teenage girl and a young man. He collected a little video. After some time, he noticed another boat pull up with two girls.

He realized after a few moments that the first boat needed a tow. He felt sort of silly having videoed the first boat, but then he noticed the older girl in the second boat digging in the sand and leaving a marker. He thought it odd and decided to record a little more video. He had plenty of disk space, so might as well be safe than sorry. As the boat rounded the island, he heard laughter from the crew.

It was mid-afternoon. No fish were biting, and there was no sign of drug movement. It was time to get some relief and replenish his water supply before it got too late in the afternoon. Just as he was getting ready to move, he heard a call from his partner, Jim Matchett, located at a waterside bar at Casey Key. Earlier that day they had received a distribution report from the Orlando field office and Jim had just validated the intelligence in person.

Kyle tensed in anticipation when he heard the smuggler's boat was leaving after the drop. But he was immediately deflated when he heard the boat was moving southward, so there was no way for him to help track the boat. This was likely the only delivery this afternoon. A quick discussion with Jim, and it was decided he should wrap up and head back to the office to plan surveillance for tomorrow.

◊◊◊◊◊

As they neared Stephanie and Ryan's dock behind their house, Stephanie jumped onto the deck before the boat was moored. She ran inside quickly. It had been over thirty minutes since she had originally called Shelli, so no one dared get in her way. Shelli walked over to the pool, sat down, and dropped her legs in to cool herself. Ryan helped tie up the boat and talked with Nikki as they headed toward the house. Nikki noticed scuba gear and spear guns stacked at one side of the pool.

"Learning how to dive?" asked Nikki.

"No, I just got a new regulator and BC vest and was checking it out before trying it for real," said Ryan. "I love to go spear fishing."

Stephanie returned looking relieved. Since she had to get ready for dance, Shelli and Nikki said their good-byes. Stephanie hugged Shelli and thanked her again for coming to her rescue. As Nikki was hopping in the boat, Ryan jogged up and asked for her number. Nikki blushed and thought briefly of Cody. Cody was extremely nice to her and treated her with respect. She knew he liked her a lot, but he was either afraid or didn't know how to expressed his feelings to her. She'd give him more time to figure it out, but since there was no expressed commitment, she didn't see the harm in giving out her number to Ryan.

She reached in the boat for her phone and said, "Give me your number, and I'll call you so that you have my number." Ryan responded, and Nikki hit Send to transfer her mobile number.

"Great, thanks," he said with a smile. "I promise I will not be calling you for a tow!"

As the girls were heading back home, Nikki noticed the fisherman on the seawall near the Siesta Key Bridge was gone. *Guess he had no luck*, she thought. Shelli's phone rang. She looked at Nikki and said, "It's Dad."

Shelli answered, "Hi, Dad, what's up?" She paused while

listening. "Yes, we're heading north now and should be home in about ten minutes." Shelli gave her dad a quick replay of the day's events. A few questions later, Dad dropped the bombshell.

"Awww, Dad...really? What time do we have to start tomorrow? OK, I'll let Nikki know. See you in a little while...Love you too," she said with a sigh.

"What?" asked Nikki.

"Dad wants us to help him set up his sensor grid tomorrow. He's going to talk about it at dinner. We start at 10:00 a.m. I really dread it."

"That's what I figured," Nikki said. "He was talking about it a week ago. It shouldn't take but about a half a day to finish. Fortunately, it won't be hard work."

Rick Bryant had flipped on his computer in his home office to check on the whereabouts of his girls. He was the first one home and saw the message from Shelli. He gave her a call as the boat tracking software was coming up on his displays. He was comforted to know they were coming home. His daughters had a lot more freedom and privileges than many other kids their age. But his kids had always proved to be responsible. Since the financial status of the family had only recently changed, they did not grow up rich and had had a relatively normal childhood. He was glad the wealth they now enjoyed hadn't spoiled his girls, as he had seen it do in many other well-off families.

Rick was a fifty-three-year-old entrepreneur whose financial status had recently improved when he sold the business he had started ten years earlier. He had started a wide area sensor security business from his garage, and his commitment to performance and customer satisfaction had resulted in booming sales. He eventually decided to sell when he realized he was missing too much time with his family. He had no shortage of offers and took the one that most benefitted the company and his workers.

Rick was a workaholic. But he also played hard when he had time off. He loved everything to do with the water, including fishing, kayaking, diving, boating, and hunting for prehistoric shark's teeth with his kids along the beaches from Stump Pass to Nokomis. He also had learned to fly and had recently updated his license to include seaplanes.

His love of outdoor adventures had rubbed off on his daughters. Nikki had learned scuba, and both daughters often went snorkeling and kayaking with him. Rick had stayed in shape over the years through a regular regimen of weights and running. Since moving to Sarasota, his daily exercise routine consisted of a mixture of swims out in the Gulf, kayaking, and running on his treadmill or on the nearby Lido Beach.

When Rick and the family arrived in Sarasota, they knew exactly what they wanted in a house and where. After years of coming to Florida, it was no question that Sarasota was going to be their new home. The house they chose was a five-bedroom, Key West-style house painted sea foam green, with white trim and a white tile roof. The three-car garage, screened pool, large home office, media room, and boat dock in the back on the canal, plus the great location, sealed the deal for the family.

Rick loved his home office. It had a large bay window in the rear of the house that overlooked the dock and pool. Two tall palms framed the window, and the beautiful tropical plantings by his wife rounded out the view. He had a powerful computer with three LCD screens. The computer was networked to his rugged notebook PC with sunlight readable display, which enabled him to take his work with him wherever he went. He had multiple high-speed Internet access points, which enabled him to stream live video and sensor feeds. He had a large LCD display on the wall, which was used for presentations and as a situation display for his field sensors. He had the ability to see and sense his cars, home and most importantly, his family.

After only two months of moving to Florida, he decided he would open a new firm that specialized in ocean sciences. And true to his nature, this expanded into more unique types of "hardware." This time things would be at his pace, however, and it gave him plenty of time with the family.

He had been able to buy an old boat storage facility in Sarasota that had Gulf access. He converted it into labs, shop, and offices. He often referred to the work office as "the Lab." He particularly liked the large bay doors on the waterfront side of the building that allowed boats to pull right into the facility. He had purchased a large fishing boat and refurbished it with a new engine and with two large davits. It had room to store lots of equipment on deck, and the bridge looked as modern as any cruise ship. He was able to get several of his employees from his old firm in Virginia to move down and join his new adventure. The rest he hired from Florida universities. A total of eleven employees plus Rick worked with no real management structure. The difference between his new company and his old one was that he had complete flexibility in what he did without the constant worry of revenue. His staff was completely able to run the business, and his day-to-day involvement was by choice, not because it was required. And if the day was pretty, which it often was, he had the luxury of taking it off without having to travel anywhere to enjoy himself.

Rick had been working for months on an idea he had many years ago. He was excited because tomorrow he was going to launch the first production units. He had made quick friends at the coast guard, Sarasota police, and the sheriff's office. After a few months working with him, these organizations quickly understood that Rick was there to help with any and all of their security needs. The prototype sensors he had funded himself and placed in Charlotte Harbor had been hugely successful. The proposals Rick submitted to the Department of Homeland Security leveraged this success and had resulted in funds for products that were going to help both the city's and nation's security.

Rick was still watching the girls' progress when he heard the door to the garage open. Danielle was home. Rick heard her enter the kitchen, and in a few moments she walked in with a glass of lemonade in her hand. Rick briefed her on what he knew of their daughters' activities and told her they would be home shortly.

Ten minutes later Shelli and Nikki walked in through the back door.

"Mom," yelled out Shelli as a long, drawn-out word. "I have dance team practice in thirty minutes." Danielle came out of Rick's office, acknowledged her daughters with a smile and a kiss, and began the ritual of the dance mom.

A few hours later, after dance was over, everyone convened at the dinner table. At the completion of the meal, they bussed their plates. Danielle reached for the homemade key lime pie in the fridge, and Rick herded the girls down to the media room for a briefing of tomorrow's activities.

Rick's family was instrumental in the success of his first company. Rick loved to tell the story of how he once did a security radar demonstration to a general at his facility. The general was impressed with the technology, but commented, "It's great, but it needs to be easy enough for a third grader to operate. It needs to be almost intuitive so that very little training is needed. We can't hire scientists to operate it in the field."

Fortunately it was a holiday for the schools, and Shelli had come into work with Rick. Rick called Shelli into the demonstration room and asked her to show the general how the radar worked. Shelli proceeded to conduct a demonstration for the general. The general was impressed and asked Shelli what *radar* stand for.

"Radio detection and ranging," she said. She continued to explain how radio waves reflected off of objects and were detected by the radar. The general asked how old she was.

"I'll be seven in a couple of months," she replied. Rick won the contract. Although the family didn't have to help often, Rick still requested their support on occasion with the new company.

While still enjoying their dessert, Rick started up the PowerPoint presentation and summarized the state of the sensors.

"As you know, the prototypes were very successful in Charlotte Harbor. This led to the DHS contract we got many months ago for production. We've finished the new sensor buoys, which consists of a data buoy complete with a short-range radar, thermal imaging cameras, sonar, underwater cameras, wireless communications, and a solar panel charging system. Both printed and broadcast news media have released notices to the public that new channel markers with radio transponders are being installed throughout Sarasota Bay and all waterways southward to Lovers Key. Lovers Key is just below Sanibel and Estero Island. You girls must keep all of this a secret. We don't want the general public, and more importantly the criminals, to know the true nature of the buoys."

"But, Dad, isn't that an invasion of privacy?" Nikki asked.

"Good question," said Rick. "We're using these assets for monitoring true criminals. It will not be used for issuing boat speeding tickets. When the radar detects moving objects, the cameras will be pointed automatically at the objects, and video transmission back to the command center begins, as does recording. The software then begins its behavioral analysis. We've developed a learning system to monitor the sensors. Over the next few days or even weeks, the system will learn what is typical and will only trigger alarms when there is something out of the ordinary.

"So we're not really spying on people, we're letting the system automatically find the criminals, and only then will we review the data of that event," continued Rick.

Shelli asked the all-important question. "So what are we supposed to do to help tomorrow?"

"I need Nikki to drive the boat," Rick said. "I'll work the davits and lower the buoys into the water. And you are to stay at home and verify we can communicate to each buoy from my office displays."

"Why are we doing this and not your employees?" she asked.

"The guys at the office have put in a ton of overtime to meet tomorrow's deadline. I just couldn't make them work another Saturday. Plus, I really miss you two too much during the day, so I thought it could be fun to do this together."

Shelli sighed and shook her head. "Dad, you're hopeless."

Chapter 5: *A New Life on the Sea*

It was late in the day, and the air was humid. Juan Ortiz was spying the clouds growing in the west as he cruised in his sloop up the west coast of Florida. It was September 1715, and after experiencing a number of hurricanes over the last few years, Juan got nervous whenever he saw tall clouds forming in the distance. In fact, a hurricane caused him to be where he was now. In July a great hurricane had sunk eleven Spanish ships full of gold, silver, and jewels onto the jagged reefs on the east coast of Florida.

Juan was the quartermaster, basically the second in command, on the *Isabella*. The *Isabella* was one of a number of salvage ships sent by Spain to search, find, and return the lost treasure home. The thought of the long voyage to Spain, the bad food, and the reward of measly pay had started to eat at Juan. So he began talking with the navigator, master gunner, and the carpenter about the riches in the cargo hold and how they could be wealthy beyond their dreams if they took the ship. The navigator, master gunner, and carpenter talked to the cooper, boatswain, and even the cook about the quartermaster's ideas. It was agreed to mutiny and maroon the captain on one of the many small islands they would encounter in the Spanish Main.

Marooning the captain was akin to a death sentence for the man, but he was staunchly supportive of their mission and Spain. He would surely hang anyone who thought of piracy. The captain had been a navigator himself once and was a collector of maps. He would not even let his own navigator use or see the entire collection. Juan planned to use these maps to set up a new base of operation for his men. If they ran out of gold, they would turn to piracy.

The mutiny had been successful. They left the captain marooned on a small island off the southern tip of Florida. The crew had voted Juan the new captain, which was not a surprise to Juan. The ship stores were full of enough food to make it back to Spain, so the main concern was avoidance of the British and Spanish warships as well as other pirates and privateers.

The detailed maps they confiscated from the former captain's quarters included the entire Gulf of Mexico. After studying these maps, Juan and his navigator thought about heading up the west coast of Florida. The navigator had heard talk of a place named Zara Zote that had a sheltered bay with great numbers of fish and pleasant winters. After discussing it with the crew, Juan decided this was the ideal place to settle. It was off all the main routes, so British and Spanish navies would not likely search for them. It would be defendable, and the bounty of the sea would sustain them. They had not heard any rumors of pirate camps in this area, so their only concern was the local Indians. However, they had also heard that many pirates traded with the Indians on the west coast.

It had been more than four weeks since they had marooned the captain, and they were slowly making their way north along the west coast. Winds had been calm until the last two days. The cook brought Juan some hard tack, cheese, and rum to drink. The hard tack was stale. Juan beat it on the table and noticed a plump, gray maggot work its way out. Good, thought Juan. At least the bread still had some value and was not totally bad. A skinny maggot meant the bread was totally spoiled. At least rum could not go bad, he thought as he sipped from his cup. It wouldn't have mattered, though. It would be gone before it would have spoiled anyway.

He didn't know what lay in store for him, but he was prepared. They had twelve cannons, plus plenty of powder, grapeshot, cannonballs, and chain. They had multiple chests of gold, silver coins, and jewels, so they could buy or trade for their needs. It was well known throughout the Spanish Main that pirates hid in the many islands on the west coast of Florida. Juan had asked the navigator to make sure their course was far enough off the coast to keep their sails from being spotted easily from shore. But with the clouds forming, he didn't know how long they could stay this far out from the coast.

At least he felt good in his sloop. It was as fast as they come. But it was full, which slowed them down some. However, Juan thought the ship was still amply fast to keep their distance from chasing pirates. If the storm came closer and they had to go near the coast, then he'd pull the sloop into the shallow bays for protection from the storm. The sloop was an excellent class of ship for shallow water bays, due to its shallow draft.

Just then his new quartermaster, Fernando, knocked on Juan's cabin door. "Come in," said Juan in Spanish.

"Sails sighted south of us, sir," said Fernando. "Looks to be another sloop, sir, and we cannot make out its colors."

Juan leapt up from his chair and rushed to the upper deck. He took the spyglass and looked out to the distance. Only the top of the sails was visible. It was too far to see the ship's flag—even its color. If it was a solid black or red, it would mean pirates. They would need to keep true to their course, but prepare for the worst. By this time, everyone was on the deck seeking to get a view of the distant ship.

Juan turned to the navigator and directed him to estimate how much time they had before they would be overtaken by the pirates. He also wanted to know how far they were from Zara Zote. This required some measurements and observation to answer. The navigator estimated speed using dead reckoning. At this distance, if the distant ship had a two-knot speed advantage over the *Isabella*, they would close on them in three to four hours. He could refine this answer in another hour of watching the boat. After some careful observation and comparison to the maps, the navigator believed they were just north of the harbor entrance to Punta Gorda. At their current rate of speed, they would be at the entrance to Zara Zote in about three and a half hours.

Juan's heart almost stopped. The harbor for Punta Gorda was a known haven for several pirates. The course was taking them far from the coast—far enough to keep them from being spotted from the shore. The ship must have been on the water when the *Isabella* passed by the mouth of the harbor. That would have allowed them to see the *Isabella*'s sails, and would account for the sudden appearance.

Juan ordered the crew to assemble around him.

"We must prepare for a fight," said Juan. "Prepare the cannons and arm yourselves. Gather all that is not essential and be prepared to throw it over the side to help our speed. Officers, meet in my quarters in ten minutes. We must prepare a plan in the event these are pirates."

Juan looked for the sun to check the time, but it was no longer visible. The clouds were rapidly moving toward them from the west, and the distant rumble of thunder could be heard.

Chapter 6: *Deployment*

It was Saturday morning at ten o'clock. Shelli was at her dad's office in front of the monitors. Nikki was on the boat with her dad, Rick, who was operating the davits. They headed out to northern Sarasota Bay and began dropping the buoys. Each buoy was held in place by a concrete block attached to a hefty chain coated with a urethane skin for long life. They continued until noon and stopped for lunch at Marina Pete's on the eastern shore of the Bay. Since Marina Pete's was a short distance away over the John Ringling Boulevard Bridge, Danielle and Shelli met Rick and Nikki at the restaurant. They discussed their progress while they ate. Rick suggested they put in about two more hours and then call it a day.

Once they finished lunch, Rick and Nikki returned to the boat. They continued to the mouth of the south entrance to Sarasota Bay and then backtracked to move into Roberts Bay. As they passed the Siesta Key Bridge, Nikki looked over to the park on the west side of the bridge and noticed that another fisherman was sitting in almost the same place on the seawall as the guy she had seen the day before. He was not the same person, but she had to do a double-take to verify this. She noticed he had a fairly big tackle box and a white and yellow fishing rod.

They were making slow, but steady, progress. Although Nikki had to keep the boat steady for her dad to drop the buoys, it was not a challenge for her. So she had plenty of time to monitor her surroundings. She picked up her phone to check for messages and noticed she had missed a call from "Unknown." She checked for voice mail, but didn't have any.

They were well south of the last of Edwards Islands when Rick's cell phone rang. Nikki noticed a look of concern on his face. Putting his free hand on his forehead, he looked quickly back at Nikki and then turned away and ended his call. He walked toward the bridge and opened the door.

"It's time to wrap it up for the day and head back," he said.

"What's wrong, Dad?" asked Nikki.

"Oh, I'll discuss it with you when we get back."

This was unlike Dad, Nikki thought. *I hope it's not something bad.* Her dad phoned Shelli and told her they were finished for the day. Then he asked to speak with Mom. He walked back out on the deck near the stern of the boat and faced aft. Nikki couldn't hear what he was saying, but his demeanor told her something unusual was going on. After a few moments he hung up and began strapping the remaining gear down for the transit back to the lab.

He was noticeably quiet for the entire trip to the Lab, and didn't say much on their drive back home. The only thing notable he said was, "Thank you for helping today—you did a great job."

When they arrived home, Shelli was in her room and Mom was in the kitchen. She had poured them two Cokes in tall glasses with ice. Nikki sat down and looked at her dad.

"So, Dad, what's going on? You've been weird since getting that call this afternoon."

Dad lowered his head for a moment, and Mom walked up next to Nikki and sat down beside her.

"My friend at the sheriff's office said the coast guard found two dead bodies floating offshore last night," said Rick. "One body was a man who had arrived from Atlanta yesterday. He has a wife and two children who just got the news."

"Oh my God," interrupted Nikki. "That's just horrible. No wonder you were upset."

"I'm not finished," said her dad. "The second person found dead was a local fishing guide." He paused a moment. With wet eyes he looked straight at Nikki and said, "It was Cody, honey."

Chapter 7: *On the Road to Orlando*

Having made his drop-offs on Friday in a timely manner, Johnny Gates was again heading to Orlando for Saturday's delivery. Today's pickup location was from Indian Mound Park in Englewood. While waiting for the merchandise to be delivered to this location, Johnny had a drink at one of the several bars along Dearborn Street, on what used to be the hub of the town. Since the area is struggling to reinvent itself, the bartenders and servers at the joint paid extra attention to everyone entering its doors. This is exactly what Johnny didn't want—attention. But he managed to keep to himself and nurse his drink until it was time for the pickup.

When it was within ten minutes of the drop, he paid his tab and headed to Indian Mound Park, which got its name from the mounds of shells left by the Indians. He would park close to the water and wait for the boat to arrive. People were regularly launching boats at the newly improved launch, and there were always people picnicking or walking their pets. The park overlooked Lemon Bay, which was wide at the park location. His drug-running partner came through Stump Pass from the south, under the bridge to Englewood Beach, and was right on time. A quick exchange and Johnny was on his way.

As he was driving up I-75 north, he turned on his FM radio to listen to some news just as he passed the exit for Fruitville Road. He rarely got to watch TV to see what was going on in the world, so it was part of his ritual to listen to the news for a while on each day's trip to the Orlando distribution house. The sun had started to set when he heard that an Atlanta man and local summer fishing guide had been found shot to death off the coast from Charlotte Harbor. The story suspected the culprits were modern-day pirates from the Caribbean. The guide was a young man from Sarasota who worked when he was home from college for the summers. *Poor kid,* thought Johnny. *It's terrible to see anyone that young gunned down.*

Even though Johnny's line of work was criminal, Johnny never thought of himself as one. He just took advantage of a market that would exist whether he was involved or not. His part of this system was almost insignificant, and the likelihood that he would be caught was slim. He never saw the results of the drugs he transported in his daily life, so he felt distant from the criminal element that employed him.

Johnny saw the traffic up ahead in the middle and right lanes slowing down as he was nearing the University Parkway exit. This was the Sarasota Airport exit, and with all the summertime visitors, you occasionally experienced a slowdown here. He looked in his rearview mirror and over his left shoulder, and then signaled to move left. He looked again in his rearview once he had moved into the new lane and noticed a truck two cars back pull into the left lane as well. He thought he remembered seeing the same truck behind him when he pulled out of the gas station on Jacaranda Boulevard. It had Virginia tags.

Johnny always drove the speed limit and obeyed all traffic laws when delivering the merchandise. He was told by his Orlando counterparts to be alert and to look for anyone who might be watching him. If he thought he was being followed, he was supposed to call it in. He never used the same phone on any day. A new phone was given to him for the next day when he dropped off the merchandise. That made eavesdropping a little harder. He kept his eye on the dark truck and continued to head north.

Once Johnny passed the exit for I-275 to St. Petersburg, he moved to the middle lane again. The truck he had been watching had fallen to a position of four cars behind him and was still staying in the left lane. But a mile farther up the road, he noticed the truck moving to the middle lane. Johnny started to tense and wondered if he should call in. After a few moments, he thought that it could still be a coincidence and he'd appear foolish to his bosses if he called in a false alarm. He would wait to see if the vehicle followed him on I-4 to Orlando. If it did, then he'd exit off of 566 in Plant City. Several restaurants, a Starbucks, and gas stations were located there. If the vehicle was still with him, he'd call it in.

When he came within a mile and a half of the I-4 interchange, he signaled and moved to the right lane. The traffic from Tampa on a Friday afternoon was always thick, but he had managed to drive safely and keep an eye on the tailing vehicle. He watched for the truck to move. A full minute passed. Even though he was almost on the ramp, he noticed the truck had still not moved over. As he took merged on I-4, he was relieved to see that the truck had continued north on I-75. He'd been paranoid and as a result had sweated a long portion of the drive unnecessarily. He stayed in the right lane of I-4, switched to satellite radio, and settled in for the remainder of his drive to Orlando. He was oblivious to the white van that had merged onto I-75 about five miles from the I-4 interchange and that was now following him four cars back. The white van radioed the black truck to tell them to head back down to Sarasota.

The DEA had now identified two delivery points for drugs into the United States. They would keep following Johnny until he repeated a pickup site. After that, they'd start mapping the routes along the waterways. They had used this methodical approach to find the Orlando distribution center, and it would be only a matter of time before they had the entire ring and sources under arrest.

Chapter 8: *Honor the Dead*

Danielle was a fit fifty-three-year-old and the world's best mom, according to Rick. She had sacrificed career opportunities to be able to be an integral part of her daughters' lives. Driving the girls to dance, kung fu lessons, and school activities filled much of her time. Once both girls were in school, she continued to work part time in volunteer art education programs. Her art degree and her enthusiasm were welcomed by all the local schools in their community.

When they moved to Sarasota, Danielle kept busy with home décor and outdoor plantings for the first seven or eight months. But she soon found that with her daughters being more independent and her husband busy at work, she needed a new direction.

It was about that time that she learned of a new opening at the Ringling Art Museum. The Ringling family of circus fame had been instrumental in the history and growth of Sarasota and the surrounding area. The art museum was one of their many cultural offerings to the community. The position was for a docent, or art gallery guide. The position required a keen knowledge of art history and the ability to communicate with others. It also didn't hurt when Danielle when she mentioned she was fluent in French during her interview. She got the job, which kept her busy four days a week. The new home and new job suited her well.

But seeing her oldest daughter this way was breaking her heart. Nikki was not only her daughter; she also had become a good friend as she entered adulthood. They talked to each other daily, even when her daughter was in college. And Nikki had helped often over the last few years with Shelli's dance competitions, which required numerous costume and makeup changes.

After an hour of being consoled by her and Rick upon receiving the news, Nikki had gone to her room and stayed for a full day. The only time she came out was when the sheriff came by to ask a few questions. The sheriff's office was involved because their jurisdiction is up to nine miles offshore in the Gulf of Mexico. During the sheriff's visit, he apologized for the phone calls Nikki had received from his deputies. One of his deputies had found her name on Cody's recovered phone. Once the sheriff saw the last name of the phone contact was Bryant, he realized she was Rick Bryant's daughter. At that point, he decided to take over the case personally. The sheriff gave Nikki his card in case she thought of anything that might be important to the case.

Danielle brought Nikki food during the first day, which she half ate. Danielle didn't know if Nikki and Cody were in love, but it was clear they had grown fond of each other. The fact that Nikki had stopped seeing other guys was a sign of growing commitment. It didn't help things that Nikki and Cody had planned another date the day after his death. A funeral instead of a date was a harsh reality.

On the second day after Cody's death, Rick went up to see his daughter in the morning. Rick was always upfront with his kids, but it was hard to tell Nikki why the casket would be closed for the wake. But she would probably read it in the papers, so he thought it best that he be the one to tell her. Another flood of tears came as Rick held his daughter close.

◊◊◊◊◊

The funeral was two days later. The number of people attending was immense, since Cody had lived in Sarasota most of his life. Nikki had a hard time at the closed coffin wake. Her sister held her hand throughout the whole ceremony. Although Danielle knew Cody's parents, they were not close. But any parent can imagine the pain of losing a child. She and Nikki were one of the first to give their condolences. Danielle and Cody's mom hugged a long time without a word. When they released, Cody's mom said her son was fond of Nikki, and she was going to miss seeing Nikki around.

As Nikki was leaving the funeral with her family, she noticed Ryan and Stephanie getting into their vehicle. She should have known that they probably knew Cody, since they were longtime Sarasota residents too. A sudden wave of guilt flooded her thoughts, and she fought back another crying attack. She felt upset with herself that she had been thinking of another guy while Cody lay dead or dying. She buried her face in her hands and then collapsed on her mom, who was sitting next to her. Danielle fought back her own tears as she put her arms around her daughter.

Chapter 9: *Murder Investigation*

The day after Cody's funeral, Wednesday, Rick and his employees got an early start and worked late on the deployment of the sensors' buoys. Since each sensor buoy could cover three kilometers, they were able to finish up to Boca Grande by the end of the day. On Thursday they worked late again and made it south to Lovers Key. Everyone was tired, but it was a relief to get it done.

While near Cayo Costa on their lunch break, Rick stopped by the prototype buoys to copy the contents off the internal drives onto his notebook PC. The east or bay side of the island was a favorite boating destination; the island's popular small cabins could be reserved. The buoys were still operational. They were being used by state park rangers and were also patched to the marine patrol unit's command center of the Charlotte County's Sheriff's Office. These earlier prototypes only had cameras installed and did not have the radar, as the newer models did. They also did not have the meshed network that Rick had added to the new buoys. The meshed network allowed the buoys to talk to one another. If a buoy failed, the wireless communications stayed intact because of the "healing" ability of the network. Each prototype buoy had a direct gigabit network, but it still took a full hour to copy the video data from the four buoys.

It was nightfall by the time Rick got back home. Nikki had taken Shelli to dance practice, while Danielle was busy cooking dinner. Rick gave Danielle a kiss and briefly described his day. Danielle did the same while Rick helped set the plates and silverware. They were going to eat out by the pool.

Upon finishing his table chores, Rick walked back into the office to bring up the feeds coming in from the buoy network. He had a forty-one-inch monitor on the wall, which he was using as his situational awareness display for the buoy network. A big coastal map extending from Tampa Bay in the north to Marco Island in the south showed buoy locations on the display. Although the sensor grid did not extend to these extremes, they would eventually do so in the next phase of the project. Whenever something was detected and tracked by the radar, the buoy icons would change from green to yellow. When the behavioral software thought it to be unusual, it changed from yellow to red. At that point the operator could click on the icon, and the track history and video replay would appear on a pop-up window.

Rick heard Shelli and Nikki arrive in Nikki's white Audi Q5. Moments later they poked their head in the door to say hi. Rick told them everything the team had done during that day. Then he explained the situation awareness display.

"It's SAD," Shelli said.

"What's sad, honey?" Rick asked.

"No, it's S-dot-A-dot-D-dot—SAD," she said, managing a smile. They all moaned.

The sheriff called while they were eating dinner. Rick excused himself and went to his office. He enabled the audible speaker on the phone.

"We've had some developments on the Cody Foster case, Rick," said the sheriff. "We need your help with some images we've got here. It would be great if you could come by the marine patrol office after lunch and we can bring you up to speed."

"Sure thing, Bob," said Rick. "I'd be happy to help. I'll be there at around two o'clock."

"Great, see you then. Bye."

Rick went back to the table and let the girls know what the sheriff wanted.

"Since I have everything up and running, I now need to do some tests on the sensors before conducting the acceptance tests with the customer," Rick said. "But I don't feel like doing it by myself." He looked at the girls.

"Dad, did you say something?" Shelli responded quickly. "I'm having trouble hearing you." Rick smiled.

"I said, would you girls would like to go redfish fishing with me tomorrow off of Boca Grande?"

"Yes!" Shelli said.

Danielle spoke up. "I have off tomorrow, and I was going to go shopping with the girls."

Shelli looked torn—shopping with Mom or fishing with Dad. Both were always fun.

"I'm not really in the mood for fishing right now, given what's happened," Nikki said. When Rick heard this, he immediately wished he'd not mentioned fishing.

"Why don't we split up?" Danielle said. "Shelli, you go with your dad. You guys could stop at the restaurant on the beach at the end of the island. I know you like it. After eating you can go over to the sheriff's office together. I'll take Nikki shopping, and tonight we'll meet back here, have dinner, and take a walk down to the St. Armands Circle for ice cream."

They all agreed.

Next morning Rick and Shelli headed out on his fishing boat. First stop was to pick up some live shrimp at the small bait shop at New Pass on the north side of City Island. Shelli liked to go here because the shop owner always let her pick out big shrimp and scoop them out with his small net into their bait bucket. Once done, they hopped back on the boat and cranked it up.

Instead of going out to the Gulf the short way on New Pass, they headed east around Sarasota Sailing Squadron and then southward, under the Ringling Bridge and out by Big Pass. Rick did this so that he could test the new sensor buoys. His route would be recorded by his new sensor buoys, so he could replay the data when he got back home later.

The boat ride was going to be almost fifty miles, which would take them over an hour to get there. This was still much faster than a car, though, and more fun, in Rick's opinion. He let Shelli take turns piloting the boat. He pulled into the pass north of Gasparilla Island and went under the causeway. They passed through the opening of the old railroad line that used to connect the island to the mainland before the causeway was built. They then moved out to the sandbars south-southeast of the fishing pier on the island. He had caught redfish here a few times in the past when paddling his kayak.

Shelli was excited when she caught the first fish, which was a saltwater catfish. Rick removed it and threw it back in. They slowly moved south along the bay side of the Gasparilla Island, and by lunchtime they had caught a number of quality fish, including some redfish, Spanish mackerel, and spotted sea trout. They stowed their gear and motored around the southern tip of the island. Once clearing the tip, they turned northward on the gulf side of the island, and shortly thereafter they beached the boat at the little seafood shack they both enjoyed.

After their meal of fresh grouper Reuben sandwiches, they took off up Charlotte Harbor to Punta Gorda. Since the sheriff's office was near the airport on Utilities Road, they would have to dock their boat and take a taxi. They decided Fishermen's Village was the best place, since it had public docks and they knew they could get a taxi quickly. It was going to take Rick and Shelli about forty minutes to get there, which would put them at the village at about half past one. That was plenty of time to make their two o'clock appointment at the sheriff's office. Rick called the sheriff to let them know their plans.

As they pulled up to the docks, Shelli pointed to the parking area next to the restaurant, and Rick saw Sheriff Bob Huggins waving. Rick docked the boat and grabbed the notebook PC that he'd brought with him. The two of them made their way to the sheriff. Rick put out his hand.

"Bob, it's good to see you. We were going to take a taxi over. You didn't have to pick us up."

"Hi Rick and Shelli," said Sheriff Huggins. "It's good to see you too. It was no problem coming over to pick you up. I know you're busy, but the reason

I called you is that I think you might be able to help us find Cody Foster's murderer."

They arrived at the sheriff's office and were greeted by a number of his staff. The sheriff suggested that Shelli talk with the dispatcher and "help her out." They convened in a conference room, where pictures, maps, and a host of other papers were spread out. Someone brought Rick a coffee, and they all sat down to go over what they knew.

"Rick, this matter is confidential, and we don't want any of this to leak to the media," said the sheriff. "So we ask you to keep what you hear today to yourself. Lieutenant Kevin Williams is commander of the special operations section. The marine patrol unit falls under his command. Lieutenant Williams will take it from here."

"Nice to meet you, Rick," said the lieutenant. "I know now that your daughter Nikki had been dating Cody for some time before the incident. We're sorry that we had to bother her the other day, but we hope you understand."

"I completely understand," said Rick.

The lieutenant nodded and then continued.

"Since the marine patrol unit has jurisdiction out to nine miles, the coast guard handed over the full investigation to us. We've been putting the pieces together, but we have run into some stumbling blocks, and we need some outside help."

"I'm here to help any way I can," said Rick.

"What I'm about to show you is not pretty, so I hope you have a strong constitution," the lieutenant said. He reached for pictures and spread them out.

The pictures were nighttime shots of the scene when the coast guard and later the marine patrol unit arrived. The scene was gruesome. Floodlights lit up a large area around the incident to the point that it almost looked like daylight. Body parts were floating in the water, and the water was red around Cody and his Atlanta customer.

"Both people were shot at a relatively close range with a machine gun," said Lieutenant Williams. "The coroner said Cody was killed instantly by a shot to the head. The Atlanta man was killed by shots to the jaw, neck, and chest. Given the number of rounds expended, it is clear they wanted no survivors."

"It looks like the pirates were thorough," said Rick.

"That's just it," said the lieutenant. "We don't think they were pirates. We believe they were drug smugglers."

Rick looked surprised. "I thought that it was pirates being reported on the news."

"That's what we let the news crews believe," said the sheriff.

Rick thought a moment.

"You don't really think Cody had anything to do with this," he said. "He was an outstanding young man with lots of potential. I had him checked out when Nikki started dating him more seriously. She doesn't know I did that, by the way, so please don't mention it to her."

"At first we did think he was involved," said Lieutenant Williams. "There was no sign of theft, and we had no idea who the Atlanta guy was. A pirate would have snatched anything valuable, yet all valuables were either floating or on the bottom. But when we started checking on Cody and the Atlanta man, we realized they truly were victims. Then we began to question why boats would be sitting that far off shore at dark."

"Boats?" asked Rick. "How do you know there was more than one boat?"

The lieutenant pulled a miniature recorder.

"This is the recording we copied on the night Cody was killed."

The lieutenant started playing the recording. Rick was startled to hear Cody's pleas for help. After a few moments, Rick heard Cody's voice say, "This is the *Marlin Hunter*, and we are under attack by pirate boats at Channel Marker 4."

The lieutenant stopped the player.

"Note that he said pirate boats, with an s. This was an open channel, and it was Cody's mention of pirates that caused the news media to conclude it was pirates."

"Well, then, what made Cody think they were pirates?" asked Rick.

"We think he may have been thinking about some of the reports of pirates down in the Marco Island area over the last six to eight months," answered the lieutenant.

"We also had divers go down and check the sunken boat," he continued. "It was shot up badly. But from their report and from the analysis of their underwater photos, the bullets seem to come mainly from two directions. The sizes of the holes also indicate that two different calibers were used. So we're thinking two boats."

"It appears from the voice recording that you had boats on the way fairly quickly," said Rick. "How did they get away so fast?"

"As you know from coming here today, it's a good twenty-five minutes for our fastest boats to get from the docks to the mouth of Charlotte Harbor," said the lieutenant. "And they were at channel marker 4. That was plenty of time for a racing style speedboat to disappear."

"Did the coast guard send their copter?" asked Rick.

"Yes, they did. The only way they could have totally evaded us was that at least one boat was a very fast speedboat. They could have shot up the boat and then made a wide swing away from us. It was pitch black, and their speed would have given them the ability to stay out of sight while we were racing there as fast as we could."

"What about the second boat?"

"We don't know for certain," replied the lieutenant. "It could have also been a fast boat. Or it could have been a regular fishing boat that left earlier. The fact that they caught Cody's boat meant both boats were faster than the average boat, since Cody's boat was no rowboat. It could move."

"It appears you've made a lot of progress," said Rick. "How can I help?"

"One way the boats could have eluded us is if they went southwest and entered the islands and inlets. We checked video from all the docks in the area and saw no boats come in after the time of the murders. So they had to have hidden in the islands and waited until morning. Traffic on the water by morning would pick up and make it difficult for us to isolate them. We then began thinking of your buoys. Your prototypes were out on Cayo Costa recording video."

"Yes, they were," said Rick. "If no one was manually operating them, the cameras would have been performing a 360-degree tour. There would have been video recording at ten frames per second all night."

"Yes we know," said the lieutenant. "But that is a lot of data."

"I had ten terabyte of disk space installed to make sure we could get good quality records for a long while. There's no need to have a high quality thermal camera if you then lose quality with poor compression software. Might as well have a web cam if you were going to do that."

Rick paused and then he understood. "You need my help searching the video fast."

"Precisely!" said the sheriff.

Rick pulled up his rugged notebook PC.

"I stopped by yesterday and downloaded all the data from the buoys," he said. "We use it for diagnosis of the system and for algorithm training. I've also got our new behavioral analysis software and our video motion detection software—or VMD as it is sometimes called—on this computer. I'll use the VMD software to first look for gross motion changes in the thermal imaging data. Thermal works both day and night, so it's better than looking at the CCTV camera images. I'll then feed that data into the behavioral analysis software to look for irregularities. But this is still going to take some time."

"No problem," said the lieutenant. "We'll wait."

Rick pulled up the programs and initiated the search beginning at noon the day Cody was killed, to noon the next day.

"It's cranking away. This might take a couple hours to finish."

"As the lieutenant said, we can wait," said the sheriff, "but can you?"

"Do you have an Internet connection that I can access?" asked Rick.

"Yes we do," replied the sheriff.

"I need to get Shelli back. I can leave my notebook with you and then access it from my home office via the Internet. Then I can call and talk you through what it finds."

"That will be perfect," said the lieutenant.

"I have a question, though, Lieutenant Williams," said Rick. "Even if you find a boat coming in or even leaving the area at that time, how will you tie this to the murders?"

"We may be able to use the video to get search warrants to board those boats to look for clues."

Rick shook his head to indicate he understood. "It's too bad we hadn't replaced the Charlotte Harbor lighted channel markers with our new buoys," said Rick. "They were close enough to the number 4 marker for the radar and camera to have recorded everything."

Then Rick got an idea.

"I just remembered something. NOAA, the National Oceanographic and Atmospheric Administration, has a drone they've been flying over the Gulf. They've been using it to map the remaining oil slick from the big offshore oil spill. I thought it would be good to tie in the thermal camera feeds to our command center to give a wide area perspective, so I called them. It's a long shot, but maybe they were flying over on the night of the murder."

The sheriff and the lieutenant looked at each other in surprise.

"But they haven't returned my phone calls," said Rick. "You know how Big Brother is."

The sheriff spoke up quickly. "I can bet you they will respond to a subpoena. Give me that number and a contact."

Rick gave the sheriff and the lieutenant the information, checked the progress of the software, and then fetched Shelli. Shelli said she had fun and got to direct some of the deputies out on patrol. The sheriff had one of his men drive Rick and Shelli back to their boat. In a few minutes, Rick and Shelli were on the water and heading home.

Chapter 10: *Pirates*

Three hours had passed since the distant ship was spotted by the crew of the *Isabella*. In that time they had discovered that the ship was indeed a pirate ship. But there was another problem. As the pirate ship closed, they spotted a second set of sails following the first ship. Both vessels were sloops and about the same size as the *Isabella*.

It would not be much longer before the ships would be within firing range of their cannons. The lead pirate ship had already fired one round as a message to stop and be boarded. By continuing their run northward, the *Isabella* crew had invited the full rage of the pirate crew.

It was almost dark now, and the winds were blowing hard from the west. This helped speed them to their destination, but the light rain falling was unwelcome. Lightning was almost on them, and they were still another thirty minutes from Zara Zote. Of course, there was also the matter of what could be done once they did get to Zara Zote.

But after a short while, the officers had designed a plan for the attack. They knew that even though they were well armed, none of them had the battle experience of the pirates. And two ships would not have followed this far just to let them go. There was going to be loss of life; perhaps everyone would perish. So they had nothing to lose by attempting their outrageous plan and everything to gain if they survived it.

The master gunner began instructing the cannon crew on the plan. He pressed the crew over and over to look back to him for every shot placement. If he were killed or went missing, they were to continue the assault under the direction of any other officer. Juan watched as the other officers began to instruct the crewmen on their jobs and when they should carry them out. The most important thing heard again and again was to keep their eyes on their commanding officer when the roar of cannon fire began. It was impossible to hear anything when the cannons were firing. Juan felt fortunate to have the loyal crew that was preparing for battle before him now.

It was unnerving to the crew to wait for the attack to begin. Pirates normally had only a few cannons; they relied on manpower over firepower. The typical maneuver would be to cripple the ship by taking out its masts and sails. They would use grappling hooks to pull the vessels closer and then board with overwhelming numbers. Having significantly more cannons on the *Isabella* could help keep the pirate ships at bay, but it came at a sacrifice. The pirate sloop would undoubtedly be faster and more maneuverable without all the weight of the cannons and ammunition, which made them harder to hit.

At just under two thousand yards, the pirate ships began their maneuvers. They started to separate, with one ship positioning so that it would be on the starboard side of the *Isabella* and the other ship to the port side. They knew that the cannons on the *Isabella* would have a range of at best two thousand yards.

As they closed to 1500 yards, Juan told the quartermaster to begin the plan. The quartermaster ordered their flag to be raised. Juan had had the carpenter fashion a flag of a skeleton in a pool of blood. It was hoped this would momentarily confuse the pirates. As soon as the flag was raised, the master gunner started the cannon fire. He had arranged for two aft cannons to continuously fire at the two ships. They had a crew of sixty-two. Firing each cannon took two to six men, with the larger cannons requiring more men. The more men assigned to a cannon, the faster they could shoot. Most of their crewmen were on the twelve cannons round the sides and the ship's stern.

The aft crew was using large round shot. It was not accurate, but it could reach the ships. As they fired, the master gunner used the many misses to adjust the bearing and tilt of the cannon. The pirate sloops continued to maneuver to make them more difficult to hit, but after the tenth shot, the first ship was hit at its bow. Deck timbers buckled, and a massive number of shivers, long wooden splinters, flew toward the stern of the ship. But the ship did not slow its approach.

The master gunner continued his assault on the ships, but it took a moment to position the crew on the side cannons, including the small swivel cannons. He spoke with large gestures, since the noise was deafening. The side cannons were loaded with chain shot, the swivel cannons with grapeshot. The chain shot and grapeshot were the deadliest ammunition. Both were capable of mutilating a number of people at the same time. The grapeshot was a small iron ball the size of one to two grapes in diameter. These were packed in cans to increase lethality. Chains either had large balls on the end or were packed in a similar way as grapeshot. Chain shot could take out the mast.

At less than one thousand yards, the forward pirate ship started firing at the *Isabella*. Moments later the second and more distant ship began firing. They were wildly off at first, due to their maneuvering. They did not fire rapidly. The combined firing of both ships was about half the rate of cannon fire from the *Isabella*. Juan was now able to tell at this distance that the forward ship had one large forward cannon, and two mid-size and two swivel cannons on the side. The second ship seemed to have only three total cannons—two on the side and one forward. So the *Isabella* had an advantage when it came to firepower. Juan could see and hear the pirate crew wildly yelling and cursing on the deck of each ship between the cannon fire. Each pirate ship had a crew larger than the *Isabella*'s crew. Juan prayed their plan would work.

The storm was now at full force. The wind was howling, and the *Isabella* had picked up speed as it continued to tack the wind. Lightning illuminated the skies as nightfall was almost on them. The deck became slippery as water sheeted on its surface.

Suddenly the aft port cannon suffered a direct hit, which put it out of commission and instantly killed two crewmen. The aft starboard cannon crew was dazed, and two were holding their ears, clearly in pain. The master gunner merged the remaining aft crewman and continued firing the starboard cannon. This allowed the lead pirate ship to halt evasive maneuvers and close in faster on the *Isabella*. The pirate plan was clear. They were going to attack the *Isabella* from both sides. By staggering their ships, they could safely fire at point blank range at the broadside of the *Isabella* without hitting each other.

The aft cannon crew managed a hit on the second ship. It hit square on the deck, and the master gunner watched pirate crewmen rise in the air and land in the water. Since most pirates couldn't swim, they would perish soon, if the percussion hadn't killed them already. That was the last shot the aft cannon crew made that hit anything. The rocking of the ship in the storm and the speed and maneuvering of the pirate ships were just too much for the crew to compensate.

The boatswain, who was the best sailor on the boat and whose responsibility included the sails and tackle, stood ready near the mast with two crewmen. All three of them had hatchets in their hands and were awaiting word from the quartermaster. *Isabella*'s master gunner had arranged five cannons on each side of the *Isabella*. All swivel cannons were to aim at a 45-degree angle toward the bow of the ship, while the larger cannons aimed straight out.

The lead pirate ship started to pull along the port side and had their cannons ready. The swivel cannons were aimed directly at the *Isabella*'s cannon placements, while the larger cannons aimed straight out from the side of the ship.

The port side pirate ship had what looked like at least seventy crewman on deck, with pistols, daggers, and cutlasses. The foul language was unbelievable and would have been almost unbearable if it were not for the howling of the wind. The swivel cannons on the pirate ship fired grapeshot shot across the deck and took out three of Juan's men. It was a brutal sight. Arms and legs were sheared from the bodies, and streams of blood from the limbs shot over the deck. Holes peppered part of the jib sail.

As the first larger cannon on the pirate ship neared the center of the ship where *Isabella*'s mast stood erect, the quartermaster gave the signal, and the boatswain and two crewmen cut the lines of the main sail. The sail tumbled to the deck under the increased weight caused by the rain. The *Isabella* immediately dropped speed with only its jib responsive to the wind. At this moment, the larger-size cannons on the pirate ship fired chain shot. The sudden drop in speed of the *Isabella*, however, caused the shot to be well forward of the mast. Since the second cannon was timed from the first cannon fire, it too missed the mast. Had the chain shot from either cannon hit the mast, it would have either weakened it or cut it down. Unfortunately, one of the *Isabella* crewmen standing in front of the mast did not fare well. When the shot passed, his lower body stood motionless for a moment before dropping to the deck, with his head and shoulders totally missing from his upper torso.

At the same moment in time, the master gunner fired the two large side cannons filled with chain shot at the first pirate ship. Like a bowling ball, the chain shot from the first cannon cleared a lane by cutting several pirates in half. The second cannon obliterated the stern rails and severed the ropes on the aft sail. The lowering of the *Isabella*'s sails had caused the first pirate ship to lurch ahead, right into the line of fire from the *Isabella*'s swivel cannon grapeshot. Over twenty pirates were cut down by these cannons. The pirate ship raced ahead of the *Isabella*.

On the starboard side, the second pirate ship approached fast. With no mainsail, the *Isabella* had less speed and maneuverability. The second pirate ship used this opportunity to alter its course so that it was going to literally scrape by the *Isabella*. The aft cannon crew on the *Isabella* moved forward to support the starboard cannon crews. The sails had been rigged with two sets of lines, and the boatswain immediately had the crewmen raise its sails just as the second pirate ship bow crossed the stern of the *Isabella*. With a sudden burst of speed, the *Isabella* was then steered sharply to the starboard side. This turned what would have been a light scrape with the second pirate ship into a hard collision. The bow of the pirate ship plowed into the starboard side of the *Isabella*. The pirate ship jolted at the impulse force. This sudden reduction in speed launched most of the pirate crew airborne, and several landed in the water. The master gunner had the starboard swivel cannons aimed forty-five degrees to the stern of the *Isabella*. At the point of collision, all these cannons fired, and a good number of the still-standing pirates were mortally wounded or simply diced. The force of the collision had caused the pirate ship's cannon crews to falter, and they did not get shots off with their cannons.

As the two ships pushed forward, the force of their forward momentum won out, and the two ships were forced to straighten out. Only one of the *Isabella*'s larger side cannons fired, and this hit and damaged the mast of the second pirate ship. The second cannon crew could not fire, as two were killed from pistol and muzzle fire from the pirates. The pirate ship began throw grappling hooks to the *Isabella*'s starboard side, but the combination of winds and crashing ships caused their aim to be off. Several of the *Isabella* crew drew their cutlasses and began cutting the lines that did catch.

Although more than forty pirates had just lost their lives in the first wave of the attack from the two ships, Juan knew they were far from safe. It was pouring rain, and with the exception of the lightning that was filling the sky, darkness had fallen all around them. He quickly moved to the bow of the ship and began looking for the first pirate ship. The darkness and the rain made it hard to see anything more than a hundred yards in front of them. Then a brilliant flash of lightning came down, lighting up the sky long enough to see the first ship moving fast to the port side of the *Isabella*. With all the tactics and collision with the second pirate ship, the first pirate ship had time to move ahead and then come about for a second attack.

It was then he saw a black man standing at the bow of the ship with his cutlass pointing ahead. Runaway slaves made up large percentages of pirate crews. And as pirates, they enjoyed equality unlike anything they had experienced before on land. This former slave looked like he was the captain.

The first pirate ship had moved all its cannons to the port side of its ship. Juan quickly turned around to see that his port side crew was scattered all over the deck. The continual collision and gun exchange with the second pirate ship, coupled with the storm, had caused chaos on *Isabella*'s deck. Juan watched helplessly as the first pirate ship opened fire on the *Isabella*. Its mainsail filled with holes, and the mast took a direct hit, but was still standing. A full quarter of the crew was lost by the time the ship passed. Several of the crewmen on the second pirate ship were killed by the exchange, as it had stayed side by side with the *Isabella*.

With visible damage to the mast, the boatswain began lowering the mainsails to keep the mast from breaking under the heavy winds, and then trimmed the jib to help regain some power. But at the same time, the second pirate ship boatswain mirrored the move and kept his ship glued to the *Isabella*. The pirate crew on the second ship started a wave of pistol fire, which allowed the grapple hooks to catch and hold. The first three pirates jumped onto the *Isabella* with swords in one hand and pistols in the other.

As the pirates moved toward the center of the deck, Juan watched as the boatswain responded. He reached for his pistol. Before his pistol could be drawn, one of the three onboard pirates fired his pistol at a distance of two yards from the boatswain. Juan watched in what seemed like slow motion as the large caliber shot passed through the eye socket of the boatswain and left the back of his head. More pirates began to jump onto the ship, and hand-to-hand combat broke out. The crewmen were trying to hold their own, but they were being overwhelmed. The master gunner plowed his way past Juan and headed below deck swiftly. Juan pulled his cutlass and blocked the first pirate he met, who was swinging downward with his cutlass. In a fast and fluid motion, Juan plunged his dagger in his left hand into the ribs of his enemy. The pirate dropped in agony and then quickly grew lifeless.

Juan saw the first pirate ship pull up along the port side of the *Isabella* and start throwing lines over. The deck of the *Isabella* was soon flooded with pirates from both ships. The crewmen slowly began to move closer to Juan to form a barrier. The black man Juan had seen earlier jumped onto the deck of the *Isabella*. He was huge, and his muscles were rippling as he struck with his sword. Once spotting Juan, he made a beeline directly for him. He sliced at Juan's crewmen as he walked, and they dropped like melons. As the black man neared Juan, it became clear to Juan that this was futile. Juan dropped his sword and put his hands up. He yelled to his quartermaster and navigator to do the same. It was over.

As the man came to Juan, he pushed his sword tip to Juan's neck and said in English, "Kneel to Caesar, you pig! How dare you think you can stop me?"

Juan said nothing. He had learned English in his youth and could understand most of what the man said. But he decided to pretend he could not. "*Que*?" said Juan. "*No hablo Inglés.*"

The man placed the broadside of his sword on Juan's shoulder and pushed down. Juan went down on both knees. The man called for a pirate crewman to come forward. He approached and greeted Juan with a few curse words in Spanish.

The translator, while holding the side rail of the heaving ship, announced loudly that this was Black Caesar. Both the translator and Caesar had to yell out every word, with the storm beating down on them and the crashing sounds of the ships as they scraped against each other in the swells.

"You are very clever," said Caesar, "but you cannot defeat the king of the pirates." As he talked, he marched with his cutlass held high. His pirate crew began scouring the *Isabella* for treasure, food, and anything they could carry. All the pirate booty was piled on the deck on top of large old sails that had been spread out. Anticipating this, Juan had left one small stash of gold coins worth a handsome amount in plain sight for the pirates to see. It was a small fortune, but nothing compared to the treasure that they had hidden. He hoped that in finding this, the pirates would cease looking so diligently.

Black Caesar approached Juan and continued, "You have killed many of my men today, but you all will pay with your life." He paused and shouted to the top of his lungs, "Dead men tell no tales" for the entire crew to hear. With this, Caesar raised his sword to take a final blow on Juan.

But at that moment a low rumble shook the beams of the ship. Caesar looked around confused. Then he ran to the side. Bubbles began surfacing from below the water's surface. And then seconds later, he began to see rats popping up on the water. They immediately began swimming to the open water and to the first pirate ship.

"It is my ship," said Juan in perfect English. "And if I can't have her, no one can." His master gunner, who had gone below deck behind the false wall they had quickly erected, had set off the charges that were set into place prior to the battle. This was their last resort in the event they were boarded.

Caesar tilted his head as if he could not believe what the captain was saying. Then with a grin Caesar said, "Take your wretched ship, Captain, and say hello to Davy Jones for me!" Caesar ordered his men to quickly take the booty and regress. They all scurried back to their ships like the fleeing rats before them and cut the grappling lines. Both pirate ships maneuvered away to the port side of the *Isabella* and out to deeper water. They were going to let the *Isabella* sink where she drifted.

Juan jumped up off his knees and commanded the crew to prepare to launch the longboats. The pirate ships were now over five hundred yards away and could not see what they were doing on deck. As far as the pirates were concerned, the crewmen of the *Isabella* were all walking dead. Juan and his remaining crew loaded onto the longboats as the *Isabella* began to list. It was a perilous departure from the *Isabella*, but they made it without incident. They paddled as hard as they could toward the shore, which was only visible during the flashes of light. By the time the *Isabella* sank, the two longboats were out of site of the pirate ships.

Juan could not believe the plan had worked. But the cost was great, and he felt sorrow for the crewmen who had followed him to their death. Most of the officers had survived, and they remained loyal. *At least this was not all for naught,* he thought as he looked down. For the seat he was sitting on was not part of the longboat. It was one of several chests of gold, silver, and jewels that he and the officers had hidden while the crewmen were eating their last supper before the pirates attacked. Both longboats were heavy with the treasure and crew.

Chapter 11: *Guilty Feeling*

Danielle and Nikki were returning home from their day shopping when Nikki's phone buzzed with a text message. She looked at it, sighed, and powered off her phone.

"Who was that?" asked Danielle.

"Ryan," said Nikki.

"Aren't you going to text him back?"

"No, I'm trying to avoid him," said Nikki in a deflated mood. Danielle knew something was bothering Nikki, but she didn't want to press her. Danielle didn't want to nag her with questions, given all that she had been through.

They arrived at the house and found Rick and Shelli were out back tying up the boat. Shelli gave her big smile and told them what a great day they had. She was especially pleased that she had caught more fish than her dad and that she got to be dispatcher at the sheriff's office for a while.

Nikki headed to her room and Rick to his office.

Perfect, thought Danielle as she reached for cookies to share with Shelli.

"So, Shelli, did Nikki and Ryan get into some kind of argument lately? I know you two had seen Stephanie and Ryan about a week ago, but did anything happen between those two?"

Shelli chomped down on a cookie.

"No. They seemed to get along pretty well for the short time we were with them. Nikki helped clean and dress a cut on Ryan's foot. And later when we were leaving, Ryan asked for her number and said he'd like to call her sometime."

Oh, that explains it, thought Danielle. *Nikki probably feels guilty about exchanging numbers with Ryan, given what happened to Cody.*

"Pardon me, honey," said Danielle to Shelli. "I need to go talk to Nikki about something."

"No problem, but don't forget we're supposed to walk tonight to get ice cream," said Shelli as she reached for a Coke in the fridge to wash down the cookie. When Shelli finished her snack, she picked up her phone and sent a text to Stephanie. It was the weekend, and she had a cool set of activities planned for tomorrow. That is, if Mom approved it.

Danielle knocked on Nikki's door and was invited in. She stopped and stared for a moment at Nikki sitting on her bed. There sat a beautiful, athletic woman with shoulder-length brown hair and the same drive to succeed that Danielle saw in her husband. But seeing Nikki crying made her remember the day when Nikki was eight years old. She had come into Nikki's room to find her sitting just the same way on the bed, crying because some boy had said she wasn't pretty. She remembered telling her that the boy was both silly and blind, and to just ask her dad if she wanted to know the truth. She was fine in a few minutes. Things were far more complicated now that Nikki was older, and affairs of the heart were no different. Danielle hoped she could help this striking grown woman the way she helped that pretty eight-year-old girl long ago.

"Hi, honey, can I come in?" asked Danielle.

"Yeah, sure," responded Nikki without looking up. Danielle sat down next to Nikki and gathered her thoughts for a moment.

"You know, honey, you really ought to talk to Ryan. He's not guilty of anything. He'd probably be a good person to talk to now."

"Are you kidding?" said Nikki. "I don't even really know Ryan. I've only talked to him once, and I don't think it's really right to get involved with anyone, after what's happened. It just doesn't feel right."

Danielle saw the sorry in Nikki's eyes as they watered up.

"I didn't say you needed to date him or anything like that. But you don't want him to think you dislike him. I'm sure by now he's found out that you and Cody were a couple, and he probably just wants to see if you're OK."

Nikki looked up at her mom as a tear came down her cheek. She spoke in a feeble voice.

"You're right, but I feel really uncomfortable about this. I think Ryan does like me. He gave me his phone number the day Cody was killed. I feel just awful that I actually thought about calling Ryan when I left him that day."

"Honey, you are a healthy, normal, vibrant young adult. Although you and Cody were dating, you had not committed to anything more—right?"

Nikki shook her head no. Danielle put her arm around Nikki and held her close.

"Unless you have some mystical powers I'm not aware of, you cannot see the future. You can't play these what-if games and second-guess what might have been. You couldn't have done anything to change what happened. Cody will always hold a special place in your heart. Honor him, honey, and remember him for the good times you had—not for some momentary, perfectly normal thought. I am sure that Cody would not want you to be miserable forever. You are entitled to mourn, but you will need to start to look beyond this. Maybe Ryan or some of your girlfriends would help get you mind off of Cody."

Nikki didn't say anything for a minute.

"Mom, I've never known anyone close to me who has died except for Great-Grandma. And that wasn't quite the same. What's the typical time a person should mourn before moving on?"

Danielle smiled. "There are no steadfast rules on this, honey. It's up to you, but I think it wouldn't hurt to have a little fun with your friends." Danielle stood up and headed for Nikki's door. She paused when she opened the door and looked back.

"You have always made me very proud, Nikki. You have a smart head on those shoulders, and you're more logical than you think. You get that from your dad. But logic doesn't always apply when it comes to love, life, and death. All the feelings you have are perfectly natural, but just don't let them consume you." She continued after a moment. "I'll leave you to your thoughts. I'll be in the kitchen if you need me."

With that, Danielle closed the door and headed down the hall toward the kitchen.

Nikki sat for a moment thinking of what her mom had said. She was glad she had finally talked to someone about it.

"Good ole Mom," she said out loud. With that she took a deep, cleansing breath and wiped the tears from her eyes. Then she got up and headed out of her room to find out what was going on with the rest of the Bryant clan.

Nikki walked first to the kitchen and then followed the voice of her sister out to the pool. She found Shelli sitting across from her mom at the glass table, which held a beautiful bouquet of sunflowers in a fancy blue vase, a pitcher of lemonade, and Tervis Tumbler sailfish cups. Shelli was trying to gain approval for the plan she had concocted for tomorrow.

"Mom,...please?" concluded Shelli. Danielle smiled at Nikki when she walked out.

"Shelli and Stephanie have come up with quite a set of plans for tomorrow. They want to go Venice Beach look for shark's teeth. Then have lunch at Osprey's Nest while in Venice. Of course they want to stop in Nokomis at the orange grove store for the chocolate and lime soft-serve ice cream. The mall comes next in the afternoon, and then they'll end the day with a barbeque picnic on South Lido Beach Park."

Danielle exaggerated a deep breath when done.

"Wowww," said Nikki. "That's really a packed day. How are you getting around?"

"Ryan said he could drive us down to Venice if we paid for his lunch at Osprey's Nest," Shelli piped up. "And he needed to look for some new jeans, so he was OK going to the mall too. He even said he'd pick me up."

Nikki immediately perked up. *That might be a good time to say hi to Ryan and apologize for the missed calls,* she thought.

"How are you getting to South Lido?" asked Nikki.

"Well," said Shelli, dragging out the last letter. *Here it comes,* thought Nikki. "I was hoping you could pick us up in the boat from Stephanie's place and then moor on the beach at South Lido," said Shelli with a not-so-innocent smile on her face.

Nikki thought a second and then agreed.

"I'll load a cooler with some burgers and drinks, and we can cook on the grills in the park."

"Awesome," said Shelli as she picked up her phone. "I'll tell Stephanie."

"Hold on a second," said Danielle. "I didn't say yes yet." Shelli and Nikki both looked at their mom. "Yes, it's fine," she said. *It will be good for Nikki.*

Shelli immediately texted Stephanie and got a reply a few milliseconds later. "Ryan wants to know if he can come with us to the barbeque. He said he'll bring the music and will help with the cooking." Nikki smiled wide for the first time in a while.

"It's OK with me," she said. "It would be great if he came."

Another flurry of fast fingers set the plans in stone. Shelli ran off to start picking out her wardrobe for tomorrow.

Nikki and Danielle poured some lemonade and enjoyed the breeze for a while. Then Nikki turned to her mom.

"Thanks, Mom."

"For what?" asked Danielle.

"For being you," said Nikki with a grin.

Danielle remained silent while grinning. Life was definitely better here in Florida. The tough high school years were gone, as was the tension that was once commonplace between her and her eldest daughter. It was so nice to be both mother and friend. Before that thought settled in her brain, she heard the distant yell from Shelli.

"Mommmm…where's my pink swimsuit? Did you wash it?"

Chapter 12: *Clues Surface*

While his girls planned the next day's activities, Rick was in his study accessing his notebook PC that was still running down at the sheriff's office. *Still another hour to go, but the pattern buffers are successfully determining normal versus abnormal patterns*, he thought. Rick hoped they had captured an image of the boat involved in Cody's murder. He called the sheriff to let him know the progress and said he'd call back in about an hour to summarize the software's findings.

Meanwhile, he checked on his new sensor buoys. Rick wanted to verify that the radar had detected Shelli and him that morning as they took the boat southward to fish. All was good with the radar detection. Video should have been recorded with each radar detection. A quick check of some of the video proved that the cameras and network video recorder was working well. The pattern buffers were collecting data at a fast rate, but unlike the small number of the prototype buoys he was investigating for the sheriff, the new sensor grid coverage would take days to collect enough information to make intelligent assessments.

Movement by the pool caught his attention. He looked out the bay window to see Shelli skipping excitedly away from the pool while Danielle and Nikki remain seated. It looked good to see Nikki smiling after being so sad for a week. Maybe she was starting to cope better with Cody's death and move on.

His mind drifted back to days in Virginia when his first business was still young. Danielle held the household together while he poured all waking hours into the business. Long trips overseas and long hours at the office made for tense times at home. Fortunately his family supported him, and it was because of them they were now living the sweet life they had always dreamed of in Florida.

Deep in his daydream, Rick was startled when the phone rang. Caller ID stated it was the sheriff's office. He looked quickly at the time display on his PC and noticed that there was still another fifteen minutes or so to data processing completion.

"Hello," Rick answered the phone.

"Hi, Rick. This is Bob."

"What's up Bob?" said Rick. "We're still a few minutes away from having some answers."

"I've contacted a few people at NOAA and persuaded them to help us," said the sheriff.

"That's great. Do you have a contact for me?"

"Yes, and I've got them on the phone. You want me to conference you in?"

"Certainly."

Rick heard a click and then seconds later another click, followed by the sheriff's voice.

"You still there, Rick?" he said.

"Yes, I'm here," said Rick.

"Dr. Simon Clark, meet Mr. Rick Bryant," the sheriff said.

Rick and Dr. Clark exchanged greetings. Rick asked if Dr. Clark and the sheriff both had Skype accounts, and they both concurred.

"I'm at my computer now, and I have a corporate account," Rick said. "Contact me and I'll conference us." He gave them his account name, and moments later both the sheriff and Dr. Clark had joined in on a conference. Rick had both video feeds side by side on his display. A quick confirmation of both video and sound allowed the video call to continue.

"Dr. Clark, I put in a request some time ago to get access to the feed for from your drones monitoring the Gulf."

"I found that request, Mr. Bryant, which had been shelved with no action. Sorry, it wasn't my call. But Sherriff Huggins', er...um, strong request got a quick clearance from my superiors."

Rick looked at the sheriff and smiled. He could only imagine what a lively telephone conversation that had been.

"The initial request was to add the drone feeds into my security network, but the request became more important given new events," said Rick.

"What are you looking for, Mr. Bryant?" asked Dr. Clark.

"Please call me Rick."

"And Simon is fine," said Dr. Clark quickly in return.

"On the Friday before last, a fishing guide and his customer were gunned down brutally offshore from Boca Grande Pass," Rick said. "We believe these two may have stumbled on a drug ring making deliveries. They were murdered past the last lighted buoy, which I believe is near the range of your drones flying along the coast. It is probably a long shot that one was flying over at the right time, but it's worth the effort to search your video records if it helps us find the killers."

"I see," said Dr. Clark. "We have a total of ten UAVs, unmanned aerial vehicles, on this project. But we only fly two of the drones, as they are often called, at any one time along the area you mentioned. And although that doubles the odds, the probability of capturing the event on video would still be very low."

Rick noticed the dejected look on the sheriff's face.

"The first thing to do is to determine if one or both of the drones were flying during that time," Dr. Clark continued. "What was the time of the murder?"

"It was about two hours after dark that they were killed, according to the latest report from our coroner's office," the sheriff said. "Give or take an hour."

"So that's about a three-hour search window," said Dr. Clark.

He looked at a second computer screen and began clicking with his mouse.

"A quick database search shows that two drones were indeed flying along the coast during that time. Both have five-axis, gyrostabilized thermal cameras, of course. Each camera has a 640 by 480 focal plane array and one-thousand-millimeter lens. Those are our newer drone assets. They fly at about one thousand meters altitude, so it should be able to easily see detailed features if they were looking in that direction."

"I assume that the thermal cameras are cooled three to five micron wavelength cameras with InSb detectors and three or more fields of view," said Rick. He pronounced the acronym *InSb* as "ins-bee."

Dr. Clark looked at him surprised and said, "Yes, you are correct. I see you know your thermal camera technology."

"I've worked with many sensor technologies over the years," replied Rick.

The sheriff was starting to look a little confused.

"The cooled technology permits clear images at much longer distances than uncooled thermal cameras," Rick explained. "Three fields of view means the thermal camera has three zoom levels. Unlike CCTV cameras, such as your camcorder, thermal technology has just started implementing continuous zoom. In other words, these are excellent cameras for our needs."

"Oh...OK," said Sheriff Huggins.

"It will take us three hours to view the video at standard frame rates and about one and a half hours to view it in fast search mode," said Dr. Clark.

"Simon, I have video search algorithms in my sensor suite that should be able to do that in about two or three minutes," interrupted Rick. "It would take about fifteen minutes to download the data over our high-speed Internet socket. That is, if the database resides on a network that has a broadband Internet connectivity."

"Give me a couple of minutes, and I'll copy this segment of the database to our semi-public FTP site," Dr. Clark said. "Then you can access it at this address and password."

Rick saw the address and password on the conversations window on Skype. Within a few minutes, the data download had begun. Rick checked the status of his notebook PC located at the sheriff's office, which was searching the data collected from his prototype buoy array.

"Bob, it appears the search is done on the video data from the buoys," he said. "As you recall, the results are for a full four terabytes of video data collected over weeks of operation. Sixty-two abnormal events had been identified over the search time."

"What determines an abnormal event?" the sheriff asked.

"First, the software must search the entire video database to determine what is normal. This might seem to be easy, but we had to enter many parameters such as tidal changes to weather patterns to night versus day activities. There has to be enough data across such parameters as weather so that weather itself doesn't trigger an abnormal event. Even such things as cloud shadows on the ground could trigger abnormality if all we had were perfectly clear days in the majority of data. The program then starts building rules for normal behavior in the video scenes. We're using the thermal data since it is in grayscale versus full color as in CCTV video. This will make for faster rule generation."

"But wouldn't identification be easier in full color?" the sheriff asked.

"Not necessarily for the computer. But once we've isolated any facial features, we can view the color video on the CCTV camera. That video was recorded at the same time as the thermal images."

"You said there were sixty-two abnormal events," asked Sheriff Huggins. "Can you narrow that down to see if any of those sixty-two abnormalities occurred on the night of the murders?"

"Yes we can," said Rick. "I'm sorting the events now by date and time."

Rick paused to wait for sorting to be completed.

"That's strange," he said. "There were four abnormal events the night Cody was killed. I would not expect that many events in that short of period."

Rick asked the sheriff to take a look at the notebook PC.

"Don't have to do that, Rick," the sheriff said. "We added an LCD projection screen to your notebook. We have it up on the wall for the lieutenant and the rest of us to see."

"Two of the four events occurred before the time of the murders," said Rick. "I'll ignore those and pull up the two of interest. Look up on the screen. The video histogram on the bottom of the screen shows motion activity over time. Note that during the time of the murders, very little activity was seen from any of the cameras. Motion detection is accomplished by comparing each new frame to the average frame content in each look direction. Since it was late, no one at the state park or the sheriff's office was controlling the cameras, so they were touring 360 degrees around each buoy. At about the time of the murders we have a spike in activity, which is what probably triggered the software to record it as abnormal."

Rick clicked on the video reference and then dragged over the time indicator to select a ten-minute window of time centered on the event. Then he clicked the Play button on the display. The video showed the camera was rotating between stationary azimuth angles. Each new angle stop was ten degrees from the last angle. It stayed at each stop for about two seconds, which allowed it to collect twenty frames of data at each stop.

It was after four minutes and two full revolutions that the camera picked up a boat moving and then stopping in the leeward side of Cayo Costa. It was a fishing boat, with three people on board. The people were easily distinguishable because they glowed from body heat. Differences in heat were what the thermal cameras are designed to detect. About two minutes later, a speedboat came racing fast up to the fishing boat and stopped next to it. The software that controlled the cameras was programmed to keep the camera trained on large movements for an extra fifteen seconds, so each event had about thirty seconds of video.

"This might be our guys," said Rick. "Bob, didn't you say there were at least two boats involved?"

"Yes. But it really amazes me that your software calls this an abnormality. Anyone looking at this could easily think they are just finishing up a day of fishing. It would be hard to use any of this as evidence."

"Let's look at what prompted the recording," Rick said quickly. "The program shows there were two event triggers for the first boat's arrival. One trigger was the time of night. A boat pulling up at that time of night seems to be irregular. The rules engine shows most boats pulled up from six to seven in the morning, at around noon, and just before dark."

"What was the second trigger?" asked the sheriff. Rick clicked on a screen icon that summarized the findings.

"It detected a weapon," said Rick excitedly.

"Replay the scene again," said the sheriff. Rick replayed the event. They could see the men were holding something in their hands, but it was difficult to make out it was a gun.

"How did the program detect this as a gun?" asked the sheriff. Rick clicked on the DSP False Color button on the display.

"The program has digital signal processing, or DSP, filters that are employed continuously. One filter I constructed was a weapon filter. The program searches for three characteristics of weapons. Any two will cause the filter to log an event. The three characteristics are shape, temperature, and frequency response. Let me enable the filter. Anything meeting two of the three characteristics will appear in a bright blue color."

As they stepped through the frames, they saw the software algorithm initiate a blue color area on the display. Clearly outlined there was the outline of an automatic machine gun.

"There it is," said Rick. "It's still not that clear, but the program believes the shape is consistent with a machine gun. And given the heat intensity, it is certain it was fired within thirty minutes or so. Otherwise the color intensity would have been in the much cooler frequencies."

"Can you make that image any clearer?" asked the sheriff.

"Just a second. Let me pull up the CCTV images."

"But it is dark and there should be nothing on the daylight cameras," said the sheriff.

"That may be true, but the daylight CCTV is sensitive to low light. The moon was providing a little light that night. I'm going to go to grayscale and then equalize the intensities across all frequencies."

When he did, a collective "Aaahhh" came from Simon, Rick, and Bob. The image clearly showed the outline of the machine gun.

Rick pushed ahead to the second video segment and was able to see two machine guns, one of which hung over the shoulder of a man.

"OK," said the sheriff. "We're making some progress here. But we need to identify the men on the boat and the boat registration number on the side. This would help us link the boat to the vicinity of the murder at the right time. It's circumstantial evidence, but it's still useful."

Rick went through the frames of both video segments, but only partial numbers were visible on the fishing boat. Rick sat stumped for a moment, but then he looked as if he had an idea and began clicking more controls on his display.

"What is it?" asked the sheriff. Rick continued clicking with his mouse and stayed focused at his display.

"These images came from one of the two middle buoys, he said. "The buoy closest to the southern tip of Cayo Costa did not have any abnormalities that night. It must be more common to see boats coming in late around the tip of the island. I'll play the video sequence at about the time these boats would have crossed by the buoys."

After a few moments, the most southern buoys video started to play. Right on cue, the first boat came into view. Since its presence activated the motion detection filter, the camera stayed on the boat as it passed. Before the side of the boat came into view, Rick slowed down the video play to slow motion. The boat operator had seen the lighted buoy and cut close by it before turning northward on the leeside of the island. As the boat came broadside to the buoy, Rick froze the frame. As if on cue, Rick and the sheriff read out loud the three-inch-tall registration numbers on the bow of the boat.

"That's exactly what we needed," said the sheriff excitedly.

Dr. Clark, who had been mostly silent, looked awed.

"That's just amazing," he said.

Rick repeated the steps and came up with the second set of registration numbers for the speedboat.

"We got two boats with armed men within the vicinity of the murders," said the sheriff. "The video shows their guns had been fired within the time of the murders. And we have their boat registration. This is really good. But we still don't have proof they killed Cody and his client."

"Can't you compare the bullets from the bodies to these guns for a ballistic match?" asked Rick.

"We could, but it is our experience that they destroy these weapons after use to keep from incriminating themselves. However, you have given me enough here to issue warrants for search and seizure of anything we find on the premises of the owners of the boats."

"Maybe the video we collected will help," Dr. Clark said. "It appears the video download from our drones is complete."

"Right," said Rick. "Let's start the quick search."

Chapter 13: *Time Forgets*

Even though Juan and his remaining crewmen had survived what should have been certain death by the two pirate ships, they were not out of trouble.

The storm was still raging and the waves were topped with violent whitecaps. The navigator fortunately grabbed the map of the area before he boarded the longboat. As best as he could tell, they were near the mouth of the big bay at Zara Zote. The crewmen kept their heads down and rowed hard. The faster they could travel, the more control they had over their course. No one wanted to see the boat capsize. Even though the captain and one other could swim, neither of them wanted to try to swim in the waves that were now crashing down on them relentlessly.

After what seemed to be an eternity, the lookout on the bow of the boat shouted that he spotted the inlet. This was a wonderful sound. The navigator strained to get a better view, but there was no visibility except during lightning strikes. It took several more minutes before the navigator recognized the pass and signaled the crew. The two longboats struggled in the breaking waves and finally reached the calmer waters of the bay without a single loss of life or an ounce of treasure.

Juan shouted to the navigator and the lookout to search for the shelter of a river or the leeside of an island. Juan was looking for this for three reasons. One, they would need a source of fresh water. When they hurried off the *Isabella* they had to load either people and provision or people and treasure. They had opted for the latter. Two, they needed shelter from the wind and weather. And three, they needed to hide from the pirates. If Black Caesar or his pirate crew had seen them escape the sinking ship, he would be undoubtedly unhappy about the outcome and would come seeking revenge. This order from the captain was met with groans from the crewmen as their muscles strained from the physical demands of rowing.

It wasn't far before they realized that the land to their starboard side was an island. Juan ordered the crew to maneuver down the waterway on the leeside of this island. As they moved down this waterway, Juan dragged his cupped hand in the water; he kept sampling its salinity and spitting it out. The water was clearly brackish, but the salt content was quite thin. A fresh water source must be nearby. After a few more moments, the flashes of lightning revealed two or more little islands in the middle of the waterway. Given the men were exhausted and the current location was providing a good relief from the wind and surf, he ordered them to beach on one of the little islands. They could stay there for the night, get their bearings in the morning, and make a decision as to where they should go next after some sleep.

The boats beached on the sandy shore of the biggest of the islands. From the looks of it, thick green mangroves covered part of the island's beach areas to the east. Elsewhere were beach grasses and brush. No trees greater than twenty feet tall were visible anywhere on the island. The beaches were elevated by at least two yards high above water level, so they should be safe. If there was a chance for a flood, it should have already occurred, given the rainfall rate over the last hour or two. Juan walked a little around each side of the island. *This is a defendable position, with only one direction that enemies could approach. Fresh water is nearby, and we already know there are fish in the waters.*

"We will stay here for the night," Juan said out loud. "Remove the treasure from the boats and bury it in the soil inland. That way we can flee quickly if we are attacked and can return for the treasure when the threat is gone. We will flip the boats so that we can be protected from the direct line of fire if pirates come for us. We are near fresh water, so the first thing we will do is search for this when the sun rises in the morning.

"We will have two men on lookout at all times," he continued. "Shifts will be on the hour so that we stay alert. The navigator and I will be on the first watch." Juan wanted to make sure he had the first shift, because he was not certain the pirates would give up so easily tonight.

The men settled in for some sleep while the navigator and Juan started their watch. The navigator pulled out his map.

"Captain, I have looked closer at the map and there is no detail on this inland area. However, given the condition of the water here, I would say that we should continue on this course to seek water. "

"Agreed," said Juan. "Finding water is the most important thing. Where there is fresh water, there will be game to kill. And although the men are not fisherman, they can try to use the netting we brought to catch fish. "He looked off in thought. "We'll be fine." *At least I hope so*.

The navigator put away his map in its leather tube and sealed it with wax. The two of them remained silent for the rest of their watch.

The sun was rising when Juan was awakened abruptly.

"Wake up, sir," said the quartermaster. "We have visitors."

Juan bolted up and peeked over the edge of the longboat, expecting to see approaching pirate longboats. Instead he saw local natives in canoes behind patches of mangroves on the west and east sides of them.

"What do you think the natives want, sir?"

"They may have been alerted by the cannon fire last night and watched us beach last night," Juan said. "They may have decided to wait for morning to assess the situation."

A few minutes passed, and he noticed that the Indians were starting to close.

"Let's not try to provoke them, but we should be prepared to stand our ground if necessary," said Juan. His crew stayed low and made sure their pistols were ready for action.

"Sir, I will volunteer to stand without weapons and introduce us," offered the quartermaster. "If we show them we are friendly, perhaps we can arrange to trade with them."

After some discussion with the crew, Juan agreed. The quartermaster rose and walked between the two boats and stood a few steps forward of them.

"Greetings," said the quartermaster slowly. "We are here as your friends and look forward to…"

Juan heard the quartermaster stop talking in midsentence at the same instant he heard a *thunk*. Before Juan could look up again over the longboat, the quartermaster landed between the two longboats on his back, with his eyes wide open. He was dead. Looking slightly forward, Juan saw the arrow in the center of the quartermaster's chest.

"Avenge your quartermaster and make every shot count!" Juan shouted to the crewmen. "Pair up and have the best marksman fire. The other crewman will reload. Keep firing until you kill all the savages!"

Juan reached over the longboat and fired at the closest canoe, which had closed to only ten yards from the island. The front of the native warrior's chest splayed open, and he slumped over.

There were two or three warriors per canoe, and in the case of this closest canoe, there were two. The cook was the next to fire and took out the second warrior in the canoe. The navigator handed his pistol to Juan and asked for the empty pistol in Juan's right hand. Juan stuck his head up just in time to have an arrow bury its flinthead into the longboat just below his face. It startled him momentarily, but he continued to fire at canoes to his right.

"Crew in boat two, take out warriors to the left. Boat one will get those on the right!"

The warriors kept coming and dropping. Only three of Juan's men had been hit, which was amazingly few, given the number of arrows embedded in the longboats. Although many men had survived the onslaught, the boats were effectively ruined for use on the water.

Juan fired again and felled a warrior emerging from the water. He turned to the navigator for the reloaded pistol. The navigator had a grim look on his face.

"What?" asked Juan.

"You have two shots left," said the navigator.

Juan had known this was coming. He was surprised they had enough powder between them to make it this far. He turned and saw the worried look on his crewman. Half of the crewmen behind boat two were out of ammo completely. They were running out of options. He turned to look behind him. The dense brush and small trees that were protecting them from behind due were also trapping them from any hope of retreat.

"We need ideas, gentlemen," Juan said. He looked up and fired at yet another warrior.

"Sir," said the navigator. "We do not have any choice. There are too many of them to kill with our pistols. We must let them attack and hold them off with our cutlasses until it gets dark. They waited until morning to attack us, so maybe they will stop at sunset. If so, we can then escape in their canoes." It was a dire plan. It was even more farfetched than the plan they'd had to escape from the pirates. But they had survived the pirates. His thought was interrupted by another shot from one of the crewmen at another warrior leaving his canoe.

"Men," said Juan in a voice that could be heard by all crewmen. "You have been a loyal and brave crew. We have expended our ammunition, and our only choice is to let them approach close and take them with our cutlasses. I know you are tired, hungry, and thirsty, but we must prevail. I will fight by your side until we defeat them or die. Whatever it may be, I am proud to be your captain. Now prepare for the invasion."

The men roared in fervent cheer. If they were to die, they were going to make it a hellish chore for their enemy.

The warriors must have realized from the absence of fire that they had nothing left to fear from the pistols. They landed on the beach, raced to the longboats, and dived over them with bloodcurdling cries. As they cleared the longboat, they encountered the blades of the *Isabella* crew. Two and three warriors at a time plunged to their death. Within just a few minutes, the pile of lifeless warriors draped over the longboats and on the ground around the boats was making it difficult for new warriors to reach the crew. But that did not stop them. The warriors started climbing the bodies to reach the crewmen.

Juan felt the pain in his arms from the fatigue of the continual swing of his blade. He looked for a second at his crewmen. The Indian warriors' pace of attack was too fast for them. They could not kill fast enough. Boat two had only four men left alive. All of the crewmen still living were covered in their fellow crewmen's blood or the blood of the warriors. They had no choice; they had to make a run for it.

"To the canoes, men," he shouted. "We must try to escape. Follow me!"

With that Juan charged to his left at a canoe that was about to drift free of the beach. He cleared the end of longboat two and the pile of dead bodies around it. As he passed the last warrior body on the open beach, he leaned forward into his fastest sprint toward the rocking, drifting canoe. He was three yards from the canoe when he felt an incredibly sharp pain in his neck. The invisible force spun him around, and he almost fell.

With his dagger in his left hand and his cutlass in his right, he dared not drop them to reach for his neck. The pain was unbearable. He felt wetness on his sleeve. As he looked down, he saw a spurt of bright red fluid shoot from his neck and spray his sleeve. Another spurt shoot out as his heart took another beat. The shaft of the arrow that had impaled in his neck was barely visible to his blurring, peripheral eyesight. Being in the open had made him a sitting duck for the bowmen.

Dazed, Juan turned around toward the longboats to see his navigator looking at him in horror. Juan tried to talk when another severe pain shot into his side. Seconds later there was another pinch to his leg. Shock had set in, and Juan's pain receptors were shutting down. He felt himself stumble, and his vision started to fade. He strained to focus and had a couple seconds of clarity to see the point of a knife pierce through the lips of the navigator. The navigator fell dead forward toward Juan with the hilt of the knife protruding from the back of his neck. More pinches in his arm and torso accompanied a feeling of calmness as Juan's vision went black. He fell to the ground with his cutlass and dagger still clutched in his hands.

On a warm and sunny morning in November 1715, more than one hundred Native American warriors and the remaining crew of the *Isabella* expired on a remote beach of a small island where no one would ever find them. The remaining warriors retrieved their fallen brothers and gave them a king's burial. Although many of the Native Americans died, their spirits lived on for a few generations in the stories of their tribesmen before European diseases would erase them from existence. The crewmen of the *Isabella*, however, were left to rot away. The crabs and maggots feasted until the bones were clean. The sands of the beach slowly consumed their skeletons, and the boats turned to dust that the rains washed away to the sea. Their names and fates would be lost to history forever. Dead men tell no tales.

Chapter 14: *Blood in the Water*

Rick launched the search of the drone video data that Dr. Simon Clark had provided him. Instead of a normal fast-forward search through the video, Rick had first isolated the latitude and longitude coordinates stored in video header and quickly pulled out only the video associated with the stretch of ocean where Cody's murder had taken place. Dr. Clark had already minimized the amount of video data to cover a three-hour window around the approximate time of the murder before providing it to Rick.

"It appears there were four passes by two separate drones along the murder location at that time," said Rick. "I've reduced the amount of video down to just those four passes for a segment of two miles centered on the murder location."

He clicked a few more times on his mouse as he talked with Dr. Clark and Sheriff Huggins over Skype.

"The drones are flying at about eighty miles per hour, so the video over this area lasts about a minute and a half. The drones are flying long elliptical paths in a north-south orientation. Each leg is one hundred miles, and the end of the ellipse is just south of Sanibel Island. So we're catching the end of the leg southbound and the beginning of the leg northbound. We were sort of lucky in this instance. Had the event taken place near Venice or Englewood, we would have more time between passes. This would have resulted in only two drone passes instead of four over the same period of time."

Rick started playing the video. The resolution of the video was incredibly clear—much more so than the video collected by the buoys. The images looked like they had been filmed by a black and white camera in broad daylight.

"The clarity is amazing," said the sheriff.

"That's what an extra seven hundred thousand dollars will buy you," said Rick with a smile. Rick was streaming the video from his office computer back to his notebook PC, which was sitting in the sheriff's office in Punta Gorda.

The video was not straight overhead; rather, it was taken at about a forty-degree tilt down angle from the side of the drone.

"We look out from the side for two reasons," said Dr. Clark. "We can cover a larger area than just looking straight down. Plus, we look at the same patch of water from two look directions. On the southbound leg, we look at a swath of water in the direction of the shore. Then when we turn and fly northward, we orient the path so that we are looking at the same swath of water surface from the opposite side. This allows us to build a 3-D model of the surface. Since the thermal image can penetrate the surface of the water, we can see also below the surface a few meters. With two drones flying the same flight pattern, we get twice the updates of the surface swath over the same amount of time."

As he finished talking, a boat came into view on the video. Rick slowed down the play speed, and the sheriff immediately recognized Cody's boat. It was confirmed when the heat signatures of two people could be seen. The boat quickly moved out of view of the drone, and moments later two other boats came into view. They appeared to be adrift in the water.

"Are they the guys we saw in the buoy video?" asked the sheriff. "How can we determine if they are the same guys we saw on the buoy cameras?"

"Let me check something on the buoy data," Rick said. He paused the drone video and pulled back up the video that had the Florida registration of the two boats collected by the buoys. "Any boat built since 1972 has to have a hull identification number on it. It's a twelve-digit number placed on the boat by the manufacturer. The first three numbers are the manufacturer's ID code. The next five numbers are the production or serial number. The next two numbers show the month and year, and the final two show the model year. It's normally found at the boat transom."

After another moment of looking at the video, Rick stopped the video to see the first boat's hull number just barely visible.

"There it is. Time to cross reference the hull number to a boat model number."

After another minute, Rick said, "Got it!" He pulled up the manufacturer's Web site. "Here's the drawing download webpage. It should have a plan or top view drawing of the boat."

In a few moments a window of the boat's drawings popped up on the display. He clicked and dragged the plan view onto a separate window. Then he clicked and dragged a snippet of the frozen video from the drone. He compensated for distance and resized the image.

"It's a match," Rick concluded. "That is the same type of boat as the first boat in the buoy video data."

"But we still have no video of the actual incident," said the sheriff.

"Right," said Rick. "We still have three more passes to view."

Rick selected the next video clip. This video was filmed on the northern pass by the same area, which means the view was from the east. They again saw Cody's boat moving, but more in a eastward fashion. The other two boats were following him. In the last couple of frames, a bright flash of light appeared on the lead boat, which was the high-speed boat.

"That's gunfire," said the sheriff. The third pass, which was the southward track of the second drone, showed all boats stopped. One boat was in front of the bow of Cody's boat, and the other was just off the starboard side. A spotlight was switched on by the boat on the starboard side, which caused the camera to become jittery for a moment before it compensated for the light intensity.

"That's the camera automatically adjusting to the light," commented Dr. Clark.

"Here's our last chance," said Rick as he clicked on the last video segment. "This is the northward leg of the same drone flight. It's only a few minutes later than the last video, but that could be too late."

The video came up on the three boats in about the same positions. Simon, Rick, and the sheriff were quietly and intently watching the video. Cody appeared to be standing with his hands up. He made a move, but then stood back up. Suddenly bright flashes came from a gun on the boat with the spotlight, which was a fishing boat. Drops of bright fluid spattered all over the boat and water surface as Cody's body danced with the cadence of the flashing lights. Cody dropped and slumped over the edge. A stream of the same bright fluid was visible on the outer hull and pooled on the water's surface, where it dimmed and merged into the cool darkness. The clip ended shortly thereafter.

The quietness was interrupted by the sheriff.

"I need all the video we've viewed tonight cataloged and copied into a form we can show in the courtroom."

"I'll get on that," Rick said. "We'll cut it on a DVD. I'll put in a few introductory comments to show what we're seeing."

"Please be sure to include those screenshots of the boat numbers too," said the sheriff. "We'll need that to show the judge for the search warrants."

The discussion continued for a few more minutes. The sheriff wanted to make sure he had some of the technical lingo down as well. He then wrapped up the session with a few words.

"Dr. Clark, I want to thank you for your support on this matter. I think you might want to seriously consider convincing the powers that be at the NOAA to work with Mr. Bryant. We had little chance of a conviction before tonight. Now we have actual video that could put someone in prison for this act."

Dr. Clark agreed with the sheriff and thanked Rick for the "fascinating interchange." He signed off after the sheriff reminded him that he had to keep everything confidential until the case was solved.

"Rick, that was some impressive bit of work you did tonight," the sheriff said. "I almost felt like I was in school there for a little while. I am sure we're going to be using you and your technology again in the future."

"Thanks. I was more than happy to help."

"Help? Why, you've done more than just help. I'm going to make sure Cody's parents know what you've done." He paused for a moment and rubbed his neck. "I hate to even ask for this, but we're probably not finished needing your services on this case. Do you think your new buoy system can be used to locate these guys? I have a sneaking suspicion that they will cover their tracks and will be difficult to find."

"We can certainly use the buoy network to search for sightings of these boats. But we don't have a good full facial shot of the bad guys. We just have a few profile shots. But I'll enter all this into the system for continuous search."

"Thanks. It's much appreciated. I'll see if we can get you some kind of consulting contract. I'd feel better about taking up so much of your time anyway."

"Don't worry about that now," said Rick. "I'm more interested in seeing those criminals put behind bars. We can talk about the long term after this is over."

Chapter 15: *Beautiful Day*

Shelli and Stephanie were riding in the backseat of Ryan's Jeep Wrangler. The sky was blue with light, patchy white clouds. The girls were giggling at their own jokes and eating the chocolate and lime soft-serve cones they bought at the local orange grove store in Nokomis. Their long hair was in ponytails to keep it from wrapping around the cones as the wind whipped by. Ryan had his shirt off while driving and was singing to himself with the songs on the radio. When they pulled up to the stoplight at US 41, he reached to turn up the volume as U2's "Beautiful Day" came on the speaker.

Stephanie loudly spoke up.

"Hang a left and then cut over on Albee Road to the beach road on Casey Key. It's too pretty out to go to the mall right now."

"OK," said Ryan. He was enjoying the day, which was not steaming hot for a change. "I'll take the beach road up to Blackburn Point and then get back on 41 again. That would put us just a few minutes from the mall."

"Cool," said Stephanie.

They crossed the southern bridge to Casey Key and then headed north. The island narrowed in a number of places, which gave them beautiful views of the beach on one side and the Intercoastal Waterway on the other. The road was lined with beautiful mansions and palm trees. The manatee and dolphin mailboxes that dotted the roadside were no match to the beauty of the real dolphins they saw playing in the Intercoastal Waterway at one spot.

By the time they reached the end of the island, the girls had finished their ice cream cones. They had begun planning their list of stores to check out at the mall when Ryan turned right onto Blackburn Point

Road. As they approached the small bridge, a van pulled out quickly in front of them, causing Ryan to slam on his brakes. The driver of the van rolled his window down and waved an apology.

"Jerk!" yelled Ryan as he shot his middle finger in the air. The girls looked at each other and then threw back their heads in laughter at Ryan's gesture.

◊◊◊◊◊

Inside the van, DEA agent Kyle Thompson was sitting in the front passenger seat. This was the second time the suspect they were tailing had picked up drugs here at the tiki bar. The pattern was now repeating, so they had located all the drug drop-off locations. The suspect was going to leave the parking lot and begin his long drive back to Orlando. The agents were intently watching the suspect when the driver pulled out of the parking lot across from the tiki bar a little too quickly.

"Shit, Jason! You pulled out in front of that Jeep. You got to pay attention when you're on stakeout. You're lucky the suspect is far enough ahead not to see that."

"Sorry," said Jason as he opened his window to wave at the Jeep.

Kyle looked into the large mirror on the passenger side, which magnified the view behind.

"I recognize those kids in the Jeep," he said. "They were on the boat that stopped at Edwards Islands about a week ago. I saw them pull up there when I was on stakeout at the Siesta Key Bridge. Remember? I was fishing at the seawall that day and captured some video of them."

"Do you think they are involved in this?" asked Jason.

"No, I think it's just a coincidence. They're locals. But it's a small world, ya know."

Once they hit US 41, the van turned north and so did Ryan and the girls. The van moved to the right lane, and Ryan accelerated past them on the left. Ryan shook his head as he drove by the van without looking at the driver. As they passed, Shelli glanced back and saw both men looking at her. She noticed the man on the passenger side had a UVA cap. She saw

Virginia plates when she glanced down.

"He's not a local," shouted Shelli as she turned forward to Ryan. "He's got a University of Virginia cap on. He's probably here on vacation."

"That explains the poor driving," Ryan shouted back.

Ryan, Shelli, and Stephanie headed to the mall, which was busy. After a couple of hours of shopping, Ryan had had his fill of the mall. He got to thinking about tonight and the opportunity to see Nikki. So he started a thirty-minute campaign of nagging that was successful in getting the girls to agree to leave. They got back in the Jeep and headed north toward Siesta Key. Bags filled with the girls' purchases rattled in the front seat of the Jeep.

Once they arrived at Ryan and Stephanie's house on Siesta Key, Shelli and Stephanie went to the pool and took a dip. Ryan put the top back on his Jeep and headed inside for a quick snack, since he didn't have any ice cream. The time was about five o'clock in the afternoon when Shelli decided to give Nikki a call.

"Hi, sis," answered Nikki. "Did you guys have a good day?"

"It was awesome." Shelli proceeded to describe the day's events in detail. "Oh, and we almost hit a van that cut us off! We think they were on vacation. Ryan shot them the bird once he got the Jeep under control."

"Why do you think they were on vacation?" asked Nikki curiously.

"One guy had a UVA cap on and they had Virginia plates." Nikki thought a moment.

"I just saw someone with a UVA cap on. I can't remember where that was, though. I wonder if it was the same guy."

"Who knows," said Shelli. She began describing what she had bought at the mall.

"What time do you want me to pick you guys up?" asked Nikki once Shelli had finished. "It gets dark now at around eight o'clock. We should already be set up on the beach by then so that we don't have to fumble in the dark. Plus, the raccoons really come out to raid the picnic area just as its turning dark."

"Just come on now. We'll be ready by the time you get here."

"OK. I've got the boat already loaded with coolers, blankets, and coals for the grill."

"Great. See you in a little while."

"On my way," said Nikki as she hung up her phone.

Nikki found her mom and dad sitting by the pool. She let them know where she was headed and then jumped in the boat. She did one more check. Four life preservers, flashlights, radio, coolers, lighter, coal, blankets, towels, and a change of clothes in case she went in the water.

"Check, check, and check," she said as she checked the last few items. She cranked up the boat and headed out.

The day was indeed beautiful, she thought as she passed under the Ringling Bridge. In the morning she had hit Newton's Bagel off Tamiami Trail, or Route 41. A large mocha Frappuccino and a spinach bagel with veggie lite cream cheese started the morning right for her. She got the grocery shopping done early for tonight's cookout and then was able to spend a relaxing day down at Lido Beach.

She slowed as she passed under the north Siesta Key Bridge and looked to her right at the seawall, where a few people were lined up fishing. It was then she realized where she had seen the man with the UVA cap. It was on the seawall the day she came down to rescue Stephanie. The man had been fishing there. It dawned on her that it was the day after Cody's death. The thought saddened her. She was in a daze for a few seconds and the shook it off.

"Enough of that," she said out loud. "I'm going to have a good time tonight with the girls." *And Ryan,* she thought.

Nikki rounded the first of Edwards Islands and was reminded of the object that cut Ryan's foot. She made a mental note to herself that they should make a stop on the way back. If nothing else, it would be a good distraction.

Nikki pulled up at the dock. Stephanie and Shelli came out immediately, carrying Shelli's new purchases and her purse. Shelli's phone was, of course, in her hand.

"Hi, sis," said Shelli as she skipped up.

"Hello, girls," said Nikki. She looked up to see Ryan wearing a T-shirt, cut-off jean shorts, and his sandals.

"All aboard, Ryan," said Nikki.

"Aye, aye," said Ryan with a big smile as he swung his legs over onto the boat. Nikki grinned. She had forgotten just how attractive Ryan was.

They took off back into Roberts Bay and rounded the biggest island.

"Let's stop back at the island to see what was on the beach that cut your foot, Ryan."

"Are you joking?" said Stephanie. "I spent enough time on that island."

"Relax, sis," snapped Ryan. "You used the restroom before we left home. You'll be fine." They all laughed as they remembered Stephanie's "pee" dance.

Nikki cut the motor and drifted the boat up onto the beach. Ryan jumped off the bow and pulled the boat firmly on shore. He lifted his hand and helped Stephanie and Shelli off the boat. He gave a big smile again as he held Nikki's hand and helped her off the boat.

"Thank you kind, sir," said Nikki in a British accent. Ryan half bowed and swept his arm toward the beach in front of them.

"After you, me lady," he said in an attempted British accent.

As they moved higher on the beach, Nikki said, "I put a big rock over the object so that no one else would step on it." After a few moments, Shelli announced she had found the rock. Everyone came around it. Nikki bent down and moved the rock. The object was no longer visible. She rested on her knees and slowly began to move sand away from the spot the rock had been sitting.

"Careful," said Ryan. "My mom made me go get a tetanus shot after I told her what I had done that day." After a few sweeps of her hand, Nikki felt the object.

"Here it is," she said.

"I put a small shovel in the boat," said Nikki. "I brought it in case we need to put out the coals for the cookout." She looked up at Ryan. "It's in the back of the boat under the blankets."

Ryan jumped back on the boat and fetched the shovel. He handed it to Nikki, who was still kneeling next to the object.

Nikki slowly and carefully shoveled more sand away from the object. The sand was dry and was easy to push away.

"It's a long, relatively thin piece of metal," Nikki said after a minute. The metal was encrusted with dead barnacles and had long lost its luster. Those metal parts that were exposed were heavily rusted. After about a yard of metal had been exposed, they saw more curved metal coming off the main beam. Nikki brushed with her hand now in a slower, more careful manner.

"This looks like a sw…" Nikki stopped in midsentence. Stephanie gasped as Nikki wiped another handful of sand to expose a white-gray object about a half-inch long.

"Is that what I think it is?" said Stephanie. One more wipe exposed the second joint of a skeleton finger.

"Eeewwww," said Shelli at the same time as Ryan said, "Cooool." Ryan continued, "It's a skeleton hand holding a sword!"

"We've got to call someone," said Nikki. "We shouldn't go any further. We don't know if this is a murder scene, a historical site, or both."

Nikki thought a moment. She remembered when the sheriff came by to see her after Cody's death that he left her his card. Nikki got up and said, "Shelli, you call Dad and tell him what we found. Tell him that I'm calling Sheriff Huggins."

Nikki jumped on the boat and picked up her purse. Inside her wallet was the sheriff's card. She dialed.

"Hi, sheriff, this is Nikki Bryant. I need to report something we just found at the northernmost end of Edwards Islands." She proceeded to describe what they had found.

After a couple of minutes on the phone, she hung up.

"Sheriff Huggins said he was going to call the sheriff's office here in Sarasota to respond. But he's coming up too." Shelli had also just hung up with her dad.

"Dad said that the local sheriff was probably going to come. He and Mom are going to stop at the office and pick up one of the workboats and meet us here in about fifteen minutes. He said not to touch anything and leave if there is any sign of trouble."

The local sheriff, Mike Steele, was the first to pull up. He greeted the girls and Ryan, and they immediately walked him over to the dig site. Moments later, Rick and Danielle pulled up in the smaller of the workboats. Rick couldn't ground the workboat, so he had to anchor it in shallow water. He carried Danielle from the boat to the beach and set her gently on the shore. They walked up to shake hands with Sheriff Steele, whom he had met a few times before when planning the buoy project.

"So what's the plan?" asked Rick.

"This looks more like an archeological site, so I've called the University of Florida to tell them to be prepared to come over," replied Sheriff Steele. "But I've also called the forensics team to get here immediately, in case it is a homicide."

"Any need for my kids to stay here?" asked Rick.

"No. I've given them a clipboard for their statements. Once they've finished, they can leave. We may need to contact them again for more questions if this becomes a murder case." The sheriff paused for a moment, thinking about what he had just said. "But it will be just as witnesses, not suspects."

"Good," said Rick. "We'd like to stay, if possible, at least until Sheriff Bob Huggins arrives from Punta Gorda. I have some news for him on Cody's case, and I'd like to give him an update."

"No problem. I've got some news for Bob as well."

By half past six that evening, Nikki, Shelli, Stephanie, and Ryan were on their way to South Lido Beach. On the short boat ride, they were all talking about the find. Ryan was standing next to Nikki at the helm, and Shelli and Stephanie were sitting near the stern. Nikki looked back at them and shouted over the roar of the motor, "Remember what the sheriff said. We cannot tell anyone about this until it's been released by the sheriff's department."

"We know," said Shelli. "Dad told me he didn't want to hear about any text leaks to my friends, either."

When they arrived at the beach, Ryan leapt off into the water and repeated his now-standard task of pulling the boat to shore. One other boat was there, along with a few people who had driven to the park. They found a nice picnic table at the edge of the tall trees, but still on the beach. They unloaded all their supplies and started setting up for the picnic. Ryan started the grill. The girls pulled out the big beach blanket and put a tablecloth on the picnic table. Since the raccoons were well known for their snatch-and-grab tactics at this park, they remained seated at the picnic table talking while the food was cooking.

It was nearly dark, and they had finished their dinner when Shelli received a call from her mom.

"Hi, Mom," said Shelli, answering the phone.

"Are you guys still there at the Island?" asked Danielle.

"We're about to head back home."

"Sheriff Huggins finally arrived and we're talking to him now," continued Danielle.

"What about the body we found on the beach? Was it a murder?"

"I don't want to talk about it too much now, but it looks like it's a historical site. But still no contacting your friends about this. We'll talk about this more when you get home." Shelli agreed and said good-bye.

Shelli relayed the news from her mom. This started another round of speculation amongst the group. It was decided after a few minutes that there was just too much excitement to stay at the park. They wanted to find out more details about the site they found, so they decided to pack up and head back to Nikki and Shelli's house before it got pitch black. They cleaned up their trash and packed it and the rest of their gear back in their boat. Stephanie called her dad to let him know where they were headed.

They were off in less than ten minutes. Nikki was at the helm when Ryan spoke up.

"Better take it slow. It's hard to see what's in the water at dark."

Nikki smiled. "Are you kidding? Do you know my dad at all?" Nikki turned on the display on the console in front of her. She pressed another button, and a crystal-clear view forward popped up on the display as if it were daytime. "That's a high resolution thermal camera image."

She pointed to the display in front of Ryan.

"Turn on your display right there. That one is tied to the radar. If the radar detects something on the water, it will automatically point that camera at the object. It's just like…uh, never mind. It's cool, isn't it?" She almost told Ryan about the sensors on the buoys, forgetting momentarily that her dad said she was not to tell anyone about their capabilities.

"Yes it is," Ryan replied. He looked directly at Nikki. "Your family is cool. You must be really happy."

Nikki thought about what he said and looked back at her sister, who gave her a quick wave.

"Yes, I am. It felt good to have the cooler night air blowing across her face. She began thinking of the day again. "It was a beautiful day today, wasn't it?"

"And you can't beat the scenery," said Ryan, with his eyes still fixed on Nikki

Chapter 16: *No Detours, No Exceptions*

Frank was moving the boat southbound and was talking to his partner, Greg, for this run. They had just dropped off the drugs again to Johnny and were starting the long boat ride back to Charlotte Harbor. It had been a beautiful day to be on a boat. The only regret was that they forgot their own cooler and didn't have a thing to drink.

They were about a half a mile from the Intercoastal Bridge on Albee Road when Greg said, "Hey, you know, I'm real thirsty, Frank. I don't think I can make it all the way to Charlotte Harbor without something to drink. There's the southern bridge up ahead to Nokomis. How 'bout stopping at Seagull Alley for a drink? Remember, they have that dock you can pull right up to. We could grab a quick beer and then make up some time out on the Gulf."

Frank shook his head.

"No can do. We are not supposed to make any stops unless we have an emergency. Being thirsty is not an emergency."

"Come on, Frank. We've been doing this for a while now and haven't had an incident yet. We've earned the right to stop just this one time. I promise I won't forget the cooler again." Greg had pitiful-looking eyes when he was begging. It seemed funny to Frank that the man with the gun was begging.

"Maybe we can if we call in," said Frank. "We can tell them we forgot our cooler, and maybe they'll let us stop."

"Hell, no. You know what the boss will say. 'Get your ass back here now and no stops!'" mimicked Greg. "It won't take us more than fifteen minutes to stop for a beer. Hell, get yourself a water if you're worried. But don't call it in."

Frank paused for a minute, thinking about what Greg had said.

"Well, OK. But we have to make it quick. And only one beer, Greg. Swear to me you'll only drink one beer, and you'll not beg me to stay longer. Swear it!"

"I swear," said Greg with his hand over his heart and a three-finger salute in the air.

◊◊◊◊◊

Hans lowered the handheld clear parabolic dish. He had heard enough from the two operatives over the remote listening device. He removed the headphones and started his black Mercedes sedan, which was sitting on the long sandy boat ramp that paralleled the Intercoastal Waterway just north of the southern bridge to Nokomis Beach. The boat ramp was wide enough for cars to park on either side and still have room for boat trailers to be towed and be moved into the water.

He let Frank and Greg pass by his position at the end of the ramp. He put the car in gear and slowly followed them. He still had his window down and could hear the white sand that stuck to the treads of his black tires make soft clicking sounds as it was hurled upward to impact the back bumper and back wheel wells.

Hans turned right at the end of the sandy boat ramp road, passed over the concrete bridge, and then went left on Casey Key Road. He passed the bridge and Albee Road and turned left a tenth of a mile later into the parking area of a little park that sat on the waterway just south of the bridge. He saw the drug boat across from him tied at the dock. Frank and Greg were sitting in the screened-in patio area, already talking to the waitress. With the car running, Hans pushed a button that released the truck latch. He walked to the back and picked up a long black leather case. He brought it back into the car with him and opened it. Inside was a pistol with a variable power scope. He picked up a long black tube that was threaded on one end. He screwed the tube, which was a silencer, in the end of the pistol barrel.

Hans waited patiently in the comfort of his air-conditioned car with its plush tan leather seats. Black was a less popular color for cars in Florida, but it was his favorite car color. He loved his car. It reminded him of his homeland, which he could never see again. Although he had traveled the world, he had never found anyplace he loved more than the beautiful scenery, the great changes brought by the four seasons, the food, and the people. Even though Florida had a healthy population of German transplants and tourists, he rarely had time to socialize. He disliked the humidity and flat landscape of Florida, but his job didn't give him much time to think about it. It was when he was alone like this that he missed his country the most.

Motion on the dock at Seagull Alley brought Hans back to the present task. He watched as Frank and Greg boarded the boat and started south toward Venice. Hans started his car, pulled back out onto Casey Key Road, and drove southward to the end of the key. This was called the North Jetty of Nokomis, even though it was at the southern extent of the island. Across the Venice Inlet sat the South Jetty, which was part of Venice. There was a small building at the end of the road, sitting right on the jetty. The building was a combination fish camp and restaurant that served beer, wine, soft drinks, hot dogs, and of course, bait and fishing tackle. A big red sign with a fish identified the restaurant and the live and frozen baits it sold.

The area in front of the restaurant and to the side was a sandy parking lot and boat launch. Small boats and kayaks used this spot. Hans knew that it was normally not crowded here, and today was no different. He parked under a nearby palm tree so that he would be able to see the Waterway. The tree was one of a line of palms and pines that separated the parking lot from a park with picnic tables and grills. The park bordered the waterway and was sometimes visited by fishermen, but not today. He rolled down his window and then picked up the pistol, chambered a round, and laid it on his lap.

The location offered a wide vantage point of the intersecting waters of the inlet and the waterway. A long island park only accessible by boat was directly east of the point, and another island sat south of that, further blocking waterfront eyes from seeing what Hans was about to do.

He waited until he saw Frank and Greg slowly moving down the waterway toward Venice Inlet. He looked around one last time to make sure no one was watching and that no boats were near. Hans rested the barrel on his sleeved arm and aimed at the boat. He could see Frank clearly in his scope. He was laughing at something Greg had told him.

"You know better, Frank. Time to teach you a lesson," said Hans quietly to himself without taking his eye from the scope. He slowly squeezed the trigger, and a quick *thup* sound accompanied the kick of the pistol. Bright red spewed from Greg's head, and he immediately fell forward toward Frank. Frank's shirt and face had blood spatter all over it. Undoubtedly there was plenty inside the boat.

"You caused the death of your partner by breaking the rules, Frank," said Hans to himself.

Hans put the gun into its case and got out and returned it to his trunk. His cell phone rang as he shut the trunk.

"Hello," said Hans as he looked up and watched the boat. He could see that Frank was panicking on the boat.

"Boss, this is Frank. Something horrible just happened. I just saw Greg's head explode from some sort of gunshot. I didn't hear a thing. He was in the middle of a sentence and then splat and it was all over."

He was looking around but had not seen Hans. "Boss, I didn't see anyone. There was no problem with the drop, and we were on our way home."

"Calm down, Frank," Hans said slowly. "Get a hold of yourself. Did you stop anywhere?"

There was a long pause.

"Well, uh, sir...we did stop to get a drink, 'cause we accidently left our cooler," said Frank.

"What's the rule on that Frank?"

Frank was again quiet for a moment.

"We're not supposed to make any stops, sir. We're supposed to come straight back."

"That's right, Frank. Rules are made to be followed. If you don't, you and maybe all of us pay the consequences. Do you think you've learned a lesson today?"

"Yes, sir, Boss! I promise I'll never do it again."

"Take off your shirt and dip it in the water," said Hans. "Rinse out the blood and then wipe your face and arms."

Frank looked around and was talking to himself. He clearly did not understand how Hans knew he had blood on his face and arms.

"Rinse it again and then wipe any splatter off the inside of the boat." He watched as Frank cleaned his face. "Hurry now. Then go out at least a mile out from shore and then turn south for another mile. Dump Greg out into the water there. Make sure to tie your anchor to his legs so that he won't float. The sharks will take care of him. Wet down your shirt and clean out the rest of the blood. Then cut up your shirt and throw it in the water. Understand?"

"Yes, sir," answered Frank, still with a shaky voice.

"Good. Now get moving. Don't speed, though. You don't want to do anything to cause you to be pulled over by the marine patrol."

"Yes, sir," replied Frank.

Hans hung up and got back into his car. He watched Frank drift as he continued to clean up the boat. As Hans turned around to leave, he looked one last time to see Frank starting up the boat and then turning toward the inlet. Hans turned on his classical music station and slowly drove back north on Casey Key Road.

Chapter 17: *Preparation for a Sting*

Agent Kyle Thompson and his partner had been following the suspect's BMW Z4 coupe since it had left the tiki bar. Given they almost had an accident at the drug pickup point, Kyle thought it best that they peel off early. He radioed Jim Matchett, another DEA agent who had been watching this suspect over the last week, to pick up the tail. A few moments later, Jim pulled up in an unimpressive sedan they had rented at Sarasota Airport for the day. Kyle waved to Jim, who like himself was sitting in the passenger seat. The suspect looked like he was going to take a different route to I-75. They veered left on US 41 just past the Sarasota High School, while the suspect continued straight on US 301.

"Jason," said Kyle, "let's go get an early dinner and then head over to the command center downtown." The DEA had moved in a large number of people for the sting operation and had their temporary command center at the Sarasota sheriff's office. Most agents were flying in from DC via Atlanta or direct flights to Tampa. The rest of the agents came out of the Tampa and Fort Myers offices.

"We've got a meeting tonight to plan tomorrow's arrests. I don't know how long things will go tonight, so we better eat while we can."

Jason kept his eyes on the road while listening.

"I can eat any time of day, so now sounds good to me," he said. "How about Bobby Caribbean's at St. Armands Circle?"

"Not on our per diem," said Kyle. "Its Del Burrito or Railway Pizza tonight."

"Stakeouts are tough when you are lactose intolerant," Jason moaned.

Five miles northeast of Kyle's position, Johnny was about to enter I-

75 off Fruitville Road. Nothing seemed out of the ordinary. A near accident between a Jeep and van on Blackburn Point had caught his eye, but neither of those vehicles had followed him. Ever since he had seen that black pickup truck follow him for a long time a few days ago, he had been uneasy over the last week of driving. He knew that he was probably being paranoid, but his employer was paying him to be extra careful. And there was no room for mistakes in this business.

◇◇◇◇◇

Johnny turned on his radio and listened to the news. He hadn't heard any news update on that fishing guide who was killed by pirates. He had asked his contact in Orlando if that was tied to their shipments, but was told not to talk unless it was about his merchandise deliveries. Johnny's work didn't give him much chance to socialize, so he talked to almost anyone who would give him the time of day. That made life a little lonely, but his paycheck more than made up for this inconvenience.

His hopes were to do this job for a couple of years and sock away a nice nest egg. He'd move on to something more legitimate then. After a few minutes of the top news stories, Johnny decided to switch to a jazz station. It was relaxing background music while he was thinking about the upcoming events and life in general.

Tomorrow it was back to Indian Mound in Englewood. He'd have off a day after that delivery. He was thinking of maybe staying in Orlando after the delivery and checking out some of the hot spots there. But for now, he had to keep focused. He looked down and saw that his daydreaming had resulted in him going faster than the speed limit. There was no sensory feedback or warning for this, because his BMW suspension made him feel like he was almost stationary on a cloud. A quick glance in his rearview mirror showed a state policeman in the middle lane about four car lengths back. He tensed, slowed down, and moved slowly to the middle lane. He wasn't going noticeably faster than the surrounding cars, so maybe he'd be OK. The cop didn't come closer and eventually exited before the I-275 interchange.

Easy sailing from here, Johnny thought.

Jim Matchett was in the sedan following Johnny three car lengths back. The suspect, whom they now knew as Johnny Gates, was sticking to his normal game plan. The only hiccup was the momentary speeding he had done for a short section of road. Given the number of times he had made this drive, it wasn't surprising thathe would probably daydream from time to time. Jim had to radio the local state police dispatcher to have the officer who was following Johnny back off. Fortunately Johnny didn't seem to freak out and do something rash. Almost getting a speeding ticket seemed to have awakened him, and he was now driving at the 70 mph speed limit.

After they reached the I-4 interchange, the next DEA agent picked up the tail, and Jim and his fellow agent turned around and headed back toward Sarasota. They had a meeting to attend tonight. Jim was excited to get on with the bust. This surveillance was getting to be boring. He missed home and the family. He had been home only one weekend over the last month.

Jim's home in Ashburn, Virginia, wasn't necessarily any cooler or less humid than Florida in the summer, and his commute into Washington was absolutely horrible. But he missed the comforts of his own bed, the rat race with the kids' extracurricular activities, and the much more healthy and appetizing food made by his beautiful Italian wife. They lived only an hour and a half from the cooler, green mountains. He loved to camp sometimes on the weekends and fish in the streams and lakes that dotted the mountains of western Virginia.

He especially loved the fall season when the air was crisp, and the trees were full of reds, yellows, and orange leaves. He loved looking up at the clear sky and watching the stars at night while wrapped in his sleeping bag. It reminded him of camping with his parents out West in his youth. Only the brightest stars were visible in suburbia. Light pollution had spoiled the night skies. But in the mountains in the fall, the skies looked alive, and he could stare for hours. The sounds of nature were his music, and the nights he spent there always afforded him a peaceful night's sleep.

His phone rang, and he answered, "Hello, this is Jim."

"Hey, it's Kyle. We picked up some snapper and pepperoni pizza and brought it back to the command center. It's not bad once you get used to it. We'll save you some."

"Oh, lovely," said Jim in an expression of dread. "Can't wait." He put his finger to his head and pretended to pull the trigger. He heard Kyle chuckle.

"See you in a little while," said Jim as he hung up his phone.

After an hour-and-fifteen-minute drive, Jim pulled up to the sheriff's office. He walked toward the meeting room and opened the door, which was like walking through a wall of cheese and fish smells.

"Wow," said Jim as he entered. "Is that fresh fish? It's got a pretty strong smell."

"Who knows," replied Kyle. "It's deep fried fish nuggets on the pizza, so you can't really tell if it's frozen or fresh. But it's not too bad. At least it was when it was warm. You'll have to microwave it now, if you want it warm."

"Yum, yum," said Jim. "Cold, smelly, fish pizza? I don't think so. I'll stick with the pepperoni."

"Let's get started," said the director of the DEA's Tampa office. The Tampa office was the closest and largest office on the Gulf Coast of Florida, so it was given the lead on the investigation. Director Jack Dusauriss began the briefing.

"We are all aware of the importance of Florida to the drug trade. With eight thousand miles of beaches, it offers ample opportunity for drug runners to move product in from the Caribbean, Mexico, and Columbia. The majority of drugs enters into Miami and then moves to other cities north for distribution, including Orlando. It's mostly cocaine, marijuana, and heroin coming into the country.

"As you know, we've located what we think are new players with entries into the country from Charlotte Harbor to Sarasota," the directory continued. "Kyle, Jim, and the crew from our office have been following the mules, which are ferrying the drugs to a distribution point in Orlando. Since heroin use is really high in Orlando, and given the size of the containers, we believe it is either heroin or cocaine or both being smuggled in."

The director paused while he pulled up a map onto the LCD projection screen.

"The map shows all the routes that drugs are being moved from the beach communities to Orlando. As you see, there are four main pickup points on the water. We know that the drugs are entering from the open ocean in fast speedboats coming in at night. They then transfer the drugs to fishing boats on the backside of these islands along the entrance to Charlotte Harbor."

He was pointing to the string of islands from Gasparilla Island to Sanibel Island.

"We haven't been able to find the exact locations, but we'll have the water assets out tomorrow to follow the full movement on the water. The drugs are transferred via the inland waterways to the four pickup points from Placida to Sarasota."

The director flipped to the next slide, which showed pictures of four people taken at various local sites.

"Four drug mules are moving the drugs each day. They pick up the drugs at three different times of the day at one of the four pickup points. No two mules pick up from the same site on any day, and it appears all their pickup plans come each morning as encrypted e-mails. We haven't been able to decipher their rotating encryption key, so that means we require four surveillance crews at the pickup points."

He continued the briefing by describing the locations of each of the crews along routes between the four pickup points and the I-75 and I-4 interchange.

Kyle interrupted. "How are we covering all the water routes?"

"Each land-based drug pickup point will also be monitored by two crews in boats, since the drug runners always have two exit routes from each pickup point. I've asked the sheriff's department to help with this. They have marine patrol divisions with boats and experienced crews. Sheriff Mike Steele in this office is contacting the other sheriff offices now to coordinate the waterside surveillance and arrests."

"We'll start by making arrests of these four mules tomorrow and the distribution point in Orlando where the drugs are delivered," the director continued. "We'll follow the boats back to their base locations. We'll arrest all the boat operators in the late afternoon and find out their pickup points. That will lead us that night to the open water pickup points. But we need to make sure that when we make the arrests tomorrow, we shut down their communications so that they do not spook the distributors in Orlando or their open ocean boat smugglers."

"How are we going to stop phone calls?" Jim Matchett asked. "They could get suspicious and make a call any time."

"We've got engineering crews in the garage right now adding cell jammers and interceptors to each crew's vehicle," the director said. "The jammers emit high-power radio transmissions at the same frequencies used by all US cell providers. Once the cell phone is jammed, we can connect to the phone and talk directly to the mule to persuade him to pull over, if necessary. But you must stay within five hundred meters of him to make this work. This device is not directional; it works 360 degrees around the vehicle. It is not to be turned on until you get on the interstates. We don't want to interrupt the cell transmissions of too many citizens, or we'll take more heat than you can imagine."

The director began establishing the exact timetable of events and all what-if scenarios. Even though the entire plan would be provided on paper to all crews, Kyle was soaking up as much of the details as he could mentally. In the heat of the chase, there was often no time to look down and read through a bunch of paper. Crews had to be ready for any situation that could develop and make adjustments as needed.

Chapter 18: *Murderer is Revealed*

Nikki and Shelli arrived at their boat dock with Ryan and Stephanie well after dark. After stowing the gear and hosing down the boat, they headed inside. Ryan carried the cooler full of leftovers. As they entered the house, they found their mom waiting for them with hot cocoa and slices of key lime pie from the local supermarket. Although not as good as Danielle's recipe, the kids always liked it. The pie had a graham cracker crust and was ringed with whip cream dotted with almond slices. Danielle grinned as she saw Ryan's eyes lock on it.

"Where are Dad and Sheriffs Mike and Bob?" asked Shelli.

"They're in Dad's study," Danielle said. "Let's head into the den, and I'll ask them to come out and give you the latest news."

They picked up their beverages and plates and headed into the den. A minute later, the two sheriffs walked out with Rick and said their hellos. Danielle met them with some pie and drink.

Sheriff Steele spoke up first.

"The forensic team said the site was not a modern-day homicide. They cleared one full body and stopped. There was no blood and human tissue on the bones and only the skeleton, leathers, and metal seemed to have survived the years at the site. Since this is not a legal matter, the sheriff's office turned this over to the state to figure out what to do with the remains.

"Just before we left to come here, a University of Florida archeology professor arrived," the sheriff continued. "He looked at the sword and some of the other metal around the body and was saying it might be as much as three hundred years old. They found arrowheads in the sand as they were clearing it from the skeleton and even found one stuck in its vertebrae. So the poor soul must have been killed by local Indians."

The sheriff said that the professor was on his phone calling the university and the Smithsonian as soon as he saw the arrowheads and the dead man's gear.

Nikki, Ryan, and Stephanie were listening with their eyes wide open.

"Do you think he was a pirate?" asked Ryan. No one had noticed that Shelli was on her iPod Touch until Danielle glanced over at her and asked, "What are you doing, Shelli?"

"I'm googling," said Shelli. "Pirates were the first thing I thought of when you said the remains were three hundred years old, so I looked up pirates in the area at about that time."

"While you're doing this, I need to update Sheriff Huggins on my latest findings," said Rick.

"And I've got to talk to both of you about what we have going on in the area with the DEA," said Sheriff Steele. They finished their pie, thanked Danielle, and headed into Rick's home office. Nikki, Ryan, and Stephanie crowded around Shelli as she keyed search phrases into the search engine.

Rick sat down at his computer, and the two sheriffs sat across from him. The large situation display was on the wall to the left of Rick and the right of the sheriffs.

"Thanks again, Rick, for all you did on the video search," said Sheriff Huggins. "And thanks for the loan of your notebook PC." said Sheriff Huggins. Sheriff Huggins had returned the PC, which was now sitting on Rick's desk.

"You're welcome. And it is the buoy data that I want to talk to you about."

"Before you go into this, would you please bring Mike up to date on what we found already?" asked Sheriff Huggins.

"Certainly." Rick proceeded to summarize the findings as of yesterday and showed a few key snapshots and videos.

"Impressive," said Sheriff Steele. "But you said you had something new to tell us."

"Yes, I do. As you recall, Bob, I ignored two of the four events yesterday when I was doing the search. I focused only on the video data collected at the time of the murders. Two events, however, occurred earlier in the day." Rick maneuvered his mouse and selected a video segment to play.

"The first video segment was taken late afternoon on the day of the murders. The first, or most northern buoy, captured this video. Note that the time is about five o'clock. Watch this now."

The three men watched quietly as a speedboat came into view and stopped next to a small fishing boat. The boats were only about one hundred meters from the buoy. Rick froze the video.

"Using the boat's registration number, I verified that the boat in this frame is the same speedboat we saw later in the night at the scene of the murder. What triggered this event as abnormal is visible in the next few moments."

He resumed the video. In a few moments he froze the video.

"There—a transfer of a cooler from one boat to the next. Remember that the software learns over time what is normal and abnormal. The program thinks boats don't normally do this apparently, or at least not in the weeks over which the video was collected."

"Well, this is a new twist," said Sheriff Huggins. "So we have more players."

"Yes, but that isn't all," said Rick. "We have another event to watch." He pulled up the second video segment and started it. The video had a beautiful scene of the bluish green water and Cayo Costa in the background. The same speedboat seen in the early video clip approached another larger fishing boat moored within twenty meters of buoy two.

"That looks like the fishing boat we saw in the video of the murder yesterday," said Sheriff Huggins.

"It is. In the next few seconds you'll see why this caused the abnormal trigger event to record all of this." In the video a man in the fishing boat picked up a black item that was easy to distinguish.

"He's got a machine gun," said Sheriff Huggins. "It is clearly visible."

"And watch this...now," said Rick, clicking on the freeze frame button. The man in the boat with the machine gun turned around and looked directly in the direction of the buoy. The frame froze with the man's face in the center of the frame. The man was about fifty-something, tall, and had a heavily receding hairline.

"Now let's pull up some other pictures," said Rick. He pulled up partial views and side profiles of a man with the same physique taken near the time of the murders from all the video reviewed up until now. Then Rick pulled up the overhead thermal images from the aerial drones. He played the segment of video with the man shooting Cody. He froze the video on a sharply focused frame of the man with the gun.

"Check out the heat signature," said Rick. He zoomed in on the man. To a thermal camera, skin will appear brighter than skin covered by hair or clothing. There was a pale V in the top of the man's head, with much brighter V's pointing in the opposite side on either side.

"The man has a receding hairline," said Sheriff Steele.

"And check out his shirt pattern," Rick said. "The heat pattern from his skin on his arms and chest in the thermal shot is consistent with the exposed skin in the daytime camera shot. He kept on the same pale yellow and white aloha shirt that night. Gentlemen, we've now got a picture of the man who killed Cody," said Rick excitedly as he zoomed in on the color frame from the buoy camera.

"This is fabulous," said Sheriff Huggins.

"I've forwarded this shot and those of the other accomplices on the boats to both of your offices via encrypted e-mail," said Rick.

"That is perfect," said Sheriff Huggins. "We've got an address from the Florida registration number. When we checked on the address, we found it ended up being twenty feet beyond the end of a pier. So this picture is a great find and puts us back on the killer's tracks."

"I need to give you an update as well, Bob," said Sheriff Steele. "And given what I've just seen, I think you need to hear it too, Rick."

Sheriff Steele pulled out the folder he had been carrying and placed it on Rick's desk. He opened it and spread the contents on the table. He quickly described the DEA surveillance operation and showed the map of drug movements. Rick and Sheriff Huggins studied the photos and maps as Sheriff Steele described the arrest plan for the next day. Rick's face lit up when he saw one of the photos of the small fishing boat that had delivered the drugs and the photo of the blue cooler.

"Look at these two pictures," said Rick. "The small boat is the same boat in the video I showed you tonight that met with the speedboat at Cayo Costa. And the cooler is the exact same cooler we saw passed between the speedboat and the small fishing boat."

"You're right," said Sheriff Steele. "I believe Cody stumbled onto this drug operation and was killed for it. The DEA wants our marine patrol units to arrest these small boat operators tomorrow. But they wanted us to also find the open ocean connection and drop-off points. It appears from your Cayo Costa buoy video data that we've already found the missing parts of this. We've got to let the DEA know. They are still meeting in my office."

"Let's go," said Sheriff Huggins. "I'll call Lieutenant Williams while we're on the way, so he can organize the boats early in the morning. I also think we should allow Rick to come too."

"I agree," said Sheriff Steele. "The DEA guys might be tense about it at first, but I'm sure they'll be happy Rick's there once they see all of this."

"I'll bring my notebook PC," Rick said. "It will take me about five minutes to transfer everything to it."

"I'll head on now to the office," said Sheriff Steele. "I'll let them know you'll be there and quickly brief them on your work, Rick."

"Rick can come with me when he's finished transferring the data," said Sheriff Huggins.

After Sheriff Steele left, Rick continued transferring data.

"I'm also going to open the link to our new buoy sensor network. I just added the screen shots of Cody's killer and his associates, and the registration numbers and boat descriptions into the search filters. Any new sightings of the men or the boats will cause an alarm. Plus, I've started searching the database for sightings that may have been collected thus far. We don't have enough data to have abnormal trigger events, but the database can be searched for these events now. Since we're not training the database, just searching it, it should be completed in about ten minutes for all the sensor buoys from Sarasota Bay to Lovers Key."

"Wow—this technology stuff never ceases to amaze me," said Sheriff Huggins.

As Rick and Sheriff Huggins were leaving, they passed through the den to say good-bye—most likely for the night.

"Dad," said Shelli, "I found some reference to Sarasota back in the 1700s. It is believed the name *Sarasota* came from the local native name for the area, Zara Zote. A bunch of pirates were known to stay around the areas from Charlotte Harbor to Tampa. One of the most well-known around the time of our skeleton was Black Caesar, a former slave. It turns out there were two Black Caesars from the 1700s to 1800s, but the first one was known for the saying, 'Dead men tell no tales.' Maybe that skeleton was Black Caesar. History says he did bury his treasure for safekeeping. Maybe he had a treasure he was protecting."

"Who knows, sweetheart," said Rick. "But it is too early to know anything now. And I wouldn't get your hopes up. It could be weeks before they find anything. I've got to go, though. Don't wait up for me."

"OK, honey," said Danielle. "Be careful," she added, knowing it was fruitless as soon as she said it. The rest of the kids said good night as well. Rick went out the front door with his notebook PC in hand. He and Sheriff Huggins got in the sheriff's car and headed to Sheriff Steele's office.

"Rick, did you tell Nikki you found Cody's killer?" the sheriff asked as they were riding in the car.

"No – I haven't told anyone.   I appreciate you not mentioning it back there at the house. Nikki had a really good day today, better than she's had since she heard the news of Cody's death. I just couldn't bring her down by telling her. I will probably do so tomorrow."

Ten minutes later, Rick and Sheriff Huggins arrived at the Sarasota sheriff's office. Sheriff Steele had just finished a quick introduction of Rick and his work with Sheriff Huggins' office.

"Here's Rick Bryant and Sheriff Bob Huggins now," said Sheriff Steele with a gesture of his hand. "Mr. Bryant, could you please give the gentlemen here a briefing of your findings."

Rick spent the next twenty minutes giving a summary of the findings. Everyone looked a little stunned when he was finished. Jim Matchett spoke up and confirmed that the boat Rick captured on video was the boat that was dropping off drugs to the mules.

"We've submitted the pictures you gave the sheriff to the FBI to see if we can come up with some IDs," said Kyle. "It will take a few minutes before we hear back from them."

The DEA director, Jack Dusauriss, reintroduced himself and the others in the room. Afterward, he repeated a short version of their findings. The map of the drug runners' routes, the same one Sheriff Steele had shown him earlier, remained on the overhead.

Rick opened his PC and hooked up his video output to a second LCD projector.

"That looks like the Google Earth map program you have the routes overlaid on there," said Rick. "Let me pull up the results of the search I've done on our buoy data. I haven't seen it myself yet. I entered the faces of the criminals and the boat numbers and photos we captured on the Cayo Costa buoys into the database search parameters of the new buoy sensor grid data. Facial and shape recognition algorithms pull just the video clips of interest.

"I'll first plot the latitude and longitudes of the same Google map that you have." As Rick clicked on his PC, dots started peppering the map. "Let's connect the dots."

Lines formed. "These are the boat patterns of the drug runners on the water."

Kyle Thompson stood up and moved the two projectors so that the two maps aligned on the projector screen. A long, drawn-out "Aah" came from the group.

"This is going to greatly simplify tomorrow's arrest plan," said Kyle.

Jim Matchett was handed a note by the dispatcher. He stood up and went over to the PC attached to one of the two LCD projectors.

"I just got a note that the FBI confirmed the IDs of the guys on Rick's pictures and video."

Jim pulled up his email and opened the attachments.

"Looks like the majority of the guys involved in the murder were professional killers or enforcers," he said. "Our triggerman popped up on Interpol. He's been involved in all kinds of criminal activity. He was a mercenary earlier in his career. He's worked for everything from drug lords to art thieves. He's German—Hans Schmidt is his name, or at least that's what he goes by. He's managed to elude prison entirely. He's always had some kind of benefactor get him out of his predicaments. He is wanted now for art theft in two countries and embezzlement in another."

Jim paused while he read the email. "Funny, though. The mules and boat taxi-men had either no priors or just petty crimes."

While Jim was talking, Rick combined the map data and added DEA and sheriff crew locations for both land and water drug routes. He then printed copies for all the crews. Jim Matchett passed them out and reminded everyone that these were classified and could not be misplaced or given to anyone outside the room.

When Rick finished, Sheriff Huggins addressed everyone.

"I am fully aware that the purpose of the DEA arrests tomorrow is to shut down this drug ring. The sheriff's department of course supports this effort. In case you weren't aware, Rick's daughter was Cody Foster's girlfriend. He wouldn't say anything to you because he's that kind of guy." Rick looked down at the mention of his name, knowing that everyone in the room was now looking at him. "But I will say that it will be the Punta Gorda Marine Patrol Unit's number one mission to grab those suspects involved in the murder. I request that the DEA agents in the room remember this tomorrow when they go after these criminals."

Soon after Sheriff Huggins' speech, the order came to close down for the night. Everyone was ordered to go home or to the hotels and get some sleep. Everyone was to report back at 7:00 a.m. sharp tomorrow.

"Rick," said Sheriff Steele as he reached to shake his hand, "we really appreciate your help on this. You have been incredibly supportive, and we may never have known who Cody's murderers were without your cooperation." He let go of Rick's hand. "Tomorrow is going to be dangerous," said the sheriff, "and I don't want to put your life in danger. So you'll have to sit this one out."

Sheriff Huggins grinned and looked down, knowing what was coming next.

"Sorry, Mike, but that's just not going to happen," replied Rick quickly. "I really want to see this through. I still think my company and I can be of assistance tomorrow."

"There could be gunfire exchange tomorrow if anything goes wrong, and we can't risk your life," rebutted Sheriff Steele.

"Mike, I have some tools," said Rick with a special emphasis on the word *tools*, "that could be helpful to your teams tomorrow. Plus, I've supported the US military in some pretty harsh places, such as Iraq. I've got my own bulletproof vest that probably is better than yours."

Before Sheriff Steele could argue another point, Kyle walked up and asked, "What tools?"

"Sheriff Huggins, since you drove me here, could you drop off Kyle and me at my company office?" asked Rick. "I think you guys would like to see what else we do beside buoys." He turned to Sheriff Steele. "Of course you're welcome to come too, Mike."

"You've peaked my curiosity," replied Sheriff Steele. "I'll follow you."

When Rick, the two sheriffs, and Kyle entered the company's front door, they were unimpressed at first. It was the standard lobby and receptionist's office. Nothing on the walls indicated what they did. They looked somewhat more interested when Rick showed them around the front offices, which consisted of electronic labs, a command center, and software modeling labs.

"Very high-tech," said Kyle, just to be polite. For a field officer, this was not what Kyle thought of as helpful tools.

"Thanks, but this is just the support offices for what really goes on here," said Rick. He headed down the corridor to the bay and opened the door.

"Gentlemen, welcome to Marine Science Systems, LLC." The mouths of the three visitors opened as if they had seen the most gorgeous woman in the world standing naked in front of them.

Rick chuckled as he looked at their expressions.

"This is like being in a law enforcement officer's best dream," said Kyle in awe. "Do you actually make all this stuff?"

"We either make each item or retrofit it with some special features. This hardware was all built for the purpose of demonstration. We built them all under our own R&D, research and development, funds. They are what you might call our 3-D catalog of products. All are fully functional."

Rick walked around the room, describing each piece of hardware. As he finished, he stood in front of them and said, "Gentlemen. This equipment could use some actual field trials, so I'll make them available if you wish to try them out tomorrow. My only condition is that I am in on the action."

The three men looked at one another and shook their heads. In unison they said, "You're in."

Chapter 19: *The Night Before*

It was past midnight when Rick slipped into bed. Danielle stirred, so Rick stayed as still as he could not to wake her.

"Late night," said Danielle without moving.

"Sorry to wake you," said Rick quietly. "The meeting went later than expected." She remained still and quiet for a few seconds.

"You took them to the office, didn't you?"

"They needed my help, so I thought it the prudent thing to do."

"Yeah, right," said Danielle as she rolled over. "So, let me guess. You can use it if I can come along. Did I get it right?"

Rick looked at her in the dark. "How do you know me so well?"

"Thirty years with a broken record. It's not too hard to figure you out, honey."

Rick lay still for a while. It was hard to just go to sleep with all he had racing through his head.

"I know you're probably sleepy, but I need to ask you something,"

"What is it?" asked Danielle.

"I found out who killed Cody today. I provided the information to the DEA, Mike, and Bob. It's a good chance that they'll get him and his buddies tomorrow."

"That's great, Rick. How did you do it?   And who is it?

"It's a long story, but the man's name is Hans Schmidt," answered Rick.   "I used the buoy video and some high-flying drone video to get a picture of the killer and his accomplices. That allowed the sheriff and company to track down his name."

"I'm impressed," said Danielle excitedly. Rick smiled, but then appeared to be somewhat less enthusiastic. He had a look of dread. "What is the question?"

"I'm wondering how to tell Nikki tomorrow. She looked happy today, and I just didn't want to bring this subject up with her. Got any suggestions?"

"Nikki is tougher than you think. Just tell her what you found and let her know the law is going after him. She'll be happy to know you were the one responsible for identifying the murderer. I'm sure she'll be OK, and the sooner you tell her, the faster she'll get over it."

"OK, I'll get her up tomorrow morning and give her the news. I've got to be at the DEA command center by seven o'clock in the morning."

"Well, you better get some sleep. That's earlier than you're used to waking up since moving to Florida."

"Nonsense. That's how early I get up when I go to fishing."

"Yeah, but you normally go to bed before eleven o'clock the night before," added Danielle. "You've been burning the candle at both ends. Remember you're not twenty anymore."

"I have plenty of time to relax when I get old. You know I can't sit still."

"Just be safe tomorrow. Let the law do their job, and you keep your head down. Shelli will be upset if you're not around to go fishing with her anymore."

"I'll be fine," said Rick. "I've got my technology to protect me. And no need for you to get up in the morning. I'll get something to eat on the way."

"Don't worry. I wasn't planning to. I don't want you to think that I support what you're doing. But I also know there is nothing I can say to stop you." She paused for a few seconds. "Good night, and get some sleep."

"Good night, sweetheart," said Rick as he kissed her. Danielle closed her eyes with the kiss and settled in to sleep quickly.

Rick rolled over with his eyes wide open. Something was nagging him about the drug ring. The cartel was taking precautions in their operation with the encrypted e-mails, four pickup points, and varying times of the day for pickup. But it seemed that it was awful easy to figure out the routes. The amount of money being spent on the operation was quite large. So why use such inexperienced mules and boat operators? Well, it was late, and the morning would be here soon.

Chapter 20: *D-Day Preparation*

Nikki awoke slowly to a gentle hand on her shoulder.

"Wake up, sweetie," said her dad while sitting on the edge of her bed. "Sorry to wake you so early, but I need to let you know some news before I take off to help the sheriff's department and the DEA."

Nikki sat up and rubbed her eyes. She turned and looked at the time. It was 6:30 a.m.

"What are you talking about, Dad? Why are you up so early?"

"Yesterday I was able to isolate the face of Cody's killer on the video from our buoys. The FBI was able to associate a name with the killer's picture. Cody's probably not the first person this man has killed."

Nikki suddenly came alert with the news.

"What, you've found Cody's killer?"

"We know who he is, and the DEA and sheriff department is going to try to catch him today."

"Dad, you're awesome," said Nikki as she reached and hugged her dad. This surprised Rick.

Nikki continued as she released him. "Are you going to help them find him?"

"I'm going to help in whatever way I can, honey," said Rick. "I've got to go now, but I'll let you know if we get him."

"OK, Dad. But be careful." Rick kissed her on the check and got up to leave the room. "Love you, Dad."

Danielle was right. That was much easier than I thought it would be, thought Rick as he headed out of the house.

He got into the SUV he brought home from the office the night before. The vehicle was retrofitted by Rick's company with a tracking radar that can work while the vehicle moves, a 360-degree field-of-view thermal and daylight camera, broadband cellular and meshed RF networks, and a command center with video monitors in the visors.

The radar had a sloped, low-profile, aerodynamic dome, with a color that matched the vehicle's paint color. The radar and camera were installed on the top of the vehicle and could be elevated even when driving, using a scissor lift that welded into the roof. This allowed the operator to see over taller vehicles. The camera optical zoom was equivalent to a one-hundred-times zoom. The video display on the command center was a seamless, simultaneous view in all directions around the vehicle.

When the radar detected an object, a pop-up red square would appear on the video display to highlight the detected shape. As the object moved, the red square stayed locked on it. The command center also displayed a moving map, which could plot the symbols with a line indicating the direction the object was moving. The symbol was a car, boat, person, plane, or square, if the system couldn't figure out what the object was.

The vehicle had a larger aftermarket alternator to power the sensors, and heavy-duty shocks to permit better off-road performance. It also had run-flat tires, which allowed the vehicle to continue down the road, even if the tires are shot or the vehicle runs over spikes or nails.

Rick hoped this vehicle would be useful in following the mule's car at a longer and less noticeable distance. Rick had installed his own cell jammer last night before driving it home. It impressed Kyle that he just had these lying around.

Rick arrived at Sheriff's Mike office at 6:55 a.m. As he pulled in, he saw most of the DEA officers and sheriff's staff standing outside, looking at the hardware brought over from his company's bay. As Rick got out of his vehicle, he heard Kyle describing the features of his hardware with enough enthusiasm to make any used car sales manager proud.

"Just correct me if I get something wrong, Rick," Kyle said.

"You've got a sales position with my company any time you've had enough of helping the DEA save the world."

Kyle grinned.

"Here is the vehicle I like best," he continued. "It's an off-road vehicle similar in appearance to the military's Hummers, but it's better. It's built for Florida specifically. It has a smooth ride on the highway, as I can attest, and although I didn't take it off road, I saw from Rick's videos that it is more than capable. It has a winch in the front with a launching grapple hook, bush guard, and overhead high intensity lights that can rotate via joystick. These would be great for the Everglades. It has radar and thermal cameras like those on his buoys, and a command center that is all-weather, since it can be driven open air like a Jeep. The ragtop keeps the rain off when needed. It has run-flat, off-road tires, and even the spare is a run-flat.

"And my favorite is that this is also a boat. Yep, you can drive it right down in the water. You press the gas pedal when it starts to float, and it retracts the wheels, and its drivetrain switches to spin the four props in the back. It will do one hundred miles an hour on the road and forty miles an hour on the water. Rick calls it the *Gladeator*." He slowly pronounced the name "Glade-e-ate-tor."

Kyle continued as he strolled over to the boat sitting on its tow trailer.

"This is the *Spearfish*. It's Rick's company's idea for the next offshore patrol boat. It has the radar and camera, of course, tied to a waterproof command center. It's fast, but it still can't catch the fastest cigar boats out there. But that was not its intended use. It was designed to be able to move fast to those who need help, propel bad guys as needed, and have plenty of room for rescue if necessary. The steering console is bulletproof—that's why it is surrounded by half-height metal and bulletproof glass in the front and sides. The hull is dual walled and bullet resistant, and the foam inside the walls is self-sealing, so it will not sink from bullet holes.

"It is fitted with a mini-PAD, which stands for Precision Acoustic Device," Kyle continued. "This can pinpoint sound in the direction it is pointing. The radar can also point and fire this automatically. The sound is louder than a jet engine, and it also can project a sound that disturbs the inner ear and makes people sick. The *Spearfish* also has a water cannon, which can be used to repel people away. To top it off, it has underwater cameras, a watertight stowage for guns, a grapple launcher that would make pirates of old jealous, a hardened bow for charging a beach, and a cell jammer that Rick added last night."

"What's this, an ATV?" asked Jim Matchett. He was standing beside what seemed to be some sort of modified four-wheel all-terrain vehicle

"That's the ATAWT, or the all-terrain all-water transporter," Kyle said. "It's an all-terrain vehicle and Jet Ski in one. It has some extra features like winch, and the front windshield and the metal crest in front of the handlebars and steering column are all bullet-proof. It's amazingly fast on the water. Again, great for the Glades and even around this area, with all the water hazards we have."

Kyle moved on to show the crowd the vehicle that Rick had driven in. Rick moved in to begin setting up his notebook PC and network in the sheriff's office. By the time people began to slowly meander into the command center, Rick was finished with the setup and had even tied the sheriff's helicopter camera feed into the cellular network as well. Still at the command center checking his buoy sensor grid, Rick turned to watch the staff walking in pairs or small groups all discussing the vehicles. Director Dusauriss finally stood up and started going over changes, in light of the new hardware they had at their disposal.

As the group stood up and began to group in their assigned pairs, Rick noticed the dispatcher come in to talk with the director

"Attention, folks," the director said. "The encrypted e-mails for today's drugs plans were sent out. Let's get going, people. I want you set on your posts within the hour."

Rick left his notebook PC and the meshed network up and running at the command center as he walked out with Jim Matchett to his vehicle.

"I'm driving," said Jim.

"I expected that much," said Rick. "I should be at the command center controls anyway, in case I have to coordinate with the other vehicles."

Traffic lights turned red in both directions from the sheriff's office as the long line of vehicles came out onto the road. Last to leave was a truck pulling the boat on its trailer and a second truck with the ATAWT loaded in the bed.

Chapter 21: *All Quiet on the Gulf*

Shelli awakened to the sound of wind blowing the palm fronds against the windowpanes in her room. She sat up, stretched, and vaguely remembered someone kissing her sometime earlier. Probably her dad, she thought. She stood up and looked out her double-pane windows to see that it was cloudy. It looked like there might be rain today.

After a bathroom stop, Shelli followed the smell of coffee to the kitchen, where Nikki and Danielle were sipping from large white mugs.

"Good morning, honey," said Danielle.

"Morning," said Shelli, still not quite coherent.

"Would you like some breakfast?" asked Nikki. "I made some croissants and crepes."

"Yeah, that sounds good. Where's Dad?" "I think he came in real early and kissed me on the forehead."

"He's off at the sheriff's office today rounding up bad guys," Nikki replied.

Shelli's eyes became more alert. "Really? Did they make him a deputy?"

"No, honey, but they are going to be using your dad's vehicles and sensor grid today," replied Danielle.

"Dad is going to let them use those? Those are his pride and joy toys."

"Yes I know, but he used those as carrots. He allowed them to use them only if he could participate in the arrests."

"Now, that sounds like Dad," said Shelli, with emphasis on the word *that*.

"What are you doing today, Mom?" asked Shelli once she started eating her breakfast.

"I am too worried about your father today, so I'm going to go down to the museum and help with the upcoming social event. It will help keep my mind off of him. It's going to be a luncheon and closed viewing of a rare collection from Japan. It's a fund-raising event with only wealthy patrons and benefactors being invited."

"Do you need any help, Mom?" asked Nikki.

"Sure," said Danielle. "There's no pay involved, but if you're interested, I'd love the help."

"I'll help. Let me just get out of these PJs. What should I wear?"

"Oh, shorts and a T-shirt are fine."

Shelli spoke up. "Mom, I'm going to stay around here, if you don't mind. Stephanie might come by later after her dance class. Plus, if Dad needs anything I'll be here to answer his call."

"That's actually a good idea, honey." said Danielle. "Just keep your phone on."

As soon as Danielle said the last statement, she knew they were wasted words. *What teenager leaves her phone off?*

Danielle and Nikki left for the museum while Shelli stayed behind at home. Shelli didn't have a plan for the day—certainly nothing as grand as her plans yesterday. She didn't feel like going to the beach on the overcast day. Maybe she would just watch some TV. That's one thing she noticed about living in Florida. There was so much she liked to do outdoors, she didn't get to watch TV very much. She thought about it a little more. None of them watched TV much, except for the occasional movie. The lifestyle suited their family.

Her phone rang. It was Stephanie.

"Hi, Steph," said Shelli. "What's up?"

She listened as Stephanie told her the plans for her day.

"OK. See you about two o'clock then. Have fun," said Shelli as she hung up. *Well, Stephanie was going to go with her mom shopping and then to her dance class. So I have a few hours to kill before then.* She turned on the tube and it wasn't long before she saw a commercial for the Pirate's Lookout, a local seafood restaurant. Shelli thought about the skeleton they had found on Edwards Island. *It's time for a little Internet study.* She headed to her room. Her dad thought it was good to have a nice, comfortable desk, good PC, and fast Internet connection in each kid's bedroom. That was a major design element for the room, which had a tropical theme overall.

"Let's see," she said out loud. "Let's check out what it was like in Florida in the 1700s."

◊◊◊◊◊

A little over seven miles away from Shelli's house was where Johnny Gates lived. Today was the last day this week he had to work. He'd be off tomorrow. It was nearly ten o'clock in the morning, and he had already heard the "ding" from his computer, which indicated he had another e-mail. It was likely to be his assignment for today. It should say his pickup point would be Englewood. He opened the e-mail. Sure enough, Englewood it was. He read the short message fully. Nothing special today, and he closed and deleted it as he was always instructed to do. He checked today's mobile phone and verified it was working by calling the operator and asking for a local restaurant number. It worked.

He looked out through the sliding glass door to his balcony and noticed the heavy cloud cover. He turned on the TV to see the weather forecast. The forecaster announced showers today, with periods of heavy rain. There was a 50 percent chance of thunderstorms.

"Great," said Johnny out loud. Johnny hated driving in the rain in Florida. The rain could be blinding, and thunderstorms were often severe. "White-knuckle driving," he had once heard it called.

"What to have for lunch today?" he asked himself. Maybe he'd go to Café Italiano just a few miles north on Route 41. The owner was born and raised in Pitigliano, Italy, and had come first to the United States and developed a savory menu of fine Italian dishes in his restaurant. Johnny loved the Rustica sandwich with polenta fries, and he looked forward to it. Then he thought of his day off. *I guess it's time to check online for a hotel for tonight, since I'm going to hang around Orlando tomorrow. I'll go check out the shops at the big mall and see what's new at the theme parks.*

◊◊◊◊◊

At lunch, Shelli was thinking of something to eat in the house. Nothing appealed to her. She started thinking of going back to Mango Tango for something light, but decided against it. Her mom was worried about Dad. No need to worry her anymore. Then she saw the bananas in the fruit bowl in the table.

"I guess it's peanut butter and banana sandwich for lunch."

Before closing the browsing window, she saw the article she was reading about Florida treasures. Then an idea came to her. She walked into her father's office and looked on his desk. Although her father always scanned the business cards into his computer database, he usually kept the cards in a binder as well. She opened the binder and found the card of the University of Florida professor who had come to Edwards Island.

She dialed the number on the card and heard the professor's phone ringing.

"Hello, Dr. Carlisle speaking."

"Hi, Dr. Carlisle. This is Shelli Bryant. My sister and I were the ones that found the skeleton. Well, uh, my dad asked for me to call to check on the progress. Is it too much trouble to get an update?" she asked, somewhat embarrassed.

"Hi, Shelli. The sheriff told me to give your family updates whenever you called, so no problem," replied Dr. Carlisle. "The site is amazingly preserved. We've found twelve skeletons thus far, and we believe there are a lot more. Almost all of them had some sort of metal or oil-coated leather that survived. We're cataloging it all, but the quantity of items is so large, it will take weeks to finish."

"Wow. How much longer will you be digging?"

"Several more days. We have to finish this fairly quickly, since the elements start affecting the skeletons as soon as they are exposed. We have ten students, photographers, and faculty crowded on the beach with brushes, trying to get this done quickly."

"Is it possible for my friend Stephanie and me to come and help?" asked Shelli. "We both love history and are thinking of being archeologists. We promise not to do anything except what we are told!"

A long pause followed. "This is not an uncommon request, and we usually say no," said Dr. Carlisle. "But I guess this is a little different given that you're the discoverer. Plus the sheriff requested that we cooperate with your family on this dig. I suppose we can let you and your friend come and help, but you'll have to leave if you can't follow instructions."

Shelli jumped up and down when she heard Dr. Carlisle approve. It was all she could do to keep from screaming.

"Call before coming," said Dr. Carlisle. "We'll have to close today if the rain gets too bad."

"Yes, Dr. Carlisle. Thanks again! Bye!"

She jumped around the room for joy. She couldn't wait to tell Stephanie. She looked at her watch and saw she still had an hour and a half to go before Stephanie arrived. She finally calmed enough to sit and finish her sandwich. She hated to tell the white lie about loving history and wanting to be an archeologist. But it was only a little white lie. She had hated history until they had found the skeleton. Since then she couldn't read enough of the history of Florida and about the ways of pirates. And she did like to collect fossils when she was a little kid walking around some of their campgrounds in upstate New York when she was little.

"Wait, that's paleontology, not archeology. Oh, well, it's close enough. Both are ancient studies!"

After what seemed to be forever, Stephanie arrived.

"I thought you'd never arrive," said Shelli. "I've got something fun planned for the afternoon."

Stephanie laughed. "That doesn't surprise me. You always have something planned. But how much trouble are we going to get into this time?"

"Today we're going to be archeologists," replied Shelli. "I've got us an invite to Edwards Island to help Dr. Carlisle with the dig. Isn't that wonderful?"

Stephanie looked at Shelli weirdly. "Digging in the sand for skeletons? That doesn't sound fun, that's freaky," said Stephanie with a sound of disgust in her voice.

Shelli now laughed. "Don't you see? This is like going on a treasure hunt. These had to be pirates to be in this area during that time in history. And if they're not, then we'll say good-bye and head back home."

Stephanie thought for a few moments. "OK. That is, if you promise me we'll leave if it gets too gross."

Stephanie called her brother Ryan, and in twenty minutes, he arrived with the boat. Shelli called her mom to let her know she was going to the island. It took a few minutes of convincing, but once she heard

Ryan was going, her mom reluctantly agreed to let her go. They were heading away from the Bryant dock minutes later. Shelli called Dr. Carlisle to let him know they were heading to the island. He said they would be there for about two more hours.

When they arrived at the island, Dr. Carlisle greeted them. Ryan told the girls he would be back in two hours to pick them up, if he had not already received a call from them. Then he headed back home. Dr. Carlisle introduced them to the university staff working on the site and gave them a quick tour. Canopies had been erected to protect against rain and to protect from the sun's UV rays. Each site with a skeleton had been roped off, and small tags and markers were posted all over each dig site. Two photographers were taking pictures, and one videographer was taking video of each site to document the find.

A few college students with brushes were painstakingly brushing lightly through the sand around the skeletons and in the areas adjacent to them.

"This is what you'll be doing," said Dr. Carlisle. "When you find anything, you'll immediately come for me or one of the other staff members."

He walked toward a set of tables with an overhead tarp cover and continued talking.

"Once an artifact has been documented, it is moved to these field preparation tables, where they are further cleaned and prepared for shipment back to either the university or the Smithsonian labs." Dr. Carlisle continued on with how things were packaged and protected for shipment.

Shelli was absorbing everything she saw and heard from Dr. Carlisle. She was surprised at just how interesting this all was to her. She could tell that Stephanie was perhaps not as interested, but was eager enough to stay focused.

"What happens when they get back to the university and labs?" Shelli asked.

"They get a detailed cleaning and are documented further in photo and video. Those that are most interesting are sent for spectral analysis to determine the materials and carbon dated as necessary for the age. However, in this case, with so much detailed metal and artifacts, very little dating is needed. OK, I've got a lot of work here before we finish up for today. I'm assigning you to Paul Guthrie. He's one of our grad students assigned to organize the student labor and digs. He'll tell you where to dig. I've asked him to put you at one of our more interesting specimens."

With Dr. Carlisle in the lead, they walked back to one of the sites, where a skeleton lay face down. Paul and two other students were working to clear out the sand in and around the skeleton. They were about halfway through the skeleton.

"Paul, I'd like to introduce you to Shelli and Stephanie," said Dr. Carlisle. "They were two of the four kids that discovered the site. They've come to both work and learn. Can you please help me out here and show them how we clear the site and such?"

"Sure, no problem," said Paul. "I'd be happy to show them the ropes." Dr. Carlisle gave a half wave gesture and walked back to the benches of artifacts.

"You two really stumbled on an awesome site here," said Paul.

"Yeah, it was pure luck," said Shelli. She quickly described how they found the site.

At the end of the story, Paul said, "Cool. Well, we've found a bonanza of skeletons and artifacts. These fellows had the fight of their lives...which they didn't win. Over half the skeletons had arrowheads next to them or inside them. Those that weren't killed by arrows must have died from stab wounds."

He walked toward the head of the skeleton and knelt down.

"This poor fellow died a horrible death." Paul pointed at the base of the back of the skull. The hilt of a knife was visible. "He got a blade shoved through the base of his skull and out of his mouth."

A cold chill went through Shelli, and she saw Stephanie shudder at the mention of the knife.

"That sounds just horrible," said Stephanie. It was clearly hard for her to look at it.

"I know it looks a little gruesome, but be thankful it is just skeletons you're seeing," said Paul. "You get used to it after a while."

"Well, he probably died quickly," said Shelli.

"Since his spinal column would have been severed and the base of his brain ruptured, I would expect he just dropped and died immediately," said Paul. Another shudder went through Stephanie as she released an "Eeewww. Gross."

"OK, here are your tools. You guys clear around his rib section while I reach in and clean inside the chest cavity," said Paul. Just the thought of what Paul had just said made Shelli nearly heave. But at the same time, it was fascinating. Shelli and Stephanie kneeled on either side of the skeleton and worked from the outside to brush away the sand with the short-handled brushes. Paul kneeled beside Shelli and with a long-handled brush pushed the sand in both girls' directions.

After more than an hour of tedious labor, Shelli noticed something brown in the sand under the skeleton's sternum. She touched Paul's shoulder and pointed to the object.

"What's that?" she asked.

"I don't know," Paul said. He asked for Shelli's brush and gingerly brushed more sand from the object. The edge of a rounded surface started to emerge.

"Go get Dr. Carlisle," Paul told Shelli.

Dr. Carlisle followed Shelli to her dig site. He saw the oiled leather tube partially uncovered from the dry sand and knew exactly what it was.

"My God," said Dr. Carlisle. "It's a map tube. Chances are the leather has completely dried and will fall apart with a touch."

"If there are any maps inside, would they have survived?" Shelli asked.

"Not likely. If the leather tube is compromised, the map would have gotten wet. Mold would form, and eventually the map would rot away."

Dr. Carlisle and Paul continued to brush sand away with gloved hands. Dr. Carlisle held the tube with both hands as Paul brushed. After thirty minutes, and with sweat pouring down his forehead, Dr. Carlisle rose with the help of two students. His legs had gone numb from not moving for so long.

After he started to regain sensation in his legs, he started to move toward the field preparation tables. Paul walked beside him on one side, and Shelli quickly came up on his other side. Staying focused on the tables, Dr. Carlisle stumbled on a mound in the sand. Since he did not want to drop the map tube, he came down to one knee. As his body shook from the impact, one elbow hit his kneecap, and he heard a *click* sound from the map. He looked around at Paul in disbelief. Paul and Shelli helped him up and moved quickly to the field table.

"I believe my stumble may have broken what seemed to have been a wax seal. This tube is in better condition than I thought." He sat the tube down on the table. Then he picked up a magnifying glass and held it over the tube.

"This is an old tube that was likely used to store the nautical maps used by the navigator," he said. "This is a very ornate leather case—expensive for its day. The leather was undoubtedly coated in oil to make it weatherproof. This flaky material around the top is what is left of the wax seal. It seems heavy for leather, so sand most likely got inside.

"I would normally carefully ship the whole thing as is," Dr. Carlisle said. "But in this case, I believe we should open it in case there is a slim chance of seeing any pieces of the maps. The case may partially crumble due to its condition, but that will happen anyway, since it has now been exposed to the air."

With one hand on the top, Dr. Carlisle slowly pulled the sleeved top upward off the main body. As he did so, an irregular-shaped piece of the leather about half an inch in size fell off. A dull material was seen underneath. Dr. Carlisle looked surprised.

"The leather surrounds a metal tube," he said without looking up. "This is exceptionally rare. This metal lining is why the tube felt heavy."

He continued to open the tube. Shelli, Stephanie, Paul, and the other students crowded around with the videographer and photographers, who busily documented every moment. When the top cleared the tube body, they all gasped at what they saw. There was paper rolled inside.

"Dr. Carlisle," said Shelli, "I thought you said it was doubtful any maps would have survived."

"Yes, I know. The navigator fell forward onto the tube. That would have pushed it into the sand. I'm sure it took a year for the body to fully decompose and for all his clothing to rot away. The tube was well oiled, and there was a healthy amount of wax around the lip of the top. In those days, they used linseed-like oil on the metal to keep it from rusting. The oil used on the leather probably kept the tube lubricated. This was high up on the beach, and the sand up here probably allowed rainwater to leach through quickly to the waterline of the brackish water that flows through here. That allowed for it to stay dry most of the time."

The doctor slowly rubbed his gloved fingers over the edge of the paper.

"It's intact," he said. "It feels like laid paper, which was the cotton paper they used during that time period." He pulled out the paper slowly, and it came out as several rolled pieces of paper. He sat the tube down carefully and then asked Paul to help him unroll the paper. Shelli caught a view of a shape that looked like an island.

"It is a map," she said. "It's in black and white."

"The majority of maps were printed in black and white during those days," Dr. Carlisle said. "During the 1600s they switched to copper plate printing. Color maps were black and white maps that were colored by an artist or map painter. And it is definitely laid paper."

"What's laid paper?" Stephanie asked.

"They made it from wet cotton strands laid over screens to dry. It's thicker than the wood paper we make now and is more textured, as you can see. It's more robust than any paper we make today. If it were printed on today's papers, called woven paper, it would be mostly dust. Woven paper has high acid content, so it will age much, much faster."

They looked carefully at the topmost map, which appeared to be a map of the western coastline of Florida.

"This is probably the last map the navigator looked at before he was killed," said Dr. Carlisle. "He was probably looking for fresh water. They clearly must have come from a ship in the Gulf. They probably used rowboats to make it here. The water is shallow, and a schooner could not have made it here."

The doctor slowly moved the map aside to see the second map.

"That's Florida and Cuba," said Paul, pointing at the features on the map.

"Look at that line," said Shelli. It was a line drawn with notations at almost regular intervals to the side of it. The line started on the east coast of Florida and was drawn all the way to the mouth of Sarasota Bay.

"It appears the navigator was making a record of their trip so that he could repeat the trip if necessary," said Dr. Carlisle. "The notations are the position readings he made from observations of the stars at night."

Stephanie had quietly grabbed her phone and was recording everything Dr. Carlisle was saying. She also was able to get the second map in her video before Dr. Carlisle quickly prepared the maps and tube for shipment. About that time, Stephanie heard a boat motor and saw her brother pulling up on the beach. She touched Shelli's arm and pointed to her brother.

"It's that time already?" Shelli asked.

"Yep," said Stephanie. "We've got to go. The skies are going to open up any minute."

The rain started by the time Shelli and Stephanie were at the north Siesta Key bridge on their way back to Shelli's house. They were talking loudly to Ryan about what they had seen and done. They were talking so fast that Ryan was having a tough time keeping up.

As they passed under the bridge, they had no idea that a man in one of the homes on Roberts Bay to the south of the bridge was putting down his binoculars. The waterfront estate was huge and sat on Flamingo Avenue on Siesta Key. Its view was eastward toward Edwards Islands and was private, except from the gawking eyes of boaters passing by. From the privacy of his screened patio, Jacques had been intently watching the events on the island all day. His waterside security cameras were also filming the events.

Just before the kids left, there was a flurry of activity. They must have found something important. He had to find out more about those kids. They had been snooping around the islands for days, and they must have found something to attract this much attention. This could be yet another fruitful business venture. His main business, which was in international trade, had its ups and downs. But it had yielded him a comfortable existence, and he had substantial assets in banks all over the world.

He loved antiquities and was a collector. His businesses allowed him to maintain substantial fine art pieces, which had made him a respected and well-known buyer in the art world. Although the duties of his business took up more time than he liked and kept him on the road, Jacques' new large home on Siesta Key gave him plenty of space to exhibit many of his art treasures.

He called his head of security.

"Yes, sir," said his security chief.

"I need you to find out more on the kids we've been seeing over on Edwards Islands. Pull up the video from the security cameras and ask around," said the man with a French accent.

"I'll get right on that, sir," said Hans.

Chapter 22: *A Day of Surprises*

The day had gone without a hitch so far. Three of the four mules were now under arrest. The distribution center in Orlando had been raided, and law enforcement officials had worked out a deal with the distributors to continue with the operation under DEA supervision, in return for leniency in their jail sentence. Once all the players were arrested, the DEA would close the center down permanently. The three boat operators were all under surveillance now at a dock site in Placida. The last boat operator would also be arrested as soon as he transferred the drugs to the mule. He'd be made the same offer as the Orlando dealer in turn for wearing a wire and going back to his pickup point.

The team was now surrounding the Indian Mound Park drug drop-off point in Englewood. The last mule, Johnny Gates, would be arriving soon. Once he made the pickup, he would be arrested, and they would start tightening the noose on the rest of the international drug ring.

Rick and Jim Matchett were parked behind the funeral home off of West Dearborn Street. The business sat right on the water and even had a dock. It had a clear view of Indian Mound Park, which is why it was chosen. Sheriff Steele and one of his deputies were in their plain clothes at one of the picnic tables at the end of the parking lot at Indian Mound. DEA agents also sat low in their black pickup truck backed up to a boat trailer near the Indian Mound boat ramp. Johnny would have to drive by them to park his car. Another sedan was following Johnny to Englewood from Sarasota, relaying position updates to the team as they neared.

Indian Mound Park sat on the east side of Lemon Bay. The western boundary of the bay was Manasota Key, which was an island with many exclusive homes and three major beaches. The middle beach park, called Blind Beach Park, stretched from the beach on the Gulf side to a kayak launch on the bay side. The beach was frequented by petrified shark tooth hunters. Most people who went to the beach had no idea of the kayak launch, since it required a four-wheel drive to get to it most of the year. The kayak launch sat across the bay from Indian Mound. Lieutenant Williams was on the ATAWT at the kayak launch site. He had pulled the ATV out into the shallow water and had his binoculars trained southward.

Kyle and Jason were in the Gladeator at the intersection of McCall Road and Route 776, which ran north and south from Port Charlotte to Venice. McCall was a shortcut back road from Old Englewood and Indian Mound to 776 southbound. If Johnny made a run for it south, Kyle could cut them off.

Sheriff Huggins was on the *Spearfish* with another deputy. They were moored at the private docks of colorful new condos on Beach Road.   These condos had views of the tall bridge to Englewood Beach to the east and Lemon Bay to the north. Sheriff Huggins and his deputy were ready to cut off the southern exit route for the boat transporters after the drug shipment was dropped off. Sheriff Steele's marine patrol boat was moored further north of Lieutenant Williams off the shore from Lemon Bay Park. A helicopter was now flying toward Englewood from its base at the sheriff's office in Sarasota.

Rick was monitoring the feeds from all the assets. He had also installed monitors and tracking systems inside the DEA's vehicles and sheriff's office boats. The buoy monitoring system was already tracking the movement of the drug boat heading north from Charlotte Harbor. He notified everyone via voice-over-IP, commonly written as VoIP, on the encrypted cellular network he had established. Everyone in the sting operation was able to watch what was going on their vehicle or boat monitors. During the morning operations, Sheriff Huggins had said it wasn't the lack of information they had, but the overwhelming amount of it that was almost confusing. So Rick had limited the video to only what was pertinent at that moment in time.

The group was poised for this final takedown. As soon as Sherriff

Bob gave the word, Rick was ready to initiate all the jammers he had installed on his boats. The DEA agents would activate their jammers as well.

The agents following Johnny reported that he had turned onto Dearborn and appeared to be stopping for a drink at one of the bars. Watching the buoy sensor grid, Rick notified the group that the last transport boat had passed the Boca Grande Causeway and was heading north at about 15 mph. A DEA agent pretending to fish near the bridge at the causeway confirmed the sighting. It would take the drug runner about forty-five minutes to arrive at Indian Mound at this rate.

◇◇◇◇◇

Johnny walked quickly into the Mexican restaurant bar on Dearborn to keep from getting wet in the light but steady rain. He ordered a Corona Lite and some tortilla chips and salsa. *Nothing unusual*, he thought as he took his first swig of beer. The beer was refreshing after walking in from the muggy outdoors. The taste of the lime wedge he had squeezed in the beer was appealing. The salty chips were fresh and tasted good with the spicy cilantro and lime salsa. *I've got about thirty minutes to enjoy this before going to the park*, he thought. The baseball game was on the TV at one end of the bar, and the local news and weather was on the TV at the other end.

Johnny quietly sat watching a little bit of both for about ten minutes. The first beer was gone quickly. "Another, please," he said to the bartender as she walked by. *She's new...and hot.* He was prepared to start small talk with the bartender when he glanced above her at the TV exclusive report. The news was showing a phone video taken of a person being arrested by undercover police on Placida Road. Johnny noticed that the face of the person was not visible, but he was clearly in handcuffs, being escorted to a sheriff's cruiser. The video was grainy due to the low quality of the camera on the phone, but it was clear enough to alarm Johnny when he saw the sheriff open the truck and pull a blue cooler out of it. He was so absorbed in the video that he didn't see the bartender set the beer in front of him.

The reporter ended the segment saying that nothing else was known about the event, and the sheriff's office had no comment when called and asked about it. Johnny looked down and immediately felt flushed as his mind raced. He began to allow his brain to process what his eyes were seeing and realized he now had the new beer in front of him. He picked it up and downed half of it without stopping. *Wonder if that is one of my fellow transporters. The cooler looks like the ones I transport. Maybe the law has figured out their distribution routes. Am I being followed?* Then he remembered the black truck that had followed him a week ago.

Paranoia set in and Johnny became fidgety. He looked around the bar to see if anyone was watching him. No one looked suspicious, but how would he know? He got the bartender's attention and told her he was going to the restroom and to please ring him up.

As he passed by a window that overlooked the parking lot, he looked out for a few seconds. *No one there,* he thought. He continued into the restroom, satisfied no one was sitting in his vehicle watching the place. He couldn't get the thought of being caught and arrested off his mind and realized he was just standing in front of the stalls just staring. An urge came on him, and he quickly pushed the door open to the stall and threw up. He kneeled over the commode for almost five minutes with dry heaves. He was still shaking as he slowly stood up. He walked over to the sink and turned on the cold water. With cupped hands, he splashed water on his face and then wiped it dry with paper towels.

I've got to pull myself together. It could be just a coincidence, but I've got to be prepared. He thought of calling his Orlando contact, but then realized an important fact. *If one of the transporters had been arrested, his Orlando contact would have sent an encrypted text message to warn them.* He left the restroom and made his way back to the bar. He opened up his prepaid business phone and checked for text messages. No texts from the Orlando contact had come in. He suddenly felt better. *Of course I would have been contacted—they would have wanted to stop the drug flow, if the police were making arrests.*

Johnny looked at his watch—ten more minutes before he had to leave. He took out his 4G touch screen phone and clicked the icon that pulled up Google Maps. *I better be prepared, just in case the police do try to catch and arrest me.* He started mapping out the routes of escape from his present position to Orlando. He saved each route so he could pull it up from his favorites, if necessary.

After paying his bill, Johnny left the bar. The rain was still falling steadily as he jumped in his car. Before pulling out on the street, he paused and looked in the adjacent parking lots for other suspicious cars. No black trucks or suspicious cars caught his eye. He pulled out and headed toward the park. As he did, he saw a car in his rear view mirror pull out of the corner store onto Dearborn. He hadn't noticed the car earlier. He tensed as he turned right onto Magnolia and then right again on Green. He pulled over on the grassy shoulder to see if the car was following him. He was relieved to see the car turn the opposite direction and drive away. He pulled back onto the road and made a left onto Winson Avenue, which dead-ended at Indian Mound Park.

As Johnny pulled into the park, he quickly looked toward the water to see how far out he could see in the rain. Visibility was still good, and there were no lightning strikes. He pulled into a parking space and waited for his delivery. Although it was still raining, he got out of the car, adjusted his shirt, and put on his raincoat. This all allowed him to do an inconspicuous survey of the area. Nothing much was around, except for a couple of guys at a picnic table talking and laughing. He couldn't see the entire boat ramp parking area due to the trees and foliage blocking his view, but the rain was keeping things relatively quiet.

A few moments later the boat came up. He said hello to the boat pilot and his buddy and asked him if everything was OK. They said everything was fine, but they wanted to hurry up and get out of the rain. Their rain slickers were plastic and undoubtedly hot. He said good-bye and returned to his car, loading the cooler into his trunk.

He waved as the guys started away from the shore and walked back to his car door. He looked one more time around quickly and noticed one of the two guys at the picnic table was looking at him, but then looked away. Johnny hopped in and started the car. He sat for a minute and watched the two men at the picnic table. They didn't look his way again, so he put the car in gear.

Johnny pulled out of the parking space and was slowly driving though the boat parking area when he saw a black truck parked in front of a boat trailer. His heart skipped a beat. He gently stepped on his brake to slow down and kept his eye on the cab of the truck. He didn't see anyone in it, but he was still worried. The road curved right to the exit, but he moved slowly, adjusting his rearview and side mirrors so he could see the parking lot.

The parking spaces at the boat parking area were slanted in the direction of the exit and were long enough to accommodate a truck and its boat trailer. The black truck in the last parking spot was mostly obstructed by a truck beside it. Johnny purposely drove at a snail's pace to see if the truck started up. With only the right headlight and bumper corner visible, he saw the light go on. The overcast skies made it dark enough outside for the lights to automatically come on as the truck started. *Oh, shit, they're after me!* Johnny floored the gas pedal, and his tires squealed as he bolted down Winson Avenue.

The DEA agents in the truck realized their mistake and shoved the truck into forward gear. The trailer wasn't attached to the hitch, so the driver turned sharply left toward the exit. The BMW coupe was speeding off. The DEA agent in the passenger seat called up the team and quickly told them the mule was fleeing out of the park.

Johnny knew he was in trouble.   About a quarter of a mile ahead of him, a sedan pulled across the road and blocked the end of Winson Avenue. He slammed on his brakes and turned his car hard to the left. The back end of his rear-wheel-drive car spun around, causing him to face the black truck that was leaving the parking lot. To his left at fifty yards was Fray Street. He floored it and turned left before the truck could intercept him.

Johnny set his phone on his dash cradle and raced ahead. The road was a straight shot to 776, but he had to cross three intersections before 776. All of them had stop signs, but Johnny kept his foot down. He was fortunate to clear all of them without incident. Just before hitting 776, he looked back in his rearview mirror to see the black truck several intersections back. He was losing them.

He exploded out of Fray onto the multi-lane highway 776 and immediately saw cars slamming on their brakes on both sides of him. There was no median, just a large two-direction turning lane. He turned hard left to purposely cause his rear end to slide. He accelerated and then spun the steering right to put the car into a controlled sideways slide facing north. A car narrowly missed him in the southbound lane as he continued sliding into the left-hand lane of the northbound traffic. A motorcycle in the left lane dropped and tumbled as the rider lost control of the bike. With squealing tires, Johnny moved northward at fast as he could push the car. He was turning right at the Dearborn intersection when he glanced back and saw the black truck enter 776. It now had a blue flashing light on top of the passenger's side.

Traffic would be light on Dearborn, which turned into State Highway 777. If he could make it to River Road, he'd have a clear shot to Interstate 75. Johnny figured he could take I-75 a short distance, then jump off and abandon his car, if necessary. He could get a taxicab and make his way to Orlando as fast as he could.

Orlando! I've got to let them know we've been discovered. He picked up his phone and had begun to dial when he looked up in his rearview mirror and was surprised to see a BMW SUV coming up on him. He checked his speed—85 mph.

"Holy shit," he said out loud. He set his phone back into the cradle and put both hands on his steering wheel. He looked up ahead and saw the road veering again to the left. He took it, accelerating to 90 mph with rain steadily falling.

Several minutes later, Rick looked down at his map display.

"This is five miles of single lanes. We have two lights to cross before we get to the Interstate. This is going to be challenging." They approached traffic, and Johnny passed it at breakneck speed. With the traffic terrified by his actions, passing became even more difficult for Jim.

"Don't worry if he gets a little more ahead of you. He's three hundred meters ahead of us now, and my jammer has a range of 1,200 meters. It's better than the ones the DEA installed on its vehicles. I use a directional antenna to give me more range. The radar also has a lock on him, and I've got the camera image of him on my display."

"Good," said Jim. "This is just crazy driving."

As they neared I-75, Rick said, "We've got the sheriff's men approaching I-75 up at University Parkway to support the DEA guys already there. Unfortunately, the other DEA guys behind us just hit the intersection at Route 45 and are continuing to fall behind. That is, except for Kyle. He is two miles behind everyone else, but he is closing on all of us. He must be at the max speed of the vehicle, which is a hundred miles an hour."

Johnny entered the I-75 cloverleaf with his tires squealing. He floored it on the on-ramp and jetted onto the freeway. Jim managed to make in around the circular on-ramp, although not as fast as the coupe they were following.

"He's propelled to almost one thousand meters ahead," Rick said. "You now need to close the gap so he can't make a call." Jim entered the freeway and floored it. The motor continued to rev as the BMW X5 hit 100 mph. He leveled out his acceleration.

"What are you doing?" asked Rick.

"Kyle said the top speed was one hundred this morning when he was going over the features. I didn't want to blow the motor and lose him completely."

"No, that's the Gladeator's limits," said Rick. "You should be able to well exceed 160 miles an hour with this. It's got a four-hundred-horsepower, 4.4-liter motor. Johnny's got a three-liter motor with a hundred and fifty horsepower less than yours. Even with the extra weight of the vehicle, sensors, and an extra person, you should be able to catch him on the straightaway."

Jim stomped the gas pedal and caught up to Johnny quickly.

"He's headed north, and we've got the ability to block the road at University Parkway on command," said Rick. "You're slowly gaining on him. We are nineteen miles to the University Parkway. You're doing 123 miles an hour on average right now, so that will put us there in nine minutes. The sheriff's office has just notified us they've placed FDOT work crews at all the northbound freeway entrances from Laurel Ave to University Parkway at the north. That will reduce the chances of an accident."

◊◊◊◊◊

As the chase on I-75 was underway, the men who had dropped the drugs off had headed southbound to return the boat to the dock. Frank was at the steering console, while Will kept a watchful eye out for anything out of the ordinary. Frank was skittish after the murder of his previous partner a few days ago.

Frank and Will were within about four hundred yards from the bridge to Englewood Beach when they saw a boat leave from a private dock and move rather quickly toward the center of the waterway. Will looked in his binoculars and saw the sheriff's uniform.

"This is not good," he said. "The boat ahead is from the sheriff's department. I've got an illegal machine gun and two pistols. We can't let them take us."

"What do you want to do?" asked Frank.

"We can't outrun them, based on the size of their motor," said Will. After a few seconds of thought, he had an idea. "Let's get closer. I'll pick up the machine gun and spray them with bullets. They'll drop down on the boat for cover. I'll then shoot near the waterline to see if I can sink them or at least make them take on water. That should give us a chance to escape."

"But you could kill one of them," said Frank with a concerned look on his face. "They'll throw the key away for killing a law man if they catch us."

"I've got two strikes against me already. But let's get on with it. We don't have much choice."

At about three hundred yards from the officers, Frank and Will heard the voice of the sheriff. The extremely loud voice hurt both smugglers' ears. It appeared to be coming from the flat panel box near the bow. Before the sheriff could finish his message telling them to stop, Will picked up the machine gun and starting firing. He told Frank to speed up and head right for the boat. He continued to fire, but he was concerned to see that no one on the boat did anything but stand behind the pilot. He noticed the square box speaker rotated upward so that its steel base was visible. He thought he was missing the boat entirely until he saw a ricochet spark on the speaker.

"Something is not right here," yelled Will over the roar of the motor. They were now inside two hundred yards. "Stop and prepare to turn around. I'll try for the waterline." He started firing again at the waterline. He marched bullets along the water until they impacted the boat. Again the people onboard didn't flinch, and the boat didn't look like it was even being hit.

"Turn around and get out of here," he said to Frank. Frank opened the throttle wide open and headed north. The deputy onboard was at the helm. He started the boat forward.

"They've got some kind of bulletproof boat and we'll never outrun them," Will said. "We've got to call for help." He picked up his phone and pressed the preprogrammed speed dial number for help. He put the phone to his ear and heard no dial tone or ringing. He tried it again with the same result. Then as he was about to hang up, he heard Sheriff Huggins' voice.

"Stop your boat, drop the gun, and raise your hands. You are under arrest."

"Holy crap," said Will. "They're talking to me on my phone."

Will tried to think of a way out of his predicament. He saw Frank had the boat at full throttle. He tried to think about the local geography. Then an idea surfaced.

"It's raining, but there are always people at Blind Pass Beach looking for shark's teeth. There's a point that is on the Lemon Bay side right over there."

He was pointing to the thin strip of land to their left. "On one side is a kayak launch. It looks like someone is sitting there on an ATV. We want to go to the other side of the point—the side next to the beach parking lot and Manasota Key Road. The water's shallow, so the sheriff's boat may not be able to follow.

"I once went fishing at the end of that inlet," he continued. "It's a small path running from the water's edge up to the road and parking lot. You'll have to run aground into the mangroves and sea grapes. We'll jump out and make a run for either the parking lot or the beach."

Frank looked at him with worry and fear. "That's not much of a plan," he yelled back.

"You got a better idea?" asked Will. Frank looked at him for a few seconds and then shook his head no.

Will looked back and saw the boat was gaining on them quickly. They were one hundred meters from the point, and the sheriff's boat was about the same distance from them. As Will turned around, he saw a Jet Ski on his right coming toward them. He looked into his binoculars at the Jet Ski.

"Where the hell did that come from?" said Will in disbelief. "It's another sheriff deputy."

"I don't know, I was focusing on the point," answered Frank.

Will lifted his machine gun and fired at the Jet Ski. He saw the officer duck low behind the windshield. Although the Jet Ski slowed somewhat, Will soon realized the bullets were deflecting off the windshield. *I don't get this. Did they send frickin' James Bond and MI-5 after us?*

Frank and Will made it past the point and kept the boat at full throttle. They saw the sheriff's boat and the Jet Ski enter just behind them, but the boat began to slow down. "We're going to have to run for it when we hit the mangroves," shouted Will. "That guy on the Jet Ski might stay with us, but he'll think twice about jumping off of it to come after us when I fire at him."

It took two painfully long minutes, but bullet fire prevented the Jet Ski from coming alongside the boat. The sheriff's boat cut back power to their motor—the water was now shallow, and they seemed worried about bottoming out. At the last minute, Frank killed the motor, and then he and Will dropped down low at the stern of the boat as it ran into the beach-less shore. The mangroves made horrific scratching sounds as its branches acted like thousands of eagle talons grabbing at the sides and bottom of the boat.

Will had inserted his fifth clip into the machine gun just before they hit the shore. He now grabbed the fully loaded gun and the pistol and leapt out of the boat into the mangroves, which immediately scratched his right leg and tore his shirt. Frank grabbed the second pistol and followed. Will heard Frank curse at the mangroves when he hit the ground. They had crashed on the shore only two yards from the sandy path, which was itself about a yard wide. But it took them a few seconds to muscle their way through the mangroves. Will turned and told Frank to run for it while he fired at the Jet Ski.

Will smiled as he saw the Jet Ski operator slow his approach.

"That's right, you bastard," yelled Will, holding his machine gun with both hands. "You're afraid to get off that thing and come after me." He fired shots at the Jet Ski, which just ricocheted off. But the Jet Ski kept coming. Will tried to maneuver to get a side shot at the operator, but the path was not wide enough. It was then that he noticed four wheels lowering from the sides and into the water. Will's smile faded. *What the hell?*

He continued to fire as he backed up on the path. The wheels of the ATV spun and then came in contract with the sandy bottom in front of the path. At that point the machine gun stopped firing; it was out of ammunition. Will pulled out the pistol that he had shoved in his pants. By the time the gun was level, the ATV hit him squarely and knocked him back. Without stopping, the ATV drove over Will and headed for Frank, who was now looking back while running through the parking lot.

Lieutenant Williams glanced back quickly to make sure the first boat smuggler was not getting up. He wasn't getting up; in fact, he wasn't moving. Lieutenant Williams looked forward and cranked the throttle. This launched the ATV directly at the second smuggler. The smuggler tripped while looking back and fell. Knowing it was over, he threw the pistol aside and raised his hands while seated in the sandy parking lot.

Lieutenant Williams jumped off the ATV and drew his revolver. At that moment, a sheriff's patrol car pulled in, and two officers exited quickly with their guns drawn. Frank offered no resistance. Lieutenant Williams asked the other two officers to read the boat smuggler his rights. The lieutenant ran to Will, who was now coming to and holding his head. The lieutenant kicked Will's guns out of the way and told Will that he was under arrest.

Although he was bruised badly and had an extremely bad headache, Will had the strength to ask, "Are you guys special forces or what?"

Lieutenant Williams called for an ambulance and found out they were already on their way. It was then he realized that their helicopter was hovering above them. They must have called it in.

Within five minutes the ambulance had arrived. The medics examined Will and said it appeared he had a slight concussion and must go to the hospital for observation. This put the sting operation in a dilemma. They needed to get the two operators to agree to return to the smuggler's dock. Fortunately, the lieutenant was able to talk to the emergency room's chief doctor, who said if his staff could do a quick examination of the patient, they might be able to release him. So the sheriff's helicopter landed, and the lieutenant, Will, and one medic climbed aboard and headed to Port Charlotte Hospital.

Meanwhile, Sheriff Huggins was able to pull the smuggler's boat out of the mangroves, using rigging lines and the powerful motors of the *Spearfish*. The boat had a number of new scratches, but was still functional. They would have to make up some story for Frank that explained the damage.

Law enforcement officials brought Frank back to his boat, and he climbed in with Sheriff Huggins and a deputy from the patrol car. His second deputy followed in the *Spearfish*. They had to run the boat at full throttle now to make up for the twenty-five minutes they had lost in the chase. Even at full throttle, by their calculations this was going make their arrival eight to ten minutes late to the dock. They could claim the rain slowed them down, but they'd need to come up with a story for the scratches on the boat.

Frank was given an offer to get off with a light sentence in the local low-security prison if he cooperated in the sting operation. He was against it at first, because of the murder he'd seen by his employer. But the sheriff was able to convince him that he'd not have a chance if he went to a federal prison. So Frank reluctantly agreed. The only thing now was to see if they could rush Will back by helicopter to the boat before it arrived at the Placida dock. As they were racing southward, Sheriff Huggins wondered how the land chase was going.

◊◊◊◊◊

Jim Matchett and Rick were still closing in on Johnny Gates in their BMW X5 at a speed of 138 mph. They had just passed the Clark

Road exit. University Parkway was in three exits. With the traffic now gone as a result of the blocked freeway entrances, Johnny was picking up speed. The radar on the BMW X5 was easily tracking Johnny, and the thermal camera was locked on him.

As Rick was watching Johnny flying down the road, he heard a *beep* from the computer.

"Holy cow," said Rick.

"What?" asked Jim.

"The buoy sensor grid is lighting up on Lemon Bay," said Rick. Rick clicked to watch the live video feeds coming in from the buoy camera. "The boat smugglers are about to be captured. It looks like they were trying to make a run for it, like Johnny."

Rick continued to watch for a few moments as the sheriff and lieutenant caught the smugglers.

"Got 'em," said Rick.

"Good, one more to go," said Jim.

Just then another *beep* was emitted from the speaker on the computer command center. The interceptor had detected a cell phone call. They were less than four hundred meters away, and the jammer was blocking the call. Rick enabled his PC microphone and said what Jim had told him, "Johnny Gates, this is the Drug Enforcement Agency. Pull over now, or you will be stopped by any means. You have no chance of escape."

There was a pause.

"Screw you," replied Johnny.

After ending the call, Johnny increased his speed. Jim was staying with him as they both continued northward. Rick had broadcast the messages as VoIP to all the other vehicles involved, so the roadblock went into effect on I-75 north at University. The entire team planned for a potential violent ending. All traffic heading north that was behind them was stopped and directed off the Laurel Road exit. All traffic heading southbound was stopped just north of University. So the freeway consisted of just Johnny and them.

◊◊◊◊◊

Johnny was cresting the slight hill at the Fruitville Road exit when it came to him why there was no traffic on the road.

"They're setting up a roadblock to trap me," he said out loud. He strained to see ahead, but the rain was limiting his view. He looked down at his phone. He had one mile before University Parkway. Maybe he'd try to get off there.

Johnny glanced back and saw that the car following him was slowing down. He looked forward and saw the flashing lights of the roadblock about half a mile ahead. Pure instinct set in. Johnny slammed on his brakes and pulled his hand brake. The wet road and the low center of gravity sent the car into a continuous 360-degree spin. Tires screeched loudly and shuttered violently as it spun. All Johnny could think of was flipping over and being crushed under the car. After four full spins, the car came to a complete stop facing southbound. Without a moment of hesitation, he squealed tires as he accelerated south on the northbound lane.

Johnny looked at the faces of the two men in the BMW as he passed by them. The driver had fierce look on his face while the other man had a look of surprise. He looked back in his rear-view mirror and saw the BMW screech to a halt. The car then lurched in reverse and in a fluid motion spun 180 degrees and vaulted toward him. *Great*, thought Johnny. *I've got a damned race-car driver following me.*

◊◊◊◊◊

Kyle and Jason had just entered I-75 and were miles behind Rick and Jim. They watched Jim and Rick's icon on the command center display move first north and then reverse directions and head south. The command center also showed traffic was blocked at Laurel. This was going to prevent them from being any help to Rick and Jim.

"Jason," said Kyle. "Look at the map. What likely routes would Johnny try to escape on if he exits the freeway?"

Jason looked at the map. "Clark Road is my bet. That's also Route 72. They could take that westbound back into Sarasota or eastbound toward the host of back roads and Myakka State Park."

"How do we get to east 72?" Kyle asked.

"Pull off the first chance you get. There's a small road about two miles ahead that heads north." Kyle pulled the vehicle over immediately and looked at the display.

"That road is going to be too congested from the traffic being routed off the south roadblock at Laurel," he said, pointing at the display. "Let's take this route. We can go just a quarter of a mile back, or southbound, to enter it."

"That's Well Field Road," said Jason. "But that doesn't really make it to 72."

"Yeah, I know," said Kyle. "We'll get off on this road, which does go to 72." He was pointing to the intersection.

As they started to move again, Jason said, "But that's Vicker's Head Trail. It can barely be called a dirt road."

"I know, and it's nine to ten miles from where we are now to 72 on that road. But I bet this vehicle can make it," said Kyle, with a devilish look on his face.

Jim and Rick were following Johnny southbound on the northbound lane at a dangerous speed. Rick was scanning the map looking for escape routes.

"If he figures out that the reason there's no traffic coming this way is another roadblock, he'll try to make a move to get off of this freeway," said Rick. "The best route to escape would be Clark..."—he looked up and saw Johnny veering to the left toward the on-ramp for the northbound freeway—"...Road," Rick said, continuing his sentence. "Just like that."

◊◊◊◊◊

As Johnny was going down the ramp, he saw the highway department had a truck on the side of the on-ramp and a wooden sign stretching across the on-ramp. The intersection beyond the wooden barrier was clear of traffic. His only choice was to go left or eastward on 72. There was no way he could turn sharply enough at his current speed to the right or westward. Johnny lifted his foot off the gas pedal and pressed on his brake and clutch. He shifted down two gears and then lowered himself in the seat just before he plowed through the sign. Wood flew everywhere, and he heard glass break, which was his passenger side headlamp.

Johnny quickly rose in his seat as he struggled to keep the car under control. As he squirmed, the light turned green for the cross traffic. He slid across two lanes of oncoming traffic and hit the front driver's side corner of a VW bug that was attempting to miss him. As he slid across the female driver's view, he could see the terror in her wide-open eyes. He broke the driver's side headlamp and gouged his front panel. But his car was still drivable. He cut across the grass and sand median and quickly merged into the passing lane of the eastbound traffic.

As he revved up the motor, Johnny gave a quick glance over his left shoulder to see if the BMW SUV was following. His pursuers now had a blue flashing light and a loud siren, just like he had seen on the black truck in Englewood.

"Damn," said Johnny out loud. The BMW SUV made it clean through the intersection and was quickly closing on him again.

Johnny looked at his map on his phone. The built-in GPS gave his position on Route 72 as eight miles from the road to Myakka River

State Park and thirty-eight miles from Arcadia. Myakka was a popular park for locals and tourists to watch hundreds of alligators that lived in the park. The park had a number of roads running north, in case he needed to take that escape route. Arcadia was a small town with five roads entering and leaving the town. Route 17 runs north-south through the town, with the northbound route going to Orlando. He had to stay attentive now, since the road went from two to one lane. Even slight traffic could complicate escape.

Rick looked down at his display and saw the blips of four vehicles merging to help with the chase. He saw Kyle and Jason heading on a dirt road northbound to intersect at 72. Rick smiled when he saw Kyle was going about 60 mph on the road.

"Kyle is pushing the Gladeator hard from a dirt road that runs into 72 about two miles beyond the turn-off to Myakka River State Park," said Rick. "And we have two sheriff's office vehicles and a DEA vehicle that will be entering 72 behind us in less than two minutes."

"How far is Kyle from 72?" Jim asked. "This mule is still smoking fast."

"At our rate of speed and Kyle's, I'd say he's going to be cutting it close. There will be only a few seconds to spare."

◇◇◇◇◇

Johnny was cursing as he came out of the curve on Route 72. At a quarter of a mile from the entrance to the park, the road widened, and a left turning lane opened up for traffic going into the park. About ten cars sat in this lane waiting to turn left, and two cars in his lane were driving slowly. A car in the oncoming lane was slowly pulling into the park as well.

"Why the hell are people going to a state park late in the afternoon on a rainy day?" He was too close to think of what he should do. He instinctively knew he could only pass on the right-hand side of the road in the sand and grass shoulder. He was afraid to hit his brakes as he starting pulling his passenger side wheels off the road. Instead, he pressed the clutch and downshifted. This caused his front end to swerve back and forth, but he was able to keep his car in control as he zoomed by the stopped cars. The tension released slightly in his shoulders as he pulled his car back on the road.

Johnny looked back and saw that the driver of the car he had passed in his lane was frightened so badly that he had pulled over onto the shoulder. This caused the BMW SUV to be totally blocked. Now was his chance of getting some distance on the SUV. He increased his speed as he passed over the river bridge.

As he neared a curve a minute later, he saw a bright-green, military-style vehicle pop onto the road about a quarter of a mile beyond the curve and park across the road. In a flash, he saw two people get out of the car and position on the side nearest him. He immediately pressed his clutch and brake to slow his speed.

"Crap," said Johnny in disgust. "Where the hell did they come from?" With great effort, he was able to slow the car two hundred yards from the strange-looking vehicle and turn around. As he accelerated away, he saw gunfire in his direction. But he couldn't tell whether any hit his car. As he sped back toward the state park entrance and the BMW SUV, he saw the two people getting back into the strange car.

◇◇◇◇◇

"The fool is going to try to escape through the park," said Jason. "I just entered the distance calculator on the display. If we take the dirt road to our right just three hundred yards ahead, we'll hit the main park road in 2.6 miles. It's 2.7 miles for the mule to get to the same spot. We have straight dirt roads, and he has curvy paved roads. If we push it, we should still beat him to that intersection."

"Well, let's do it," said Kyle. Kyle turned right on the dirt road and smashed through the gate that blocked the entrance to the public.

As they sped along, Jason continued to monitor their progress on the display. "Umm," he said aloud as he studied the screen. He pushed the button, and the current map displayed on his command center projected on the windshield in front of Kyle like a 3-D hologram.

"Wow," said Kyle, surprised. "Why didn't you put that up before?"

"Sorry," said Jason. "I just saw the button and pressed it."

"Cool!" Kyle said. He mashed on the gas, and the Gladeator moved down the trail with dust flying behind them. "Contact Rick and let him know that Johnny is heading that way.   Tell him to let Johnny enter the park. We'll trap him there."

◇◇◇◇◇

Rick saw Kyle's movement on his command station display and then got the warning call from Jason.

 Rick turned to Jim and said, "Johnny Gates is heading right for us. Pull across the road and let him take the park entrance. Kyle is taking a back road in the park and is going to block him from the north We'll have him captive on the park road."

"Right," said Jim.   He quickly jumped out and stopped all the approaching cars from the west and then pulled the BMW across the middle of the road.   Twenty seconds later they saw Johnny approaching the intersection.

◇◇◇◇◇

Johnny saw car movement as he neared the park entrance intersection. Cars were blocking the road, but the park entrance was clear. They were expecting him to do this. He worried a split second about a trap, but didn't have any choice but to go for the opening. His tires squealed on the road, and his rear end fishtailed as he turned in. He clipped a car parked in the exit lane with his rear bumper and fender. The fender was crushed, and the bumper peeled back, but his car had no problem accelerating away from the intersection.

Johnny was driving the car as fast as he could and still maintain control. No cars were in front of him, but he did see several pass him on the way out of the park. *Good,* he thought. *They haven't had time to block this road. Maybe I have a chance.* He came to the first bridge about a mile from the park entrance and saw a large number of people standing along the bridge in the rain looking into the river. He hit his brakes to avoid running over people and beeped his horn as we went through. A small boy stepped off the curb just ahead of him, but a man on the bridge grabbed the boy before he was hit. The man shot Johnny his middle finger and yelled something as Johnny raced by much too fast. *That was close. It's one thing to risk my life, but I can't imagine killing a kid.*

After crossing the bridge, both sides of the road were lined with dense live oak trees draped with Spanish moss and palm hammocks. As he passed the pull-off for a trail to the canopy walk, he looked at his map and saw there were no other intersections for three-quarters of a mile. He kept the speed up as fast as he could.

As he neared the upcoming intersection, Johnny knew he had to make a choice: go right or continue straight. Right could eventually lead him back to Route 72 much further east. Straight offered him a number of choices: east, west, north, and south. Since the right looked more like a farm road, he decided to go straight. Just as he was about to enter the intersection, the bright-green military-style vehicle appeared from the right and pulled directly in front of him.

Johnny hit his brakes and prepared for impact. Just then he noticed a dirt road to the left. He jerked the steering wheel to the left. His back end swerved to the right, and his rear quarter panel hit the front wheel of the military vehicle. *My car looks like a gnat compared to this thing.* The collision stopped him, but he quickly dropped into first gear, and his tires spun as he lurched ahead. As he did so, the entire quarter panel ripped off and fell on the road.

Johnny realized he was driving to the end of a power line road as soon as he had pulled away from the military vehicle. Tall poles with power lines framed the dirt and grass road on both sides. It was less than a quarter-mile long and dead-ended in the Myakka River. He saw the power lines stretching to the other side. He instantly had an idea. *I'll ditch this vehicle, swim across the river, and try to escape by foot on the other side. They'll never catch me.* He was young and fit from his daily workout regimen, and he had no doubt he could outrun anyone trying to follow him.

The battered BMW coupe reached the end of the power line road and plunged into the river. The chilly wall of water from the impact traversed the body of the vehicle and drenched it completely. The vehicle started to sink quickly. The airbag went off and engulfed Johnny. He immediately started waving his arms to push the bag off of him and reached for his seat belt. The car started listing to the right as Johnny freed himself from the vehicle and pushed off downstream.

Without a second thought, Johnny started swimming for the opposite shore. After about twenty yards he looked back and saw the military vehicle approaching the river's edge at the same time the last trapped air bubbled up from the roof of his BMW. He looked forward at the shore about sixty yards ahead of him and swam like there was no tomorrow. After a minute more of hard swimming, he looked up again to see that he was not far from the opposite shore. He looked back and couldn't believe his eyes. The military vehicle was entering the water! This river was way too deep for it. He turned around and continued to swim.

A few more strokes, and he started feeling with his feet for the bottom. Suddenly he felt an incredible pain in his leg, and he was instantly pulled underwater. He opened his eyes and looked down to see a dull red fluid filling the water below him. As he reached down, he felt the snout of the large alligator that was biting his leg. He kicked wildly with his other foot on the head of the alligator. Not realizing that the alligator had tough protective eyelids, he continued to kick. Johnny started to feel lightheaded when he remembered he had a pocketknife. He reached in his pocket and fumbled as he felt himself being pulled deeper. He opened the knife and plunged it into the alligator's softer skin under its lower jaw. It immediately let go of his leg, and he pushed himself to the surface.

As Johnny exploded to the surface, he gasped for air. He felt dizzy and disoriented. His vision was blurry, but he still couldn't believe what he was seeing. The military vehicle was coming right for him on the water. It had converted to a boat. He waved wildly, not caring now that he would be arrested. He needed to be saved from this beast that had grabbed him. The boat was within ten yards when the alligator bit again. This time it pulled him down hard and fast. As the alligator pulled Johnny into a death roll on the bottom of the river, Johnny lost consciousness quickly. He never got to find out why people were coming to the park this late on a rainy day.

In the winter months, days were pleasant in Florida, and visitors to the park could see hundreds of alligators swimming in and sunning near the river. In the summer, however, the gators loved to lie on the bottom of the river for long periods of time to escape the high heat of summer days. This kept the body temperatures lower and conserved their energy for afternoon and night-time feeding. Rainy summer days allowed the alligators to surface a little earlier than normal to start feeding. Johnny was the first meal this afternoon.

As dusk came, Kyle circled the last place he saw Johnny before going under. The dark red trail flowing down the river was attracting more alligators. He called Rick and Jim, and they arrived at the shore as he pulled up in the Gladeator. It was now dark.

"I'm going to drop my winch hook and see if I can pull up the car," said Kyle to Rick and Jim as they got out of their vehicle. Jim had left his headlights on bright to light the surface of the water. Kyle turned on his bright overhead spotlights as he positioned the Gladeator over the spot where the BMW coupe went down.

After a few minutes of trying, Kyle yelled back that he had hooked the sport coupe. He kept the winch reel loose as he motored back to the shore. He lowered the wheels and drove up on shore. With the winch locked and the parking brake on, he powered the winch and pulled the battered BMW coupe out of the river. As the car came to rest on the eastern river shore, Jason walked around to the driver's side and pulled the keys out of the ignition. He walked to the back of the car and opened the trunk. Lying on its side, but still sealed, was a wet blue cooler.

Jason sat the cooler down on the ground and opened it up. Inside were bags of white powder.

"Looks like we closed them down," said Jason. "It's a pity this guy had to die, but he was a real idiot to try to escape as he did."

The command station beeped in the BMW SUV and in the Gladeator. Kyle, Jason, Rick, and Jim crowded around the BMW command center to see what it was.

"It's a video call from Sheriff Steele," said Rick. He answered the call and saw Sheriff Steele's face pop up on the display.

"Great job catching that mule," said Sheriff Steele, with a worried look on his face. "But we've got a problem."

"What?" asked Kyle, looking over Rick's shoulder.

"The coolers we confiscated from the other three mules had only one bag of the real thing on top and the rest were just baking powder," the sheriff said. "It doesn't make sense that there would be only one bag, given how much money was being spent to move the drugs."

Jason ran back to the cooler and took out his pocketknife. He lifted the top bag and cut it open. Then he cut the bag below it. He felt the consistency of the white substances in both bags. They were not the same. He licked his finger from the second bag.

"It's baking powder," he said. Jason walked back over to the command center at the BMW and told the sheriff.

"It's the strangest thing I've ever seen," said Sheriff Steele. "The guy just got eaten by alligators for what would have been not much more than a misdemeanor possession charge. What a waste."

Rick thought for a few seconds as Kyle, Jason, Jim, and Sheriff

Steele continued to talk. He remembered thinking the night before that something just wasn't right about this operation. The DEA had said that all the mules and smugglers were petty thugs or people with no records. He thought back to how the drug routes were so regular that the buoy sensor network he had laid in the waterways considered it normal behavior. Given the aggressive methods used by Florida drug enforcement, this drug cartel just seemed too predictable. Then it dawned on him.

Rick interrupted the group as he shouted, "This whole distribution network was a decoy. It was set up to give the real distributors a warning and to keep us occupied while the real distribution occurred either at different times or over different routes or both."

"You mean this Johnny character and the others we arrested were expendables?" asked Jim.

"Precisely," replied Rick.

Rick looked at his watch and back up at the screen.

"Sheriff," said Rick. "I see from the display that the last drug smuggler boat is almost back to Placida."

"That hasn't gone the best," said Sheriff Steele. "One of the two boat operators was hurt in the chase. He had a mild concussion. But the hospital has cleared him, and we have our chopper rushing him back to rendezvous with the boat minutes from now."

"This decoy development changes everything," said Rick. "We need to change our plans." Rick went over his plan in the next few minutes, and then they loaded back into their vehicles and headed southbound to Placida.

Chapter 23: *Clear as Mud*

"Hi, Shelli," said Danielle into her Bluetooth headset. She was driving back from the museum with Nikki in her Infinity G37 light metallic blue convertible. Shelli had encouraged her to buy it, and she hadn't regretted it since the day she brought it home a year ago. Danielle liked driving the car in Florida—especially at night, when the air was less muggy and the temperatures were cooler. But with the rain falling, she had to have the top up.

"Hi, Mom," answered Shelli.

"Your sister and I are on our way home," continued Danielle.

"Good. I can't wait to tell you about my day, Mom. It was incredible!"

"That's good, honey. Did you hear yet from your dad?"

"No, I haven't. And there are no messages from him on the phone."

Danielle looked at Nikki with a frown. "OK, honey. We'll be there soon. Love you. Bye."

"Bye, Mom," said Shelli and hung up.

Danielle had stayed busy all day trying to keep her mind off Rick. It wasn't the first time Rick was doing something a bit crazy. But even after all these years of marriage, she still hadn't got used to it. Before kids, she used to go on some of his adventures in the great outdoors. But as Rick became more successful, the adventures became somewhat more dangerous and usually were out of the country. She thought when Rick sold his first company, he'd be back to just outdoor adventures again. But she should have known better. Rick couldn't relax for long. He'd raised the kids to be just as adventurous, although Nikki and Shelli were resistant to some of his more strenuous activities.

"Don't worry, Mom," said Nikki, sensing her Mom's feelings. "You know Dad. He'll be in the thick of things for sure, but he always comes home. He can't stand to be away from us very long." Danielle smiled as she turned right off of Route 41 and headed toward the Ringling Bridge. She knew Nikki was right. The fact that Rick hadn't called meant the operation was still underway. Rick had warned that he might not be in until very late. As she approached the bridge, she tried to put Rick out of her mind. Darkness was almost on them, and the rain continued to fall at a steady rate. She gripped the wheel firmly as she rose over Sarasota Bay, which was starting to get choppy as the winds picked up. *White-knuckle driving*, she thought.

◊◊◊◊◊

Rick met with the entire crew of the DEA and the Sarasota and Punta Gorda sheriff's offices at the small boat dock and ramp to the north side of Gasparilla Island Causeway entrance. According to the smugglers Frank and Will, the home dock for the smugglers was the marina just down the road about a mile. Behind the marina was a trailer park, which consisted of modern trailers with concrete driveways, porches, and palm trees lining the roads. They were all supposed to meet for dinner tonight at the seafood restaurant at the point in Placida, where the road curved from southbound to eastbound. The new bridge completed in 2010 passed over Coral Creek, which emptied into Gasparilla Sound between the restaurant and the marina.

By boat, the distance from their current position and the marina was one and a half miles. By foot on Gasparilla Road, it was only six tenths of a mile. They were as close as they could get, and were in fact a little worried they could be spotted. Frank and Will were now five minutes late for the rendezvous back at home port. The rain was coming down hard now, and winds were causing the palm tree fronds of the trees surrounding the boat ramp to rustle and bend.

Frank and Will were bugged with the latest wide bandwidth, low power audio transmitters used by the DEA. They were each given separate code words that triggered they were in trouble.

More than twenty men were now being positioned around the marina. Four boats from the sheriff's marine patrol were now in position. Rick's *Spearfish* boat was positioned near Little Dog Island, which was a circular island that sat halfway between the Gasparilla Island and the entrance to the Gasparilla marina. The ATAWT was on the beach on the south end of Gasparilla Island. ATVs were commonly used to patrol beaches in Florida, so it was not conspicuous. Since the Gladeator did draw attention, it was parked next to the BMW SUV at the boat ramp. The helicopter that had dropped off Will and Lieutenant Williams was now grounded due to the weather.

Frank and Will had explained to the officers that they picked up the drugs from their contact offshore on the east side of Cayo Costa, which of course was confirmed by the video data from the buoys. Just as with the mules, they received e-mails in the morning to tell them if the pickup and delivery that day was going to happen or not. And they received text messages if anything changed during the day. There were eight of them in total—four pilots and four armed security men.

The meeting tonight was an update with their bosses. This happened once a week and always at the same restaurant. The speedboat operator was always there with a security detail of well-built, well-armed men. Present at some of the meetings was an older man who looked like he was in his fifties. He spoke good English, but with an accent. He sounded German, but they knew he could speak French as well, since they had heard him speak it over the phone. No one knew the names of the German man or the speedboat operators.

The restaurant was accessed from a branch drive off a circular road, named Fishery Road. Fishery Road was lined with a few shops, a bait shop, and a few cottages that were rented offices. At the far end of the circular drive was the dock. Fishing trawlers and fishing charter boats lined the dock. Fishery Road began at an intersection with Gasparilla Road.

Frank mentioned a memory from when he first started working as a boat pilot for the smugglers. At the end of one of the weekly meetings of the group, he had left the restaurant to have a cigarette, since no smoking was allowed inside. The German had left a few seconds before him. Frank thought he saw the German man walking around the side of the restaurant, which was Fishery Road. With the lit cigarette in hand, Frank pretended to be taking a stroll in the same direction. From the safety of darkness, he watched as the German entered one of the cottages at the end of the road on the left. Frank never mentioned it to anyone for fear he would be killed for knowing too much.

With this information, Rick had created a plan.

"Frank and Will need to leave now," said Rick. The two headed to the boat, started it up, and pulled away from the dock.

"We're going to listen in on the meeting that will occur in twenty minutes at the restaurant," he continued. "The meeting will not likely go long, because the speedboat will need to leave in forty-five minutes if it is going to make it out to the site of Cody's murder. If there is a drug source, that's where we will find it. The rain and wind are not going to let up for at least another hour. Of the boats we know about, the smuggler's speedboat is the only boat they have that will be able to go out in this weather. Only the *Spearfish* will be fast enough and seaworthy enough to follow it. It's been agreed that Jim Matchett and Lieutenant Kevin Williams will operate the *Spearfish*. They're listening in now from their console command station. Jason wanted a shot at driving the ATAWT, and he's listening on his waterproof dash display. My only worry is that the drug pickup tonight will be cancelled due to the weather."

Rick looked over his shoulder to see Frank and Will head out of sight. "We'll record everything being said at the table through the audio on Frank and Will. I've also got a toy here that will be useful after the meeting in the restaurant is over."

Rick went to the back of the BMW SUV and opened the trunk. Rick pulled out a slide-out tray that had a black case. He opened the case and pulled out a black device that had four large circles with propellers in each; the center was a large oval with two cameras.

"This is the Quadricopter. It has four propellers that act as both lift and steering. In the center are the processing heart, two cameras, and a microphone."

"Wow, cool!" said Kyle. "It looks hard to fly. How do you control it?"

"It's very easy to control. But we don't have time to go over that now. We've got to move."

"Agreed," said Sheriff Huggins.

The team dispersed to their vehicles and departed from the parking lot of the boat ramp. Everyone who wasn't already in position moved to his spot over the next fifteen minutes. Rick and Sheriff Huggins were in the BMW X5 in the parking lot of the restaurant. Sheriff Steele and one of his deputies were following the group of drug boat operators and their security partners to the restaurant.

The drug smuggler group arrived at the seafood restaurant on Fishery Road. The rear of the restaurant sat right over the edge of blue green waters of Gasparilla Sound and had glass across the entire back wall. On clear days the sunsets were beautiful to watch. People normally desired to sit at the tables near the windows. Today, however, the view was dark and damp. Few people had ventured out to eat tonight.

Toward the front of the restaurant, larger tables allowed small and large groups a little privacy and plenty of room. Wall mounts of the tropical and freshwater fish of Florida were found along the ceiling beams. A rectangular-shaped bar sat to the rear and right of the restaurant. A rear entrance to the restaurant was next to the bar, and led to a long boat dock for fisherman to have access to the restaurant. The restaurant was well known to locals for its good seafood, great key lime cheesecake, and for being featured in the movie *Out of Time* with Denzel Washington a few years ago. Adjoining the restaurant was a larger building that was a fish market, part of which was unused and in dire need of repair.

The smugglers were all sitting at a large table to the front of the restaurant when the speedboat pulled up to the restaurant dock. The boat operator and three large men walked into the rear entrance and headed straight for the table. They sat quietly at the end of the table. A few minutes later, a man entered the front of the restaurant with a large, hulking bald man leading the way. He walked to the table and stood at the other end. He seemed to be in his fifties, but was clearly fit. He dressed in military-style kakis pants, brown shoes, and was wearing a long-sleeved, denim shirt. He had a loose-fitting black jacket on, which was wet from the rain. He didn't take the jacket off at the front door, mostly likely because it concealed a gun.

"Gentlemen, we have had another week of successful deliveries," said the German. "However, two of you were late arriving today. Frank and William, can you explain why you were more than ten minutes late today?" He made it a point never to call Will by his nickname. "Need I remind you what will happen to you if I find out you are lying?"

In the parking lot, Rick and Sheriff Huggins had seen Hans and his bodyguard entered the restaurant. They had seen Hans walk from the side of the restaurant, but couldn't see any sign of the vehicle that they might have arrived in. "Did anyone see where Hans and company came from?" asked Rick over the VoIP network.

"We're behind the restaurant on Fishery Road, and we saw them come out the second to last cottage," said Sheriff Steele.

"Well, did anyone see their vehicle or boat?" Rick asked. "I know Hans's boat was last seen going from Cayo Costa in this direction." Rick relayed the fishing boat registration number and the black Mercedes description. A round of no's came from all the parties, except for Sheriff Steele.

"A few minutes ago we saw a black Mercedes arrive and park in front of the cottages on Fishery Road," said Sheriff Steele. "Hans and another man exited the car and went straight to the restaurant."

"Good," said Sheriff Huggins. "We're set to follow him if he goes from here by land."

"Are there any lights on in the cottage?" Rick asked.

"No," replied Sheriff Steele. "I don't think it would be wise to snoop at this point. They probably have burglar alarms and maybe even surveillance systems and man traps in the place."

"We'll have to wait then until they go back to the cottage and turn some lights on," Rick said. "Then hopefully we can use the Quadricopter to eavesdrop."

Frank broke into an immediate sweat when he was questioned. He and Will exchanged worried looks with each other that would have told any professional gambler they were guilty of something.

"Well, we hit a downpour of rain on the way down, and I had my head down for a bit trying to keep the rain out of my eyes," he said. "I guess I was looking down too long at one point. When I looked up, there was another boat coming across my bow out at the Palm Island Ferry crossing. It scared the shit out of me, and I turned the boat sharp starboard and ran into the clump of mangroves just south of the ferry landing."

Frank could tell his story sounded credible as he told it.

"It was pretty tough getting the boat out of the mangroves. The bum that cut me off didn't even come back to help me. Anyway, I realized we were late and tried to make up the time, but I was afraid I'd call attention to myself and kept slow from there back. I landed at the restaurant dock instead of the marina to make sure I wasn't late for the meeting."

Frank could feel the sweat bead on his temple and slowly work its way down. His only hope was that Hans hadn't seen the chase scene earlier today. Flashbacks of his partner's head exploding were still haunting him.

Hans was quiet for a moment, clearly wondering if what he had heard made sense.

"William, you know what happens to people who don't follow the rules," said Hans. "I'm sure Frank here has told you the consequences. You don't look all that good, William. What's the matter?" Hans paused as he watched Will squirm. He continued, "Do you agree with Frank's story?"

Will answered immediately, "Yes sir. He's telling the truth. When he turned sharp to the right, I fell off the seat and hit my head on the transom. I still got a nice headache and bump on my head, sir." Will lifted his bangs with his hand so that everyone could see his bump.

Rick and the sheriff were holding their breath as they were listening to the audio transmissions from Frank and Will's wires.

"It wasn't an Oscar performance, but they did sound convincing," said Sheriff Huggins. "They won't kill them in the restaurant, but we need to be ready if they take the two of them out of the restaurant." Rick notified everyone over the VoIP network to be prepared if they needed to save Frank and Will.

Hans was quiet for a moment; shaking his head slightly up and down before he started to talk.

"Well, Frank taught us something today. We need to get a pair of goggles on each of the boats. Pilots should put those on when it starts to rain so that you can see well. Frank did the right thing and didn't panic. William, you get that bump looked at on your day off tomorrow. It doesn't look good. One of the speedboat crew will relieve you and go with Frank, if you have to sit out a day or two." Frank and Will looked at each other and took a silent deep breath.

Hans looked at the end of the table at the speedboat operators.

"The rain is supposed to start subsiding in about an hour, and the wind has already dropped a good deal. I'm going to call our contacts in a few minutes to make a schedule change for pickup tonight. I'll tell them we're leaving an hour later. I'll not be personally going tonight; I have a meeting to attend. So it will be just the speedboat going out tonight." Hans then looked at the others. "For those of you that have the day off tomorrow, enjoy it. I'll remind you that I expect you to stay out of trouble. You should all be sober when you appear at work Monday. Any questions before we adjourn and you guys eat your dinners?"

Back in the BMW X5, Rick checked the Internet on the command center and confirmed what Hans had said. "Hans is right," said Rick over the network. "The front has almost passed, and the winds are now relatively calm. So it appears we're going to have to stay positioned for another hour before things happen."

Sheriff Huggins asked to talk. Rick handed him the mike.

"And it looks like we'll have three groups to watch," said Sheriff Huggins. "Rick and I will stay with Hans, wherever he goes. Sheriff Steele, if he doesn't mind, can follow the pilots go back to the trailer park, and Jim and Lieutenant Williams will follow the speedboat out to pick up the drugs. They can use the thermal camera to follow with their lights off. Kyle and the other DEA agent with him will stay with the Gladeator in the boat ramp area at the Causeway as backup for either the *Spearfish* or Rick and me."

Rick interrupted, "Sorry, sheriff, can you hold it a second? There's a question in the restaurant." They were all ears as they listened to the conversation.

One of the pilots spoke up. "I have just one question, boss. I was watching the news today and saw what looked like my mule being arrested on the news. Was that my imagination or was there trouble?"

Hans looked upset with the question for a moment, but then calmed himself before answering.

"I checked in with our distributors in Orlando and have been in contact with all the transporters.   There has been no disruption in deliveries, so everything is in order. Whatever you saw today on TV had nothing to do with our operation."

The pilot looked relieved.

"Oh, OK boss. I was a little worried about it," said the pilot.

"Believe me," said Hans. "I would have called off the meeting tonight and sent you gentlemen text messages to lay low until we regrouped if our operation was compromised. OK then, good night, gentlemen."

Rick and Sheriff Huggins were relieved when they heard the news. It was good they had gotten to the Orlando distribution dealers before Hans called them.

Hans left the front of the restaurant and headed toward the cottage office with his bodyguard walking beside him, holding an umbrella for both of them. The two remained silent as they walked.

Rick waited until they cleared the side of the restaurant before he got out of the SUV. He opened the tailgate, pulled out the Quadricopter and set it on the ground. With a quick switch of the power button, the copter lifted up about a foot off the ground and hovered. He left it hovering and walked back into the vehicle.

"How do you control it?" asked Sheriff Huggins. Rick opened up the glove compartment and pulled out a thin touch screen PC tablet.

"With this," Rick said. Rick powered the tablet on and pressed the animated icon with a capital Q and four whirling propeller blades to launch the control app. The forward camera came up on the tablet and two main controls. Tilting the display in a particular direction made the copter move in that direction.

"What happens if the wind blows it hard?" asked the sheriff. "How do you stabilize it?"

"It does that on its own using an accelerometer," answered Rick.

Rick guided the Quadricopter at rooftop level to the cottage office. The cottage was white with aqua -colored trim. Four windows were visible from the sandy road, and a small portico framed the front door. It sat across from a small green area filled with palms and oak trees and a couple of picnic tables. Beside the cottage was one tall palm and pine tree to the left of the cottage.

One of the many changes that Rick's company had requested from the Quadricopter manufacturer was a change in the motors. The standard motors had a high-pitched whine. They weren't loud, but easily detectable at a distance. The new motors where whisper soft and almost undetectable. Rick also had ordered the product to be weatherproof, which was a good thing, considering the present steady rainfall. Cameras were swapped by Rick's company to be near-IR CCTVs with LED illuminators that worked out to about one hundred meters. And new software was added to allow point-and-click positioning using a map interface.

Rick switched to the bottom camera and lowered the copter to the top of the windows in the front of the building. The field of view was adequate to still see about five feet inside the window at this elevation. Only the feet of what appeared to be the bodyguard were visible. Rick steered the copter around to the side and then the back of the cottage, where a second light came on.

Rick lowered the copter to the top of the window and was startled when Hans reached for the window lock and then opened the window. He stuck his head out and looked in both directions. Rick raised the copter higher into the darkness until Hans put his head back in. He left the window open. Rick lowered the copter slowly and saw that Hans was sitting at a desk in front of the window. There was a small netbook on the desk that Hans powered on. A briefcase was open at the end of the desk and contained what looked like pamphlets. Rick tried to zoom, but the double-pane glass was still wet from the rain and it distorted the image too much. The audio picked up nothing but the muffled keystrokes on the PC and the rustling of paper.

"How long can you hover there?" asked the sheriff.

"About ten more minutes," replied Rick. "It's hard to tell exactly, because of the rain and wind. If the copter has to continually adjust to keep level, it will cause the batteries to drain faster.

"Let me see what the bodyguard is doing," said Rick. He moved the copter around and saw no other light but the one room in the front.

"I'm going to lower the copter to eye level. The light reflecting from the inside of the window should keep us from being detected." As the copter lowered to the top pane window, Rick flipped back to the forward camera. A couch and coffee table sat to the right. An LCD TV hung on the wall to the left of the room. The audio was picking up the local news channel.

"Nothing to see here," said Sheriff Huggins.

Both Rick and the sheriff jumped when the bodyguard call out, "Hans, the weather is coming on." Hans walked into the room moments later.

"This is our chance," said Rick. "What channel is he watching?"

"I heard the jingle for Suncoast 7 News," said Sheriff Huggins.

"Here, look up that channel on the command center while I go to the back window," Rick said. He quickly steered the copter back to the other side of the building while the sheriff searched the Internet for the live web-cast.

Rick aligned the copter with the open window as best as he could, looking forward. He switched to the bottom camera since it allowed to him to see the windowsill as he went through it. The copter was about twenty-one inches wide, and Rick thought the window opening seemed to be about thirty-two inches wide. The copter easily flew through the open window. As the copter passed over the desk, papers rustled on the desk from the downdraft of the blades. Rick hovered around the room and saw that it was a combination bedroom and office. The door to the room was closed. A long black case sat open on the bed.

"That's a marksman's pistol—very accurate," said the sheriff. The copter moved over to the end of the desk, where Rick could see a folder, a few receipts, and the upper-left corner of a pamphlet. Rick zoomed in the camera and could see a picture of a diver's underwater scooter on the pamphlet.

"Hans must be into diving or at least interested in it," said Rick.

"Tell me when the weather's over," said Rick. I'll have to leave the room by then."

He switched to the forward camera and aligned the copter with the PC screen.

"It's a spreadsheet," said Rick. "It has days of the month across the top and rows labeled merchandise number one, two, and three. Plus, it shows weekly expenses of their staff salary, houses, and meals. He's created a ledger of the operation."

"There is nothing really incriminating, though," said Sheriff Huggins. "But look at the amount of merchandise. That's thousands of kilograms per week."

"That's what I was saying earlier, Bob," said Rick. "We've busted the decoy ring today. It's like the canary in a coal mine. It's obvious that they have a much larger operation."

"Crap," said Sheriff Huggins, realizing he wasn't paying attention to the broadcast. "They are finishing up the five-day forecast. It's just about over." Rick elevated the copter level with the lower windowpane and aligned the copter with the open window. He switched back to the bottom camera and slowly started easing the copter through the window opening.

About halfway through the window, they heard the door open. Rick accelerated through the window and upon clearing the windowsill, spun the copter 180 degrees and elevated the copter quickly. He switched back to the forward camera and saw Hans standing in the doorway looking back to the other room.

"I'm going to work a little longer, and then we'll head back north," said Hans. He turned forward and looked around the room suspiciously.

"You think he saw us?" asked the sheriff.

"I don't think so," said Rick. Hans walked directly toward the desk, but looked at the floor in front of it as he walked. He bent down and picked up a piece of paper on the floor. "The copter must have blown it off the desk when I passed over it." said Rick.

Hans looked quickly at the computer and briefcase and then stuck his head out of the window and looked around outside. As he did, Rick quickly lifted the copter to the roofline.

Hans stuck his head back in the window, and Rick and the sheriff heard him yell out to his bodyguard to check for anyone outside. A light off a back door entrance came on and lit up the back of the house. Rick pushed the copter over the roof of the house and kept it hovering there.

The bodyguard came out of the back door with his pistol drawn and held low to his waist. Hans showed up on the front portico with his pistol in hand. The barrel of the gun pointed down, and it was held close to his hip. The bodyguard walked around the perimeter of the house while Hans stayed in the front.

"Oh, no," said Rick.

"What is it?" asked Sheriff Huggins.

Rick replied with a worried look on his face, "The battery indicator is flashing. We're almost out of juice."

"If that thing drops, it will slide right down the A-frame roof," said the sheriff. "The whole world will hear that."

As the bodyguard came back around to the front, Hans talked a moment to him and then Hans walked inside. The bodyguard lit a cigarette on the portico and looked around.

"We've got seconds now," said Rick.

Sheriff Huggins grabbed the mike again. "Mike, do you have a clear sight to the cottage office?"

"Yes we do," said Sheriff Steele. "We're at the bait shop, and I'm watching through my field glasses."

"Can you see the copter?"

"No," said Sheriff Steele.

"I'll move it forward over the porch roof," said Rick.

Sheriff Steele came back on the speaker, "Now I see it."

"Good," responded Sheriff Huggins.

"There's trees all around these cottages, and the copter is about to fall out of the sky. We need eyes to tell us when we can move."

"OK," replied Sheriff Steele. "Get ready...now move out slowly over the road and toward us. He's looking toward the docks in the opposite direction. Wait...wait...OK. Go, go, go!"

Rick had the bottom camera on and could see he had cleared the front of the porch. He tilted the copter right and accelerated to the top speed of the copter. About twenty feet from Sheriff Steele, the battery died. The video screen went black, and Rick and the sheriff saw a "Lost Connection" message on the tablet screen. The copter blades slowly stopped spinning, and the copter glided the remaining distance, hit the top of Sheriff Steele's vehicle and bounced off the other side onto the sandy parking area.

The bodyguard turned quickly and looked in Sheriff Steele's direction. He walked a few steps onto the concrete walk in front and looked again in the direction of Sheriff Steele. Sheriff Steele and his deputy had shifted low in their seats and didn't dare move. After a few moments, the bodyguard threw the cigarette butt down on the porch and put out the glowing embers with his shoe. Then he turned around and went inside.

"Wow, that was close," said Sheriff Steele. "It fell out of the sky and landed on the top of our car. I thought for sure he was coming over here. I'll wait a few more minutes before we open the door and pick up the copter. He might be looking out the side window that's dark right now. I don't want to take the chance he'll see our door open."

"That's fine," said Rick. "Let us know when you have it and when you see them getting ready to leave."

"Roger that," said Sheriff Steele.

One hour later the time was nearing for the speedboat to leave for the ocean pickup. The boat pilots and their security detail had finished their dinner and had just left to go back to their homes in the trailer court. Kyle, Jim, Sheriff Steele, and Jason were reporting in regularly over the VoIP network.

Sheriff Huggins spoke up as word came in that the speedboat was leaving for the rendezvous.

"Didn't Hans say that he was going to call his contacts for a change in pickup time? The cell interceptor never picked up any telephone calls on their cell phones, and the wiretap we put on the phone line from that building never picked up any calls."

"Yes, he said he was going to call," Kyle answered from the Gladeator. "But I don't think there is anyone to call. I think it is all a hoax or decoy, as Rick said, and he just mentioned it for the sake of the pilots. I think our only key to finding out what is going on is to follow Hans."

"I agree with Kyle," said Jim. "We've picked up a minuscule amount of drugs from two-bit mules. The race boat operator is going out in bad weather, and would you as a drug dealer risk losing any significant amount of drugs by going out in this weather? I think the boat will go out, stay a few minutes, and then come back empty-handed. And notice Hans was smart enough to avoid going out himself."

"It would be good if we can at least confirm that tonight," said Rick.

"Remember to give them plenty of room when you follow them, Jim and Kevin. And as the sheriff said, use the thermal camera for your eyes. Keep all lights off, if possible."

"Roger that," said Lieutenant Williams.

After a couple of minutes, Jim told the group that the speedboat had passed by them on the way to Boca Grande Pass. All members on the team soon saw the thermal image from the *Spearfish* camera as Jim pulled out from Little Dog Island to follow the speedboat. After thirty minutes, Jason reported the speedboat had cleared the pass and was heading into open water. A full two minutes later, Jim and Lieutenant Williams passed by Jason in the *Spearfish*.

As predicted, the speedboat went out five miles off the coast and performed large circles before returning to Gasparilla Marina in Placida. Although disappointed, no one was surprised that nothing happened. The speedboat crew retired for the night with a call to Hans to let him know they had completed the run.

While the speedboat was approaching Boca Grande Pass on its way out, Hans and his bodyguard had left the office and were now heading northward in *Hans's* black Mercedes. Rick and Sheriff Huggins were following Hans in the BMW X5 at about a quarter-mile back. Kyle was following in the Gladeator by another quarter-mile back.

Hans ended his drive in Sarasota on the last point of land before crossing over the Ringling Bridge to St. Armands Circle, which was called Golden Gate Point. A circular road ran around the perimeter of the point and was lined by condominiums. Hans entered an exclusive condo that overlooked Sarasota Bay. The building had large balconies on the waterside, and the roofline had multiple domes, which resembled mini versions of the Duomo in Florence, Italy. *Obviously the drug business was fruitful to Hans,* thought Rick as he watched Hans enter. *I'm sure the other residents would be horrified if they knew who lived in their building.*

Kyle entered the end of the circular drive and was followed up by more DEA agents and deputies. Rick and Sheriff Huggins were parked on the street in front of the condo complex next to the one Hans had entered.

Sheriff Huggins brought up the mike. "It looks like Hans is down for the night. This is a gated condo complex, and we don't know how many friends Hans has here. So we'll wait until Hans leaves again before going in and checking out his condo. The pilots are down as well in Placida. So I suggest the second shift of deputies and agents take over and those of us involved today get some sleep. We'll regroup tomorrow at Sheriff Steele's offices at 7:30 a.m. We may have another long day."

"Thanks to all those who participated today,"Kyle said. "It wasn't how we expected it to go, but at least the dealers don't know we're closing in. Hopefully tomorrow will bring better success. Good night, everyone."

The relief agents and deputies took over all surveillance. They traded places with the day crew so that the high-tech vehicles remained in the field. Sheriff Huggins dropped off Rick at his house.

Rick entered his house at half past ten that night, hungry and tired. Everyone was still up, and Danielle pulled out a plate of food she had saved him. In between bites, Rick gave a short summary of the day, which was fascinating to the family.

"Basically everything is clear as mud," ended Rick. Shelli gave Rick a quick synopsis of her day's activities at the island as she massaged her father's shoulders. Rick kissed his girls good night and headed to bed. The rest of the family followed suit.

Chapter 24: *What's Next?*

At a quarter of seven that morning, the Bryant family was at the breakfast table. Nikki and Shelli volunteered to make breakfast, which started with a fruit parfait of raspberries, blueberries, and blackberries with layers of non-fat frozen yogurt. After that, they made mini bagel sandwiches of eggs, turkey bacon, and a little butter. OJ and coffee in his favorite "I Love Dad" mug accompanied Rick's meal.

"Delicious indeed, girls," said Rick, wiping his mouth with the paper napkin. "Well done and very filling."

"What are you going to be doing today?" asked Shelli. "It sounds funny to say, but the drug dealers are really smart, aren't they?" Shelli was referring to the frequent TV ads that depicted drug users as being dumb and lethargic.

"These are not the run of the mill drug dealers, honey," answered Rick. "There was a lot of money and significant planning. Their decoy scheme fooled all of us. It's almost like starting all over again with the investigation."

"I can't believe you were cool and calm enough to steer the Quadricopter into that bedroom, Dad," said Shelli. "I would have been a bundle of nerves. It would have been bouncing off the walls if I were controlling it."

"I'm not as good with video games as you girls are. But I've been practicing a lot with the copter, so it felt pretty natural to me."

"You didn't mention what you saw in *Hans's* room," said Nikki. "Or is that classified?"

Rick smiled at the funny emphasis Nikki put on the word *classified*. "No, it isn't classified. Let me get my tablet PC, and I'll replay the data. But don't tell anyone what I'm going to show you."

Rick retrieved his backpack, which contained the tablet PC, powered it up and started the video. Nikki, Shelli, and Danielle gathered around behind him to watch.

"Who's that?" asked Shelli when she saw the feet of the man sitting in the front of the cottage.

"I don't know his name, but he seems to be a bodyguard to one of the main players."

Then they saw Hans enter the room.

"And that?" asked Shelli.

"That's Hans Schmidt."

"What's the scoop on him?" asked Nikki. Rick hesitated for a moment. *Should I tell her or not?* Thinking back to his wife's conversation about how tough Nikki was, he decided it was OK to answer.

"He is Cody's killer, honey," said Rick. Nikki's expression changed immediately. She was quiet for a few seconds, clearly struggling for what she was going to say.

Feeling the eyes of the family looking at her, Nikki turned and walked away a few steps. She thought she had cried all she could, but the sight of Cody's killer made her eyes go wet. She felt her mom's hand on her shoulder. She turned toward her and saw a tear forming in her mom's eyes.

Nikki could tell instantly her mom was not crying for Cody, but for her. She suddenly felt a wave of courage come over her.

"Enough of this," said Nikki as she wiped the water from both eyes. "Keep going, Dad. I want to see the rest of this." Rick turned back to the tablet PC screen. He was about to restart the video, but stopped. He closed it and opened the email client.

"It gets a little more interesting from here," said Rick. "Let's go see the video on my large office screens."

They all followed Rick to his office. They sat in the chairs while Rick opened the email he had received from his tablet PC and started up the attached copter video. He fast-forwarded it to the point where the copter was hovering just outside the rear bedroom of the cottage. He resumed the play at normal speed.

As they watched, the copter entered the room and hovered over the pistol and then the briefcase.

"I didn't see much here in the briefcase, except some literature on underwater scooters," commented Rick as he freeze-framed the image of the briefcase contents.

"Oh, those are so cool," said Shelli. "Remember back at spring break when Stephanie and I went to the beach birthday party for one of our friends?" Everyone shook their heads yes and she resumed.

"Well, they had a lot to do there. They had Jet Skis, beach tennis, water polo, and two underwater scooters. Everyone had a chance at the scooters. We couldn't go deep because we only had masks and snorkels, but it was really fun. They didn't go fast like a boat, but it was a lot faster than I could swim."

Shelli pulled out her phone and started clicking on the screen. "I took some video from the beach of Stephanie using one."

Rick reached in his desk and pulled out a USB cable.

"Here, plug this in." Shelli plugged the other end of the cable into her phone while Rick plugged the USB end into his computer. Moments later Rick had it up on the same large display as his copter video. He pressed Play to start the video.

They all quietly watched the video. Then Shelli spoke up again.

"See, here's where Stephanie started her turn with the scooter." They laughed as they heard Stephanie squeal through her snorkel. She was going fast enough for a small bow wake to form off her forehead as she plowed through the water. They kept watching the mini video clips of people riding the scooter, including one Stephanie had taken of Shelli on the scooter.

"I had it going as fast as it could go here," she said.

The next clip showed the dad of the birthday girl kneeling on the ground over the two scooters.

"What's he doing there?" asked Rick.

"That's Belle's dad changing out the batteries and adding the bracket for the two," replied Shelli.

"What bracket?" asked Rick.

"Oh, we mentioned it would be cool if we could put two together and go even faster. Belle's dad heard us and said he could do that. He pulled out that bracket from the back of his car. He said he used it when he goes scuba diving with his underwater video camera."

"Really," said Rick. "That's very interesting."

"Yeah, he said he could mount the video camera, his spear gun, and his game bag on it, and the two scooters would pull him and all of that around."

Rick stared at the screen while the video clips continued. He was deep in thought when he heard Danielle say, "Rick...hello. Anyone there?"

"Sorry. Seeing that video made me think of something."

"What?" asked Nikki.

Rick pulled up the map display for his buoy sensors. Since being deployed, they were fully operational and were busy looking for anomalies and the last programmed search, which was Hans Schmidt. He zoomed out on the map until the whole western coast of

Florida was visible on the display and then turned back to look at his family.

"We thought we had uncovered a drug ring, but it turned out to be a decoy to keep the DEA and local law enforcement busy while some other much larger operation was underway," said Rick. "But just what is that other operation?"

He turned to his three-screen PC and began clicking on the mouse, which brought up Google Earth. He zoomed in to Boca Grande Pass and slid it up to the large display for everyone to see. He also opened up his browser and entered the Web site for the underwater scooter on one of his three desktop screens. He opened up a spreadsheet window on a second desktop screen. He could easily slide the applications from one screen to another and up to the big screen.

"Now let's assume the drug cartel is using scooters to move drugs underwater," Rick said. "They could use two or even four scooters together to take a load from out at sea to the shore."

"But they would be seen if they were coming onto a beach," interrupted Nikki.

"And they'd draw attention to themselves if they tried to bring it up to a boat in one of the harbors or a public place," said Danielle.

"Right," said Rick. He thought for a moment. "It could be they drop it off at a private residence."

"But wouldn't neighbors be suspicious of this?" said Danielle.

"Most likely. Well, let's not focus on how they get them from underwater to the shore. Let's focus on the transfer from offshore to the underwater scooter."

"Those scooters last a good while, Dad, but their batteries would have to last going out to the sea and coming back in," said Shelli.

"Good point, honey," said Rick. "Let's look up some statistics on the scooter's Web site." He brought up the specifications page of the scooter.

"OK. The specs say the scooter lasts 1.5 hours underwater and can go 5.3 kilometers per hour. So let's enter this in the spreadsheet." Rick typed in the data. "So 1.5 hours times 5.3 kilometers per hour, divided by two for the round trip—the scooters could go 2.65 kilometers in one direction before turning back around for home port."

"How would the operator stay under that long, Dad?" asked Nikki. "I usually can get about fifty minutes out of a scuba tank at moderate depths."

"Another good point, sweetie," said Rick. Rick pulled up a dive-planning site on the Internet. "The site here says fifty-four minutes at fifty feet is about the maximum time underwater for an aluminum tank. Since they'd want some safety margin, let's set this to forty-five minutes. So forty-five minutes underwater would mean the diver could only go half the distance I calculated for the scooter."

"What if he was using two tanks?" said Nikki. "He'd get twice as much time, or 1.5 hours."

"Perfect," said Rick excitedly. "So he could use two tanks to move the drugs the full 2.65 kilometers and back."

"What next?" asked Shelli.

"Well, if we assume Hans Schmidt is still involved in this, which I think he is, then he'd probably be within driving distance of where he lives. I don't think he'd drive any further south than Placida. To the north, there's a lot more traffic. He could possibly get on the north end of Anna Maria Island, or even get to the beach at Fort DeSoto via I-75 and I-275."

He zoomed the Florida map to show the mouth of Tampa Bay to Boca Grande Pass.

"Now they would need to go a respectable distance off the coast to keep watching eyes from seeing, if it is an ocean-bound vessel bringing the drugs in. So the majority of the underwater distance would have to be in the open water, not in a bay."

"But, Dad, I think someone would have been suspicious if people were moving that many drugs that close to shore," said Nikki. "All the inlets are busy from Tampa to Boca Grande, and it would have to be lots of trips, even with four underwater scooters."

"You're right, Sis," said Shelli. "Dad, how many trips would the scooters have to make in a week to move those drugs?"

"Well, let's see," said Rick. "There was on average about twenty thousand kilos on the spreadsheet we saw on *Hans's* computer per week. If we assume they are moving drugs seven days a week, that means almost three thousand kilograms per day. Just estimating the payload of four scooters, that's nine to ten trips back and forth."

"If it was 1.5 hours per trip, that would take fifteen hours per day for ten trips," said Nikki.

"Realistically, they would need four divers and four rigs at a minimum," Rick said. "And that would still take about four hours to complete the daily deliveries. The divers would get their workout for sure. But even that is way too long for the drug boat to stay on site with that much drug onboard."

"Do you think they would have lowered it overboard onto the bottom and left it there to be picked up?" asked Danielle.

"Perhaps," said Rick.

"They could relay the GPS coordinates of the drop point," said Danielle.

"Unless they surface, the divers would not be able to receive GPS signals underwater," said Rick.

"Is there some other way we're not thinking about to get the drugs to the divers?" said Nikki. "Something we're not considering. I wouldn't expect something like a plane or helicopter. That would require flight plans, and it is even more noticeable than a boat. May something underwater—maybe something like a...."

At this point an idea popped into Shelli's head, and she and Nikki both blurted out, "...submarine!"

"Holy cow, girls," said Rick. "That could be it! As you know from the water-based sensor research I have been doing lately, I have looked at almost everything a sensor could be mounted on. Whether the sensor was radar, camera, or sonar, I looked for vehicles or vessels to put them on. I went to a marine show in Tampa not too long ago, and I got a chance to talk with a company building personal subs. These can fit as few as one person to over a dozen people."

Rick clicked with his mouse to open his presentation software and selected a file he had received from the sub manufacturer. A slide of a personal submarine popped up. It looked like a water drop on its side. It was painted a shiny yellow and had window portals along the side and big glass front. The entrance was a more streamlined version of the classic submarine sail and hatch.

"Here it is. Every time I see this presentation, I want to start humming "Yellow Submarine" from the Beatles. It is twenty-six feet long, seven feet wide, and eight feet tall. The marketing literature shows it painted yellow. It has a payload capacity of several thousand kilograms, and it can operate up to eight-hour missions in waters deeper than five hundred feet. It would be absolutely perfect for transferring the drugs to the divers!"

He looked at his girls and saw bewildered looks.

"Honey, where in the world would the subs come from?" asked Danielle.

Rick laughed. "From their mother ship, of course!" He clicked ahead a few more slides.

There on the screen were drawings of a ship with a cutaway showing the personal submarine sitting inside the hull on the keel. It sat on a cradle, which lowered into the water for deployment.

"See, this shows the drawings of the North Sea fishing trawler that the company was being paid to modify. It has a range of over five thousand miles and has full medical facilities, recompression chamber, and facilities to recharge the scuba tanks. It has what's called a moon-pool in it. It allows the divers and passengers to enter the sub and water without being seen on the deck of the trawler."

"That is just way cool, Dad," said Nikki. "So the fishing boat picks the drugs up from the Caribbean or South America and brings them way offshore from the coast of Florida. The sub takes them from the boat to a point about two kilometers from shore, and then the divers and scooters carry it somewhere on shore. It is never seen by plane, boat, or even satellite."

"You've got it, honey," said Rick. "This is a very possible scenario. And with that quantity of drugs moving in, it can be easily afforded. The boat is about one hundred and forty feet long, and it takes a minimum crew of about ten people to man it. Well done, girls!"

Rick's phone began to vibrate. He picked it and answered it. The girls could only hear Rick's voice in the conversation.

"Good morning, Bob. You're out front to pick me up? Great. But call into Sheriff Steele's office. Tell them we are going to be a little late. I want you to come in and see what we've pieced together this morning. OK." Rick hung up. "Shelli, can you run up and let Sheriff Huggins in, please? Thanks."

Shelli quickly jogged out of the room.

About a minute later, Sheriff Huggins entered Rick's office. Rick stood up and shook his hand as the sheriff was saying his good mornings to everyone. Rick proceeded to explain how they had created a possible drug movement scenario from watching the Quadricopter video. He described in detail the concept of moving the drugs from the mother ships to the personal submarines and then to the scooters. Nikki used her dad's notebook PC to make some measurements for Rick while he talked.

"That's a lot to take in, Rick," said Sheriff Huggins. "And pardon me if I say it sounds a bit farfetched. But this case has been anything but normal, so I guess I should be a little more open-minded."

"I know it's hard to believe, and we're not in any way certain about our hypothesis. But I was about to do something here that might prove that we're right." Rick turned back to his PC. "As you know, the sensor grid consists of buoys with built-in cameras, radar, and wireless communication. But you may not remember that each buoy comes with an array of hydrophones and an underwater array of CCTV cameras. The array of hydrophones allows us to tell the direction of detected objects underwater, and the CCTV camera images are automatically snapped when such detections occur."

"What triggers the detection?" asked Sheriff Huggins.

"They basically sense pressure, so sound waves and someone moving by causes a pressure wave that triggers detection. Divers and perhaps even the sound from the propellers may trigger a detection. The bad news is that we do not have this tied into the automated detection and learning system used by the radar and cameras of the buoys yet. So many fish and wildlife in the waters are big enough to trigger it, such as tarpon, turtles, manatee, sharks, dolphins, and the like. We have to let it run all the time and must review each buoy's underwater data manually. And I haven't had the time to look at any of this."

"With all those buoys you have running up the Intercoastal Waterway, it will take a long time to review the data," said Sheriff Huggins. "I don't think we have the time."

"We do have several things that can help us reduce what we have to search," said Rick. "We know that the longest distance that these divers can go is 2.65 kilometers in one direction. They are not likely coming ashore on the beaches. That would be way too easy to be discovered. So they need to come into some harbor or inlet. Plus, these subs cannot operate in shallow water. They will need at least twenty to thirty feet of water to keep from being accidently hit by the keel of a passing boat. That's why we think the scooters are a good bet, because they are highly maneuverable, even in a couple of feet of water."

Rick turned to Nikki. "I just asked Nikki to measure the distances where there are 2.65 kilometers from points in harbors and inlets out to twenty-five feet of water. What did you find, Nikki?"

Nikki took the mouse and keyboard control from her dad and started her summary.

"I found three locations that met the criteria Dad just mentioned. From north to south between Tampa Bay and Boca Grande Pass, they are the inlet at Beer Can Island, Venice Inlet, and Stump Pass. I don't think Beer Can Island is a good area, though. They would have to cross under the bridge between Longboat Key and Anna Maria Island, and there is always a lot of activity there. Of the three, Venice Islet has the best and shortest access and would be my bet."

"Very good, Nikki," said Sheriff Huggins. "I'm not as familiar with the Venice Inlet. I'm sure Sheriff Steele would be, though."

"Venice Inlet is fairly deep, but does have a lot of traffic," Rick said. "Fishermen are regularly present during the day on the jetties on each side. But it is too wide to cast to the center, so the divers could move through there without too much trouble."

"It's easy to get snagged on the jetty rocks," said Nikki. "If they hooked the divers or their sleds accidently and lost their hooks, the fishermen wouldn't think twice about it." said Nikki.

"Let's now look for events at Venice Inlet on the buoys," Rick said. "We have one floating west of Snake Island just out of the boat traffic lanes. That one has a clear underwater and top water view of the inlet. We have another one floating near the marina at Albee Road Bridge to the north, and one south of Bird Island. So if the divers enter and head north or south from the inlet, we should be able to see them. Let's start with Snake Island. I'll select this week's events and then scroll through them."

They all watched intently and Rick scrolled through each detection and subsequent video for the week. Just as Rick had indicated, they saw several dolphins right away. They loitered a long time, and the event resulted in a large number of detections. Rick jumped ahead an hour and continued.

The next detection was a manatee calf and her mother. They moved much slower than the dolphin, and Rick had to jump ahead again. The next detection showed an object coming from the north toward the buoy. Rick played the video.

A dull yellow blur became visible on the underwater video. It eventually turned into four slightly brighter ovals and a dark blob behind it. The water was murky, which made it difficult to see clearly. But the object became clearer before turning to go out through the inlet. Rick backed the video up and paused it when a diver with two scuba tanks and four scooters were broadside to the buoy camera.

"Well, I'll be," said Sheriff Huggins. "You were right. They've made underwater sleds using brackets and scooters. The divers are heading out to the Gulf through the inlet. It appears there's no cargo on the scooter sled. Can you see if we pick him back up on the way back?"

"We should be able to," said Rick. "He has got to be back at this point within one hour and a half, or he'd be out of air." Rick looked at the detection logs and saw a detection one hour and fifteen minutes later in the direction of the inlet. He clicked on the video to play it, and in a few seconds they saw the dim glow of yellow heading toward the Intercoastal Waterway.

"There are the underwater scooters," said Shelli. "Wow! Look at the big long tubes between the scooters. They're huge."

"And the rounded front of the tubes helps them cut through the water better," added Rick. "Those tubes can hold quite a bit of drugs."

"My goodness," said Sheriff Huggins. "What time was all this?"

Rick replied, "About four o'clock, Bob. I'm sure there's a lot more of these events. We just happened to pick the first one here. We'll have to go through them to find all the events."

Sheriff Huggins' cell phone rang.

"Oh, wow, we've lost track of the time," said Sherriff Bob, looking at the time on the phone display. "We were supposed to be at Sheriff Steele's office fifteen minutes ago." He answered and told them to hold a second.

"Rick, we have enough here to go after these guys. Can we go back to the Mike's office and report this?"

"Sure," said Rick. "I'll need about thirty more minutes to transfer the video to my notebook PC. It will take a long time to download all of this over the Internet connection at Sheriff Steele's place."

Sherriff Bob stood up and walked out of the room as he talked. A minute later he came back in.

"Go ahead, Rick. They'll wait for us before they get started. Apparently there has not been any movement at *Hans's* condo. So take the time you need."

"Sit down here, Bob," said Danielle. "I'll bring us some coffee."

"That would be most appreciated."

Chapter 25: *Underwater Transporter*

Rick had finished gathering the data he needed and was preparing to leave his house with Sheriff Huggins. Danielle pulled him aside in the kitchen.

"Rick, before you leave I need you to remember that tomorrow I have our big fund-raising event at the museum. I'm going to be tied up again some of today and all of tomorrow. I might get Nikki to help me. So remember that if you're trying to reach us."

"OK, honey," said Rick. "Is there anything I need to help you with?"

"Goodness, no. But thanks for asking. You take care of yourself." She kissed Rick and watched him kiss both of his daughters as he headed out the door.

As Shelli and Nikki watched their dad leave, Danielle asked, "So what are you girls doing today?"

"I don't know, Mom." said Shelli.

"I don't have any plans, Mom," said Nikki. "Do you need help again over at the museum?"

"That's nice of you to ask, Nikki," answered Danielle. She thought a bit about what she had to do. "I tell you what, if both of you help me for about two hours, we could all go do something together when we finish. Maybe go out for lunch and shop?"

"Sure, Mom," said Shelli. "That sounds good."

"Sounds good to me too," said Nikki.

"Let's get showers and head out," said Danielle.

Rick and the sheriff arrived a few minutes later at the Sarasota

Sherriff's office. They found the whole DEA crew, Sherriff Mike, and his deputies already discussing the case.

Kyle stood up and cleared his throat.

"The director couldn't be here today. He's got some other important business he had to attend to. He sent me a text message and asked me to take over until he returns. He has not been informed on yesterday's events. I did leave him a message to call me. I'll fill him in once he does. So let's get started.

"We know that yesterday did not turn out the way we expected," said Kyle. "But Rick told me they had some good video that could help us. Before we start, could we get a report on activities last night at the stakeout at *Hans's* place."

One of the night-shift DEA agents stood up and reported that all was quiet. No one came or went from the building. They had a person watching with a night vision scope from the parking lot at Marina Pete's, which had a clear view of all the balconies on the waterside of the condominium. Kyle thanked the agent and told him to go home and get some sleep.

Kyle turned and addressed Rick, who had already plugged his notebook PC into the overhead LCD projector.

"OK, Rick," said Kyle. "Wow us."

Rick smiled and began going through the video clips he had shown his family and Sheriff Huggins earlier that morning. Everyone immediately perked up, with many disbelieving headshakes. He left off the part about the submarine and the mother ship.

"What I've been able to do since I showed Sheriff Huggins these about an hour ago is to isolate times and the general area the smugglers are operating inshore." Rick pulled up the Google map.

"Unlike the decoy operation that spread up and down the coast, the actual operation takes place solely at Venice Inlet and the Intercoastal Waterway to the north. In fact, based on the acoustic arrays on my buoys, I've determined that the offload site is somewhere north of Snake Island here and south of the marina at Albee Road Bridge." Rick pointed to the area using the mouse cursor.

"The buoys' acoustic arrays and underwater cameras cannot see as far underwater as the radar and thermal cameras can see above water. The range between the two buoys at these two positions is three quarters of a mile. The underwater camera range is about a quarter of a mile, so that means we're blind about one quarter of a mile in this area. Here, between this large house and just south of this houseboat."

"Mike, is there anyone living in those houses that would be on your watch list?" Sheriff Huggins asked.

"No," replied Sheriff Steele quickly. "We've never had complaints at those residences. In fact, they are likely to call us if there's a problem with tourists or speeders."

"Is there anything new in the last year or so that has changed at the Nokomis Beach area?" Jim Matchett asked.

Sheriff Steele thought for a moment. "I'm not aware of anything." Mike swung around and looked at his deputies. "Do any of you know if there have been changes around there?" One of his deputies raised his hand.

"Yes, sir. There used to be two houseboats, but they left, and the land and docks were up for sale for much of 2010. The land was purchased eventually, and another two-story houseboat moved in about at the turn of the new year, if you recall. Our marine patrol was asked to help keep traffic clear on the waterway while it moved into place."

"Oh, yes, I remember that," said Sheriff Steele. "But we haven't had any complaints, have we?"

"No, sir," said the deputy.

"These underwater sleds could be going to that houseboat," Kyle said. "We should check it out." Kyle turned to Rick. "So we see drugs being moved into the inlet, but where are they coming from?"

Rick explained his belief that these could only be connecting with an underwater personal submarine, which in turn was coming from the belly of a mother ship. A series of "Wow" and "Oh" preceded Kyle's next statement.

"Come on, Rick," said Kyle. "I was blown away about the scuba diving sleds, but please forgive me if I'm a little skeptical about subs."

Rick pulled up the Web sites for the submarines and mother ships.

"It is real, Kyle. I've put in a call to this company to see if they can give us their customer list. But no one has responded, since it's a Sunday. It really is the only logical choice I see. My logs on the acoustic array show about four to twelve transfers on average a day by two to three divers. Sheriff Steele or the coast guard or even local fisherman would have been suspicious of that much traffic at two kilometers off shore from Venice Inlet."

"Well, I asked you to wow me, and you can consider that mission accomplished," said Kyle. "OK, then. Unless you know where the subs were going, we need to find the mother ship. Perhaps we can take the sheriff's helicopter out and see if we can find the boat."

"I think that might draw suspicion if we fly way out from the shore," Sheriff Steele said. "We rarely do something like that unless there is an emergency or we're chasing someone."

"Just how far out do we need to search?" asked Jim. "Do you have any idea?"

"The subs can handle an eight-hour mission," Rick said. "Assume they must sit on station three to four hours waiting for divers, and that they must make a round trip." Rick used the PC calculator program. "They can travel about six knots, so that means that in the remaining four to five hours, they can travel 13.8 to 17.3 miles offshore. Since the divers are going a little more than a mile offshore, you can say about fifteen to nineteen miles as a maximum."

"So we need to look for ships big enough to hold that sub at a distance of up to nineteen miles from Venice Inlet," said Jim. "That doesn't seem that hard."

"I assume you guys want to catch both the sub and the mother ship," said Rick. "Although I said the subs can go for eight-hour missions, they keep air onboard for about forty hours. This is for emergency situations. They keep extra fuel as well for the same reason. So if they are tipped off, they could be considerably harder to find."

"What do we do about this?" asked Kyle. "Suggestions, anyone?"

"Between Sheriff Huggins and my department, we probably have enough boats to cover the water," Sheriff Steele said. "But we need some way to detect the subs."

Kyle quickly spoke up. "It's good you have those boats, Mike, and we will definitely need them for backup. But I think the smugglers will figure out something is going on, if sheriff's department boats full of officers start scanning over their area of operation."

Sheriff Steele nodded in agreement. "You're probably right." He paused and then continued. "The coast guard has got to be informed. One of their main charters is drug interdiction, and they will want to be all over this raid. It's a perfect fit for their teams. I'll contact them—the nearest branch is the St. Petersburg sector."

"Good idea," said Kyle. "The coast guard probably has enough resources to pull an all-out assault and take out the divers, sub, and mother ship."

"That's true," said Sheriff Huggins. "But we don't know the extent of the drug ring on the land side. All we think is that maybe the smugglers are using a houseboat. But where does it go from there? And how? I think we need to be careful and not rush the...basically, pirates...and take the chance of tipping off the onshore distribution arm of this. Plus, remember, I want to make sure we get all those involved in the killing of Cody and his client."

Jason, who had been quiet for most of this, raised his hand and began to speak.

"You know, we can try all we want, but this is a large, well-funded operation. They established a whole fake drug distribution scheme just to keep us occupied and to act as an early warning to them. Who knows what security systems they have in place and how far-reaching their operation is on land? They don't know we stopped the decoy operation, and haven't discovered we know about the underwater drug movement."

"So we have some element of surprise, but as of tomorrow morning that is gone," Jason continued. "Tomorrow is when the decoy operation is supposed to start up again, and that's not going to happen. So I say we take out what we can while we can. Right now we have a good chance of taking out the key element with minimum chance of casualties. We barely have enough time to organize anything, so I say let's get moving on some sort of raid now. Maybe we can interrogate the players after we nab them and hunt down the rest."

Everyone listened intently to what Jason was saying, many nodding their heads in agreement.

"Well said, Jason," said Kyle. "How long were you sitting there writing that speech?" Jason smiled, and chuckles from the group broke up the serious mode of the room.

"OK, then let's suppose we make an orchestrated attack on both the land and water at the same time?" said Kyle. "The coast guard can certainly take care of the water side, and the DEA and sheriff's department can take care of the land side. How are we going to coordinate this?"

Sheriff Steele came back into the room.

"We've got a coast guard officer heading this way now," he said. "He said he'll be here in forty minutes."

"Wow, that was a quick response," said Sheriff Huggins. "While we're waiting, let's pull up the map of the Venice area and start planning."

Rick moved quickly to pull up Google Earth again and zoomed into the Venice Inlet.

"Thanks, Rick," said Sheriff Huggins. "We can at least start planning on the land side and perhaps the Intercoastal Waterway while waiting for the coast guard to arrive."

The group started to discuss how the resources of the DEA and sheriff's department would be used. Although ample vehicles and boats were available, it was decided that only the DEA undercover vehicles and Rick's BMW X5 would cover the area at Nokomis Beach Park jetty and the dockside of the houseboat. The Gladeator would be parked at the boat ramp further up the road, just north of Albee Road, so that it could cover escape routes on the Intercoastal Waterway northbound and the island road that headed north to Blackburn Point Road. The sheriff's department vehicles would park as inconspicuously as possible in a perimeter of a radius of one to two miles in all directions from Nokomis Beach. The remaining DEA agents would watch Hans in Sarasota, while Lieutenant Williams was in charge of monitoring the activities of the decoy crew further south in Placida.

With his permission, Rick's *Spearfish*, the ATAWT, workboat, and personal boat were to be used close in around the inlet. The buoys near the inlet and north and south of the inlet gave "eyes-on" underwater. The ATAWT looked like a regular Jet Ski from a distance and could sweep back and forth across the inlet at about five hundred yards out. This was not uncommon to see during the summer months when Jet Ski rentals were at their highest, next to the Christmas holidays.

The *Spearfish* would pretend to be trolling for fish at about a kilometer offshore, and the workboat, which was a fishing boat in its former life, would take up trolling at about two kilometers offshore. The *Spearfish* and workboat had sophisticated side-scan sonar already, so they would use this to locate underwater operatives.

Rick had called in two of his employees, Paul and Gerry, to install a fish-finder system on the ATAWT. Gerry had received the DLL, dynamic link library software, from the manufacturer a few weeks earlier and had already integrated it into the display used on the ATAWT and other vehicles. It was good enough for a poor man's diver detection system.

The sheriff's department boats would cover routes further north and south of the Intercoastal Waterway under the pretense of spot-checking licenses.

"That just leaves the open water plan," said Kyle just as the coast guard officer walked in.

Sheriff Steele stood up to introduce the officer.

"Gentlemen, this is Coast Guard Captain Mitchell Harris. He's in charge of the St. Petersburg Sector of the coast guard."

"Hello, gentlemen," said Captain Harris. "Good to meet you. Mike gave me a quick briefing of the events leading up until today. You've been very busy. And which one of you is Rick Bryant?"

Rick stood up and shook the captain's hand. "I'm very impressed with what the sheriff has said about your contributions," the captain said. "We may need to talk more after this is all over."

"It would be my pleasure," said Rick.

The team introduced themselves and brought the captain up to speed on their plans. Rick went over the videos of everything from the UAV video to the buoy's above-water and below-water videos. Pictures of Hans and the other members who were working with him were also shown. The captain requested that all the materials be emailed to his key staff in St. Petersburg.

"How do you propose to arrest those on the mother ship and the sub?" asked Kyle.

"We have several cutters that are available," said the captain. "I'd say it would be best to use three of them—one to the north, one out in deeper water, and one to the south. The cutters should be able to overtake any larger boat if they make a run for it. We can set up two helicopters to be prepared for two missions. One would have divers to intercept the sub as it nears the mother ship. The other would have an assault team that can be lowered to the ship's deck. We have a few rigid hulled boats in the Sarasota and Port Charlotte areas for patrols and rescue. We can have them ready offshore if we need additional backup. They're fully armed and very fast."

"That should do the trick," said Jim. "How long do you think it will take to be in place? It's now almost ten o'clock, and I suspect we're pushing it to be ready for today's four o'clock drug movement."

"I think we can meet that deadline, and I'll call now to get things moving," said the captain. "But as I understand it, we have not yet confirmed the hypothesis that there are personal subs in use, or even if there is a mother ship?"

"That is correct, sir," said Rick. "We only discovered the diving operation in Venice Inlet this morning."

"Well, I suggest that we commence with the operation, but I will have one of my helicopters fly over the area where we think the mother ship might be and confirm the hypothesis," said Captain Harris. "I checked before coming down and saw that we have a helicopter heading south now in the Sarasota area about five nautical miles off the coast."

"That's excellent," said Rick.

"It appears then that we have the plan," said Kyle. "The only loose ends I see are who makes the call on when to start the arrests, and how are we going to communicate with each other. Having been an employee of Uncle Sam's for many years, I can pretty much guarantee we don't use the same radio hardware."

"I am familiar with the sheriff's department, DEA, and coast guard communication gear and can tell you they are nothing alike," said Rick. "But we know my voice-over-IP cellular communication systems in all the DEA and sheriff's vehicles and boats worked well during the decoy sting operation. And since my vehicles and boats use the same communication system, it makes sense to use it for all land and Intercoastal Waterways communication. I have also installed it in the sheriff's dispatcher's office."

"Perhaps we can get a coast guard radio placed at the dispatcher's office, as well as getting a direct line established to the coast guard's communication officer at St. Petersburg," Rick said. "The dispatcher and communications officer will make sure all communication is then relayed to all players on both sides."

"Excellent idea," said Captain Harris, reaching for his cell phone. "I'll call and make this happen. I think it would be easier if I stayed here, if it is OK?"

"You are most certainly welcome to do so," said Sheriff Steele.

Kyle inserted the answer to the last question remaining.

"The communications question is answered, so we still have left the person who will initiate the sting. I propose that we wait for word from Rick when the divers are detected. Once he reports the first diver, mark your watches, and we'll commence the operation from that point in time. I'll give the word to the landside arrests, and Captain Harris gives the command to execute waterside arrests. Aborts can only come from Captain Harris and me." Everyone agreed to the plan.

"I'd like to make one request, Captain Harris," said Rick. "Is it possible to divert the helicopter off the coast of Sarasota to land here at the sheriff's helicopter landing site? I'd like to retrofit it with a video link so that we can watch your copter's video from here."

"Of course," answered Captain Harris.

With this, the captain immediately went to work directing the coast guard assets and getting communications worked out. The rest of the team broke up and began tasking deputies and DEA agents to their assignments.

Chapter 26: *Private Showing*

Danielle, Nikki, and Shelli were busy for the first hour continuing to get things ready at the Ringling Museum for tomorrow's luncheon. The room for the luncheon was one of the outer galleries, with tall ceilings and windows that overlooked one of the flower-laden courtyards. Nikki had made up the place cards for all the benefactors, and Danielle was placing all the flower arrangements at their proper locations. Shelli had been rolling the napkins in a fanciful way and placing the silverware.

After the first hour, Shelli asked if she could go to the office and do some additional online study about the pirates and local history in the 1700s. Amazed at her daughter's seemingly sincere interest in history and the dig on Edwards Island, Danielle consented.

As they neared the end of their two-hour commitment, a co-worker, Sharon, approached Danielle. Following her was a well-dressed man. Danielle noticed right away the fine Italian leather shoes and his diamond-studded analog divers watch. He was looking around the room as he followed Sharon, but came to quick attention when he was introduced to Danielle.

"Danielle Bryant, this is Jacques De Sores," said Sharon.

"Nice to meet you, Mr. De Sores," said Danielle.

"Call me Jacques," he said with a thick French accent.

"*Comment puis-je vous aider aujourd'hui?*" asked Danielle.

"*Quelle belle surprise! Je suis desole Je ne pourrai pas assister le privée exposition d'art demain,*" answered Jacques.

Danielle saw the puzzled look on Sharon's face.

"He said he will not be able to come to the private showing tomorrow."

"Oh," replied the co-worker.

"I think I can take it from here, Sharon," said Danielle.

"Very well then, Danielle. Can you please escort Mr. De Sores out when you're finished?" asked Sharon.

"Certainly," answered Danielle.

Danielle proceeded in French to tell Jacques that she recognized his name immediately, since she had helped put together the invitation list. Although she had noticed his French name, she did not want to presume he spoke French until she heard his accent. Jacques presented his card to her as they walked.

Danielle walked Jacques toward Nikki, who was still checking the tables, and introduced her as well. Nikki greeted Jacques, to his surprise, in French. Danielle explained that her children went to the public school system in Northern Virginia, which had a language immersion program.

"Each school has a different focus language, but both of my children attended an elementary school that spoke French for half of each day's classes," said Danielle in French.

She continued to walk toward the nearby office, where Shelli was researching on one of the computers. Danielle introduced Shelli in French, which was the cue for Shelli to also greet Jacques respectfully in French. Jacques was noticeably impressed that three Americans in the same room could communicate with him in perfect, formal French.

Nikki continued in French and asked Jacques what his art interests were. Jacques decided to switch to English and answer. By switching to English, he knew Danielle's kids would be relieved from having to continue in such a formal way in his native language. Shelli very innocently asked him if he had any children.

"No, my wife died a couple of years after we were married, and I never remarried or had children."

"Oh, I'm so sorry," said Shelli, obviously embarrassed.

"Ahh...*C'est la vie*," replied Jacques as he lightly shrugged his soldiers. "It is why I enjoy art so much. My wife was an artist and taught me to appreciate it. I think of how she would enjoy each of my paintings if she were still alive."

It was all a lie, but most of the time it kept people distant and stopped them from prying into his past. He saw it worked when he looked at Danielle's daughters avoiding eye contact. He smiled and told both girls it was nice to meet them. They shook his hand, said it was nice to meet him, and slowly walked away.

Jacques turned to Danielle and explained that he had called the museum earlier in the morning and asked for a look at the paintings today, since he was not going to make the private show. They had graciously agreed, but said that he would get the best tour if he came right away and met with Danielle Bryant.

Danielle blushed at the complimentary way that Jacques relayed the phone conversation, but also got the immediate sense of the man's importance. The fact that he could get hold of senior staff on a Sunday morning was impressive.

Danielle said she'd be happy to give the tour and asked Jacques to follow her to the exhibition gallery. As they walked away from the office, Jacques looked back at the screen and noticed a map of Sarasota centered on Edwards Island in one open window and a pirate symbol at the top of the browser page in a second window.

Danielle took about an hour to go over the full extent of the collection of Japanese art, ending back at the luncheon room she had been preparing. As they passed the office, Jacques noticed that Nikki was now in the office, sitting next to Shelli. His view of the screen was blocked by Danielle, and Jacques didn't want to be obvious by looking around her.

About ten feet beyond the door, Danielle's phone rang. She reached for her phone and looked at the number.

"It's my husband. He's doing something really important today, and I need to take this call. Do you mind?"

"No, please take it. I'm in no hurry."

Danielle said thanks. She walked away to have a private conversation. As she talked, Jacques slowly moved closer to the office door. He listened as Shelli was explaining to Nikki some of the facts she had found.

"Sis, the island seems to have no significance in history that I can find, "said Shelli. "Sarasota Bay was home to fish camps in the 1700s for both Europeans and the natives. At the time, the Native Americans in the area were quite fierce. They eventually died off from disease and war. Native Americans from further north in places like Georgia moved down and repopulated the area."

Shelli pulled up the picture of the map found at the Edwards Island site.

"Here's the map we found at the site," she said. "Notice that the map was marked beginning about midway down the east coast of Florida. So I looked back in history at the dates written on the map for treasures known on the East Coast of Florida. You won't believe it, but in the summer of 1715 eleven Spanish ships sunk from a hurricane near what is now Melbourne. They were loaded with gold and silver. The Spanish immediately started salvaging for years to come. The date on the map was later in the same year. I think the sailors on the island were from the salvage fleet!"

"But why would they have come to this shore?" asked Nikki. "Why didn't they head east to Spain?"

"I think there was a mutiny. Apparently that did happen on merchant and military ships during that time. Just think about the temptation on the sailors when they had a ship full of treasure. If the crew mutinied, they would have to sail to the Caribbean or the West Coast of Florida. Both were pirate havens." Shelli was pointing the map as she talked.

"What do you think happened to them? How did they end up on Edwards Island?"

"I don't know for sure," replied Shelli. "But to get here, they would have had to pass by Charlotte Harbor and Sanibel Island. They could have been spotted and pursued by pirates. Maybe the men at the island were the survivors of the ship. And you can bet that if they left the ship, they didn't leave the gold and silver."

"But they haven't found any treasure at the site," said Nikki.

"Not yet. But they're still digging."

"OK then," said Danielle as she spun around. Jacques turned quickly away from the office door and walked toward her. "I'm sorry for that, Jacques. It looks like my husband needs our help. Since I believe we're done here, I hope it was OK to tell him we'll be heading there soon."

"Oh, certainly," said Jacques. "Please don't let me keep you. If you can direct me to the proper exit, I'll be on my way. And many thanks for taking the time with me here today." With that, Danielle walked him to the nearest exit, shook his hands, and then came back to gather the girls.

Jacques was deep in thought as he walked toward his sports car. It was an informative visit. The art was interesting, but the conversation he had overheard could possibly finance the art purchases and then some.

It was after lunch, and he saw he had missed an earlier call from one of his employees. He started to dial the number, but the office conversation of Danielle's daughters loomed in his mind. He stopped before completing the number entry and decided to call Hans instead. Hans would be heading to Nokomis soon, so he would call him first. He needed Hans to keep a person watching the island, in case they found a treasure.

He dialed *Hans's* phone number.

"Good afternoon, sir," said Hans.

"Same to you," replied Jacques. "We have a new task to add to our long list of tasks. We need to assign a person back at the Siesta Key house to monitor the island. I also want to add a tail to the Bryant daughters—Nikki and Shelli. We'll need to put a phone scanner with the person tailing the girls. I need to know everything they know. We want to be able to jam their phones, if it becomes necessary.

"I also need someone to break into the Bryant house and put a bug on their phones and Internet connection. While there, they need to search discretely for any information on the dig on Edwards Island. Information may be digital, so tell them to check the computers and bring a USB drive to download to, if necessary."

"Yes, sir, I'll get right on that," said Hans. "I need to head out soon for the shipment today. You know I don't trust our friends to keep up the quality and like to be there when the first of the shipment arrives. I'll start arranging for the tail and scanner while I'm driving to Nokomis."

"Thanks, Hans. Your attention to detail is why you have always been my number one man in all of our projects."

"Thank you, sir. Before I hang up, do you have any updates on your other employees' progress?"

"Are you concerned?" asked Jacques.

"No sir," replied Hans.

"I haven't heard anything, which probably means nothing major has happened. But I'm sure we're safe. I've gotten one message from them, and I'll check in later. I'll let you know if anything has changed."

"Thank you, sir," said Hans.

After hanging up Jacques considered calling his employee, but began thinking of the beautiful art pieces he had just seen. Danielle had done an exquisite job of describing the history and importance of each piece of art she had shown him. One piece was quite old and originally had made it into the country via a long journey in the 1500s. Ships trading with the Orient had brought it first to France and then from France to America via the Caribbean. This was a piece worth having. He'd make the call to the museum and inquire on its price. There would be some haggling, but in the end he'd get it for below the market price. With his past purchase history, the museum would give him a fair price just to keep him happy.

He opened his phone and called the sales manager's personal mobile phone.

"Good afternoon, Charles," said Jacques. "Danielle did a lovely job showing me the new art pieces. There's one piece I'm quite fond of. I'd like to see what you can do for me on the price."

Jacques continued to talk on his phone as opened his car door. When he shut the door, he saw Danielle pull out in her convertible with her two daughters onboard. He smiled as he continued listening to the sales manager.

Danielle pulled onto Route 41 South and headed toward downtown Sarasota.

"I'm sorry it took longer than expected, girls. I didn't anticipate having to give a tour."

"No problem, Mom," said Shelli. "I got a lot of research done and can't wait to tell you and Dad."

"Thanks for understanding, honey. Dad called at the end of the tour," continued Danielle. "I felt badly about letting Jacques wait, but I didn't want to miss your dad's call, given what he has going on now."

"Mr. De Sores seemed like a nice man" Shelli said. "I'm sure he didn't mind."

"What did Dad want?" asked Nikki.

"He called to give me an update and to ask for our help. First thing he said was to stay clear of Venice. He didn't know you guys were with me, so he told me this in case you two were going that way."

"Cool!" said Shelli. "They must have discovered something really big if he gave us that warning."

"That's not all," said Danielle. "Since your dad needs our help, we'll have to cancel shopping."

"That's OK, Mom," said Nikki. "I'd much rather help Dad if it means Cody's killer is caught."

"I figured you two wouldn't mind," said Danielle.

"Dad wanted me to drop off you, Nikki, at the office. He wants you to bring the workboat to Marina Pete's. You're to ask Paul and Gerry what changes they made and make sure you know how to work them. Especially any software changes to the GUI that Gerry would have made. GUI, stands for…"

"Mom, I know what it stands for—graphical user interface," interrupted Nikki. "What else did Dad want?"

"Your dad wants me to pick up the fishing boat at home and also bring it to Marina Pete's. Once we arrive at Marina Pete's, we're to meet with a person in the restaurant from the DEA named Kyle Thompson. He'll present us his badge, which is a gold metal badge with an eagle on top and with the letters *US* in big blue print inside the circle.

"And Dad gave me a list of things for you, Shelli, to search online. He wants you to also call Stephanie to see if she and her brother will pick up Nikki and me at Marina Pete's on their boat and bring us home. After that, he asked if we would monitor video feeds from the buoys, boats, the cars, and another feed that will be the coast guard's helicopter. He wants to make sure everything is being properly recorded and backed up. He also wants us to be ready in case he needs anything else from the office or home."

"What was it Dad wanted me to research?" asked Shelli.

"It was a few things, honey." Danielle pulled up a yellow sticky note with writing on it. "Here's the list of things he asked to research. He wants you to call him when you've finished it all. Make sure you write it all down, in case it needs to be faxed or emailed."

Shelli looked at the note. "This might take a while."

"Your father said he'd like it in a couple of hours if you can do it," said Danielle.

"OK. Will do."

As Danielle's car continued southbound, a tan sedan gained on them from behind.

"OK, sir," said the driver. "I've caught up with them. We were fortunate I was up at the airport picking up a rental car when you called. And we're fortunate that the museum is near the airport."

"Keep us informed of your location," replied Hans. "We'll bring you a phone scanner. You'll need that to listen in on their calls."

"Roger that, sir," said the driver. He hung up his phone and kept three car lengths back from his mark.

Chapter 27: *Lunchtime Exchange*

Nikki pulled the workboat into an open slot at Marina Pete's. After tying down the boat, she headed toward the restaurant. Since she hadn't had lunch, she asked for a menu and a table. She was pleased to see her friend Kristin Harmon was her waitress. Nikki told her she had just talked with her twin sister a few days ago at the Mango Tango and took a few minutes to catch up.

Moments later her mom entered the restaurant, and Nikki waved to her. Danielle sat down and asked, "Did you have any trouble with the boat?"

"No, everything went fine," replied Nikki. "How about you?"

"No problems, either," answered Danielle. "Any sign of the agent?"

"No," said Nikki. "I am going to order some lunch, since we didn't eat yet."

"That sounds good. I'll do the same."

A few minutes later Kyle walked in the door. He scanned the restaurant and homed in on a woman and what was clearly her twenty-something daughter. That was certainly Rick's family—just as he had described them. *He certainly has an attractive family*, thought Kyle with a little bit of jealousy. Kyle walked up to the table.

"Hello, ladies. I'm Kyle Thompson, and I hope you're Danielle and Nikki Bryant." He pulled out his badge and showed it to Danielle, who looked at it carefully.

"Hello, Kyle," said Danielle. Nikki also said hello. "It's a pleasure to meet you," continued Danielle. "Have a seat."

"I'd love to, Mrs. Bryant, but I've got to be getting those boats to their destination as soon as possible," said Kyle.

"I hope everything is going fine today with the investigation."

"It's going well, but I'm not permitted to give out much detail. I hope you understand."

"Certainly," replied Danielle. "Well, let's get you out to the boats."

All three walked toward the door. Nikki caught Kristin to let her know that they would be coming back in a few minutes. As they walked, Nikki was trying to place Kyle's face. She was almost certain she had seen him before. As her mother continued to talk with Kyle, she searched her memory. She had an eye for faces, and she rarely forgot them. When they started walking on the dock, she remembered.

"I remember now where I've seen you before, Mr. Thompson!" she said, interrupting her mother. "You were at Siesta Key Bridge Park fishing a couple of weeks ago. I passed by the bridge when I picked up our friends stranded on Edwards Island." She thought for a few seconds. "You were on stakeout, right?"

Kyle smiled as he recalled the day. "Yes, that was me. You're quite observant. That's a good quality in an agent." Nikki blushed a little with the comment.

They jumped onboard the workboat first. Just as Nikki was about to start explaining the user interface and controls, two men approached the boat.

"These are my other DEA agents," said Kyle. Kyle introduced Jim Matchett and Jason Connelly. Danielle and Nikki shook hands with Jim and Jason.

"It's a pleasure to meet you," said Danielle.

"The pleasure is all ours," said Jim. "I just want to say that your husband has been extremely helpful during this investigation. We really appreciate his participation."

"I'm sure he is thrilled to be working with your team," said Danielle. "I can't say I'm comfortable with it, but it would be next to impossible for me to stop him anyway."

Jim saw Danielle was really concerned. "You have my word, Mrs. Bryant, that we'll take care of him." With that, Nikki continued showing them the boat controls and new software.

"Is there anything about technology your family doesn't know about?" asked Kyle.

"You've been working with my dad for a few days now," said Nikki. "I've been with him my whole life. Is it really a surprise to you that we all know a little bit about technology?" Kyle smiled and shook his head no.

"Stupid question, wasn't it? When I was talking to Kyle, he said your dad's home office looks like a command center," said Jim.

"He likes to be able to monitor the office, house, his boats and cars, and pretty much anything having to do with his family," said Nikki as she rolled her eyes.

"Well, your dad's...uh, toys...have got us where we are today," said Jim.

"We better go," said Kyle. "We don't have much time to move these into position."

"I normally operate the workboat when Dad needs to use it over the weekend," Nikki said. "Needless to say, I've spent a lot of time on it. So don't hesitate to call me if you have any problems with the GUI or hardware. My phone number is listed on the VoIP console."

"Thanks Nikki," replied Kyle. "We appreciate your help." Kyle turned to look at the others. "Let's roll, gentlemen."

Kyle and Jason got onboard the workboat, and Jim jumped onboard the Bryant fishing boat. They started the boats and headed out of the docks toward the south entrance to Sarasota Bay. Jim did S-curves as he shot ahead of the workboat. If asked, Jim would say he was trying to get the feel of the boat. But anyone seeing the smile on his face would know that he was simply having fun.

Nikki watched as the boats headed away. She wished she was aboard and part of the action. She glanced around her surroundings and felt the breeze blow mildly across her face. The sun was still high in the sky, which was a pale blue. The water was almost perfectly flat and a turquoise color. *This was a good day to catch fish...and bad guys.*

She and Danielle walked back into the restaurant to finish their lunch. As they walked, Nikki pressed contacts on her phone and then started entering Stephanie's name. But then she stopped mid-name. She looked up and smiled and entered Ryan's name instead. She pushed her hair back behind her ear as she listened to the phone ring.

"Well, hello, Miss Bryant," said Ryan in an upbeat manner.

"I see you have my name on your contact list," said Nikki.

"And your picture."

"What?" responded Nikki quickly with a smile on her face. "I don't remember you taking my picture."

"You should be more observant. I took it on that beautiful day we had at the beach."

Nikki thought for a moment. "Was that when I was in my swimsuit?"

"Uh...well, yes."

"You better not give that to anyone else!" said Nikki. Ryan was half expecting Nikki to tell him to remove it, but was happy when she didn't.

"I wouldn't think of it," said Ryan. "It's all mine."

Danielle and Nikki sat down at their table. Nikki was still all smiles when she changed the subject.

"If you're not too busy, I really need a favor."

"Your wish is my command," answered Ryan. Nikki tilted her head and let out a soft giggle. "I'm at Marina Pete's with my mom. My dad has something going on today and asked if you could pick us up with your boat here and take us back to our house. Is that possible?"

"Most certainly!" said Ryan quickly. "I'll get my wallet and head out in five minutes."

"Great," said Nikki. "Oh, and my sister would be upset if I didn't ask if Stephanie can come too."

"Hold on and let me check," said Ryan. Nikki could hear his muffled yell to his sister. She could make out what Ryan was saying, but could not hear Stephanie. Ryan came back on the phone. "She said it will take her about ten minutes to get changed. Is that OK?"

"That's fine," answered Nikki. "We're eating now. We'll look for you and meet you at the docks when you arrive."

"Sounds good," said Ryan. "See you in about twenty minutes, max."

"OK. Bye." Nikki hung up.

Nikki looked up at her mom, who was grinning and shaking her head.

"What?" asked Nikki with an innocent look on her face.

"You can't fool me, girl," said Danielle. "It looks like Ryan has got your attention."

"Mom, cut it out," said Nikki as she blushed. "He's going to be here in about twenty minutes."

"He's probably tripping over himself to get here before then," said Danielle. They both laughed as they continued to eat.

Just under twenty minutes later, Nikki saw Ryan and Stephanie pull up at the docks near them. Danielle had already paid for the meal, so they walked to the docks to meet Ryan and Stephanie. Nikki made sure to wave to Kristin as she left.

As they approached the boat, Danielle turned first to Ryan and then to Stephanie and said hello.

"Hi, Mrs. Bryant," said Ryan.

He looked at Nikki and said, "Hello, Nikki." Stephanie was searching through her gym bag. She looked up and said hello to both Danielle and Nikki.

"Are you looking for something?" Danielle asked Stephanie.

"I'm just making sure I have my cell phone," answered Stephanie. "Ryan was in such a hurry to get here, I barely had time to grab everything I wanted to bring." As she said this, Ryan looked at both ladies and shrugged his shoulders and lifted his hands as if to say, *oh, well. Guilty as charged.*

Danielle and Nikki looked at each other and grinned as they remembered Danielle's comment about Ryan rushing here.

"Sorry," said Nikki. "We wouldn't have asked if we didn't think it was important."

"Oh, don't worry," said Stephanie. "I wanted to see Shelli anyway."

Danielle and Nikki went onboard. The motor was still idling, so Ryan dropped it in gear and backed the boat up. When everyone got situated, he shouted out, "OK, here we go."

As they headed away from the docks, a man at the far side of the restaurant started dialing on his phone.

"Hello, sir," he said. "I just wanted to let you know that Mrs. Bryant and her oldest daughter just left Marina Pete's. They had arrived on two different boats and gave the boats to three men who met them here. They had badges, but I could not see them well enough to know who they worked for. Those men left on the boats and headed south from the restaurant. The Bryants left with a young man and teenage girl that picked them up on a boat. It looks like they are headed north—probably back to their house."

"And is the young Bryant girl still at their house?" asked the voice on the other end of the phone.

"Yes, sir," replied the man. "We have not been able to hear any cell phone conversations there because of high interference. And we can't get too close to the house—it's secured like Fort Knox."

"OK," said the voice. "Head back to their house and see if they arrive back there. See if you can maybe get one of the guys to bring a boat up and listen in from the water side."

"OK, sir. Will do." The man hung up his phone and left the restaurant. He got into his car in the parking lot and headed toward St. Armands Circle. As he drove, he called a fellow employee and arranged the boat surveillance.

Ryan picked up speed and headed northwest toward the bridge to St. Armands Circle. He turned left and decreased speed until he neared the St. Armands Key. He headed west along the north side of the key and moved slowly under the bridge to City Island. He slowed further still as he approached the Bryant dock.

Nikki stood up and jumped off with line in hand and tied the boat up quickly. Ryan killed the motor, and he, Stephanie, and Danielle stepped onto the dock. They were met by Shelli, who came leaping down the white stone path. Shelli gave Stephanie a hug and greeted everyone. She turned and headed back up the path.

"Did you hear from your dad yet?" Danielle asked as they entered the pool area.

"No, Mom," said Shelli. "But I am going to call him shortly. You won't believe what I found out on the search he asked me to do."

Chapter 28: *Revelations*

Rick was sitting in the BMW X5 with Jim Matchett at a public parking lot at Nokomis Beach. From the lot, they could see 250 yards south to the Venice Inlet and could also see the houseboat they suspected as a drug distribution point on the Intercoastal Waterway. The houseboat was partially obstructed by trees, but they could clearly see the second story and cars entering and leaving the driveway in front. Hans had been followed to the houseboat earlier and was still there. His black Mercedes was visible in the parking lot.

Just then video started to come in from the coast guard's HH-60J Jayhawk helicopter flying offshore from Venice. The onboard forward-looking infrared, or FLIR, camera with its five-axis stabilization gave crystal-clear images. The coast guard ships and its Clearwater facility were watching the video. But the copter had also been fitted with a second transmitter that was allowing the video to be also seen by the DEA, sheriff, and Rick's BMW X5 command station. The video transmitter also had a GPS receiver, and the helicopter's position was visible on the screen.

"How far is the helicopter offshore?" asked Jim.

"It shows its position about five nautical miles north and sixteen nautical miles west of Venice Inlet," replied Rick. "It will be less than two minutes before it is due west from the Inlet."

One minute later, the helicopter pilot reported sighting a large fishing trawler. The FLIR camera on the copter spun in the direction of the boat, and the video streamed to the BMW command station. The ship had two crewmen visible on deck. The helicopter flew directly over the ship and flipped from CCTV, or color camera, to infrared. The infrared, or IR, camera allowed Rick to see heat signatures. With exceptions of the two crewmen and exhausts, no unusual heat signatures were visible to Rick on the screen from either the ship or the areas under the ship.

"There's nothing visible on the IR camera, but it can't penetrate very far underwater," said Rick to Jim. "If there are subs, we would not be able to see them underwater. And the water is too turbid to see any depth in the visual spectra. But there is no question that this ship is certainly big enough to be the mother ship. Do you think the crew will be suspicious of the helicopter flying over the ship?"

"I asked that question earlier, and Captain Harris said that it was standard procedure to check out vessels while on patrol," Jim said. "As long as they don't dwell over it, they shouldn't draw suspicion."

"Good. We're not seeing anything from the buoys yet."

"What about the boats?" asked Jim.

"I see nothing coming in from the more sophisticated side-scan sonar systems on the *Spearfish* and our workboat," said Rick. "Jason looks to be having fun on the ATAWT just out from the inlet, but I don't see anything from his acoustic sensor. My fishing boat is sitting between the ATAWT and the *Spearfish*, and it is not detecting anything, either."

"It's pretty close to four o'clock, so we should see something start happening soon," said Jim. "Let's hope we still have the element of surprise."

"Everything is in place," said Rick. "The coast guard has three of its cutters out at ranges further than the eye can see. The one heading out to thirty kilometers due west of Venice Inlet is the new National Security Cutter. The coast guard has only eight of them. It's quite formidable and should be able to take on the trawler, no matter how lethal they are."

"Plus, it is substantially faster," he said. "It's copter is ready with a team out of Chesapeake, Virginia. That special team is the MSRT—a

The Bryant Family Chronicles: Death and Gold in Zara Zote

marine security response team. They are the coast guard's special ops team for combating terrorism and drug trafficking. They're ready to drop down from the helicopter and secure the boat. A second copter from the southern cutter has a diver team ready to drop in the water and intercept the subs."

"I guess it's a waiting game now," said Jim. Just as they started to relax in their seats, the command station computer began to buzz.

"It's Kyle," said Rick, as he hit the answer button on the screen.

"Hello, gentlemen," said Kyle. "I just talked with Captain Harris. Although nothing appeared unusual about that fishing trawler on the video surveillance from the coast guard helicopter, the fact that it appeared exactly where Rick said it would and at the exact time makes us believe the trawler is your mother ship. So we're a go for this mission."

Rick and Jim looked at each other, smiled, and nodded.

"Rick, please give us the signal when you see movement. Jim, please make sure nothing happens to Mr. Bryant. We gave our word to his family."

"Will do," said Jim.

"I've not been able to update the director, which is quite odd," Kyle said. "I'm going to try to reach him again. Is there anything else I should know before I hang up?"

"I'm going to launch the Quadricopter to get a closer look at the houseboat," Rick said. "It could give us a closer look at what's going on inside."

"Good idea," said Kyle. "But make sure you aren't detected. We don't want to blow this."

"I'll be careful," said Rick.

Kyle hung up, and Rick and Jim got the Quadricopter out of the back

233

of the BMW. Rick powered on his tablet PC and started the mini-copter. Within a few moments he was back in the passenger seat and was maneuvering the copter toward the houseboat.

"The divers should be moving any minute now," said Rick. "Would you please monitor the command station while I'm maneuvering the copter?" Jim turned his attention to the display on the car console. "All the acoustic sensors on the boats and buoys are on auto-detect," said Rick. "The screens will automatically pop up video windows with a detection at any of the buoys."

"Do I have to press a record button?" asked Jim.

"No. All sensor and video data are automatically recorded."

Rick moved the Quadricopter closer to the houseboat. To prevent the copter from being spotted, Rick moved it from palm tree to palm tree. After a few minutes, the copter was floating at the second story of the houseboat. On the map display of the command station, Jim could see the position of the copter on the display. The video feed from the copter, which was appearing on both the tablet PC display and the command station, showed no sign of movement.

At this moment, the display on the command station started to beep. Rick moved the copter back from the window. The workboat acoustic sensor had picked up movement in the deeper waters west of it. On the map display, Jim and Rick saw an elongated blob of red moving eastward toward the shore.

"Holy cow," said Jim. "It's a sub! You were right!"

Another beep from the display was accompanied by a pop-up video window. The sensor buoy symbol near Venice Inlet on the map display was flashing, indicating it had detected movement. After a few moments, the underwater scooter sled came into site.

Rick quickly moved the copter over the water on the south side of the houseboat. He hit the hover button on the tablet PC display, which caused the Quadricopter to park itself in the air. He switched to the bottom camera to watch the water for divers.

Rick then quickly put in a broadcast call to the DEA, sheriff's office, and coast guard teams.

"We've got movement! The drug transfer is underway. The sub is right now crossing my workboat position, and the divers are entering Venice Inlet!"

Kyle came on the line. "OK, gentlemen, we're going to wait until we see the sub heading back to the ship. We'll board the trawler at that time and capture the sub as it docks. Then the DEA and sheriff's deputies will move in on the houseboat. Are there any questions?"

There were none, but the chatter between the teams continued over the com-link.

Rick and Jim watched the command station as the coast guard helicopter moved toward the ship. The other coast guard ships began to close in. The sheriff's vehicles' positions started to show movement as they began to move in from all directions on land.

The video-motion detection algorithm from the Quadricopter caused the command station to beep. The video from the copter showed a dark blurred figure moving below water from the houseboat. Small bubbles surfaced as the figure moved southbound out of the video field of view.

The sub stopped just west of the workboat's north-south track. The underwater sled with diver was detected by the ATAWT and then by Rick's fishing boat acoustic sensors.

"Talking about sensory overload," said Jim. "The screen is lighting up like a Christmas tree!"

"I have to admit," said Rick, "it is a little overwhelming to watch it all. I'm glad the video and detection data are all recorded automatically."

Rick's cell phone began to ring. Unlike his daughters, Rick wasn't into custom ringtones, so he had to look at the display to see that it was Shelli calling. He was too busy at the moment to take the call—too much was going on for him to talk.

"Hello, honey," said Rick. Without pausing, he continued, "I'm overloaded at the moment and can't talk. I'll call you back in a few moments."

"But, Dad, I need to tell you what I discovered," said Shelli excitedly.

"It will have to wait for a few minutes. I've got too much going on I can't talk right now. I promise to call you in a few minutes."

Rick hung up and returned his attention to the command station display. He felt bad about having to put off his daughter, but he had to concentrate on the displays in front of him. He'd call her back as soon as he could.

Shelli hung up her cell phone. Stephanie and her brother, Nikki, and Danielle stood watching her. She turned to her mom and said, "We've got to tell Dad what I found. He could be in serious danger and doesn't know it. Mom, please! We've got to do something."

Rick told me not to come to Venice, Danielle thought. *What am I going to do?*

"Let's see what's going on," she said.

Danielle went to Rick's home office. The kids followed. She sat at Rick's desk and saw the computer displays in front of her. A look of concern formed on her face. She reached for the power button and enabled the large situation display on the wall. The kids turned to the display. Danielle watched as all mouths fell open. There on the wall were movements in every direction. They could see Rick was sitting at Nokomis Beach Park—right in the middle of it all.

"Holy cow!" exclaimed Shelli. "No wonder Dad is so busy."

"He must be inundated right now," said Nikki. "No wonder he had to hang up."

"And he's still in trouble," said Danielle. Then it came to her. "Your father didn't want you girls anywhere near Venice today, so you're staying here and wait for his call. I'm going down there to Venice and tell him what's going on."

"Mom, are you crazy?" asked Nikki. "You can't go down there by yourself. I'm going with you."

"No, I can't risk you getting hurt."

"I'll go with you," said Ryan.

"Absolutely not!" said Danielle sharply. "There is no way I am going to tell your mom that I risked your life!" Before Ryan could reply, Danielle shook her finger at him. "There is no more discussion on this, Ryan. You stay here with the girls. I am counting on you and Nikki to be responsible."

"Wait a minute, Mom," said Nikki. "Maybe we can get him a message to him from his command station here."

"No, we can't risk it. We don't know if anyone else is involved and or if anyone is eavesdropping. I've got to go down there."

"Mom, you know I respect you, but there is no way I'm sitting here while both of my parents are in possible danger," said Nikki. "I've lost one person I care about. There was nothing I could do to help him. But I refuse to sit here and let you walk out the door alone. I'm an adult, and I'll follow you if you don't let me go with you."

Danielle saw how serious Nikki was. Every moment she argued was time lost getting to Rick. She turned back to Ryan.

"Ryan, I need you to promise me you will keep Stephanie and Shelli here. I want you to promise me you'll stay here and protect them while Nikki and I go to Rick."

Shelli saw her sister smile and mouth "Yes!" as she curled her arm and closed her fist. Shelli could tell her sister was definitely stoked to be going with her mom.

Reluctantly Ryan agreed. Danielle then turned to Shelli.

"Shelli, you stand by on your phone and wait for him to call you back. If he hasn't called you in fifteen minutes, call him again. It's going to take us twenty to thirty minutes to get to Nokomis Beach, depending on traffic. If you reach him or he calls you, let me know, and we'll turn around and come back. You can watch our position on the display as we drive down."

"OK, Mom," said Shelli. She really wanted to go with her mom and sister, but she knew that her mom had enough stress. "I'll let you know right away if I reach Dad. And don't worry about us. You know Dad has made this house like a fortress. No one can get to us here."

Danielle smiled. "Thanks, honey." She took a deep, cleansing breath. "Let's go, Nikki."

"I'll drive my Audi, Mom," said Nikki. With that they headed out to Nikki's car.

As they pulled down the road, a car on the street turned its lights on. It slowly pulled out onto the road and headed in the same direction. After the Bryants crossed the Ringling Bridge, they turned southward on Osprey. Osprey paralleled Route 41 and was faster if traffic was heavy on 41.

The man in the car picked up his cell phone and hit a speed dial number.

"Hello," said the man on the other end.

"Sir, the Bryants are on the move," said the man following Danielle and Nikki. "They are heading southbound toward Venice."

"Stay a healthy distance behind them, but don't lose them," the man on the other end said. "Let me know if they change their route." With that he hung up.

◇◇◇◇◇

Rick and Jim watched the command station display as the submarine remained parked offshore. Divers continued to move drugs swiftly from the sub to the houseboat. Rick had to eventually bring in the Quadricopter to add a new battery pack. He sent it right back to the houseboat and parked it in the exact same location over the divers' route. Using electronic "breadcrumbs" algorithm written by Rick's company allowed the Quadricopter to retrace the exact path back to the previous parked position.

Rick had evaluated the size of the personal submarine's acoustic signature and was able to match this with the simulated acoustic signatures of various submarines on the market. As the program checked each vendor's submarine, a snapshot picture popped up on the display. Once the match was found, the image of the submarine popped up on the screen.

"Hey, that's the yellow submarine you showed us in the meeting today," said Jim.

"Yeah, it was a pretty good bet that is was this one," said Rick. "It is one of the most popular on the market, which has resulted in a very competitive price."

"Based on my calculations," said Rick, "this is the last load from the submarine. We should see it turn and move back out to the mother ship." Jim and Rick watched the display intently as the diver headed back up the Intercoastal Waterway toward the houseboat and the submarine began to move to deeper water.

Kyle came back on the com-link and announced that it was time to take the mother ship and raid the houseboat. Almost as a side note, he announced that he had reached the DEA director and updated him on everything. The director was now monitoring the situation, but was leaving Kyle in charge.

"That's odd," said Rick.

"What?" asked Jim.

"Kyle just said that the director was monitoring the situation. I wonder where he is. I have the network firewalled, so I know he did not log on with a new connection."

"Maybe he's at the sheriff's office."

The conversation was interrupted by Rick's phone. He looked at the display. It was Shelli again. It must be important for her to call him again. He remembered that he had asked Shelli to look up some things.

He answered. "Hi, honey. Sorry I was busy and didn't call. Whatever it is, please tell me quickly."

"Dad, thank goodness you answered," said Shelli. "Mom and Nikki are on the way to see you."

"What? Why? I didn't want you guys down here,"

"Mom and Nikki were coming down to give you the information I found out," said Shelli at a speed only a teenager could talk. "We saw you were inundated when we looked at your office command station. We didn't want to send you a message over your network because we didn't know who might be watching."

"My goodness, Shelli. What in the world did you find out?" Shelli blurted it out as fast as she could.

"Dad, you gave me the names of all the DEA team to check up on. You said to send the e-mail via your encrypted link to the FBI to do the background checks. I made sure it was addressed to your friend there, Jack Hollister."

"I decided to search each name on the Internet," she continued. "I started by just googling. I got a lot of hits, but I didn't see anything unusual. But then I started searching some of the social networks. You know, Facebook, Twitter, MySpace, and the like."

"OK, uh huh." Rick acknowledged he was listening.

Shelli kept going. "On Facebook I found an interview with a DEA official talking about the capture of a drug ring. It was really short, Dad. I almost went on, but then I heard him say the expression, '*C'est la vie.*'"

"I don't speak French, honey, but even I have said that before. It's a very common expression."

"I know, Dad. But it was the way he said it. It took me a few minutes, but I realized I had heard it recently. I heard it at the museum."

Shelli slowed her speech so that the gravity of what she was saying sank in.

"A man came to the museum today to get a private showing, and Mom gave him a tour. He was supposedly a very important art collector. Nikki and I got to meet him just before the tour. I remembered his first name was Jacques. When I met him, I thought his name was familiar. So I asked Mom for his business card that he had left with her to check the spelling. The man's name is Jacques De Sores."

"I don't know anyone by that name," said Rick.

"I quickly searched the Web again and found that there was a little-known French pirate named Jacques De Sores. His claim to fame was that he was credited for burning down Havana, Cuba, in 1555."

"Honey, what..." interrupted Rick.

But before he could finish, Shelli continued on. "That's not important, Dad. It just triggered my memory. I placed the picture of the DEA official and Mr. De Sores, the art collector, on my computer screen side by side. And I typed their names under each. Although the hair is combed a different way and the clothes are dramatically different, it's not a difficult stretch to see that the two people are the same. The DEA official has a dual personality."

"Who is the DEA official, honey?" asked Rick. But before Shelli could answer, Jim touched Rick's arm to get his attention.

"I'm sorry, Rick, but you should see this on the screen." Shelli heard Jim's voice and stopped talking while Rick looked at the screen.

The last diver's track had made it back to the houseboat. But the submarine, which had been making a beeline trajectory back to the mother ship, had now begun to veer south. And the video coming in from the coast guard helicopter showed a lot of activity on the deck of the mother ship.

"What the heck is going on," wondered Jim out loud.

Rick didn't answer, but put the phone back to his ear.

"Shelli, who was the DEA official you're talking about?" Rick put his left finger in his left ear to be sure he could hear only Shelli's answer.

Shelli replied simply, "Director Dusauriss."

"What?" said Rick in amazement. "Are you sure?"

"Director Dusauriss has two identities—sort of like a superhero. But he might be more like a super-villain. Just look at his name, Dad. Jack Du-Sau-riss sounds very much like Jacques De Sores. It's sort of like a word puzzle."

"It's an anagram," said Rick.

After a pause, Shelli said, "I know I'm right. I don't know why he's doing it, but it's one and the same person. I sent another email to Jack Hollister to ask him to focus his search on both of the director's identities."

Rick's mind began to reel. He had asked Shelli to do a search on DEA personnel because the whole fake drug ring they had discovered had made him suspicious that there may be insiders involved. But he had not expected the director. He recalled from the speeches that were made by the director that he had no particular accent. So if Shelli was right, then this meant the director was deceptive indeed.

Then he recalled what Frank and Will had said when they were first interrogated before they went into the meeting with Hans at the seafood restaurant in Placida. They said that Hans sometimes talked in French to his boss on the phone. Plus, the director had been hard to locate earlier today. If he was at the museum, he would not have answered his phone when he was being escorted by Danielle.

"Dad...Dad... are you still there?" said Shelli's voice in Rick's ear as he emerged out of his thoughts.

"I'm here, honey. I know why he's doing this, but I can't talk now. I don't know who else is involved." Rick looked down at his watch. "When did your mother and sister leave?"

"About twenty minutes now, from the house," answered Shelli. "I'm supposed to call them if I reached you so that they can turn around and come home."

"Alright, honey. You do that. Very good job, sweetheart. And if you can't reach your mother, please let me know."

"OK," said Shelli and hung up her phone.

Chapter 29: *Assault*

Nikki and Danielle were now on Route 41 heading south. Osprey had eventually curved eastward and ended on Route 41. Traffic was light, so they were making good time. They were still about ten minutes from Nokomis Beach when Danielle's cell phone rang.

"It's Shelli," she said.

"Mom, I got hold of Dad and...." Shelli stopped in midsentence.

"Honey, are you there?" asked Danielle.

"I'm still here," Shelli said nervously. "The IDAS alarm, you know, the intrusion system Dad had installed last year, is going off."

Danielle was almost paralyzed with fear for her daughter, but she remembered that Ryan and Stephanie were also there. She felt the urge to tell Nikki to turn around and drive back home. But she was almost at Rick's location, and he was also in possible danger. Her mind was going a mile a minute. It was no coincidence that the intruder was breaking in now. They were probably watching the house and saw her and Nikki leave. They might think the house was empty.

"Shelli, the alarm system will call the police if anyone tries to break in. If you're not in Dad's office, you, Stephanie, and Ryan get there now. If you need to contact your dad, don't hesitate to do it."

"We're already in the office, Mom."

"What is the intruder doing now?"

"He or she is trying to get into the garage."

"How do you know it's one person?"

"The IDAS system shows only one contact symbol," answered Shelli.

"Mom, I told Dad everything. He knows now who Director Dusauriss is. He's...." The phone speaker crackled with static, and Shelli's voice dropped out completely.

"Shelli...Shelli...are you there?" Danielle put down the phone. "I got disconnected from your sister and the burglar alarm went off." Nikki saw the terror on her mom's face.

"What should we do?" asked her mom. Nikki had rarely ever heard this from her mom. She had gone through her life knowing that her mom always knew what to do and had an answer for all of life's issues. Now it was her turn to pay it back.

"Calm down, Mom. You know the house is a fortress. There's no way anyone is going to harm Shelli. We probably just went through a cell tower transition, and the call was dropped. Try calling her back." Danielle selected Shelli's name on the call list and hit the Send button. After a moment, she said, "There's still nothing...I can't get through."

Nikki picked up her phone. "Here, hit five for Shelli's speed dial."

Danielle pressed and held the keypad labeled "5." The phone dialed Shelli's number. Danielle put it on speakerphone. Static filled the quietness of the Audi.

"Something's wrong, Mom. Try calling the operator." Danielle did so, and again there was only static. Nikki knew something was very wrong. She checked her review mirror and noticed the same sedan that had been behind them while on Osprey. *Is that car following us?*

"Hey, Mom, didn't Dad mention that all the DEA vehicles and his vehicles had cell jammers?"

"Yes, he did. Do you think someone's jamming us?" Before Nikki could answer, Danielle continued, "But that would mean someone would have to be close enough to us to jam us."

"Yes, it does. And I think the sedan behind us is the culprit."

Danielle turned in her seat to look back. "Do you know if they've been following us long?"

"I believe they've been on our tail since we were on Osprey. I didn't think anything of it until we had cell problems."

"Nikki, I think we're being targeted. Maybe the director or Jacques or whoever he is knows we're on to him. Maybe that's his lackey behind us. We've got to get to your Dad pronto. He can get the sheriff's office to stop this!"

Nikki didn't need to be told twice what to do. She pushed her foot down on the pedal and lurched forward. She weaved by the two cars staggered in the lanes in front of her. From the rearview mirror, she saw the sedan pick up speed and pursue them.

"Well, that answers that question. The sedan is staying with us."

Nikki looked down at her gauges. They were moving at sixty-five miles an hour on Route 41, which was 20 miles per hour over the speed limit. She had more than half a tank of gas, and the temperature gauge was low. Dad had made her take a defensive driving class before she went to college. Plus, he had made some modifications to her car, which in his words made him feel better about her being on her own while at college. It was time to put those modifications to good use.

Nikki checked her rearview mirror one more time before she accelerated the car. "Let's see if this guy can stay with us, Mom. Make sure your seatbelt is secure."

◊◊◊◊◊

Rick looked at the display carefully. The personal submarine was continuing southbound and was nearing the edge of the maximum detection range for the workboat acoustic sensor. The video from the Jayhawk helicopter showed the mother ship deckhands had AK-47 machine guns hung over their shoulders. And nothing was coming from the houseboat or buoys.

At first he wondered if he should say anything to Jim about the director. Rick was concerned that the director may have other insiders working with him. But unless Jim was a great actor, it just didn't seem possible that he was part of this. Rick had to take the chance and let Jim know.

"Jim, it looks like the group has been tipped off about the sting operation," Rick said. "They're making a run for it."

"How in the world would they have known? You've got an encrypted network, and we know everyone on the team!"

"You've got a mole," replied Rick. "It's Director Dusaurris."

Jim turned and looked at Rick in disbelief. "What, are you serious? There's no way. We've known Jack for three years now. We've worked with him on half a dozen arrests. How can you say this?"

"I'll fill you in shortly, but we've got to let Kyle and the others know as soon as possible."

Rick's phone started ringing again. It was Shelli. Rick answered quickly.

"Dad, we've got trouble," said Shelli. "I was talking to Mom when her phone went dead. I tried to reach her and Nikki, and I can't reach them. Plus, the IDAS alarms are ringing at the house. Someone is trying to get in the garage."

Rick started to immediately sweat. He felt like his heart was going to explode from the pressure. He knew the intrusion detection and alert system was good enough to protect a king, but he'd feel better if he was there with Shelli.

"Are Ryan and Stephanie still with you?"

"Yes, they are," answered Shelli quickly.

"I'm sure I don't have to tell you that you need to stay inside and in the office. You'll be safe. The house knows your signature and has locked down all doors into the room you are in. The police will be called if the burglar makes it into the garage, and the house countermeasures will kick in. You have nothing to worry about."

"OK, Dad," said Shelli in a more calm voice.

Rick pulled down the "Display" menu item on the command station software and selected "Show Family." A heart icon showed up at his house and on Route 41. The symbols had names next to them. It showed that both Danielle and Nikki were in Nikki's car and would be coming up on Albee Road soon. At least he knew that they were fine for now.

"Shelli, select 'Display' and then 'Show Family' from the menu if you're watching my command station."

"Got it," said Shelli after following her dad's instructions. "They're getting close to you."

"I know, sweetie. I can see them too. Just hang in there, and I'll take care of Mom and Nikki when they get here. Then we'll all race back up as soon as possible. But don't hesitate to call me if you feel you are in danger." With that, he said good-bye and hung up.

Even though he knew Shelli and her friends were safe, he still worried. But now he had to somehow help Nikki and Danielle. He tried calling them and got static.

"My wife and daughter are coming here, Jim. And we've got to help them."

Kyle came over the com-link. "We have a situation. It looks like the smugglers are on to us. We're moving now to arrest them."

Nikki was going 80 mph down Route 41 southbound. She looked back in her rearview mirror and saw the Ford Edge was still behind her. They were coming up to the overpass where State Highway 682 merged onto Route 41. There were no crossroads there, and Route 41 was wide, so Nikki took the chance to accelerate even faster. She had started to pull away from the Edge when she spotted movement in her peripheral vision to the right. Coming down the sloping onramp was a Ford Mustang GT, and the driver was looking right at them.

"Mom, it looks like we've got more company," said Nikki as she motioned with her head to the right.

Danielle turned back to her. "Nikki, that's a brand new Mustang! Can you outrun that?"

As the ramp merged closer, Nikki could see "5.0" on the fender of the car. "I doubt it, Mom. That's a five-liter motor in that car. Cody loved those cars. He told me more than once that it has over four hundred horsepower."

As the ramp merged, the Mustang bolted down the road like a missile and pulled directly into Nikki's lane. Nikki knew from her driving training that the two vehicles were going to try to slow her down and force her to stop. She had seconds to react.

Using her right thumb, she pressed a button on her steering wheel that resembled a person talking. This activated the Audi speech recognition system. After she heard a soft beep, she said "Nikki Bryant." The screen on the multimedia interface popped up the message saying "WELCOME, NIKKI," followed by the words "PLEASE STATE YOUR COMMAND."

"Dad has made some improvements on this car. He added some new gadgets that he hasn't tried yet on his other cars. He made me memorize the commands and the manual. I had to go over them with him a dozen times. But that was practice—I never actually got to see it work."

"Great," said Danielle sarcastically.

Nikki spoke the words "Security mode." The screen went blank and a single cursor flashed. Nikki then spoke the words "Attack mode." The screen immediately flashed, "ATTACK MODE INITIATED."

The screen switched to two camera views—the left half of the screen was a camera view looking forward, and the right half of the screen was a camera view looking behind. A menu showing available nonlethal weapons ran across the top of the screen.

"Hang on, Mom. This is going to get a little crazy."

"*Going* to get crazy? What do you call what's been going on up until now?"

Nikki looked forward again and said, "Enable sonic system." Within seconds, the Audi grill slid away, and a black meshed surface moved forward. She spoke again, "Full power." The screen stated "SONIC SYSTEM ARMED." Below this were the words "LEVEL: 100%." Without pause, Nikki calmly stated, "Fire."

With the completion of her words, a static sound came over the car speakers. It quickly shifted pitch and then stayed steady. It was the car's active noise cancellation enabling itself and then tuning to the appropriate sound frequency. Two seconds later a dull vibration emanated through the steering wheel and floorboard of the car. Not a sound could be heard by Danielle or Nikki.

At the same time, Danielle and Nikki saw the Mustang body appear to almost ripple, and its rear and side windows shattered from the sonic blast that emanated from the front of Nikki's car. The sound had frequencies that spread over audible and ultrasonic ranges. Even though it was directional, reflections off the ground and metal could be painful to anyone nearby. The noise cancellation fortunately protected Nikki and Danielle.

The Mustang immediately dropped speed, and Nikki maneuvered to the left and passed by the dazed driver of the Mustang.

Danielle looked at Nikki. "His ear was bleeding."

"Yep," said Nikki. "And the rest of his senses are about to get a shock."

Nikki accelerated and pulled in front of the Mustang. "Enable rear E-M-P," said Nikki. "REAR EMP ARMED" came up on the dash display.

"What's EMP?" asked Danielle.

"Dad said it stands for electromagnetic pulse. It can burn out most electronics and microchips." The license plate on the back door of Nikki's car slid to the left, and a circular disk with a spiral wire protruded from its center. Nikki spoke the familiar word, "Fire."

Unlike the sonic system, there was no vibration. There was absolutely no sound detected nor any beam of light transmitted. Danielle turned around in her seat and watched as the hood of the Mustang popped open and folded back on its front windshield.

"It must have an electronic hood release," said Nikki. Smoke came from the fried electronics inside the engine and passenger compartments. The car slowed down as it veered off on the shoulder of the road. As it did so, Danielle saw the Ford Edge that had been following them earlier emerge from the smoke screen.

"You've still got company," said Danielle. "The Edge is behind you."

Nikki looked in her rearview mirror. "We're almost at Albee Road. Let's see if I can shake him."

"Why don't you use the EMP again?" asked Danielle.

"I can't. Look at the screen. The EMP has to recharge, and it's only at twenty percent. I've got to try to lose him." Seconds later she had a plan.

Nikki said, "Enable flares." The dash display read, "FLARES ACTIVATED." Then Nikki said, "Full spread." The display echoed her command by showing four activated cannons on a top-down view of the vehicle. The middle section of the back bumper flipped down and then slid inward. A one-inch cylinder protruded out and then tilted up.

Nikki waited until she was about a hundred yards from the intersection when she shouted, "Fire!" They heard four distinct *thump* sounds as the cylinder moved from right to left, ejecting four red slugs.

As she entered the Albee Road intersection, she pulled the emergency brake and brought the rear end of her Audi to the left. Then she steered to the left and hit the accelerator. In a controlled slide, she made a wide right turn. No others cars were in either lane of Albee—otherwise she would have plowed into them for sure.

The Ford Edge sedan following them was obviously surprised to see four objects flying his way. The driver was even more stunned when they exploded into four extremely bright lights. It happened so quickly, that the driver could not close his eyes fast enough and was immediately blinded. At the same time, he could hear brakes and tires squealing ahead of him and then off to his right.

The man driving slammed on the brakes, but was well past the intersection before his car came to a complete stop. His eyes were no good to him, but he was afraid of getting hit from behind. So he turned his wheel and pressed gingerly on the accelerator. A gentle bump meant he had just jumped up on the sidewalk or curb. He stopped and fumbled for his sunglasses. He put the sunglasses on, but still couldn't open his eyes without pain.

It took a few seconds more before he could begin to make shapes and colors. He put the car back in gear and moved forward into the entrance of the sandy parking area adjacent to a small field on the south corner of Albee and Route 41.

The driver, who was still squinting from the pain in his eyes, accelerated through the grassy lot. He jumped over the south curb on Albee and stopped the car facing west. He looked ahead…no sign of the car. He got out of the car to look all around him. The Bryants were gone.

The man quickly dialed his boss again. It took four rings before Hans answered.

"I lost them, boss. I think they are heading west on Albee Road." Hans paused a moment and then spoke.

"Where are you now?" asked Hans.

"I'm at the corner of Albee Road and Route 41 South," replied the man.

"Turn around and head south on Route 41 for a quarter of a mile and turn right on Bayview Parkway," said Hans. "Then go four tenths of a mile and turn into the big house on the left; the address is 1109 Bayview Parkway. Pull all the way up to the house. Go to the garage and open up the back to it. Then go to the driver's side door of the vehicle parked inside. The vehicle is unlocked. Change into the clothes on the driver's seat. Start up the vehicle and stay alert. I will contact you with further instructions.   Do you understand?"

"Yes, sir," said the man and hung up. He expected there was a lot more going on than his chase, but he wasn't going to ask his boss now. He hopped back in his car and headed south.

◇◇◇◇◇

Rick looked at his display and saw his family crossing the Albee Bridge at a fast speed. As Rick watched his daughter's and wife's progress, he and Jim continued to listen to Captain Harris and Kyle orchestrating the arrest. The sheriff was moving in his deputies quickly.

"Jim, my family will be here in a couple of minutes," said Rick. "We need to get them in this car as fast as possible. The Audi has some anti-theft and self-protection, but it's not bulletproof."

"I'll jump out and get them in here as soon as they pull up," said Jim. "But first, let's get the car started in case we have to pull up to the road."

As Jim started up the BMW, Rick's phone rang. It was Danielle. Nikki had put enough space between her and her pursuer that the jammer was no longer effective.

"Hello, honey," said Rick. "Pull into the second parking lot on the right. Make sure you pull right up to us. Jim will open the doors and get you into the BMW quickly. But don't squeal the tires. We don't want you to be seen, if at all possible."

Sounding somewhat surprised, Danielle said they were approaching the lot now.

Nikki skillfully reduced speed and pulled into the sandy lot. As soon as her back wheels left the pavement, Rick and Jim heard a shot. They looked down at the display and saw the Quadricopter video go down. Jim knew what had happened.

"The mini-copter has been hit by gunfire!" He quickly put up his field glasses and saw an open window. As Nikki pulled up beside the BMW, Jim saw a flash of light.

The flash was the reflection of the low sun in the west reflecting off the barrel end of a rifle scope. Jim opened his door and then the rear door. Before he could yell instructions, Nikki had quickly jumped out of her car and into the rear seat of the BMW. Danielle had opened her door and was stepping quickly behind the Audi to get to the BMW. The rear of the Audi was directly in line with the houseboat. Jim shut his driver door and ran as fast as he could to Danielle.

As Jim reached Danielle, he yelled for her to stand behind him. He became her human shield. They took two steps when a shot rang out. Danielle felt Jim's weight against her and heard him yell for her to keep going. She made it to the back open door of the BMW when she realized that Jim was no longer behind her. He was lying on the ground behind the Audi.

Another shot rang out, and a chip of glass popped off the windshield. Rick shouted at them to close the doors and clip in their seatbelts. He jumped into the driver's seat and pulled the vehicle directly behind the Audi, putting it between the shooter in the houseboat and Jim.

Two more shots rang out, but they bounced off the skin of the BMW and the side window.

Rick called over the com-link. "Shots fired at Nokomis Beach! Officer down! Repeat, officer down!" As he leapt out of the driver seat, he heard a flurry of chatter on the com-link from the sheriff's dispatcher.

Officers and ambulances were on the way.

Rick knelt down beside Jim and saw that his bulletproof vest had a hole in it to the right of his heart. He was still conscious, but just barely. He pulled the Velcro straps off the side of the vest and ripped open his shirt. The bullet had penetrated his chest, and he was bleeding profusely.

Jim knew he had been shot and that he was lying on the ground. His vision was coming in and out of focus. The pain in his chest was incredible. He wanted to get up, but his legs and arms felt like lead weights. He could tell that Rick was working on him.

It was a hot, humid day. But as Jim lay there, he began to feel a chill shoot down his body. He quivered as the beach breeze brushed over his skin. A blanket of some kind rested on him as his vision started to go dark. A sudden sense of calm descended on him, and sounds blurred into muffled whispers. His mind drifted to his mountain camping trips, where he lay warm in his sleeping bag watching the night skies for shooting stars and constellations. *I love the fall camping trips,* he thought. *Oh, and there's my wife and kids. They're having such a good time.* A smile came to his face as he continued to hallucinate. His neck muscles relaxed and his head rolled slowly to one side.

"Oh, my gosh! Is he dead?" Danielle's eyes were wide, and her hand was over her mouth as she spoke. Rick felt for a pulse.

"He's still alive. Nikki, please come over here and keep putting pressure on his chest. I've got to get to the command station before more people get hurt!" Nikki jumped out of the BMW on the safe side and took over putting pressure on Jim's wound.

As he leapt back into the driver's seat, Rick turned to his daughter and wife and told them to be prepared to jump into the vehicle if they needed to get away. They both responded affirmatively.

Rick then turned his attention to the display. The sheriff's deputies were crossing over the bridge at Albee Road and were closing in on his position. The MSRT was the first to attack the mother ship by rappelling down to its deck. A few of the mother ship crew appeared on deck and began shooting upward at the helicopters and MRST members, but they lasted only a few seconds. The MRST had plenty of training in firing their weapons while rappelling, so the crew with weapons was dispatched quickly. It soon became apparent that the crew on deck was acting as diversions. Soon crew members were fleeing in everything from dive suites to life boats.

Rick broadcast over the com-link. If he was wrong about what he was about to do, all the good work he and his company had provided would be quickly forgotten. But lives were at risk. Rick selected Captain Harris, Kyle, and Sheriff Huggins as the recipients.

"Attention, attention. We have a mole in the group. Director Dusauriss is the mole. He should be arrested and held for questioning."

Kyle immediately jumped on the link.

"What the hell are you talking about, Rick? He was leading this operation! He's personally been involved in many drug arrests."

Rick replied as quickly as he could. "Kyle, remember that everything was going well until you contacted the director. Plus, we've positively identified him with a wealthy alias. Why would he have an alias? I'm telling you, you need to arrest him and get him off the network. If I'm wrong, then I'll take all the blame. But if we don't arrest him, who knows what else could happen and who else will get hurt!"

There was a pause. Then the link clicked as Kyle came back on. "Consider it done. Now let's clean this mess up." Captain Harris asked the two sentinel class cutters to close ranks on the mother ship. He also called for divers to hit the water to go after the submarine. Rick listened as the captain ordered rigid-hull inflatable boats, or RIBs, to be launched for boarding by all three cutters.

Kyle and two other DEA agents were on the *Spearfish*. He was moving as fast as he could toward Venice Inlet. He had intended to assist in the boarding of the mother ship, but the attack on his officer and the Bryants was now his top priority. The coast guard seemed to be handling the water side of the assault just fine.

Kyle rounded the inlet entrance and then headed north on the Intercoastal Waterway as fast as he could. The fishermen along the jetty yelled obscenities as the giant wake hit the jetty rocks and sent water spraying them and their gear. The houseboat was seconds up ahead on the left. He radioed in that he was pulling up to the rear of the houseboat.

Rick was watching the display and saw Kyle's position updated to precisely where Kyle's radio message said he was. On an open broadcast, he said, "Kyle, the sheriff's deputies are pulling in front of the house now, so be careful."

Rick paused and then continued on the open broadcast. "Attention to everybody entering the houseboat. The gunmen in the houseboat have a high-powered rifle. He has rounds that can penetrate bulletproof vests, so be careful."

As Kyle jumped on the back deck, Rick's message caused him to pause. *Good to know about the rifle marksman before breaking into the back door.* Kyle heard a lot of activity inside. They could be destroying evidence, so he decided he must go in now.

"This is Kyle to all agents and officers. I'm going in through the back in fifteen seconds. Deputies at the front door, please enter on my mark." Kyle looked at his watch and in twelve seconds he said, "Three, two, one...go!"

Kyle stepped back two steps from the door he had been standing next to, then took one step forward and kicked as hard as he could with his right foot right next to the doorknob. The door cracked loudly as the casing splintered and the door flew open. He had his pistol in one hand and his badge in the other. The other two DEA agents entered behind him and pointed their weapons to the right and left of the door.

The room was formerly a living room, but was now the hidden entrance to the water. A rectangular hole was cut in the center of the floor, and three water sled rigs were floating in the center. One side of the hole was a staging area for the drugs being offloaded. On one wall was an air tank refilling station and a row of tanks and diver gear. And surrounding the hole and spread out on various places on the floor were eight men—four of them in neoprene dive suites—all still and lifeless. These were the divers and support crew. Kyle recognized the support crew as being the same men who had entered the seafood restaurant with Hans for yesterday's meeting.

The front door flew open, and two deputies entered with weapons drawn. Kyle made sure the deputies saw him and his badge. They nodded their head, recognizing he was an officer. Kyle motioned to the officers to check the second floor of the houseboat. He then checked the next room of the first floor.

After about a minute, Kyle came over the encrypted com-link and said, "All clear on the bottom floor. At least eight suspects appear to be dead. Call in the ambulances." Then Kyle heard the deputies give an all clear on the second floor.

"Do you have a positive ID on Hans Schmidt?" Rick said over the com-link.

"Negative, but he sure did clean up after himself," said Kyle.

"We know he was there," said Rick. "Where could he have gone?"

Kyle looked back into the living room at the big hole in the floor. Then he activated his com-link.

"There are three sleds here. But there is obviously room for a fourth." Kyle walked to the edge of the diver's hole and looked into the water. There was a dull red color to the water caused by the flow of blood from one of the dead divers near the edge of the hole. On the bottom, which was only a few feet deep, Kyle saw a gun with a silencer. Kyle spoke again on the link.

"I think our man Hans has escaped underwater. Rick, can you check on your buoys for him?"

Rick checked the display for buoys for any detected movement. "There's nothing detected by the buoys. That means his only option was to head eastward—perhaps he moved toward the island directly east, called Turner Key, and hugged its coast. The buoys would not have detected him."

Kyle came back over the link. "I'm jumping back on the *Spearfish* and heading south around Turner Key. If the deputy to the north of Albee Road Bridge could come down and cover the north side of the island, we can meet on the east side. I also need some coverage on the shoreline."

Sheriff Steele came over the com link. "This is Sheriff Steele. All available officers...move in on the eastern shore of the Intercoastal Waterways. We're looking for anyone on foot."

Kyle was happy to see the support from the sheriff. He ran out the broken rear door and jumped back on the *Spearfish*. He pushed it toward the nearby western shore of the island, and in a few seconds steered southward. He moved as fast as he could while peering in the water for signs of the sled and along the shoreline, in case Hans left the water. He motioned to one the DEA agents who had jumped on the boat with him to check the shore of Turner Key. The agent quickly jumped overboard and waded his way onto the shore.

It took less than a minute to reach the eastern shore of Turner Key. It was then that Kyle realized that the mainland shore was split into two points, with the wide mouth of a creek in the center. Homes lined the entire shoreline. Docks and boats were along most of the homes.

Kyle had an overwhelming feeling of defeat when he saw this. For every second they did not detect Hans, he had that much more time to escape. He looked to the north and saw the sheriff's deputy heading toward him. The deputy had obviously not seen Hans. Hans was a smart man, and he had likely planned an escape route in case anything ever went wrong.

Rick came over the com-link. "Kyle, given the rate of speed of the sleds, Hans cannot be any further than six-tenths of a mile from the houseboat."

Kyle looked at the GPS display on his console. He clicked on screen to enable the range rings.

"That means he has had the time to reach a large section of the shoreline," said Kyle. "We'll keep checking the shore, but we need to make sure we close off all land escape routes."

Sheriff Steele came over the com-link. "Ahead of you on that, Kyle. I've got roadblocks being set up on all roads heading into the shoreline communities around the Venice Inlet. But that's a lot of territory. We'll do the best we can."

Kyle listened as the chatter came in from the sheriff deputies along the shoreline. Just as he thought—Hans was eluding them. He continued to listen as the coast guard intercepted the submarine and successfully boarded the mother ship and captured its crew. At least there was something good in this.

"Rick, do you have an update on Jim?"

"The paramedics are working on him now," answered Rick. "They said the bullet miraculously missed his heart and spine. Once they stopped the bulk of the bleeding, he woke up. They've given him some potent pain killers, so he's pretty groggy. They are loading him on the ambulance now."

Kyle could hear the muffled voices of the paramedics working on Jim over the com-link. "Thanks Rick. Can you please make sure they get him off to the hospital?"

"Of course," answered Rick. "It's the least I could do for the man that saved my wife's life."

"Thanks," said Kyle. "I'm going to continue looking for Hans."

As Kyle slowly surveyed the coastline, he contacted the dispatcher at

Sheriff Steele's office. It was confirmed that no one had seen any sign of the director. No director and no Hans—they were working together, as Rick had indicated.

About ten minutes later additional sheriff's boats entered the area. Kyle asked them to continue the search and expand it both north and south on the waterfront. He headed back to the houseboat. Once docked, he walked through the houseboat and out toward the parking lot, where Rick and his family were still huddled around the display on the BMW.

"Rick, what's the situation?"

"Hi, Kyle," answered Rick. "The coast guard has commandeered the mother ship. They've also docked the submarine in the ship's hold. The sub and mother ship are being escorted back to the coast guard's port. The sheriff has a citywide APB out on Hans and the director, but there's no word on their capture. Jim is stable and is heading to the hospital.   I can't thank him enough for saving my wife's life. Hans was going after my whole family."

"Thanks for the update, Rick," said Kyle. "You need to head on home. We've got this under control. I don't think we'll see Hans or the director, but we won't give up until we find them."

 "I would like to get back and check on Shelli. She needs us."

"Please go. Your family has done so much, and we feel guilty keeping you here. We'll let you know what happens. If you don't mind, we'll return your hardware back to you tomorrow."

"Sure—keep the hardware as long as you need it.   We're out of here." With that he waved and got back into the BMW. Danielle and Nikki returned to the Audi. In a few seconds they were heading north back toward Sarasota. He knew Nikki would be disappointed, but at least the drug ring that was responsible for Cody's death was shut down.

Kyle got on his phone and started coordinating the forensic team for the houseboat. There were hours of processing left to complete. But for the first time in a long time, Kyle could envision the end of the mission and the return home. It had been a long, dragged-out mission, with many twists and turns. They didn't get all the bad guys, but they had shut down a major drug operation, ferreted out a mole in the organization, and had confiscated tons of drugs. Washington would be very happy...and so was he.

Chapter 30: *Retreat*

At the intersection of Bayview Parkway and Route 41 just north of Venice and south of Albee Road, a sheriff's deputy was stopping all vehicles passing by him going southbound. Just minutes earlier the deputy had received word to stop every car going southbound on Route 41 and to look out for a man with graying hair in his late fifties. A picture had been sent to the rugged notebook PC mounted in his vehicle. Given that he was in the land of retirement, it was not going to be easy to spot this man. He had printed the picture and had to keep it in his hand just to help with the ID.

Traffic was starting to back up in both directions on Route 41, but he was told to be thorough. As he was checking a late-model station wagon, he turned to see a white US postal van pulling up to the stop sign on Bayview.

As the deputy walked over to the mail truck driver's side, he noticed two people in the car. The driver seemed to be in his thirties. The man in the passenger seat had black hair combed back and appeared to be in his late forties. The deputy walked up to see the driver had the familiar mailman polyester shorts and light-blue short-sleeved shirt with the USPS logo above the pocket. The person on the passenger's side was also in a postal uniform.

"What's going on, officer?" asked the driver.

"We're looking for escaped felons," said the deputy. "Have you guys seen anyone or anything suspicious in this neighborhood?"

The driver and passenger looked at each other and then both responded, "No."

"I'm going to have to see in the back of the van," said the deputy.

"No problem, sir. It's unlocked," said the driver. After a quick search, the deputy came back up to the driver's door.

"Why are there two of you making deliveries?" asked the deputy. "My cousin is a mailman, and he always works alone."

The driver looked nervously back at the passenger. "I'm a trainee," replied the passenger.

"Oh, OK. Well, drive safely, gentlemen. You can go ahead."

The mail van moved into the southbound traffic on Route 41 without hesitation. After a few moments the driver said, "Damn, that was something else, boss. The disguises seemed to work just fine. It's good he didn't check our plates—they are as fake as they come."

"People are easily fooled into believing what they see when it all makes sense to them," said the passenger. "And we are lucky he didn't ask for our driver's licenses."

"Well, where to now, boss?"

"Take a left at your first major intersection," said the passenger. "We need to put some distance between us and the beach. I don't feel real comfortable without my pistol. I accidentally dropped it in the water when I was trying to escape the houseboat."

The driver's phone began to ring. The driver looked at the display and handed it to the passenger.

"It's for you, boss."

"Hello, sir," said the passenger.

"What the hell happened?" screamed the voice on the phone. "How did the entire US government come down on our operation, and we didn't see it? That's the whole reason we had the bogus drug ring. It was supposed to give us a warning."

"I don't know, sir," said the passenger. "We never planned on the Bryants. And to be honest, sir, you put all of us in jeopardy by not staying more involved with the DEA activities."

"Hans, you are not irreplaceable," said the irritated voice. "I will not put up with insubordination. Please tell me you cleaned up the mess at the houseboat. They still have no proof of my involvement. Only circumstantial evidence could be brought up, and my law team has already put together a defense plan. I want it to stay that way."

Hans signaled to the driver to take the left on Colonia Lane. The driver turned left and slowly drove as he tried to listen to the conversation. Hans scanned the road ahead and in his side mirror as he talked.

"Yes, sir," replied Hans. "I took care of everyone and everything. There's nothing there to link us." Hans listened to more questions. "I wiped down everything, sir. The submarine crew never met me and they do not know your existence. There's no way they cannot connect us," lied Hans as he thought of his lost gun.

"So there is only one loose end to take care of," said the voice.

"Yes, sir," replied Hans as he looked at the driver. "Just a minute, sir." Hans turned to the driver and asked him to pull over at the entrance of a large lot with a sandy road ending at some bushes. In this area of dense housing, it was rare to have an open lot with no home nearby. Hans motioned for the driver to go down the sandy road.

As they reached the bushes, the vehicle came to a stop. Hans could see a wide canal beyond the bushes. Hans handed the phone to the driver. "My boss would like to talk to you."

The driver took the phone and said, "Hello?"

The voice on the phone said, "Thank you for your help on this project. Your support and loyalty has been greatly appreciated."

The driver saw Hans move quickly in his peripheral vision, followed by a severe pain in his chest. He looked down and saw a knife buried to the hilt in his chest. He turned to Hans with a look of disbelief.

"Goodbye, Mr. Jenkins," said the voice on the phone.

Hans pulled the slumped body out of the driver's door and dragged it into the bushes on the water's edge. He then moved into the driver's seat and picked up the phone.

"OK, sir, what is your plan?" he asked.

"We need to meet. The Bryants may have ruined our business, but they may be onto something that could be very lucrative." Hans listened as the voice said where they were going to meet and what help he was going to require.

Hans ended the call with, "I will be there at about eight this evening. See you then."

Hans's phone had buzzed once while talking to his employer. He read the text message with a frown on his face. He selected his contacts list on his phone. He scrolled down the names, selected one, and pushed the Talk button. The phone was answered by a deep voice. "Hello, sir."

"Good afternoon, George," replied Hans. "Our men at the Bryants' house are having some trouble. Please bring your assault team and make it quick. Have them fully geared as if they were breaking into Fort Knox. But make sure we get the Bryant kid alive. The rest are expendable as necessary."

"Roger that, sir."

Hans stepped back out of the vehicle and placed his phone just in behind his left front wheel. He climbed back in, placed the vehicle in reverse, and proceeded to back up on the sandy road. *Time to put some distance between me and the law,* thought Hans as he continued down Colonia Lane.

Chapter 31: *Safe Flight*

Shelli was watching the IDAS monitors closely. A second detection had just popped up on the monitors. It showed the intruder was circling the house and would be just outside the window of her dad's office where they were sitting. The first intruder had returned from his car with a crowbar. She was amazed that these burglars were doing this in broad daylight. She knew from the situation displays that her parents and sister had just left Nokomis Beach. Her dad said that the house would protect them, but she shivered with worry.

"There's a man coming around to the window," said Ryan as he looked out of the office window. "I'm going out and take care of these guys."

"No," said Shelli quickly. "Dad said to stay here. There's no way for these guys to get in."

Ryan frowned. "Well, I'm no babysitter, and I have had it with these guys messing with us."

Stephanie punched her brother in the shoulder. "Listen to Shelli! If you go out there, we'll be in here by ourselves. And if they catch you, how are we going to help?" Stephanie was looking directly at him when she saw the intruder to the left side of the windowpane.

"Holy shitake mushrooms!" said Stephanie as she pointed at the window. "There's the burglar, and he's got a gun!" The girls and Ryan jumped back behind the desk. The man was wearing blue jeans and a button-down white shirt with a marlin on the front pocket. The man looked directly at them, but turned his head as if he was trying to look around the room.

"He looks like he didn't see us," said Stephanie.

"He can't," replied Shelli. "Once the IDAS system detected an intruder outside, the windowpanes became reflective like a mirror. We can see out, but he can't see in."

The intruder reached down to the bottom of the window as if he was trying to lift it. After a few failed attempts, he flipped the pistol in his hand and drew back and took a swing directly at the center of one of the panes. As he hit the pane, the girls let out a squeal.

"Be quiet, girls!" said Ryan in a whisper. "He doesn't know we're in here. He might hear you, and I want to make sure I take him by surprise if he breaks the window."

"You don't understand, Ryan," said Shelli in a normal voice. "The windows are soundproof." She was about to continue when the man took several steps back and aimed his pistol. The pistol's barrel had a silencer on the end. The slight kick and an instant white circular pattern on the window were the only indications that the pistol had been fired. As the pistol fired, Shelli, Stephanie, and Ryan ducked instinctively. There wasn't a sound to be heard.

"The windows are bulletproof," continued Shelli as she rose erect.

The intruder lowered his gun with a look of confusion on his face. He fired three more times at spots on the window close to the first impact point. The glass held up with no sign of fatigue. He hit it with his pistol again, with no luck.

He scratched his head and walked back around the side of the house. The kids watched the tiled screens on the situation awareness display as the man had walked around the house. As he moved off one window, he appeared in the next tile window. His track was being shown as a square symbol on the map display of the house grounds. The single line, or vector, as her dad had called it, that protruded from the square indicated both speed and direction. The history of the track of the person showed up as a dotted line behind the box.

The two men talked for a few moments, until one finally reached for his phone and started texting. Shelli zoomed the camera in on the phone. After a few more words, the man hit Send and then twisted the phone headset from the body and threw it in the bushes as if it were discarded trash.

◊◊◊◊◊

Rick was following Nikki northward on Route 41. Nikki had her mom in the passenger seat next to her. Rick called Shelli to check her situation.

Shelli picked up her mobile phone and answered, "Hi, Dad. I see you and Nikki are heading home."

"Yes, honey. We're heading quite fast up 41 now. I'm watching the progress of those men on my display here. It looks like they are about to give up."

"Yeah, Dad, but did you see he texted someone?" asked Shelli. "I don't know if you could read it—it was too fast for me to read. But I hit Playback at slow motion. The message said to send help. He called this Fort Knox."

Rick did not like the sound of this. And why hadn't the police arrived? Since he was getting the feeds, the police would have been called automatically. Unless the police feeds were disrupted! "Shelli, just hang in there. I'll be there in a few minutes. Remember, the house will protect you. And remember your phone."

Rick called Nikki as soon as he hung up the phone with Shelli.

"Nikki, your sister may be in grave danger! We need to get there immediately. I need you to pull over now!"

"Dad, that didn't make any sense!" said Nikki in a raised voice. "I can keep up with you! Just watch me!"

Rick interrupted in a loud voice. "Nikki Bryant, you pull over right now! I don't have time to explain it to you." Nikki pulled her car over in the car dealership to her right.

"OK, what's going on?" she asked.

"Lock your car and you and your mom get in my car."

Nikki and Danielle exited the Audi quickly and ran to the BMW. Rick rolled the window down and yelled to Nikki to sit in the front seat. As soon as they were buckled in, Rick hit the accelerator and reversed the car back onto the turnoff lane of the dealership. The car was facing north on Route 41.

"I don't have time to explain, but the kids are in great danger. We may be too late if we try to plow our way through the traffic. Reach up to your left and pull the second seatbelt strap into the extra buckle on your right. Then sit all the way back in your seat with your head on the headrest."

Nikki and Danielle did as they were told. Rick pressed a button on his console labeled Voice Activation.

"Initiate Safe Flight," said Rick. With that, padded brackets swiveled out of the headrests and dropped down over the heads of Rick, Danielle, and Nikki. The small motors in the headrest whined as the padded brackets contracted to a snug fit around the top of their heads like a baseball cap. The motors continued to whine as the padded bars dropped to each person's shoulders. When it finished, their heads and necks were immobile. A deeper motor whine started, and the seatbelts tightened around them.

With nervousness in her voice, Danielle asked, "What is happening, Rick?"

"Just be calm, honey. You'll know in just a moment. "

"That is what I'm afraid of," Danielle snapped back quickly.

Nikki saw the map display start flashing. The radar was apparently on and was reporting car tracks behind them and in front of them. Then the screen flashed Initiating Safe Flight Course...and a red line was immediately plotted on the screen. The line moved as traffic moved. Whenever cars changed lanes, the line would adjust so that at no time did it touch any car. Sometimes it moved into turning lanes when traffic was too great.

While watching the display, Nikki saw a pop-up window to the right of the map come up, and a camera image flickered on. Nikki looked at the image and after a few moments realized it was an aerial view of their house on St. Armands Key.

"That's our house! How are we seeing that from the air?" As she watched, the image showed the mystery aerial craft was moving along the streets and was speeding up the longer it flew. To the left, the map zoomed out, and more symbols appeared at the location near the triangular symbol representing their home. Another red line appeared on the screen and emanated from the location of the house. Just like the red line moving with traffic from their current position, the red line from the house started moving as the cars moved.

Rick ignored the question from Nikki. He was focused on the indicator on the upper right of the screen. It indicated the level of safety was at 90 percent. He pulled his foot away from the brakes and accelerator pedal.

"I suggest you two hold on to your armrests. Danielle, you may want to close your eyes."

Before either girl could talk, Rick said out loud in a calm voice, "Launch Safe Flight." The last word of his command resounded in the car as it dropped into Drive automatically, and the tires squealed and smoked.

The car almost jumped onto the road and accelerated at an incredible rate of speed. The vehicle made rapid, jerky movements to avoid the cars ahead and to its sides. It was clear to Nikki why they were strapped in as they were. They would have been easily hurt from the erratic motion if they were unrestrained.

Rick had adjusted his rearview mirror prior to their start so that he could see Danielle's face. He rolled his eyes and looked in the mirror.

He saw Danielle's eyes were wide open, and she had a panicked look on her face.

"Danielle, please just close your eyes." His voice brought her out of her temporary shock, and she closed them tightly.

It took a few moments before Nikki realized what was going on. Lights on all the side streets were turning red well ahead of them, so that no cars could enter the road. She glanced down and saw their position on the map and saw how the red line was moving to locations in the lanes of the road where cars were not. *The radar is detected ahead, and the vehicle computer is calculating the best route!*

Whatever was flying from home was now moving fast southbound. As its position moved southward towards them, the lights were turning red for all southbound traffic and all side roads. Nikki noticed the longer they drove, the thinner the traffic became.

She then heard the vehicle display beep. It read 100 percent safe in the top right of the screen. A second later a click sound came from under the dashboard, and she felt a deep rumble permeate through the floorboard and armrests of the car. The car literally rocketed ahead. *Afterburners…Dad installed some sort of afterburner or rocket assist to give us the extra speed.*

They were now moving so fast, the lights, cars, and buildings seem to blur as they shot by. Nikki saw a momentary shadow come across the hood of the car and then saw the display was showing aerial video just ahead of them. *Whatever that is flying above us, it is now staying just ahead of us.*

As they were racing down the road, the vehicle spoke to them. "Reaching destination in 1.9 minutes." Nikki couldn't believe it. They were at least seven miles from home, and some quick math in her head indicated that they were moving more than 200 mph. She heard someone say, "Holy cow." It took her a moment before she realized it had come from her mouth.

◊◊◊◊◊

Shelli, Stephanie, and Ryan watched as a black van pulled up into the driveway of the Bryant house. Out jumped six hooded men in black jumpsuits, holding futuristic, military-looking guns. The two men already present greeted them and talked to them for a moment. The eight of them broke up into two teams. One team headed to the front door, and the second team moved to the rear of the house.

As the kids watched the screens, they saw a window pop up on the display. The window read "Initiating home defense mode." The air from the vents in the house stopped as the vents were closed. The door of the office made a slight click sound, and a tan foam filled the gaps around the door.

Shelli and Stephanie looked at each other in surprise. They turned their attention to the screens. The men were standing around the front and back doors. They were clearly planning to enter at the same time. One of the original men at the back door reached for the door handle. One of the hooded men tried to stop him, but it was too late. When the man touched the door, he began to shake severely, and his hair began to stand on end. After about ten seconds he collapsed. One of the hooded men grabbed his pants leg and pulled the motionless body away from the door.

"Electrified door knobs," said Shelli.

"I feel like I'm in another *Home Alone* movie," said Ryan.

They continued to watch as the each team presented a long roll of thick tape. Each team cut a piece and rolled it up, sliding it into the doorjamb of both front and back doors. They moved away from the doors.

Two muffled, but noticeable, blasts startled the kids and caused them all to turn toward the office door. The sound came from within the house, but it was difficult to tell exactly from where. Stephanie looked back at the display and said, "Look! They're coming inside!"

◊◊◊◊◊

Rick, Nikki, and Danielle grunted simultaneously from the forward momentum of their bodies against the restraints. The BMW X5 had rapidly decelerated as it had approached St. Armands Circle. Although vehicles could be stopped from entering the road, nothing could be done about people. Given dinnertime was now upon them, the restaurants along the circular sidewalks were crowded with people. The vehicle had to drop out of its automated maddening sprint to manual mode.

Fortunately the occupants had become used to the sudden slowdowns and jerkiness of the vehicle by the time they reached St. Armands Circle. The fastest car speeds were achieved on Route 41 due to the fact it was a straight road for miles. But once they started to reach the center of the city, Route 41 broke off to the left and curved around the waterfront. This required the vehicle to decelerate to below 100 mph. The speed had continued to drop from there to the last deceleration point before the circle.

During the fast drive, Nikki had heard her father speak to the onboard computer and tell it to show the vehicle sensor status display. This caused the map screen to split into two separate windows—one for the map and one for a 3-D wireframe representation of the car. Nikki watched the display for a few seconds while points on the vehicle lit up.

Nikki deduced that the display was showing sensor feedback from various systems on the vehicle, such as the shocks, the transmission, the motor, and even ground clearance. When the car hit the curve around the waterfront, she saw different color indicators light up and realized that display was showing how the car was responding and correcting for the conditions on its own. It was amazing to see how fast this system could detect and even anticipate problems and react. As they had entered the Ringling Bridge, she could have sworn she heard the tire squeals still echoing off the tall waterfront buildings.

The car turned right just before the shops at St. Armands. St. Armands Circle had several concentric circles of roads. All shops and restaurants were on the inner circle; parking and homes were on the outer circle. Most tourists and restaurant goers did not know that the inner circle and its traffic could be avoided by going around the outer circle.

The BMW moved as fast as it could around the circle. Nikki and Danielle gasped as they saw the first speed bump ahead, but were relieved as they heard the air shocks inflate and then felt nothing as the car absorbed all the shock of the speed bump.

The whine of the motors began again, and the restraints retracted. Rick placed his hands on the steering wheel and his foot on the accelerator.

He turned to the women and said, "Thus concludes the second successful test of the Safe Flight Program."

Danielle burst out in a still trembling voice, "Second successful test! You're crazy!"

"I prefer to call it confident," said Rick.

When they pulled up to their house ten seconds later, they saw the dark van in the driveway and the front door lying inside the front foyer. Rick pushed a few buttons on the vehicle display and saw a map of the house grounds and video feeds from all cameras.

"Good," he said. "I'm able to pick up the security feeds wirelessly from the house." He turned to Danielle. "Come up to the front seat and call Sheriff Steele. Tell him everything that's going on. And stay on the phone until help arrives."

"What are you doing?" asked Danielle. Rick was already out of the car and was heading towards the rear door hatch. Nikki got out of her side of the car and met her father as he opened the rear door.

"Here, put this on," said Rick. He handed her a heavy bulletproof vest. "These will stop anything but a grenade. Just don't let them shoot at your face." He then handed her a lightweight black gun. It was about a meter long and was made of carbon fiber.

"This has two types of projectiles. Number one is tranquilizing darts. It's fast-acting and will put down an elephant in ten seconds, and a man in less than a second. They are accurate to seventy-five yards. The second type of projectile is rubber bullets. These will not kill a person, but they are high velocity and will hurt like hell. The gun has built-in suppression, so it will not kick when firing any type of round."

"OK Dad, got it," Nikki said. "Let's go kick some butt."

"No, you're not going in, Nikki. I need you to stay out here for backup and to protect your mom. I'm going in by myself."

"No way, that's my sister in there," said Nikki.

"That's exactly why I want you out here. I need you and your mom to be safe. I don't have time for this, so I need you to please do as I say. Will you stay out here for me?" Nikki nodded her head yes.

Rick reached into the back of the car and pulled out two long pistol-like devices. Each had a laser pointer, with high-velocity dart projectile and rubber bullets like the gun he had given to Nikki. Under the barrel of each pistol was an elliptical reflector, with a LED array on one side of center and a black disk on the other side of center. He also picked up a small case with two earplugs.

"What are those?" asked Nikki.

"They deaden loud sounds that could damage my ears, but can amplify normal speech," answered Rick. Then he slipped on a vest. Lastly he picked up a pair of glasses. The glasses had a one-inch-high antenna on one side just above the ear. The lenses were only lightly tinted, and it looked as if he was wearing a well-fitting pair of safety glasses.

As Rick passed by the driver's door, he kissed Danielle and said, "Time to get my little girl."

"You better be careful," said Danielle as Rick walked away. Nikki came up beside the car window with the gun in her hand. They watched as Rick walked toward the front door, with his khaki shorts, sockless sneakers, bowler shirt, bulletproof vest, and two pistols in his hands.

"Your father looks like a hired killer on vacation."

Rick had already concocted a plan when he reached the door. As he walked into the house, he said, "Command lights out. Hurricane shutters down." Instantly the lights went out in the house, and metal blinds dropped from the upper window seals. In a few seconds, the house was black.

◊◊◊◊◊

Shelli, Stephanie, and Ryan were watching the two groups of men moving in the house. They had already searched the kitchen and living room, as well as the theatre room. The two groups had now merged and were checking the bedrooms, laundry, and pantry. Two men were standing in the hallway that led to the office.

Shelli had figured out how to enable the speakers so that they could listen to what the men were saying.

"Where the hell are those kids?" said the tallest man.

"We've practically checked the whole house," said another.

"They could have a safe room," said the tall man. "That would be hard to find."

"Why don't they look down here at the office?" asked Stephanie. "Can't they see the door?"

"I have no idea," said Shelli. "I wished I had listened to Dad's security lectures better." They turned their attention to the screens.

After a few moments, they saw the BMW pull up to the front of the house on the camera feeds.

"That's Dad," said Shelli.

"How did he get here so fast?" asked Ryan. "He was down in Osprey when he called." They watched for a moment as Rick moved to the back of the car.

"What's he doing?" asked Shelli. "How come he didn't come right in?"

Movement in the hallway drew their attention. They listened as the man who had shot at the office window spoke. "I'm telling you guys, there's another room here. I shot at the glass, but it would not break. But it did mar with each shot. None of the windows I've seen have any sign of damage."

The tall man looked down as if in thought. He walked quickly back down the hallway and went into the family room. He looked out the window, then ran back into the hallway to the other man. He looked straight down the hall.

He slowly walked down the hallway with his gloved hand in front of him.

"I don't understand," said Ryan. "It's like he doesn't see the door."

The man took a few more steps until suddenly the camera image, which was from the camera above the office door, rippled like a stone dropped into water.

"It's a crystal projector. It's projecting the image of a wall. It basically makes what is behind it invisible. I heard about research on this, but I've never seen it." The tall man turned back to the others. "Get the other guys, we've found our targets."

As soon as the order was pronounced, the lights went off in the house. In a few seconds more it was pitch black.

"Stay where you are, men," yelled the tall man. "Night vision goggles on...now!" With that, everyone reached for backpacks and their night vision goggles.

Once the tall man donned his glasses, he shouted, "We've got company. Weapons on the ready!" He turned his attention to the office.

With his night vision on, he could see a square heat signature at the end of a hallway. The night vision allowed him to see through the crystal projector image. He stepped through the fake wall and examined the door. It was steel and sealed.

"Time to take down this door," he said out loud. He reached for the explosive tape and inserted some at the door lock and at each of the hinges.

"Oh, no," said Stephanie with a look of horror on her face. "He's going to blow our door off."

"Calm down," said Shelli. She looked at the camera at the entrance and saw that her dad was now inside. Then she looked at her phone. She stared at it for a moment.

"Bummer," she said. "I forget to back up my photos."

"What?" asked Stephanie.

"Never mind." Shelli pressed the lightning bolt key on her phone and felt a faint vibration in the phone.

Shelli looked back at the door and said, "We've got to be ready for him if he comes in. Maybe we could barricade the door." She looked around the room for something to put in front of the door. Nothing except maybe the desk would do any good. Then her eyes homed in on her dance bag. She stared at it for a moment and then smiled.

Rick headed straight for the kitchen at a steady pace. He enabled the lasers on the pistols and had one aimed directly in front of him as he walked. Rick had also enabled his glasses, which were the latest generation thermal sensors. Unlike most military night vision goggles, these were clear LCD lens. Besides letting him see at any level of light or darkness, he could see a plan view of the house. It showed him the location of every intruder. This was made possible through the antenna on his glasses, which connected wirelessly to the situation display system in his office. At all times, he could tell where he was, where the kids were, and where the location of every soon-to-be-immobilized threat was.

He knew two men with night vision goggles had moved into the family room to wait for whoever had entered the house. He paused for a moment, then quickly rolled around the doorjamb and aimed both pistols at the men. He pulled the triggers simultaneously, and the men fell to the ground instantly without a single shot being fired. Their Kevlar vests were good for bullets, but they could not stop the razor-sharp points of the darts.

Although the sound of his weapon was a whisper, the men falling to the ground made a substantial racket. He saw the dots on his eyeglass monitors move rapidly, and he prepared for the arrival of the next men. Within seconds, one man came from the laundry room next to the kitchen and two from the bedroom hallway into the family room. Rick already had raised his arms up in both directions and was ready for them. He pressed the secondary triggers on both pistols.

The light emitted from both pistols was short-lived, but as bright as the sun. The light was amplified by the night vision goggles and caused instant retina damage to all three men. This was followed by a focused sound so intense, it sounded like a jet engine was ignited in the family room. The glasses sitting on the island counter shattered to pieces. The men dropped to their knees with their eyes shut and their hands over their ears. They yelled in pain.

At the instance the lights went off on the pistols, Rick's glasses went dark to protect his eyes. And when the impulse sound was emitted, the earplugs detected the sound wave and shut down all sound from entering Rick's ears. Within a couple of seconds, the glasses went back to night vision mode, and he could hear again.

Rick shot all three men with his tranquil darts. Five of the seven men inside were down.

He checked the map display in his glasses and saw two men remained. Both were in the hallway outside the office.

The two men dropped as a reflex when the bright light and tremendous sound echoed their way. It hurt both men's ears, but neither was disabled. They had heard the men screaming and then go quiet.

"I don't know what the hell that was," the tall man said. "It was almost like a percussion grenade. Just keep your gun aimed up the hallway and take a few steps back. I'm blowing the door.

Rick knew he had been lucky with the first five men, but two cornered men with machine guns would be ready for him. His sound and light show was good only once. The power required to fire those weapons was great, and the battery source was only sufficient for one use.

Then he had an idea. *I've got plenty of darts left*, he thought. He looked at the map and moved down the wall of the family room until he saw his symbol was exactly aligned with the man standing furthest from the door. He aimed carefully at the wall with one of the pistols and fired with the rubber bullets for a full two seconds. The sheetrock wall in front of him rapidly turned into white powder. He ran out of bullets before he could penetrate the second wall. But that was enough. He fired the dart at the center of the damaged wall.

In the hallway, the tall man was ready to blow the door. The other man had his gun drawn and was pointing down the hall. *Any damn movement from anyone, and he'll be pumped full of lead*, he thought. That thought lasted two more seconds. The loud sound to his right and sting to his neck was followed by complete darkness. He fell to the ground.

But before the man hit the floor, an explosion came from the office door. Although not big, it was sufficient to bring down the office door.

Shelli and Stephanie screamed. As the smoke cleared, they saw the tall man they had been watching on the video standing before them. When the kids saw the gun in his hand, they raised their hands. Shelli still had her cell phone in her hand.

"What's that in your hand?" said the man tersely. "Drop it!"

"It's just my cell phone," said Shelli. She held it in front of her so that the man could see its screen. Then she slowly started to bend her knees to put the phone on the ground. As she dropped lower, she rotated the phone slowly so that the top of the phone case was pointing toward the man. With one knee on the ground and one foot forward, she pushed the Send button on the phone.

Instantly, two thin black wires shot out of the phone toward the tall man. Since she dared not take her eyes off her assailant, she soon found that her aim left something to be desired. But the two probes still hit the man squarely, penetrating his pants and stopping at his crotch.

Rick was startled by the blast of sound before his earplugs squelched the sound. He had to wait a few seconds before the devices returned hearing. He saw from his display that the man had entered his office. He rushed into the hall, which was full of smoke. He saw a man on the floor with a dart in his neck.

Rick heard Shelli's voice as the smoke started to thin. The man's back became visible, but looked quite strange. It didn't take long before Rick realized that the man was shaking violently where he stood. The shaking stopped, and Rick quickly pointed his weapon at the man's back and fired two darts. There was no reaction, but then he heard a crack and the man's head jerked to the left. A small white object flew up in the air in Rick's direction as the man fell out cold on the floor. Rick held out his hand, and the white object landed in his palm. It was a tooth.

Rick saw Shelli standing in front of the tall man's feet. Rick looked up and down his daughter to see if she was hurt. She smiled at him and pointed down to her feet. She had on her ballet point shoes.

"What do you get when you mix kung fu and ten years of ballet? Give up? You get a ninja assassin passed out on your office floor." She stood on her toes and did a graceful spin. Then she dipped her head and curtsied to her father. *Those hard-pointed shoes on her feet are deadly indeed,* thought Rick.

Rick hugged his daughter and greeted Stephanie and Ryan.

"Did you see Shelli, Mr. Bryant?" asked Stephanie. "Wasn't she awesome? She was like a spy with the gadgets. She leapt in the air and took out that bad guy just like Jackie Chan!"

"That's my girl," said Rick with a smile. "Now let's go see your mom and sister. They're waiting outside."

Chapter 32: *Treasures*

Morning started with the Bryant family gathered in the kitchen. They were all talking about the events of the past few days while drinking coffee and hot chocolate. Thanks to Danielle, the smell of warming butter croissants filled air.

"Dad, I'm really glad they stopped that drug ring, but I'm really upset that Cody's murderer escaped," said Nikki.

"And it's a shame that Jacques De Sores evaded capture too," said Danielle.

"I bet the museum is sad they also lost one of their best customers too," said Shelli.

Rick took a sip of coffee. "Kyle told me they have a full manhunt going on for both of them. The information the FBI was able to assemble shows that Jacques and Hans have worked together for years. Jacques once worked for Interpol under another alias. He was able to keep Hans out of prison for years. Once things got too hot for them after a string of art thefts pointed to an inside mole at Interpol, Jacques decided it was time to put some distance between him and his former employers. They've been looking for him since."

Feeling a little hungry, Rick walked over to the oven to look at the croissants. Then he turned with coffee cup still in hand and continued.

"It didn't take long before Jacques and Hans found out just how lucrative drugs were. Jacques owned a home on Siesta Key. Not too far from Stephanie and Ryan's house, in fact. He was able to infiltrate the DEA by kidnapping an agent and getting him addicted to some rather bad drugs. That agent recommended Jacques to the force before he mysteriously vanished. Jacques worked his way up the chain of command quickly. His inside knowledge of the drug trade in the Caribbean and Florida allowed him to rack up an impressive number of arrests. He had Hans to take care of any other obstacles in his way."

"Why go to the trouble of working for the DEA?" asked Shelli. "He didn't have to do that to become a drug dealer."

"I suspect so he could operate without the fear of being suddenly arrested. Maybe he just enjoyed living double lives. Haven't you ever wondered what it would be like to be someone else?" Rick paused and sipped his coffee. "Whatever it was, I'm sure he didn't expect what happened yesterday. The FBI and state police have roadblocks checking for him, plus the TSA has his picture at all the airports, train stations, and ports. He's most likely on the run somewhere in Florida. I suspect he'll be caught soon."

"I'll be happy when he and Hans are caught and are punished for what they did to Cody," said Nikki. "In fact, I'd almost volunteer to be the punisher."

"All of us feel that way," said Danielle. "I got a text message this morning from the museum. They said that the FBI is offering to turn the paintings in Jacques' home over to the museum for auction. His collection is quite a catch, and the notoriety of the case will probably result in hefty prices at auction. After commissions, the proceeds will be split with Cody's parents and a fund to help children with disabilities. It won't bring back Cody, but at least some good is coming of all of this."

They all sit quietly for a few minutes, before Shelli broke the silence. "Well, I'd like to suggest a day off for everyone. We can go to Edwards Island today. Dr. Carlisle is there one last time to finish up documentation of the site. I'd like to talk to him about my theories."

Danielle, Rick and Nikki looked at each other and grinned. "And what theory is that?" asked Nikki.

"I thought you'd never ask," replied Shelli, starting her recap. "The Spanish treasure fleet sank in the summer of 1715. The fleet sank on the eastern shore of Florida and was salvaged for years by the Spanish. They didn't get everything, and a great deal of it was later found by Kip Wagner in the 1960s. He found millions there. History said some of the salvage vessels mutinied in 1715 and kept the treasure themselves. The navigator we found at the beach site had a map that he kept notes on about the trip, and that map was found during the dig on Edwards Island. The navigator's map shows that their trip began at the same location Kip Wagner found his treasure."

Shelli took a sip of hot chocolate. "The bodies we found were probably the last of the crew that escaped fierce pirates to the south of Sarasota. Pirates were sometimes territorial and would steal from each other. If this crew was spotted going by Sanibel Island, a known pirate stronghold, they were probably attacked. Dr. Carlisle doesn't want to speculate, but I believe they escaped the pirates with treasure in hand."

"Why didn't Dr. Carlisle's crew find the treasure?" asked Rick.

"I think he's not looking in the right place," answered Shellie. She reached for her iPod Touch and pulled up her Internet browser. She scrolled to some Web sites she had saved.

"I looked at maps over time and found that vegetation comes and goes on the river area at Edwards Island. The island used to be smaller. See this picture from the 1950s. It shows the islands were smaller.

"I believe the beachfront moved northward over time," she said. "This would explain why many of the dead bodies found by Dr. Carlisle were under thick vegetation growing beyond the beachfront. The mangroves grew, captured more silt, and caused the beach to expand some. As more sand and soil were deposited, mangroves gave way to other plants."

Shelli pulled up a Web site of Southwest Florida plant life. She started reading the plant list.

"Plants such as sea grapes, palmetto, bay cedar, sea myrtle, elderberry, and sweet acacia started growing. The bigger the plant, the more likely it is located toward the center and older part of the island. And if you look at pictures of the island, the largest trees are in the center.

"Bottom line, I think the treasure is buried under the line of sea grapes and brush—maybe as much as ten to twenty feet back from the edge," said Shelli. She pulled up Google Earth and showed the location she thought they should search for the treasure. "But how can we convince Dr. Carlisle to dig there?"

"I think I know," said Rick. "We can use GPR, or ground penetrating radar. The new side-scan GPRs don't even have to pass directly over the treasure to detect it. We might be able to find the treasure without disturbing the soil. Scans along some of the paths that run into the interior of the island might be sufficient. And I happen to have a side-scan GPR at the office. I had to buy one for a project we had for the government earlier this year."

"That would be awesome!" exclaimed Shelli. "Let's go today. Please, please, please? We don't have to do it all day—we can go fishing or something afterward." Everyone agreed it would be something good to do after all they had just experienced.

Shelli wanted Stephanie to come, which meant that Ryan wanted to come, since he had heard that Nikki was going to be there. It was decided that Stephanie and Ryan would pick up Rick and Shelli and head straight to Edwards Island before Dr. Carlisle left. Danielle and Nikki would take the family fishing boat over to Rick's work and pick up the GPR and then meet the rest of the crew at the island.

Rick, Shelli, Stephanie, and Ryan arrived at the dig site on Edwards Island. Dr. Carlisle and one student were gathering the last of their gear and staging it for pickup. He smiled as he saw Shelli jump out the boat, wave, and shout hello.

"Hi, Shelli," said Dr. Carlisle as Shelli walked up. "It's great to see you. Unfortunately we're finishing up the dig."

"That's OK, Dr. Carlisle." said Shelli. "I'm not here for a skeleton dig. I'm here to talk to you about the treasure."

"Treasure?" asked Dr. Carlisle. "What treasure?"

Rick offered his hand to Dr. Carlisle. "Hello, Dr. Carlisle. I'm Rick Bryant—Shelli's father. I know you know Stephanie, and this is her brother Ryan."

Ryan shook Dr. Carlisle's hand as well. Dr. Carlisle introduced Paul, the same student aide who worked with Shelli on the navigator dig site.

"My daughter has some theories about the pirates you found," Rick said. "She thinks they had treasure."

"Oh, well, we're not even one hundred percent sure that these are pirates. We've found traces of naval uniforms."

"I've got a theory about that too," said Shelli. "But that's not important right now. Let me tell you about the treasure."

Shelli pulled the folded paper out of the backpack she had brought with her. She went to the one field table left standing and spread out the papers, which were Google Earth map printouts, a copy of the navigator's map, and a map of the location of treasure found by Kip Wagner. She proceeded to explain her theory to Dr. Carlisle. As she talked, Dr. Carlisle nodded his head.

"That's a very good hypothesis, Shelli," said Dr. Carlisle. "I believe you'd make an excellent archeologist." He walked over to one of his crates and reached for a roll of paper in one of the small crates. He unrolled it as he walked back to the table. He spread it out.

"This is a high-resolution aerial photograph of the island I acquired for the dig. It has a latitude and longitude grid superimposed on it. I've annotated all the dig sites on the island on this picture." Dr. Carlisle pointed at one of the dig sites. "Here's where we found the navigator, Shelli. That's the site you helped Paul dig. You can see from the sites that most of the bodies found were close to, or inside, the current heavy, mature vegetation line."

Dr. Carlisle selected some of the older pictures of the island that Shelli had brought and studied them for a moment. He looked back at the aerial photograph.

"Notice that the vegetation is more mature from this point on the northern side of the island and south to the center." He pointed to the area on the map about ten feet back from the current vegetation line. "The vegetation north of this area is shorter and less mature. In fact, the vegetation seems much less dense in this area. It was probably affected more by changing water levels as the island grew."

"So if they had a treasure," said Shelli, "it would be in front of the older vegetation line, because that was probably the highest beach area at the time. That is so cool." She glanced at the photograph closely. "There's a path just around the west side of the island that works its way toward the old heavy brush line. It looks like there's a small clearing near the centerline of the island. Let's go look!"

The group all walked westward and soon found the small path.

"It looks like this path was made by the animals on the island," said Rick. They followed the sandy trail full of white shell fragments through the sea grapes and palmettos and soon came to the clearing. The old growth vegetation and scattered older deciduous trees were mostly to the right or south side of the clearing. The smaller vegetation and grasses were interrupted by a ring of rocks and tree trunks surrounding a darkened patch of ground with the remains of burnt wood. Plastic bags and bits of trash scattered the area.

"It appears this site is well used as a campsite," said Rick. "No camping and fires are allowed here, but the dense vegetation would easily hide a small fire at night. It's probably teenagers using this."

"Let's dig here," said Shelli. "We're near the centerline of the island. I bet the treasure is right under this campsite!"

Stephanie jumped into the conversation. "Yeah, Mr. Bryant. My brother is strong. He can help dig!"

"Hey," said Ryan. "I can volunteer on my own. And you can dig too!"

"Don't you want to wait for the GPR, Shelli?" asked Rick. "Your sister and Mom are picking it up at the office right now. They won't be long. Plus, I think you're getting ahead of yourself. We don't have permission to dig here."

"I do have permission," Dr. Carlisle quickly interjected. "But if we're going to dig, we need to do it correctly."

"That's great!" said Shelli. "Let's get started in the most likely place. When Mom and Nikki arrive with the GPR, we can start scanning the area around the dig."

"OK," said Rick. "Let's head back and get our shovels and digging gear."

"We also need to get the aerial photo and a GPS so that we can be sure we document the dig properly," said Dr. Carlisle. They turned and headed back down the trail toward the beach.

◊◊◊◊◊◊

Nikki and Danielle arrived at Rick's office. Nikki was at the controls. She pressed a button on the console, and the sliding door opened on the building. She backed the boat into the indoor slip next to the workboat and *Spearfish*.

"Mom, I'm going up to Dad's office. We need to get the keys to the storage closet. Dad said the GPR is locked there."

"OK," said Danielle. "I'll get the extra tackle and load it on the boat. Rick said it would be useful if we have to lift anything."

Nikki took a wide stride and jumped up the steps leading to the door to the office spaces. She turned left and went down to her dad's office. The light coming from the window to the bay came in from one direction, and the window to the harbor provided the remainder of the light in the room. As Nikki rounded the end of her father's desk, she saw her mother gathering the tackle from the workboat.

She sat down at her father's desk and entered the numbered password to the keypad lock on the upper left drawer of the desk. There inside the drawer were the keys to the boats and other rooms in the office building. She read the white square tags until she saw the one labeled "Equipment Closet." She lifted the key, but then was alerted to a beep sound coming from the display on the wall.

The display was the situation display for the buoys—similar to the one her dad had in his home office. She walked to the display and saw there were three flashing buoys in a row. The southernmost buoy was the buoy moored at the northern entrance to Roberts Bay. A window with a picture popped up on the display next to the last buoy.

Nikki looked in disbelief. It was the picture of Hans Schmidt.

"Oh, my God," said Nikki out loud. She quickly ran behind her dad's desk and opened his notebook PC. The display on the notebook was the same as the situation display.

She clicked on the southernmost buoy icon and selected Play Video from the pop-up menu. The video showed Hans's boat pass the buoy. The camera stayed locked on the boat as it moved due south. Another boat passed by behind Han's boat. The display beeped again with another pop-up window. The flashing title on the window was "Gun alert," and in the window was a still picture showing the machine gun clearly in the hand of one of the people on the boat.

Nikki picked up the phone on the desk and pressed the intercom button.

"Mom, you've got to come up here quickly and see this." Seconds later Danielle entered the office out of breath.

"What is it, honey? You sounded like you were in trouble."

"I'm not in trouble," replied Nikki. "Shelli and Dad are in trouble. Look at the display. That's Hans Schmidt and a second boat, and they are heading right for Edwards Island. And they have guns."

"What?" asked Danielle excitedly. She stared at the large situation display that Nikki was pointing to with her index finger. "Oh my goodness. We've got to call the police!"

Nikki looked at the display. "It appears they were automatically notified by the program running on Dad's computer. But let me call Dad to warn them." Nikki enabled her speakerphone and said, "Dad." The phone began to ring, but then went to voice mail.

"He's not answering," said Danielle.

"Or maybe he can't answer," said Nikki. "We can't afford to take a chance, Mom. Hans may be going after Dad for revenge. He took Cody, Mom. I can't let him hurt Dad and Shelli. We've got to do something to help them."

"What do you mean, Nikki?" asked Danielle. "What can we do?" Nikki put her head down for a few seconds. She slowly looked up at the pictures of the family on her dad's desk. She focused on the far right picture, which showed her dad standing next to her with speared fish in both of their hands. She remembered the day. It was a wonderful, sunny day on turquoise waters south of Boca Grande. That was her first spear-fishing excursion with her dad.

Then she spun in the chair and looked into the bay. The freshly cleaned *Spearfish* was bobbing in the water, in the slip behind the workboat. She looked at its powerful motors and clean lines. The only blemishes were the patched bullet holes, which still needed a fresh coat of paint.

Nikki spun back around. "I've got an idea, Mom."

◇◇◇◇◇◇

Shelli and the others arrived back at the beach and started to gather equipment. Dr. Carlisle checked the GPS to make sure it was working and rolled up his aerial map. He took a clipboard out and started making notes. Paul put the digging instruments in a wheelbarrow. The wheelbarrow was made for the sand and had a large inflated tire on the front. He also loaded line and stakes to mark the dig area, as had been done on the beach dig sites.

Rick brought the cooler from the boat, which had water and snacks. Ryan pulled his boat further up on the beach and made sure the anchor line was firmly embedded in the beach. He locked the motor, since they would be out of sight of the boat for a while. Shelli and Stephanie found the video equipment and took all of a minute before they were making news clip segments as if they were reporters.

None of them noticed a boat approaching the shore. It was not until the boat touched the shore that Rick looked back and saw Hans jump off the boat with a pistol in his hand. Two other men jumped off with machine guns. The pilot cut the motor, jumped off, and pulled the boat up on the beach, before bringing his machine gun strapped to his back around to his hands.

The armed men quickly shouted to the girls, Dr. Carlisle, Ryan, Rick, and Paul to drop what they were doing and move together in front of the dense vegetation at the edge of the beach.

"Dad, what's going on?" asked Shelli.

"You kids just do what they say," responded Rick. "These men were part of the drug ring, Shelli."

"Hello, Mr. Bryant," said Hans. "It's a pleasure to finally meet you."

"The pleasure is all yours," said Rick. "What are you doing here?"

Before Hans responded, Rick's phone began to ring. He reached for it, but one of Hans's armed men approached him and took the phone. He threw the phone in the water.

"Well, Mr. Bryant, you and your DEA friends have effectively closed my business operations in the area," Hans said sarcastically. "I can't tell you how happy we were about this. Fortunately for us, we've been told that you might be able to compensate us for our losses with the island's treasure."

As Hans spoke, a second boat pulled up to the dock. Two men with guns jumped off. A third man with an expensive polo shirt, khaki shorts, and a wide-brimmed hat stayed on the boat. The hat cast a shadow on his face, which in the bright sun made his face hard to see.

"Look around," said Rick. "Do you see any treasure? The only thing that has been found here are the bones of a shipwrecked crew. Just leave now, and you might be able to get away before the sheriff's department gets here."

As Rick talked, another fishing boat passed by. The passengers looked a bit curious, but made no signs that they were alarmed at the sign of guns in *Hans's* men's hands. Hans didn't seem to care that others were watching. He was undoubtedly familiar with the mentality of most people to stay uninvolved and out of trouble. Experiences like the VA Tech massacre and other mass murders still clung in people's minds.

The person with the wide-brimmed hat spoke up. "Now, now, Rick. We know this is not true. You've made no calls, so no one knows you're in trouble."

Rick recognized the voice as the man smoothly hopped off the boat and landed on the beach. As he walked closer, he lifted his head to confirm his identity.

"Director Jack Dusauriss," said Rick.

"Jacques De Sores, the art collector," said Shelli.

"I should have known that was you," continued Rick.

"Guilty as charged," said the director.

"Yes you are," retorted Rick quickly.

"Mr. Bryant, you and your family are quite smart. I'm sure that without you, I would still have my anonymity and my very profitable business. Of course, I can create another identity, and America's appetite for drugs will make starting another distribution system worthwhile. But there's one thing I cannot get back. You've cost me my priceless art collection. I'll never be able to get this back, and for this, you and your family must pay."

As the director talked, a familiar boat was heading toward them. Rick knew in a moment that it was his *Spearfish*. As it came closer, he saw both his wife and daughter onboard. A wave of worry overcame him. He had to figure out a way to warn them.

Shelli started to talk.

"Dad, there's...," she started to say before Rick interrupted and spoke sternly.

"Be quiet, Shelli." His mean look directly at Shelli made her stop immediately. Rick turned back to Hans and the director and made the quick decision to draw attention to their plight.

Rick made a quick dash toward the director, who was now only standing ten feet from him. He managed to lay a quick right jab to the director's jaw, which caused him to fall backwards onto the sand. Machine gun fire on the sand next to Rick caused him to stop his assault. Rick looked up to see his wife and daughter veering off to the left, or west side of the island, toward Siesta Key. Just as with the last boat, none of the henchmen paid any attention to the *Spearfish*.

The director rubbed his jaw and then laughed. One of his men gave him a hand to help him up.

"Looks like I've struck a nerve with you, Rick. How touching. You should have thought about the consequences before you decided to help."

"I helped because your men murdered a friend in cold blood," said Rick. "We had no idea of your involvement in that murder or your drug scheme when we first started this. And you can do yourself a favor and just leave us before the police arrive. You still have time if you go now. I'm telling you that they know where we are and are on their way here."

"Come on now, Rick," said the director. "I have been director of the DEA for some time now, and I still have the ability to listen in on everything. No one has any idea you are here. Not a wise move for a smart man such as yourself."

It dawned on Rick that his buoys would have detected Hans or the director or both. But he couldn't let them know about the buoys. If Hans got away, he would certainly destroy the buoys, and the sheriff's department would not be able to track them.

"Do you think I'd talk over regular monitored lines?" lied Rick. "I talked to Sheriff Huggins and Mike just before we left. They are heading here as we speak—they warned me something like this could happen."

"Mr. Bryant, you take me for a fool. There is no way you'd have your daughter and her friends here if you thought there was any chance of them being hurt. So enough of this! It is time for you to tell us precisely where the treasure is. I know you and your family have figured this out."

Rick was wasting time as best as he could. He knew Danielle and Nikki would be calling reinforcements in. And if they hadn't, the buoys system would have notified the sheriff. Help would be on the way. He just hoped he could drag this conversation out as much as possible.

Rick continued on with his lie. "I told you, we don't know where any treasure is. My daughter just has a theory. We haven't worked out all the details."

Hans was noticeably irritated. "Sir, we need to get on with this. I say we kill one of them to speed the process up."

"Come, come now," said the director to Hans. "It's a mind game Mr. Bryant is playing. We'll have plenty of time for revenge. I think we should let Mr. Bryant tell us about his theory. This could be quite interesting." The director turned to Rick. "OK, Rick. Please tell me your theory. But make it quick. We might be able to allow your daughter and friends to live if you cooperate."

That was the first sign from the director that the kids had a chance. But then, the director had been living a lie and had ruthlessly directed the murders of a number of people. Rick began a quick summary of what Shelli had discovered, but with a few changes in the story.

After a few minutes, Rick concluded his summary. "We came here to start digging in the area here on the beach for the treasure—right next to the site where the navigator was found. We don't know the precise location, so it could take us a while to dig along that area." Rick pointed to an old log that had obviously washed onto shore during some weather event in the past. "We were going to start near that log."

"Very interesting," said the director. "I see you are quite the archeologist, Shelli. The good doctor here should be very impressed with you."

"I'm no archeologist," interrupted Shelli. "But I do know that you're nothing but a murderer, just like your ancestor that burned Havana and killed hundreds!"

"Ah, so you do know my family's past," said the director. "You know that it was not only Havana, but also the countryside and other nearby cities. But my ancestor was a little-known pirate, and no one really knows when and how he died. Even with all the deaths he was responsible for and his destruction of entire cities, he does not get even a footnote in the history books. I am going to make sure people will know the name of Jacques De Sores of the twenty-first century. America's dependence on drugs will give me more riches than my ancestor could have dreamed. And since I have no access to my money now, your treasure will help me re-establish my drug network."

The director paused for a few seconds and then continued. "Shelli, I can tell from your eyes that you are not the liar your father is. And I know from watching you and your father that you were coming out of a trail from the center of the island. So I think we'll retrace those steps and start digging at the real site."

The director turned his attention to Rick. "And for all of your sakes, there better be a treasure. Now pick up those digging tools and let's go." He looked at Hans. "Hans, let's corral our friends toward that site." Hans motioned with his machine gun between Rick and the tools, which meant he wanted Rick and the rest to grab the shovels and hand spades.

After picking up the tools, they all started moving in the direction of the path. Just then a speedboat came around the east side of the island at a fast speed. Rick saw it was his wife at the helm, and she was wearing earphones. Hans and the rest of his gang turned to see what was approaching the beach.

Rick saw the Precision Acoustic Device, or PAD, spin towards them, and he knew what was coming. He shouted quickly to his daughter, Stephanie, and Ryan, "Duck down on the ground and cover your ears!" He motioned with his arm to drop down. The kids immediately responded. Dr. Carlisle and his assistant Paul were taken by surprise, but followed the kids to the ground within a second.

An extremely loud tone was emitted from the PAD's directional speaker. The effect was immediate. Several of the men closest to the boat dropped their weapons and came to their knees, with their hands over their ears. The sound was designed to upset the equilibrium of those in the sound's path, which resulted in quick nausea. These men began vomiting immediately. The director and Hans were also on their knees and were visibly suffering, but Hans was further away and seemed to be able to maintain his composure.

Danielle's voice came over the PAD. "This is a warning. Drop your weapons, or you'll be fired upon." Two of the water cannons were now trained on the beach. One of the men next to Hans picked up his gun and fired at the boat. The bullets ricocheted off the glass of the helm or were absorbed by the boat's outer skin.

Danielle fired the water cannon at full force at the man firing his gun and blew him backwards across the beach. With that force and the constant flow, the man was struggling to keep from drowning. Rick and the rest of the captives turned to witness the director getting hit by a second water cannon stream. He was desperately trying to crawl up the beach away from the steam.

While the henchmen were preoccupied with Danielle, Shelli kept her eyes on the henchman who was closest to her. The man was clearly distracted and had turned both his body and gun in the direction of her mom. Shelli decided it was time to use some of her years of training in kung fu. She decided the flip kick was her best option. She took two quick steps toward the henchman and made the first part of the kick—a snap kick—to the man's groin. He grunted and dropped his head from the pain. In a fluid motion and without dropping her right foot, Shelli spun on her left and swung her right foot for a roundhouse kick to the man's head. The snap of his jaw signaled to Shelli that she had made good contact.

The man dropped to the ground, and his gun landed more than a yard from his reach. When her right foot landed on the sand, Shelli lunged forward and delivered a strong downward thrust with her fist to the man's cheek. If he was conscious, he certainly didn't look like it.

Hans fired in the air to gain control of the situation and then aimed his gun at Rick and Shelli. He shouted at the top of his voice. "Stop, or I'll kill this family where it stands!" Shelli and Rick froze. Danielle immediately stopped the water cannons, and Shelli dropped her fists. The men were all noticeably dazed, and two of them had trails of blood coming from their ears. The man Shelli had attacked remained motionless.

The director began to slowly move to his knees. His hat had been blown off by the stream of water, and his polo shirt was twisted and missing a couple of buttons. Sand covered his legs, arms, and face. He was wiping sand from his eyes.

As the henchmen and the director moved slowly, Danielle came over the speaker again at about half the sound level. It was just loud enough, however, to cause pain to the damaged eardrums of *Hans's* men and the director.

"If you kill or hurt any of them," said Danielle, "I'll cut you in half with the water cannon without a second of hesitation…or guilt."

Rick was amazed that his wife was taking this chance. It was uncharacteristic of her to take that risk. But it was the right thing to do. Hans was looking at Danielle with some indecision in his eyes. He knew nothing of her temperament and couldn't read her. Rick began to wonder if it was time for him to make a move on Hans.

It was then Rick noticed the water disturbance behind Hans. He saw a head slowly emerge from the water. Neither Hans nor his men were looking in that direction. The head had a mask on and was breathing through a regulator. The shoulders emerged from the water, and Rick quickly realized it was Nikki.

Her long wet hair was slick and shiny in the sun and draped down over her shoulders and back. She was walking on the sandy bottom with the help of a heavy weight belt. The belt countered the buoyancy of her body and scuba tank and gave her feet traction. She had on a red neoprene one-piece diving suit, which fit her like a tight one-piece swimsuit. In the rush to put on the tank, her zipper in the front was partially unzipped to reveal cleavage. Her skin was tan and glistening, with the pale blue sky and the sun silhouetting her body as she emerged from the water.

She held two spear guns—one in each hand. A diving knife was in its sheath, strapped to her left calf. As she neared the shoreline just behind Hans, she spit out the regulator in her mouth. She spoke in a firm voice directly to Hans. "Stop right there, you miserable bastard."

Rick felt as if he were reviewing the frame-by-frame footage of a sports replay, as Hans spun around with his gun barrel moving in Nikki's direction. Before he could complete his turn, Nikki aimed the spear gun in her right hand and released the spear. It hit Hans in his left shoulder. The bright red spear tip exited several inches out *Hans's* back; blood dripped from the tip. Hans shouted in pain, dropped his gun, and fell back on the sand.

Hans began to reach for his gun. Nikki marched slowly up to him with the second spear gun aimed at his face. She spoke plainly and with hate in her face. "Payback is a bitch...named Nikki. Please do me a favor and reach for that gun."

Hans stopped and slowly raised his right hand in defeat. Pain kept him from lifting his left arm. Danielle came over the speaker again and told everyone to drop his weapons. The henchmen looked at one another and toward the director, who was sitting with his hands over his ears. They were unsure what to do.

Just then a helicopter shot out from the south over the tree line. Still shell-shocked from the PAD and water cannon, the henchmen ducked as the loud helicopter rotors forced a stream of hot air down on them. The helicopter made an abrupt rolling turn to the left and then hovered low over the water in front of them. It was Sheriff Steele's helicopter.

"This is the Sarasota Sheriff's Department," said the speaker on the helicopter. "Drop your weapons, or we will fire on you." It was Sheriff Steele himself. The henchmen dropped their weapons and put their hands behind their head.

"Get down on your knees." *Hans's* men and the director followed the directions of the sheriff. Hans was still lying on his back, holding his left shoulder, obviously in pain. In an instant the island was flooded with sheriff's boats and deputies.

Rick looked around to see if Shelli, Stephanie, and Ryan were unharmed. Shelli came running to him and gave him a hug. Stephanie and Ryan were still standing, mesmerized by what was unfolding in front of them. But it soon became apparent to Rick that Ryan's eyes were locked on Nikki. Ryan walked toward Nikki and said, "Laura Croft, eat your heart out! Nikki, you were amazing."

Nikki's stern look broke, and she smiled at Ryan. Ryan looked closer at the spear gun and tank. "Wow. That's my equipment! You went to our dock and got my equipment. I'll never ever clean it—ever!"

Rick laughed and walked up to Nikki. The gun had been kicked away from Hans by one of the deputies, who was advising Hans of his rights.

"Honey," said Rick, "you are a pretty good shot with that spear gun. A shoulder shot is a tough one from that distance."

Nikki squinted in the sunlight. "I was aiming for his heart." Hans turned his head and looked a little sick when he overheard her. Rick and Ryan laughed again.

"Too bad you missed," said a voice to their right. Sheriff Steele was smiling. "Good job, Nikki. But you and your mom should have waited for us to handle this."

"I lost a friend because of that murderer," said Nikki. "I wasn't about to let him kill anyone else I know—especially my family."

"I guess I can't blame you for that," said Sheriff Steele. He turned to the man still unconscious on the beach next to the family. "And what happened to this guy?"

Stephanie spoke up immediately. "He messed with the wrong person…Shelli! The Karate Kid put him down and out in less than two seconds!"

Sheriff Steele chuckled. "These guys had no idea what hornet's nest they stirred up, did they?" The *Spearfish* horn beeped as Danielle grounded the boat on the sandy shore. She jumped out and was met with hugs by her husband and daughters.

"Boy that was exhilarating! I see why you like this, Rick." Everyone laughed and all began to recall the events of the last few minutes.

The director was being walked with his hands cuffed behind his back to one of the sheriff's boats.

"I can't believe that man wore a badge that long and was never caught," said Sheriff Steele. "Thank goodness he was stopped and that he didn't get his hands on any treasure."

"Turns out he was just like his ancestor," Shelli said. "I read that Jacques of the 1500s attacked Havana because he was looking for gold he thought was hidden there. He never found it. His frustration led him to hold and ransom many of the townspeople, but he got very little money. In the end, he failed and history has almost forgotten him."

After a few minutes of talk, Shelli spoke up. "Speaking of treasure…we still have one left to find!" She turned to her mom and sister. "Did you guys remember to bring the GPR in all the excitement?"

"We sure did remember," replied Danielle.

"And we got more digging equipment as well," said Nikki.

"Well, let's go to the site," said Shelli with a grin from ear to ear. The group started gathering the equipment. Rick and Nikki assembled the GPR equipment, Danielle brought the notebook PC, Dr. Carlisle and Shelli carried the maps and charts, Stephanie carried the camera, and Ryan and Paul lugged the digging equipment and a field table. A few moments later they were heading down the path to the center of the island.

When they reached the clearing, Dr. Carlisle laid out a grid based on the required scan pattern that Rick had briefed. Paul had not worked with GPR, so he was keen to know everything he could about it. He also volunteered to pull the GPR transceiver over the clearing in the proper pattern.

After a few passes, the 2-D images appeared on the notebook PC screen of the GPR.

"Sorry, this is an older model, and the processor is not very fast," said Rick. "It will take a minute for the 3-D view to appear. These 2-D images aren't very helpful unless you're a well-trained operator."

Shelli was standing next to the PC screen and field table they had moved to the clearing.

"How will the GPR help us?" she asked.

"The GPR, or ground penetrating radar, sends low-frequency radio waves into the ground through the antenna on the bottom of the device," Rick said. "In this particular model the radio waves are not just sent downward, but also to the sides. Reflections from objects underground or voids underground will be seen as strong disturbances into what would normally be weak or straight-line responses.

Here's an example of a something in the soil here," he continued. "It's probably an old tree trunk, judging by its length. The GPR can also pick up places where soil has been disturbed by someone digging, or can even see places where there is a change in soil conditions. The 2-D graph is not very useful in this model of GPR, other than to give us the range of objects from the unit. The 3-D graph stitches all the scans together for a coherent underground image of the whole area."

"Cool, so it's sort of like a grainy, blurry picture of what's below ground," said Shelli.

"Pretty much," answered Rick. As the 3-D image built on the screen, Shelli and Stephanie took center positions in front of the screen. Rick peeked between their heads and pointed to a space about six feet below the surface. "That's a pretty strong return. I'd bet if there's a treasure, that is it."

Dr. Carlisle was trying not to look excited, but quickly asked to see the screen.

"I assume you're pretty used to looking at GPR images, Doctor," said Rick.

"Yes, I am. It's a tool we use often. Normally not good for objects just under the surface, like the bodies we found here, but very good for objects more than three or four feet below ground."

Dr. Carlisle asked Paul to come closer and look at the image. They discussed the details with each other and then pulled out a map of the island. He spun the map around on the table for the girls to see.

"Here's a two-dimensional map we had constructed using core samples we dug every twenty feet down the centerline of the island from north to south. We use it to date the island and to figure out its natural history. We don't normally do this for most digs, but we thought it was important in this particular case, since this is an ever-changing environment."

Paul spoke up. "You can see from your GPR image that the water table is about twelve feet down. You can also see these lines in the soil, which are the tree and brush roots. The roots of these plants act as the glue to hold this island together, and the canopy they provide keeps the top sandy soil from washing away in torrential rains. The beach where we found the body had some erosion over the last few years, which caused the tip of the sword to be exposed."

Paul picked up a ruler and placed it on the map.

"Here's the dig depth for the navigator. If I place the ruler at that depth and compare it to your GPR depth, it shows the object was about two to three feet below the surface back in the 1700s. So the object in the GPR image is consistent in depth with something that would have been buried by the crew."

"That's enough for me," squealed Shelli. "Let's start digging." Both she and Stephanie almost vibrated with excitement. Paul, Ryan, and Rick grabbed shovels and started to dig in a large area around the center location of the object. Progress was quick in the first three feet. Roots, however, began to slow progress considerably below three feet.

Dr. Carlisle, Danielle, Nikki, Stephanie, and Shelli lined the pit and watched as it got deeper. Dr. Carlisle was holding the video camera and describing the events that had led up to the moment over the camera's built-in mike. In the background, the sound of the sheriff's helicopter and boats faded as they headed back to headquarters. A few moments later, Sheriff Steele appeared and stood next to Danielle and Stephanie at the sandy pit.

It wasn't long before Rick's shovel made a thud sound when it hit the ground. He smiled at Shelli, whose eyes were wide with excitement. Even though the hole was now six feet deep, Shelli knelt and put one hand on the side and jumped inside. Stephanie followed suit.

"Let me help, Dad," Shelli said. Within a few seconds, both Shelli and Stephanie were digging with hand spades. Within a few minutes, two clearly defined, sandy rectangles were visible.

At this point, Dr. Carlisle handed Paul several brushes. Paul, the girls, Rick, and Ryan started lightly brushing the sand away. After about half an hour of work, their efforts yielded two chests with brass handles on each side. The chest was made of mahogany wood and was fully brass-bound for strength.

"The wood has probably suffered from being in the sand all these years," said Dr. Carlisle. "It is unlikely we can excavate it from the site without totally destroying it. Let's document this as much as possible."

Dr. Carlisle handed the camera and video camera down to Paul, who diligently photographed and videoed every inch of the chests' surfaces. He passed the cameras back up to Dr. Carlisle, who continued to video.

Danielle rolled out a tarp next to the hole to place the chests once they were removed from the sandy pit. Paul instructed Ryan to pick up the handle on one side of one chest.

"This is very likely going to fall to pieces as we pick it up. If there are coins in here, the chest will be heavy. So keep your legs back, Ryan, so that the splinters won't drive into your leg, and coins won't bruise you."

As Ryan and Paul lifted, cracking sounds emanated from the chest. The chest was noticeably heavy, and Nikki could see from Ryan's flexing muscles that it took real effort to lift it. At only two inches off the sandy floor, a loud snap sounded out from the base of the chest. The sudden drop of the contents out of the bottom of the chest caused Ryan and Paul to jerk the chest quickly to about two feet off the pit's floor before they could react.

The contents clinked and quickly spread out on the bottom surface of the pit. The pieces of eight were still relatively shiny, and the jewels sparkled. Paul and Ryan continued to lift until the whole of the chest's contents were emptied on the floor. Shelli and Stephanie started cheering and jumped up and down. A series of "oohs" and "ahs" came from the rest of the crew.

Dr. Carlisle jumped into the pit and quickly documented the treasure. He instructed Shelli and Stephanie to kneel beside the treasure on either side and hold a few coins in their hands.

"This will be known as the Shelli and Stephanie find," said Dr. Carlisle.

"No way," said Stephanie. "I was around for the fun of it. It is Shelli that should take all the credit."

"Fair enough," said Dr. Carlisle. "So it will be the Shelli Bryant find." The picture would later make the front page of the *Sarasota Herald Tribune* and other local papers.

The group followed Dr. Carlisle's instruction and completed the careful removal of the chests and treasure. The sun was setting when the group left. Dr. Carlisle and Paul left with Sheriff Steele on his boat, just to make sure the treasure was properly protected and stored until the treasure's disposition could be determined.

The Bryants, Stephanie, and Ryan prepared to leave on their boats. Ryan and Stephanie decided they'd go home and shower and then meet at the Bryant home for dinner.

◊◊◊◊◊◊

Later that night the Bryants, Ryan, and Stephanie were sitting out in their backyard pool area. The night was pleasant as they sat around the glass and wicker table. Water and dinner salads sat on the table, while Rick cooked fresh cobia fillets on the grill. They all had their favorite beverage in their hands while they talked.

Danielle smiled and listened to Shelli and Stephanie recounting the day's events. She watched as Ryan praised Nikki for her hero-like rescue. There was no question that Ryan was completely infatuated with Nikki. Nikki was being noticeably cautious, but was clearly interested as well.

Rick was into the food. He looked a little tired from all the hours he had put in the last few days, but there was no way he was going to miss the celebration of the treasure find.

Rick took a moment while cooking to ask something.

"Nikki, I know that you happened to see the buoy feeds of Hans and his gang pop up on the situation display in my work office. And I know your mom said it was your idea to attack the way you did. But what made you think of the attack from two sides?"

Nikki smiled. "The pirates on the beach. Shelli did a good job of putting together the story of the crew and their last moments. They had plenty of weapons, but they encountered a force from all sides. In the end they met their death because they could not fight in many directions at once. I thought that if Mom distracted them, I could take out Hans. Although the director was the leader, Hans was the operational head of the gang. Taking him out would be like cutting the head off the snake."

"So I guess dead men do tell tales," burst out Shelli. They all laughed. After the laughing stopped, Shelli continued. "Hey I got a text message from Paul—Dr. Carlisle's assistant. He said the university is going to create a special showing of the items they found on the island. What's left of the treasure chest and some of the gold coins are going to be on display. Our pictures and bios of us are going to be displayed."

"Oh, that's so cool," said Stephanie.

"Hello?" came two voices from the back door. It was the twins Kelsey and Kristin. Nikki had invited them over to join the party.

"Hi, girls," said Rick.

"We rang the doorbell, and it didn't work," one of the girls said. "And we would have knocked on the front door...but there wasn't one." Laughter followed the comment. Nikki hugged them and invited them over for some drinks and a seat at the table.

"Sorry about the door," said Rick. "It appears we will be starting our remodeling project faster than we expected. In fact, a carpenter is supposed to be here any minute to fix our front and back doors. For some reason Danielle didn't want to sleep in the house without the doors."

When the food on the grill was done, they all sat down for a toast. They raised their smoothies, and Rick started the toast. "Here's to exciting adventures with friends and family. Let's hope they continue to..." Rick's mobile phone interrupted the toast. Everyone lowered her glass as Rick looked at the caller ID. It was Sheriff Steele.

Rick put the call on speakerphone.

"Why, hello, Mike. I didn't expect to hear from you tonight. I thought you'd be home with your family by now."

"I'm heading home now," replied Sheriff Steele. "But I wanted to let you know there's been a quick decision on the treasure. Dr. Carlisle, Kyle from the DEA, and I just finished a conference call with the governor's office. We all relayed what has happened over the last week and were able to convince them to release the treasure. About a third of it will go to the university for research and exhibition. The state gets a third, as you would expect. The remainder will go to your family."

The family all cheered with the news.

"Thanks very much, Mike," said Rick. "We'll make sure to put it to good use."

"That's exactly what I told the governor you would say," added Sheriff Steele. "Well, take care and enjoy a hopefully relaxing evening. And thanks again for all your help."

"It was our pleasure to help, Mike. It was nice working with you. Take care and have a good evening yourself." Rick ended the call.

"I guess we have even more to celebrate," said Rick. "Salute!" They clinked their glasses and sipped their drinks.

"What are we going to do with the treasure?" asked Shelli right away.

Nikki spoke up immediately. "What about giving some it to Cody's family?"

"Very good suggestion," said Danielle. "We should make a list of charities for a donation."

Shelli raised her hand and burst out her suggestion. "Stephanie and Ryan were a real help in the treasure hunt. And it was Ryan who stepped on the sword in the first place. So I think it's fair that they get some of the treasure. Maybe we can set up a fund to pay for their college education too! And maybe a car and..." She was about to continue when Rick's mobile phone rang again. Everyone stopped as Rick looked at the caller ID.

"Hello?" said Rick. He listened for a moment. "Oh, Kaleho. It's been a long time. What have you been up to?"

Rick stood up and walked away from the table. As he did so, he motioned for them to start eating.

A few minutes later, Rick walked back to the table, where his family was busy eating.

"That was an interesting call," said Rick. "We've been asked to help on a police case." Everyone flooded the air with questions. "Hold on everyone. One at a time." He pointed to Shelli.

"What's the case about?" she asked.

"I don't know much," answered Rick. "I just know it's a murder mystery. My friend Kaleho couldn't give me any more details until we sign the nondisclosure agreement, which he's sending me tomorrow."

"Where is the case?" Nikki asked.

"Hawaii," said Rick. Everyone immediately cheered. Rick motioned with his hands for everyone to quiet down. "Apparently my old college buddy from the University of Hawaii is now a police chief. The department was looking for some consultants to help on the case when Kaleho saw the case and treasure find reported in Internet news."

"We've made the news already?" said Danielle.

"Yep," answered Rick. "Apparently a number of news Web sites have articles on us. And that's not all. Several faxes and e-mails came in asking for our help on mysteries."

Shelli quickly pulled up her iPod Touch and did a quick search on the browser.

"Wow," she said. "Dad's right. The Web is full of the news. And look at this, Stephanie. It's the picture of you and me released by Dr. Carlisle."

Stephanie looked at the article. "Cool," she said. "The article is titled "Nancy Drew Meets Indiana Jones.""

Shelli raised her glass again. "Here's to the crew that lost their lives three hundred years ago. Their story lives on." They touched their glasses and drank to the toast. It took all of a few seconds before they began to discuss their trip to Hawaii.

◊◊◊◊◊◊

Over a thousand miles away at Chicago's O'Hare Airport dinged the

Blackberry of a man waiting for his flight. A new encrypted text message had arrived. The man scrolled down to the message and opened it. The message read, "Your visit to Florida is to be concluded in two weeks' time. Be sure your discussions with the hosts are thorough, and don't leave a mess when you are done. Your fee will be wired to your account when you've finished the meeting."

He clicked on the link and a news story with a picture of a family standing in front of a chest of gold and jewels popped up in his browser window. The man smiled as he saw it. He wrote a short text back.

"It's double my standard fee for a family." Seconds later a text came back. It said, "Agreed."

The hit man looked at his watch. It was late. He was happy to get the message before he got on the plane to New York. He would now sleep well in his first class seat to Florida instead.

About the Author

Eddie Hughes is the President, Co-Founder, and Co-Owner of Detection Monitoring Technologies (DMT), which primarily builds security radars and integrated mobile monitoring systems. Many of the products sold by DMT were designed by him, and he is heavily involved in all research activities at the company. The vehicle and boat radar systems described in this book are built by DMT.

Mr. Hughes graduated from Lynchburg College and University of Hawaii in Physics and Mathematics. He is an avid fisherman and kayaker, certified scuba diver, and loves the outdoors. His travels for his work, education and pleasure have taken him around the world and his stories capture the sites and local flavor of these exotic locations.

Mr. Hughes, his wife, and his two daughters live in northern Virginia, but frequent the Sarasota, Boca Grande, Venice, Englewood, and Placida areas of Florida several times per year.

The Bryant Family Chronicles: Death and Gold in Zara Zote is Mr. Hughes' first novel in a series of novels that are planned about the Bryant family. The next action packed novel takes place in both Florida and Hawaii. It is planned to be published in the summer 2012.

Upcoming Books and Information

Interested in more Bryant family adventures?   Visit the Deep Sea Publishing website:

www.deepseapublishing.com.

The website provides more information about the author, book signing events, the upcoming Bryant family book releases, character profiles, and more about the technology found in the books. You can also leave messages for the author and others on the blog.

Deep Sea Publishing (DSP) is a Florida-based company that sells fictional novels, children's books, teen books, and reference guides. The website supplies details on all DSP publications and the expected release dates of new material.

All Deep Sea Publishing books may be purchased in electronic or paperback formats. Check the DSP website for a list of resellers or to order the book directly at the online storefront.

www.ingramcontent.com/pod-product-compliance
Lightning Source LLC
Chambersburg PA
CBHW071246170626
46809CB00001B/86